ORACLE

Douglas E. Richards

Paragon Press

ORACLE OF DELPHI (excerpted from the *Ancient History Encyclopedia*)

"Delphi was an important ancient Greek religious sanctuary, and home to the famous Oracle of Apollo, who gave cryptic predictions and guidance to both city-states and individuals, supposedly as a medium through which prophecies were delivered by the gods. The Oracle would answer questions put to her by visitors wishing to be guided in their future actions.

"The Oracle was famed throughout the ancient world and was consulted before all major undertakings, although her messages were often obscure or ambiguous.

"Perhaps the most famous consultant of the Delphic Oracle was Croesus, King of Lydia. The Oracle stated that if Croesus went to war a great empire would surely fall. Reassured by this, the Lydian king took on the mighty Cyrus. However, it was the Lydian empire that fell, not Cyrus. A lesson that the Oracle could easily be misinterpreted by the unwise or overconfident."

ANCIENT PROPHECY: ORACLES AND THE GODS (excerpted from HistoryExtra)

"An Oracle (a priestess of the temple of Apollo) was a gateway to knowing the will of the gods, a cosmic information superhighway for understanding what lay ahead."

PROLOGUE

Soval Din Alt took a deep breath and let it out in three rapid-fire bursts, the Vorian equivalent of a sigh, as he prepared to address the two hundred young men and women before him, seated around concentric rock benches that faced the raised platform on which Soval now stood. The cold, hard outdoor structure was an enlarged replica of the first Greek amphitheater ever built, and was located near the very center of the *Earth Portal Restricted Access Zone*.

Not that any of those gathered had any idea that this was the area's official designation.

And why would they? The Vorians had visited twenty-six other planets over tens of thousands of years, and all the information learned from these visits was now in the public record.

But this was not the case when it came to Earth and humans. While the bulk of the background on these visits had been declassified, key aspects remained as secret as any piece of information on Vor.

Soval glanced up at the perfectly clear orange sky, and Vor's two principal suns, hanging serenely at opposite ends of the horizon. Both suns were more distant than Sol was to Earth, but their combined warmth kept Vor at a nearly uniform seventy degrees. A third sun was visible, even farther away, relatively tiny in the radiant sky. For a few years each millennium, Vor's exceedingly complex orbital dance gave this sun the brief honor of being second closest to the planet. Regardless, all three in concert kept Vor bathed in light. And even during the few minutes every fifty cycles or so when the suns were all set at the same time, turning nearly endless day into fleeting night, a blazing star field generated considerable light.

Soval knew that the rock benches would be strange and uncomfortable to the members of this new class, but there was no time like the present to acclimate these students to Earth and what they might experience there. Soon enough, perfect computer simulations, tied into their visual and auditory centers, would replace the familiar suns of Vor with Earth's ugly yellow ball, and the comforting orange sky would transform into a creepy, disquieting blue one.

But now was not the time for this. Let the students wrap their minds around what was expected of them. Let them continue to sit under the comforting suns and sky of Vor before Soval condemned them to years of virtual reality simulations in far less appealing surroundings.

"I want to thank all of you for volunteering for this project," he began, knowing that each member of this group had been handpicked, and a number of them hadn't volunteered as much as they had been pressed into service. Still, they were only signed on for twenty-five years, which was but a small fraction of their lives. And this was the safest duty around, so they could hardly complain.

"Now that we're all gathered here," continued Soval, "it's time I tell you just what it is that you, ah, *volunteered* for."

Soval could read the look of apprehension on the students' faces, and they were each so quiet he wondered if any of them had remembered to breathe.

"About thirty-two hundred years ago, a single portal appeared very near where you are sitting now. One that led to a planet that the intelligent inhabitants call *Earth*. This you already know from your prior studies of the known intelligent species in the galaxy, and our interactions with them. But Earth and the human race are presented merely as footnotes. And this chapter in history is taught as a series of unremarkable visits to an unremarkable planet inhabited by unremarkable natives. A planet smaller than Vor, but also denser—giving it a gravity of .96 Vor-standard. A planet orbiting a single star, with a blue sky and endless water.

"Nothing really notable about humanity, either—at least given the material that *you've* been exposed to—other than the unusual location of the species' home planet, which is a true outlier. Earth is located within a minor spiral arm of the galaxy, a sparsely populated region twenty-five thousand light-years away. It's the only backwater planet that we know of to have spawned sentient life."

As Soval spoke, a number of perfect holographic images of Earth, as well as a map of the galaxy, pinpointing the planet's precise position, appeared above his head and began to slowly rotate.

"Its atmosphere is breathable—of course," continued the instructor, "and its temperature extremes are within range of what we can survive given proper clothing and shelter. The last mundane item I'll remind you of is that its year is a bit longer than ours, so our initial visits were about twenty-eight hundred of their years ago."

Soval paused to catch his breath and then continued. "When the portal did materialize and activate, all those years ago, it let two of us through to Earth every forty of their hours, or allowed two of us to return here. Like clockwork."

He frowned. "Then, after nearly thirty years of operation, the portal abruptly disappeared. Our people stationed on Earth, by then more than twelve hundred in number, were trapped there. We had no way to communicate with them or bring them back."

Holographic images of human males and females, some clothed and some not, now loomed above the instructor's head, twelve feet tall, and began to slowly rotate as before.

"As you can see from the holograms above me, while there are marked differences in appearance between Vorians and humans, at least while naked, clothing is able to conceal many of the more obvious ones. Above the neck, the two species are close enough that we can basically pass as them, with just a few non-surgical adjustments. Which is what we did twenty-eight hundred of their years ago.

"Since then, surgical techniques have developed such that we can alter one of us to fit in perfectly among them, even naked, at least from above the waist and below the groin. No surgical techniques can yet match the precise appearance and functionality of their genitalia. But these are usually kept covered, so shouldn't present too much of a problem."

He waited several additional seconds to give the students time to study the holograms above his head. "You are also aware that, as usual, a number of these humans were brought back through the portal to Vor, where we were able to study their habits, personality traits, expressions, body language, native intelligence, and so on. We also studied their minds, from a physical examination of brains taken from freshly dead specimens, to exact digital imprints of the same, including each and every one of their hundred billion connecting and firing neuronal cells. And with that, the chapter on our interaction with a species hailing from the most remote planet we've ever visited was closed."

He paused. "At least that's the information that was imprinted into your memories and later expounded upon in school. And I have no doubt that you found humanity to be the *least* interesting of all the known intelligences that you studied."

Soval moved his ears, the Vorian equivalent of raising his eyebrows, and continued. "Which brings us to where the public information leaves off."

The Vorian instructor went on to describe in some detail certain key discoveries that had been made about humanity, and why generations of students, just like those he was addressing now, had been pressed into service.

"We have no idea if the portal to Earth will ever reappear," he said after providing this critical background. "So far it hasn't, even for an instant. But if this ever changes, we need to be ready. *You* need to be ready. At a moment's notice. And I—and others—are here to make sure that you *will* be.

"You'll undergo surgery so that you can more easily pass as human. You'll learn human expressions and general demeanor, and we'll implant engrams in your minds to make this more natural for you. We'll implant all the languages used on Earth when we were last there. And this is only the beginning.

"So far, we've waited thousands of years for the portal to reappear—in vain. More than a hundred classes like yours have been prepared to go through—also in vain. Will yours be the class that finally gets to go on the mission that you're being trained for?"

He sighed. "Admittedly, this is doubtful."

Soval waited for this harsh reality to sink in. "And even if the portal miraculously does appear during your watch, we have no idea what we'll find on Earth. Your mission might be over before it begins. Our computer modeling suggests a greater than fifty-percent chance that humanity has gone extinct since our last visit. At that time, Earth was a largely untamed and unforgiving planet, and humanity was quite primitive. Worse than primitive, in many ways the species was barbaric. Savage. Warlike. Most of them lived in squalor. Their hygiene and sanitation were rudimentary, at best, and their lives were mostly cruel, horrid, and short.

"And if their survival as a species was in question at the time of our visit, if they managed to advance technologically, their odds get even worse. Given their violent natures, if they were ever able to develop weapons of mass destruction, the chances that they have self-destructed by now are high.

"And if the portal opens and they have managed to survive, there is no guarantee that there are any Vorians still alive there. Even if our modest contingent there managed to reproduce for a number of generations, this isn't a large enough initial population to give the group the stability in numbers it might need to survive such harsh conditions and natives, not to mention any wars or cataclysmic natural events that might befall them.

"It's possible that some did survive to this day. It's even possible this modest group was able to dramatically increase its numbers and thrive. If so, this will make your mission all the easier.

"If not, when you arrive on Earth, you'll need to devote significant time and energy to getting the lay of the land. Much is likely to have changed in almost three thousand of their years. Our computers predict that you'll most likely have to learn additional languages to get by, ones that were not even spoken at the time of our last visit.

"When our people were there last, many human cultures around the globe used a barter system to exchange goods and services, while a few used a fledgling, rudimentary system of currency. But the humans did seem to value the element *gold* fairly universally. Gold was widely seen as a sign of status and power, and objects forged from this metal were almost exclusively owned by rulers. In the first decade our people were there, they stored substantial amounts of gold at hidden safe houses for future Vorians to tap into, as necessary."

The instructor sighed. "This said, we have no idea if this metal will still be seen as valuable when you arrive. Regardless, you'll need to get fully up to speed on the current state of human civilization, and learn to fit in among them. Which will likely take three or more years. If gold no longer has value, your assignment will be even more challenging.

"Either way, there is no need to be overly concerned. We'll train you well. And you'll be well versed on what you'll need to do once you arrive to achieve these preliminary objectives, as well as your final objective.

"But given all I've just told you, the odds of your success are exceedingly small. Even if a portal opens on your watch, which is unlikely, and humanity has survived, which is unlikely, and you're able to complete your mission, which is unlikely, the portal may disappear again at any time, trapping you there forever."

This time the instructor remained silent for an extended period, letting his sober words marinate in the minds of the students. "This is truly a long shot," he continued finally. "And yet we continue to play it. Which underscores just how important we think this could be. As does the time and energy we've expended over thousands of years, just on the off chance that the portal will reappear. Success in this mission could be a true game changer. And while this success may not be possible," he added, leaning forward, his eyes blazing with intensity, "we will *not* fail due to lack of readiness."

Soval twisted his face into the Vorian equivalent of a smile. "So let's get started," he said, now trying to sound upbeat. "By the time we're finished with you, you'll be more human than *they* are."

PART 1

"It is always with excitement that I wake up in the morning wondering what my intuition will toss up to me, like gifts from the sea. I work with it and rely on it. It is my partner."

—Jonas Salk

"You may know the feeling. It's the feeling you get when you've made something wonderful, and when you look back on it later, all you can say is: 'I don't even know where that came from.'

"You can't repeat it. You can't explain it. But it felt as if you were being guided.

"The Romans had a specific term for that helpful house elf. They called it your genius—your guardian deity, the conduit of your inspiration. Which is to say, the Romans didn't believe that an exceptionally gifted person *was* a genius. They believed that an exceptionally gifted person *had* a genius."

—Elizabeth Gilbert

1

Neil Marshall glanced down at his chiming phone and, as expected, the name Shane Frey appeared there. Marshall rolled his eyes. How many times would he have to go over the same ground?

Shane Frey was a supplier and future empire builder, and while Marshall had worked with the man now for several months, they had never met—at least not in person. This wasn't the way Marshall liked to do business, but given the one-of-a-kind product that Frey produced, he was willing to accommodate the man.

And at the moment, Frey held all the leverage. If Marshall played ball he was well on his way to growing his drug operation to gargantuan proportions. If he *didn't* play ball—well, the thriving organization that he had managed to create would be swept up like a feather in a tornado as Frey found another operator to take his place. It was as simple as that.

Eat or be eaten.

Neil Marshall had no idea who this Shane Frey was, or how he had managed to burst onto the scene so quickly, but his product was *next level* amazing. And Marshall was in on the ground floor. Frey had chosen to work with only three major players in the entire country. *Three.*

Marshall, who was based in LA, Isiah Schaeffer, based in New York, and Marcus Johnson, based in Chicago. All were in the process of introducing this new drug into their respective territories, and their extreme geographical separation meant that each drug lord would have all the room for expansion they could ever want.

Frey may have been new on the scene, but he had been smart to launch in the three biggest markets in America, and *only* these three—at least for the moment. He wasn't giving in to the temptation to bite off more than he could chew.

Not only was Frey the inventor of an entirely new class of illicit drug, which produced a high that couldn't be matched, he was a visionary with what seemed like bottomless pockets. He was willing to give his three initial distributors as much supply as they could ever use—free of charge. They could give samples away and sell subsequent doses for pennies, only jacking up the price when the entire nation was well on its way to becoming hooked. Which wouldn't take long given Frey's generous and forward-looking business model. And then Frey had plans to expand his empire around the world.

Marshall had been the first of Frey's three chosen dealers, and Frey had actually asked him to name the product, bowing to his superior experience on the streets. Marshall had thought about it for just a few minutes and had settled on Foria, short for *Eu*phoria, a perfect description of the state of mind the drug brought about.

Marshall would have preferred to look Frey in the eye, but Frey refused to make use of the drug lord's expensive holographic vid-call system, which made every meeting seem face-to-face. Instead, Frey's call was coming in audio-only on Marshall's cell, as usual.

"Hello, Shane," began the drug kingpin. "Glad you called. Showtime is just a few hours away."

They had only encountered one possible speed bump that could slow the launch of Foria even a little, an LA detective a little too clever for her own good. Marshall had insisted that he could take care of her. And he had really outdone himself this time, coming up with a plan that he considered a masterpiece. Sure, it would end up costing him a man—maybe two or three if something went wrong—but the expense of the operation would be borne entirely by Shane Frey.

Marshall would gladly sacrifice a few expendable members of his organization to get the job done—*especially* if it didn't cost him financially. After all, his willingness to sacrifice even those most loyal to him like pawns in a chess game was what had allowed him to rise to the top in LA in the first place. And during the past few years, with this as home base, he had gradually expanded his empire in all directions, and was confident that before too long, he would become the dominant drug lord in all of California. With Frey's new product, this would likely only be the *beginning*.

"You're positive your plan will work?" said the deep, somehow unsettling voice of Shane Frey.

"*Positive,*" replied Marshall, for what must have been the third or fourth time. "The bitch won't know what hit her. She'll never cause any more trouble again, or raise any more red flags. She has a dinner reservation tonight at six at the Dock Harbor Bistro in Santa Monica, where she's meeting a professor. The restaurant is at least a thirty-minute drive for her, so we should have two hours to operate, at minimum. We'll only need one. And I'll have a man watching the restaurant's exit to be sure she doesn't leave early. Should go like clockwork."

"Don't underestimate her," said Frey. "She's shown herself to be as shrewd as they come. And she lives in a pricey condo with pricey security."

"Don't worry," said Marshall. "I've brought in the best talent money can buy. I hired a specialist from Houston who knows her alarm system like the back of his hand. He can beat it in fifteen minutes. And I've brought in out-of-town computer experts as well, along with out-of-town muscle." He paused. "It takes a village," he added with a smile.

"Just be careful," said Frey, "and thorough. Now that Detective Abbott is on her way home, I'll initiate my part of poisoning the well. Just see to it that you complete yours."

"Don't worry, Shane. We'll be in and out, clean and efficient. No one will ever know we were there. We'll leave everything the way we found it, and clean up after ourselves."

"And then you'll lure her to her death soon after she returns from dinner?"

"Exactly," said Marshall. "And we'll have multiple redundancies, and backups for our backups, just to be certain."

Not that these precautions would be necessary. He had every confidence that Jimmy Jessup would be able to lure her to the kill zone they had set up. And just for the sake of good theater, *Jimmy* would be shot and killed as well, with her gun. Although Jimmy hadn't been briefed on *this* part of the plan. Then they would plant a bag filled with twenty grand worth of Benjamins on her corpse, along with instructions for what they wanted from her in return.

Just like that, it would be the beginning of the end, wrapped up in a neat little bow.

Marshall hated to lose Jimmy, but sometimes sacrifices needed to be made.

And Marshall was just the kind of man willing to make them.

2

Detective Anna Abbott arrived early at the Dock Harbor Bistro and watched the sun inch its way down toward the edge of the ocean, a journey that would be completed in an hour or so when this dazzling yellow orb dropped quickly below the horizon and vanished.

Anna had no idea what she was doing here, as her case load was more demanding than ever. And if she couldn't take time out to even date, what was she doing dining with a total stranger?

On the other hand, she did deserve a break now and then. And since this wasn't a date, why not dine with a man in a fancy restaurant without having to worry if they were connecting, if he wanted to sleep with her, and if she wanted to let him? Besides, her instincts had told her to say yes to the invitation, and she rarely went against her gut.

After five minutes of gazing at the spectacular sun, wispy clouds, and ocean, she turned to study her dinner companion for the evening as the hostess ushered him to her table. It was exactly six. He was punctual, she had to give him that.

She didn't feel like she was getting much of a read on him, although her instincts told her he wasn't a threat. Not that she had expected him to be, but when meeting a stranger, there was always the possibility that alarm bells might go off. Still, there was something a little off about him, which she couldn't quite put her finger on.

He had androgynous features and was baby-faced, with flawless skin that she suspected only needed shaving once a week, as even facial hair was reluctant to taint its smoothness. He was of average height and slender, with soulful brown eyes that were larger than average.

She rose to greet him.

"Detective Abbott," he began, shaking her hand, "it's truly an honor."

"Professor Vega," she said as they both sat. "Welcome." She gestured through the panoramic window to the ocean beyond. "Nice place you've chosen."

He smiled. "I'm glad you approve. And please, Detective, call me Tom."

"If you'll agree to call me Anna."

Professor Thomas Vega nodded. "Anna it is." He locked his eyes on her as if she were the only woman who had ever lived. "I can't thank you enough for agreeing to meet with me," he added.

She was still having trouble gauging him, but perhaps this was because he was so awkward in her presence, like a gushing fanboy basking in the presence of a hero.

"So you'd like to write a scholarly paper about me," she said. "Normally, I'd spend more time on small talk and ease into the main conversation. But this isn't a date—and I can't help but be intrigued."

"And I hope flattered."

Anna allowed herself a shallow smile. Vega had contacted her several days earlier and had all but pleaded to meet with her, and she was pretty sure he would have walked barefoot over a sea of broken glass to do so. He was a professor of criminology at Stanford, and although she offered to speak with him and tell him anything he wanted over the phone, he wouldn't hear of it. He insisted that it was the shortest of flights to LA, and he would like nothing more than to buy her a dinner at an upscale beachfront restaurant. After she had briefly surfed the web to verify his credentials and satisfy herself that he was who he claimed to be, she had agreed.

"So how do you know that I even exist?" she asked him bluntly.

Vega smiled. "You're the detective with the highest solve rate in LA," he replied simply. "What criminology professor *wouldn't* want to meet with you?"

"Random chance," she said dismissively. "Someone has to have the highest solve rate in LA. I've just had a lot of lucky breaks."

The professor shook his head. "Each city compares and ranks all detectives within its jurisdiction who have handled at least twenty felony cases," he said, "based on their solve rate percentages. But these are never combined into a statewide report. Even so, it's easy enough to do this by hand if you're so inclined. I don't suppose that you've ever gone to the trouble."

Anna shook her head.

"Would it surprise you to know that you have the highest solve rate, not just in LA, but in all of California?"

"Not really," she said pleasantly. "And sorry if I sound immodest."

"Not at all," replied Vega. "Because I'm not done. Turns out you have the highest solve rate of any detective *in all of America.*"

She allowed herself a brief smile. "Nice to know," she said, not seeming to be particularly impressed with herself. "So you've found what you think of as the most successful detective in the country, and you want to write a scholarly article on what makes me tick." She had guessed this from the start, but didn't want to get too far ahead of herself.

"Exactly," said the professor. "I've been studying you thoroughly for weeks now. Your success isn't because of luck. And it's not because you're only assigned open-and-shut cases. In fact, just the opposite. For some time now, it's clear to me that your captain is only assigning you the *hardest* cases. Often after others have come up empty."

Anna Abbott didn't reply.

"You're also the youngest detective in California. And you'd have made captain by now if you actually wanted the job, or if you cared about politics. Although something tells me that if you cared, and political maneuvering was important, you'd be great at that, also."

The waiter came by, took their orders, and left.

"So you want me to share my secrets," she said.

"Yes, but only for an obscure journal. It's not like I'm with the *New York Times.*"

"What makes you think I'd care if you were?"

"I've noticed you've mostly shied away from the spotlight."

"You've done your homework well," she allowed.

"Thank you. The good news for you is that my scholarly piece will be in a journal with extremely limited circulation. It will help nerdy criminologists teach future detectives to be better at their jobs, but that's about all."

"And can you write it without providing my name or precinct? Or even what state I'm in?"

Tom Vega nodded. "I thought you might want anonymity," he said. "Yes, absolutely."

She smiled. "Good. Then I'm in."

"Outstanding!" said Vega as the waiter brought a glass of red wine and placed it before Anna. The professor had elected to stick with water. "So what made you decide to become a detective?" he asked her, wasting no time beginning his interview.

"I thought you wanted to know how I solve cases," she said.

"I do, but I wanted a little background for my own sake. I won't put it in the article."

Anna preferred not to say, but her instincts continued to insist that she be open with him. She took a deep breath, and a sad expression came over her face. "My parents were both murdered when I was seven," she answered grimly. "I'd rather not go into any details," she added, "but suffice it to say that Batman and I had the same motivations for becoming crime fighters."

Vega blinked in confusion.

"Really?" she said. "You know, Bruce Wayne's parents were murdered when he was a kid, which is why he went on to become the Caped Crusader."

"Right," said Vega. "So you've wanted to be a detective since then?"

"Of course not," said Anna. "Not until much later. No seven-year-old kid makes that kind of decision. But this incident was ultimately the prime driver." She paused. "But enough about my past. Let's talk about my present. Let me tell you why I think my success rate is so high."

The professor stared at her with such rapt attention that she had the feeling the restaurant could burn down around them and he'd be completely oblivious. "I'm all ears," he said. "And, please, don't hold anything back. Take all the time you need. Err on the side of being *too* thorough."

Anna sighed. "If you insist," she replied. "But once you've heard me out, you'll be changing your mind about writing an article. And no journal will accept it anyway. Because it turns out that the crime-solving insights I'll be sharing aren't exactly *mainstream*."

Vega smiled. "Good," he replied. "They wouldn't be of any value to me if they were."

3

Tiparax Orr sat in the driver's seat of an SUV, resenting the presence of a low-ranked comrade named Fanimore sitting beside him, and focused his attention on a floor-to-ceiling window off in the distance. Two other of his comrades were sitting inside a four-door sedan nearby, assisting in a mission that had been nothing but a waste of time.

Until now.

Until, from out of nowhere, it had suddenly become more interesting than any of them could have possibly predicted.

This, at least, was a small mercy.

Still, Tiparax fumed. He despised Earth. Despised everything about it. He loathed its sun and its sky. He loathed the throngs of human beings that littered cities like this one. He loathed their feeble minds, backward technology, and irritating, singsongy languages, which hurt his throat to speak.

But mostly he hated the planet's lack of light. In an hour or so Earth's single sun would set, plunging this part of the planet into darkness, which the inhabitants' pathetic artificial lighting wouldn't come close to fully alleviating. Even during periods of the brightest sunlight, the planet was never bright *enough*.

He and his colleagues had light amplification technology surgically implanted into their eyes, the same tech their predecessors had used thousands of years earlier, which could magnify ambient light as much as tenfold. But their scientists had never gone to the trouble of eliminating an unfortunate design flaw. When the implants were in use, they turned pupils a gleaming, fiery red, and the whites of eyes into the color of human blood.

Which meant that Tiparax and his colleagues couldn't activate them in proximity to any human. His kind were already physically taller and more imposing than the vast majority of natives, with more severe facial features. Add in gleaming red eyes, and even members of this clueless species might begin to take notice.

"Hold your positions," he ordered his two colleagues in the other sedan through a comm implanted in his throat, using a language that was so guttural in some cases, and so piercing in tone in others, that it could literally hurt the ears of the natives. He and his brethren now on the planet all possessed comms in their throats and ears that could be activated using thoughts alone, and which could measure and interpret subvocal speech, making communication silent, when necessary, and all but telepathic.

"I'm calling in a report now," added Tiparax. "I'll conference you in."

Without waiting for a response, he sent a feeler to their commander, Shanifrey Doe, requesting an audio connection. While they had to pass as human, their interaction with the natives was minimal. Shanifrey, on the other hand, as the head of their entire contingent on Earth, had taken on the more demanding job of masquerading as one of them for extended periods. He called himself Shane Frey, which was conveniently close to his actual name, although annoyingly mellifluous when spoken by a human.

"Tiparax here," he said subvocally when Shanifrey opened a channel. "Fanimore is in the car with me, and I've conferenced in Eldamir and Mezzitorp as well."

"You know how busy I am tonight!" snapped the alien leader. "This had better be important."

"It is," said Tiparax calmly. "Since our quarry appeared on the radar two days ago, he hasn't done anything noteworthy. Not really. But that changed in a major way just a few minutes ago. You're really going to want to hear this."

"Are you going to *tell* me!" snapped Shanifrey, "or do I have to guess?"

"He's having dinner with your favorite detective. Right this second. The one who's becoming a thorn in your side."

"*Anna Abbott?*" said the commander in disbelief.

"Correct."

"Impossible," said Shanifrey.

"That's what I thought. They have nothing to do with each other. It's hard to imagine they'd intersect if they both lived a thousand life-times. So I made absolutely certain it was really her. I triple-checked her image against the ones you supplied earlier, using the best facial recognition programs these humans have, and there isn't a smidgen of a doubt. I don't know what to tell you. The odds of these two even bumping into each other—by *accident*—are millions to one against. I can't even *begin* to calculate the odds against them actually having *dinner* together."

Shanifrey paused for several long seconds. "Or maybe it's just the opposite," he said thoughtfully. "Maybe it isn't random at all. Maybe it answers questions about this detective that we weren't even asking. I should have seen it before. *Of course* that's why he's in LA."

As Shanifrey's three underlings considered his words, they immediately reached the same conclusion he had, and apologized for missing the obvious.

"It's a good thing I didn't let you grab him when you wanted to," said their commander. "If we had tortured him to death, we'd have obtained information, but it might have been unreliable and incomplete. But notice where he leads us when he doesn't know we're following."

"Well done," said Tiparax, giving his commander the praise he was so clearly fishing for. Shanifrey's chest-thumping was par for the course, and his second-in-command wasn't about to deny him the response he was after. "So what are your orders?" he asked.

There was a long pause. "This detective is slated to die tonight anyway," said the commander finally. "And since she has no information we need, there's no reason to change the plans I've made for her. So, assuming they part ways once the dinner is over, ignore her. Continue to stay on him as before. See who else, or what else, he might lead us to."

"Understood," said Tiparax, trying to hide his disgust. This baby-sitting duty was beneath them. There were any number of ways to have their quarry tracked remotely. But Shanifrey wouldn't hear of it. He felt it was critical that the tracking be done in person, so his men were right there to intervene at a moment's notice, depending on how events unfolded. Given what had happened, Tiparax had to concede that the boss might have made the right call after all.

Still, he didn't have to like it.

"And if they leave *together*?" asked Tiparax.

"That might not be ideal. While I find it very hard to believe we'd have anything to worry about if they did join forces, why take any chances? If they do leave together, capture them both."

"I get why we'd want to capture *him*. For interrogation. But why keep the *detective* alive? You just said that she's slated to die tonight anyway."

"She needs to die in the right *way*. Under the right circumstances. So if they leave together, capture them quickly and then knock her out. I'll tell you where to deliver her. It will complicate the plans my human associates have made, but with a little improvisation, we should still be able to achieve our goal."

"Understood."

"And Tiparax," added the commander, "if things do play out this way, I need you to knock her out *gently*. Without causing any obvious physical damage."

"Of course you do," said Tiparax bitterly, not bothering to hide his disappointment.

4

Anna Abbott was about to continue speaking when the waiter returned with their main courses, each a colorful work of art sitting in the middle of a large white plate, a fairly standard canvas used by gourmet chefs to make the various bright garnishes and colorful sauce drizzles used in their creations pop against the snowy background.

Professor Tom Vega waited as patiently as he could for Anna to sample her main course, bourbon pecan chicken, and chase it with a swallow of red wine, never taking his eyes from her, and leaving his own meal untouched.

Anna nodded. "Okay," she began, "here goes nothing. I'll just come out with it. My recipe for success. Where is a drum roll when you need one?"

Vega's face remained impassive. This professor was an odd duck, but her instincts continued to indicate that he was harmless, and very interested in what she had to say.

"My secret is simple," said Anna. "I've learned to hone and trust my intuition."

Vega's eyes narrowed, but he didn't respond.

"But that's just the punchline," she added. "There's a lot more to it than you might imagine."

"I'm sure there is," he said evenly.

"It goes without saying that this is a discussion," said Anna. "So feel free to interrupt with questions when you have them."

"Thank you. May I ask one now?"

"You just did," she said with a grin, deciding she could at least amuse *herself*, even if her audience was a bit stone-faced. "But feel free to ask another," she said, trying to keep a straight face.

The professor proceeded as if she hadn't even spoken. "How long have you been relying on this, ah . . . *intuition* of yours?" he asked.

Anna sighed. "Since the evening my parents were murdered. We had just come home from the movies, and were about to enter the house, when I got this sick feeling in the pit of my stomach. Like something wasn't right. I couldn't put my finger on it, but my mind was screaming at me not to let my parents go inside. I looked around, but nothing seemed out of the ordinary. Yet something *was*. I just felt this dread, this unease."

"Did you try to warn your parents?"

"I did. I told them we couldn't go in. But I couldn't explain why. Since I was only seven, they chalked it up to an overactive imagination. And who could blame them?"

She paused, remembering, and then drained half of her goblet of wine. "So they told me that everything was fine," she continued, "and promised we'd all be okay. Then they tried to humor me. They said that they would go inside and check it out. They'd leave me in the closed garage for just a minute, and then come get me when they made sure the coast was clear.

"I told them this wasn't good enough, that they couldn't go inside, even to check it out, but even I was beginning to question myself. I had no reason for feeling the way I felt. So when they assured me that I was worried about nothing, and insisted that I wait there while they checked it out, I finally agreed."

Vega nodded soberly. "That is truly *horrible*," he said, not needing her to spell out what had happened next. "Do you think that leaving you behind saved your life?"

"It's unclear. I won't describe the incident. But I did end up hiding in the garage. If I had been with them in the house, would the intruders really have killed a seven-year-old girl? Maybe. Maybe not."

Her eyes became moist. "But even if they had chosen to spare me," she continued somberly, "if I had entered with my parents, I would have seen them being killed. Losing them the way I did was traumatic enough. I can't even imagine the basket case I would have become had this played out differently."

Anna frowned and drained the remaining wine in her glass. "But that's the last I'll be talking about this," she said. "The key is that this incident led me to have faith in my gut more than anything else ever could have. From then on, I began to trust my intuition, even if it was faint and vague. And it has served me well."

The professor quickly swallowed the forkful of swordfish he had taken while she was speaking. "Surely there must be more to it than just this," he said.

"Plenty more," said Anna. "And don't call me Shirley," she dead-panned, unable to resist.

Thomas Vega's stony expression remained, just as she had now come to expect.

"I'm not trying to minimize what you're telling me," he said, "but this isn't much of a revelation. It's not out of the mainstream. It's the very *definition* of mainstream. Every detective who ever lived claims to rely on their gut when they're working cases. So what makes *your* intuition different than theirs? *Better* than theirs?"

"Because I make use of *true* intuition," replied Anna, "while they only scratch the surface. They trust their *conscious* mind to make observations and draw conclusions. If a suspect is shifty, or is sweating in a cool room, that makes them suspicious. Of course it does. They think they're using intuition, and they are to a very small degree. But they're mostly relying on indicators that they're consciously aware of."

"And you?"

"I rely on indicators that I'm *unaware* of. The *unconscious* is where the magic happens. Relying on conscious awareness to guide you is only marginally effective. Other detectives will go on about using their gut, but they use it much less than they think, and they fool themselves about how helpful it is. Most detectives think they have a keen sense of when someone is lying. But studies have shown that they're not much better at catching lies than the average person on the street."

"Are you saying that you are?"

"Yes!" she said firmly. "*Much* better. Their intuition helps them very little. Because *their* hunches are almost entirely rooted in conscious observation, conscious logic, conscious connecting of the dots. I, on the other hand, give myself over to my unconscious."

"I see," said the professor.

Anna shook her head. "Of course you don't. Which is why I never discuss this with others. Because it sounds mystical. But it isn't. It's pure science. But few have the interest, or patience, to allow me to fully explain."

"I wouldn't care if it *was* all mystical," said Vega. "For someone with your track record, if you told me your secret was traveling to other dimensions to consult with elves, I'd take you seriously. So please continue."

The briefest of smiles flashed over Anna's face and then vanished. "When I was thirteen," she said, "I began researching intuition. By then, it had served me well for many years. I vowed to learn everything I could about it. Was it just voodoo? Magic? Or was it not even a real thing? Maybe I was just fooling myself, remembering when my intuition was right, and discounting when it was wrong. I started researching this topic then, and I've never stopped. So while I don't have any formal training in neuroscience, I've become quite the armchair expert."

"So you believe intuition falls under the category of neuroscience?"

Anna swallowed another forkful of pecan chicken as the waiter came over and refilled her goblet of wine. "That's exactly what I'm saying," she continued when the waiter left. "And it falls under psychology as well. I wrote a piece about the powers of intuition many years ago for a psychology blog, just before I joined the force. But after that I made it a point to never delve into this subject matter, or disclose to others just how potent a force intuition has been in my life. And I've never shared the uncanny successes I've had with it, even in the piece I wrote. When I told people about it as a kid, most thought I was a nut, or just trying to get attention. I'd have had better luck telling them I could perform witchcraft."

"Then thank you for sharing this now," said Vega earnestly. "I'm honored."

"Don't be. I'm only doing this because my intuition is telling me that I should."

"That's good enough for me," said Vega with just the hint of a smile. "I'm liking your intuition already."

Anna studied her dinner companion for several seconds. You could say what you wanted about his limited sense of humor, but he was in awe of her solve rate, and relentlessly positive about her.

"So let me start explaining the science of it for you," she said finally. "The first and most important thing to know is that our unconscious minds are vastly superior to our conscious ones. Vastly."

Vega considered this statement. "Doesn't *unconscious* mean asleep?"

"Yes, but it's also defined as the part of the mind that's inaccessible to our consciousness. I often call it our *hidden mind*. While it operates in the shadows, it largely dictates everything about us. Behavior. Emotion. Beliefs. Actions. The word *subconscious* means something very similar, so I'll go ahead and use this term from here on out."

Vega nodded.

"Almost every one of us fools ourselves into believing we're in charge," continued Anna. "But we aren't. Not really. The vast, vast majority of who we are and how we behave is governed by this hidden region of our brain. Our subconscious mind is a brilliant puppet master, calling the shots while keeping us blissfully unaware that its hand is up our back the whole time. A great idea comes to me and I say, 'Wow, I'm a genius. Way to go, Anna.' But most of the time, it isn't Anna Abbott who came up with the idea. It was my subconscious mind, working on it for hours and days and feeding it to me from behind the scenes. And counting on me to take full credit.

"And it's not just eureka moments that stem from the subconscious, it's countless everyday decisions. If you're instructed to move either your right or left hand—your choice—an experimenter can tell from subconscious brain activity which hand you're going to choose before *you* even know. There have been many such experiments demonstrating that countless decisions we're certain we are making at the conscious level are really being made for us in our hidden minds."

"Why aren't these experiments more widely known?" asked Vega.

Anna shrugged. "I don't know. But if you search the web for 'does your subconscious mind make decisions' you'll find them for yourself. But it is widely known, at least, that our hidden minds take care of our breathing, the beating of our hearts, the sexual response, and so on."

"Surely the sexual response is driven by the conscious mind."

Anna grinned, but decided not to make the *don't call me Shirley* joke again. "It isn't," she replied instead. "You can't order up arousal on demand. If you're standing over a bloody, maggot-infested carcass that stinks of rotting flesh, and your conscious mind orders your arm to move, it will move. Every time. But try ordering your sexual organ to become aroused while you're gazing at a corpse, standing within a cloud of stench, and see what happens."

Vega's face contorted into a look of pure disgust. "I see your point."

"We have little conscious control of what causes us to become sexually aroused. But a rotting corpse is most likely to cause us to become repulsed. Arousal, revulsion, fear—these things just happen. We aren't in charge. And if we had to consciously think about breathing in and out, making our hearts beat, and so on, we'd be unable to focus on anything else. So all of this machinery is hardwired in."

The professor nodded. "Go on," he said.

"Almost a third of the neurons in your brain are devoted to vision," she continued. "A third. Everything you see enters your brain upside down, backwards, and two-dimensional—with a large blind spot to boot. But you don't see things this way. Your mighty hidden mind adjusts it for you. But if you think that's a neat trick, here's one that's even better. There are specially designed fun-house glasses that flip the world upside down. If you were to wear these glasses continuously, at first you'd be helpless. But after a few days of wearing them, your hidden mind would completely remap the input, spatially, and flip the world right-side up for you again."

"Seems hard to believe," said Vega.

"I suspect the experimenters were surprised, as well."

"So the bottom line," said the professor, "is that there's lots of magic going on under the hood that we're completely unaware of."

"Exactly," said Anna. "But not just unaware of. Unable to affect one way or another. But I'll say more about that later. First, let me give you one more example of the power of our hidden minds.

Imagine speaking quickly for several minutes. Now think about the hundreds of perfectly choreographed movements your teeth, lips, and tongue have to make at lightning speed to make this happen—which you aren't even aware of. Why not? Because your subconscious mind takes care of the complex task of forming words *for you*," she added. "Effortlessly. If you had to consciously control all of these mouth movements, you'd never get a sentence out."

Vega nodded thoughtfully. "After a lifetime of speaking," he said, "I have to admit that I've never really thought about the complex mechanics of it before."

"Few do," said Anna. "Reading, touch-typing, playing the piano. All very similar. All completely handled by the subconscious once you've achieved a certain level of proficiency.

"Our brains contain over a hundred billion neurons," she continued, "allowing for a nearly infinite number of potential states. Orders of magnitude more than our most sophisticated computers. Our minds put the greatest supercomputers to *shame*. It doesn't seem that way, because we aren't consciously wired for math, and computers are. But when it comes to pattern recognition, figuring out how to catch a baseball, monitoring our environment, and versatile, general intelligence, our minds are unmatched. Unfortunately, many of these capabilities reside in our subconscious, beyond our conscious reach."

She paused to let this sink in. "And even in math, our subconscious minds are quite accomplished. If the ability to calculate square roots had been important for our survival, had helped early man hunt the mastodon, I'm sure our hidden minds would have established a pathway to feed these answers to us. But we do have impressive math abilities. They're just hidden. You'd be amazed by how many complex calculations the subconscious minds of our primitive ancestors had to make to determine the proper trajectories of the spears they were throwing."

Anna took another sip of wine. "We get a glimpse of the brain's mathematical prowess from autistic savants," she continued. "Some can multiply huge numbers, or take square roots, almost instantly. Whereas we have to strain and concentrate with our conscious minds to do even simple calculations, they can tap into their subconscious, solving what to us are impossible problems with effortless ease. They just instantly *see* the answer."

"Excellent point," said Vega. "And something else I never stopped to think about before."

The detective raised her eyebrows. "And even this is just scratching the surface of what the subconscious can do. Our hidden mind knows endless things, has endless capabilities, that we can't even begin to fathom. It has an almost god-like ability to recognize patterns and draw connections and conclusions within a mountain of seemingly unrelated data. And our hidden minds are far more observant than we are, and far more astute.

"But here's the tragedy. We have a rocket engine under the hood that we can barely tap. Because while our hidden mind is far superior to our conscious mind, we have no access. We can't direct it, or control it. It's completely walled off from us."

Anna shrugged. "Now, a minuscule percentage of people do have a tiny crack in the wall that separates their conscious and subconscious minds," she added. "Which explains the math abilities of autistic savants, for example. They can somehow peer through this crack and instantly pull out the square root of any number, which their subconscious has effortlessly calculated for them. But you and I can't."

"So why are we built this way?" said Vega. "Why have such a powerful engine if we can't tap it?"

"Sucks, doesn't it?" said Anna. "But let's talk about *whys* another time. For now, let's just accept that this is the way it is. This is the way our minds are built. Our hidden mind, our subconscious, is flat out astonishing. It excels at nearly everything."

She frowned. "With the one big exception that I just noted—it's *horrible* at communicating with us. Yes, it excels at *controlling* us. At dictating our opinions, likes, who we're attracted to, and many of our actions and ideas. But this isn't the same as two-way communication. If it wants to actually tell us precisely what it's figured out, it has little ability to do so. It can sometimes find a path to reach us through dreams, which are a very poor and unreliable channel of communication. And it can trigger clammy palms, a sick feeling in the gut, an increase in heart rate, and so on. Pathetically weak attempts that most of us choose to ignore. But that's about it."

"I see," said Vega thoughtfully. "So this is your definition of intuition. Inside our heads, we have a brilliant stranger who knows a lot more than we do, and who draws better and faster conclusions. But it's a stranger who isn't able to explain *what* it knows, or *how* it knows it."

"I couldn't have said it better myself."

"A fascinating theory."

Anna shook her head. "Not just theory," she replied. "Fact. Based on any number of observations and experiments. For example, you can have study participants repeatedly choose cards from four decks, with rewards given for high cards. And you can rig the decks so that two are markedly better than the other two. Based on tiny heart rate and perspiration changes when they reached for the bad decks, scientists discovered that subjects' hidden minds, on average, figured out which two were the bad ones after choosing only ten cards. But their conscious minds didn't figure it out until after they had chosen *eighty*."

"Wow," said Vega, impressed. "If only their hidden minds had been able to share their findings."

"Exactly," replied Anna. "But as I said, while the subconscious is horrible at communication, it can control conscious responses—with ease. And with a frequency that would astonish you. In one experiment—I won't bore you with how it was carried out—men rated women with dilated pupils as being more attractive than the same women with non-dilated pupils. Turns out pupil dilation in women is a biological sign of sexual arousal. When the men were asked if their ratings had anything to do with pupil dilation, they scoffed at the idea."

She raised her eyebrows. "But their hidden minds had not only detected this subtle sign of arousal," she continued, "but had known it for what it was. And had even managed to pull strings to get their conscious selves to respond positively to it—even though they had no idea why they were doing so. And no idea that their hidden mind was manipulating them from offstage."

Anna moved on before the professor could respond. "Chicken sexers are another classic example," she said.

"Did you say *chicken sexers?*"

"Yeah. It's a thing. When baby chicks are first hatched, males and females look identical. But the females will one day lay eggs, so chicken farmers want to separate them out right away to give them preferential treatment. Turns out there is a famous school in Japan where chicken sexing masters quickly and accurately separate the chicks into male and female bins. The problem is that these masters can't explain how they choose. So poultry breeders from around the world travel to this school to train their own people. The Japanese masters stand over these clueless apprentices while they sort baby chicks, telling them if they are right or wrong every time. Eventually, the apprentices become masters, and are never wrong, even though they, also, can't explain how they're choosing."

"I see," said Vega. "So their subconscious minds have it all figured out, and even manage to control their actions to take advantage of this insight."

"Right. Our hidden mind is great at observing. Great at dictating our tastes, fetishes, and opinions. Great at controlling us. But *horrible* at explaining. Like the Oracle of Delphi. All-knowing, yet it won't give us a straight answer."

The professor nodded solemnly. "Okay, I'm sold. Intuition is real. And your theory to explain it is real also."

Anna grinned. "Are you sure about that, or is it just a gut feeling you're having?"

The professor smiled back. "So you're saying that solving crimes is as easy for you as correctly sorting identical baby chicks is for a Japanese master. You just do it, without having any idea how."

"Not exactly," said Anna. "But this would make a great title for your paper: *crime-solving techniques borrowed from Japanese chicken sexers—your complete guide.*"

Vega rolled his eyes. "I'll take that title under advisement," he said in amusement.

5

The detective paused so they could finish their meals, which they did while watching the sun melt into the horizon and vanish in the distance.

The waiter took their plates, and both ordered after-dinner coffees in lieu of dessert.

"So how do you solve cases?" asked Vega. "Are you saying you just sort of *know* who committed a crime?"

"Not at all. I use all the traditional methods. I rack my conscious mind to try to figure it out. I plan what questions to ask witnesses and suspects. But I've trained myself to pay attention when my hidden mind is trying to tell me something. Sometimes I just magically want to ask a suspect a question that doesn't seem related to the case in any way. Instead of suppressing this urge, I ask the question."

"Because you've made peace with not understanding the why of it."

"Exactly. And I try to purposely evoke these strange avenues of thought and inquiry by blanking my mind at key times, trying to push my consciousness as much out of the way as possible. I can't tell you how many times random questions and ideas that pop into my head, seemingly unrelated to anything, end up leading to a breakthrough in the case."

"I see," said Vega. "So wild ideas out of left field that no one else would seriously pursue, you explore with a passion."

"Exactly. And even when wild questions and ideas don't pop into my head, sometimes my gut tells me someone is innocent, even if they appear to be guilty, and I spend my time chasing other suspects. Sometimes my gut tells me someone is guilty, so I stick with them like glue. Sometimes my gut says to explore the case from a novel angle. And so on."

They paused as their coffees arrived.

"Have you ever had any premonitions like you did when you were seven?" asked Vega when the waiter had left.

"Yes. But I don't call them *premonitions*. A premonition is getting a glimpse of the future. I can't do that. I didn't have a premonition that my parents were about to be killed. My hidden mind had seen something, heard something, smelled something, that no conscious mind could. Something that told it we had intruders."

"But why didn't your parents' subconscious minds pick up on what *yours* did? Even after you tipped them off to look for something wrong."

"I don't know," she replied, pausing to sip at her coffee. "But I've come to believe that my subconscious is better able to tip me off than most. I don't have cracks in the wall between my conscious and subconscious the way some autistic savants do. But I seem to excel at reading the feeble hints I'm given."

"Does this mean that your technique isn't broadly applicable?"

"No, everyone can benefit from cultivating their intuition. From learning how to listen better to the brilliant stranger inside, and trust in what it's saying. Maybe not as much as *I'm* able to benefit. A genius and a special needs student will both benefit from studying for a test. But the genius will still get higher marks."

"So how do you cultivate this intuition of yours?"

"Like any muscle. I use it. Constantly. Which means focusing on the telltales—my gut, my pulse, tingly skin, and so on—and learning how to listen to what the brilliant stranger in my mind is trying to tell me. And not just listen to it, but *trust* it. Which often requires a leap of faith, as many of its prescriptions can seem counterintuitive."

"I see," said Vega, nodding thoughtfully. "So it really is that simple."

Anna smiled. "Yes," she replied. "And that complicated. But there is one more facet. One I think is the most important of all." She winced. "But I'm afraid you'll find this the biggest reach of anything I've told you."

"Try me," said Vega.

"I cram my subconscious with as much information as I possibly can. Everything under the sun. I've been doing this since I was thirteen. I get non-fiction audiobooks and play them throughout the night while I sleep. Audiobooks that describe a hundred varieties of poisonous plants, for example. Or types of locks. Or review the science of blood spatter analysis."

Vega's eyes widened. "And you've been doing this every night for fifteen years?"

"Every night. Except for the few times I was in a relationship and wasn't sleeping alone."

"Very courteous of you," said the Stanford professor in amusement. His eyes narrowed. "But are you telling me that you can *retain* all this information?"

Anna laughed. "Don't be ridiculous. I can't retain *any* of it. Not consciously, at any rate."

"But you believe your subconscious *can*?"

"My intuition tells me this is the case."

"Any scientific evidence to back that up?"

"I'm afraid not," said Anna. "But our hidden minds take in a lot more information than we know, all the time. For example, there's something scientists call the Cocktail Party Effect. People have an uncanny ability to hear their own names ring out through a heavy thicket of otherwise indecipherable conversation. Say you're in a big crowd, with chatter all around, but totally focused on your own conversation. Even though the other conversations are like white noise, if your name is mentioned, it stands out from all the rest."

Vega nodded but didn't respond.

"So how does this work? Turns out your subconscious is taking in all of these other conversations, digesting them, without you knowing it. Like a hidden sentinel, monitoring. It wants to be sure headquarters isn't bothered by this jumble of noise so you can focus on your own conversation. But if it hears something it thinks you might be interested in, it sends this to your conscious mind. Could be your name. Could be the word *spy* if you're an intelligence agent. Or the word *fire*. Or anything else that it thinks you might need to hear."

"Hard to imagine your subconscious can take in this many scrambled conversations at the same time, and sort it all out."

"Yes it is. Which is what makes it so amazing. And indispensable. An exhausted new mother can sleep through a thunderstorm, but will awaken if her baby begins to cry in another room. Her subconscious chooses not to bother her with the thunder, but immediately throws the cry to headquarters for further attention."

The professor stared at her thoughtfully. "But even if our subconscious can *hear* everything, this doesn't prove it retains it."

"I'm well aware," said Anna. "In fact, most scientists think the idea that one can absorb the contents of an audiobook while sleeping is preposterous. But there's really no way to prove it—or *disprove* it—since your subconscious isn't talking. If I listen to an audiobook on poisonous plants at night and you ask me a question about the material in the morning, I won't have a clue. In that respect, the scientists are correct. The material doesn't benefit me consciously at all."

The detective took a sip of coffee and continued. "But I don't care. Because my hidden mind now has the knowledge it needs to guide me in some future case. Say if a murder victim is found poisoned. My intuition might cause me to take a special interest in an unusual flower in a suspect's garden, without me knowing why. But when I study this flower, now using my *conscious* mind, it can help me break the case wide open."

She paused. "I'm convinced that cramming my brain with miscellaneous information has been a big help to me. I'm providing the brilliant stranger in my head with a vast encyclopedia of knowledge to cross-reference, analyze, and find patterns within, so it can then nudge me in the right direction."

"Given your spectacular results," said Vega, "it's hard to argue that this strategy isn't working."

"Thank you."

"And you say that you use this intuition of yours frequently," said Vega.

"*Continuously*, in one way or another. I'm exquisitely sensitive to it. I've been listening to my gut since you called me. It told me to meet with you and tell you my story. I have no idea why."

Anna finished her coffee and set the now-empty mug back down on the table. "During this dinner, my gut has told me that you want the best for me, but warns that I can't entirely trust you. That there's more going on here than meets the eye. Something I'm missing. Something you're hiding from me. Believe it or not, despite carefully vetting your credentials, my gut's not even sure that you really are a professor of criminology. Or that you're writing a paper."

"Which means that your gut isn't always right," said Vega with a smile.

Anna laughed. "First, I didn't say my intuition is *certain* that you aren't who you say you are. Just that the jury is still out. And second, you are correct, even if it did insist, it isn't always right. Most of the time, but not always. I have been known to misinterpret its Oracle-like ambiguous communications from time to time. And the strongest signal I'm getting is that you mean me well, so I'm choosing to ignore the more suspicious ones."

Her features suddenly hardened. "At least for now," she added pointedly.

Vega stared deep into the detective's large blue eyes. "I *do* mean you well," he said. "So it's nice that this is coming through loud and clear. And this conversation has been even more eye-opening for me than I imagined," he added.

"I'm glad," she said as the waiter brought the bill, which Vega paid in cash.

Anna thanked the professor for dinner and rose to leave. "So are you flying back home now?"

"Not tonight. I'm staying at the Camden International Hotel on Wilshire."

"Good choice," said Anna approvingly, surprised that he had such expensive taste in hotels. The Camden was only fifteen minutes away from her condo, and she passed it frequently. It was eighteen stories tall, with a soaring ground floor that served as a magnificent, expansive lobby, complete with palm trees and an atrium.

"Thanks. I didn't want to have to cut our conversation short to rush to the airport. I guess I could have driven here instead of flying. It's only supposed to be about five hours by car. But when driving to

LA, you never know if bad traffic will add an hour or two to the total travel time. And I really don't enjoy driving for that long. Even in a self-driving car."

The detective nodded. Self-driving cars had been on the market as early as 2023, but only a small percentage of the total were truly autonomous. These tended to be pricey, and most drivers still preferred to take the wheel themselves, proving the adage that old habits died hard.

Vega blew out a long breath. "Before you leave," he said, "since I am staying in town tonight, I had a thought."

Anna studied him for several seconds. Men seemed to find her looks almost irresistibly appealing. So usually she'd expect him to offer her a nightcap, hoping to get her into bed. But her intuition insisted this wasn't the case. Not this time.

"Go on," she said.

"I know tomorrow is Friday," began Vega, "and that you'll be working. But I'd love to get together again. Maybe I can buy you lunch at my hotel. But if you can't make it tomorrow, I can make myself available any time you like on Saturday. Or even Sunday."

"So you'd stay a *second* or even *third* night if you had to, just to buy me lunch?"

"Absolutely. As I'm sure your instincts have told you, I'm not trying to hit on you. But before I fall asleep tonight, I'll be thinking long and hard about what you told me. And I believe I'll be able to devise some scientific tests of your intuition. Get a gauge on just how strong it is. Right now, the proof that it's as useful as you say is your solve rate. Which is impressive, and strongly suggests that you're on to something big. But if I had additional data to put in this paper, generated by a well-controlled experiment, this would really bolster the case."

Anna considered. She found the professor intriguing, even though he was one of the occasional people whom her hidden mind couldn't get much of a handle on. "No one has ever asked me to be their guinea pig before," she said. "I don't know whether to be flattered or offended."

"Be flattered."

"If you say so," she said with just the hint of a smile. "Okay," she added finally, "you're on. I'll make tomorrow work."

"*Outstanding*," said Vega happily. "I can pick you up. Or I can pay for your transportation if you'd like."

"No need," said the detective, shaking her head. "I'll meet you in the lobby at noon."

"Great. Just be sure to bring your intuition."

Anna grinned, her eyes sparkling. "Don't worry," she replied in amusement. "I never leave home without it."

6

Detective Anna Abbott entered her spacious, multimillion-dollar condo and once again reflected on her dinner with the Stanford professor. She had enjoyed it. The food was delicious, the view magnificent, and the conversation a little weird, but also fun. She had never before been so frank about how she had solved her cases, and it had been a long while since she had last taken any real credit for this success.

When other detectives at the precinct expressed awe at her performance, she brushed them off, reflexively countering any praise with self-deprecating humor and an immediate minimization of her contributions. Many of her colleagues already harbored resentment and jealousy of her success, so she did everything she could to tamp out this fire. She would acknowledge that she thought she was a reasonably good detective, but insist that she was far more lucky than she was special, and that she had no doubt she would soon hit a spate of *bad* luck to balance the cosmic scales. And she always gave credit to everyone else around her, finding ways to pretend that even the tiniest contribution made by a colleague had been the key that had *really* unlocked the case.

She also kept her private life very private, never disclosing where she lived, and never letting anyone she worked with anywhere near her neighborhood. They were already jealous of her as a detective, so the last thing she needed was for them to learn she lived in a luxury condominium. This would lead to questions that she didn't want to answer, and even more resentment.

Anna was walking to her bedroom to change clothes when she noticed that she was sniffing the air. She couldn't detect any strange odors, so why was she doing this?

Her eyes narrowed as her intuition provided the answer: *something was wrong*. She could feel it in her bones.

Anna had become exquisitely sensitive to subconscious signals, but the signals she was receiving now were so strong they didn't require any sensitivity.

Had someone been in her condo?

She checked the locks and security footage, but nothing looked out of the ordinary. She then took a survey of her entire residence, going into one room after another, and scouring every square inch with her eyes.

As far as she could tell, at least consciously, nothing in the place had been disturbed an iota.

And yet this disquieting feeling remained.

She walked around her home once again, this time more slowly, becoming a human divining rod, counting on her hidden mind to signal her when it sensed something worth exploring.

When she approached the thick glass desk inside her home office, her stomach tightened, and she paused near her computer, listening. She lowered her ear to within inches of the petite tower that represented the guts of her expensive desktop machine, and was just able to make out a nearly imperceptible hum. A tiny fan, as quiet as they came, was operating on its lowest setting, working to cool off the densely packed electronic chips inside, indicating the tower must have heated up very recently.

She checked, but her computer had not been force-fed software updates from the web in weeks. Which meant that *someone* had used it while she was gone. *Extensively*.

Anna felt like Goldilocks. But it wasn't her porridge that was too hot. It was her computer.

Which confirmed that her condo *had* been broken into, as her intuition had indicated. By an individual or group who possessed skills that were truly exceptional. She found it hard to believe that the condo's security could be breached by anyone, no matter how expert. Not only had her security been brushed off with ease, but those responsible hadn't left the slightest telltale sign of their visit, other than the nearly inaudible computer fan, which had likely come on only after they had left.

The job had been so *clean*. So professional. So sophisticated.

She rushed around her apartment to confirm what she already knew in her gut to be true. *Nothing* had been taken. Not even the expensive jewelry that she owned but hadn't worn in many years. Which made this violation even more chilling than if it *had* been a robbery.

They had come for one reason only: to hack into her computer. To tamper with it. And they had gone to *a lot* of trouble to be sure that she never discovered this tampering.

And it would have worked—had she been *anyone* else.

Her fingers flew over the keyboard, but after ten minutes she couldn't find anything out of the ordinary, even with her intuition to guide her. Whatever they had done was well hidden. Her secret bank account was untouched, with its usual balance of slightly over twelve million dollars.

So *why* had they come? What was their endgame?

There was only one answer that made any sense: they had to be trying to frame her. They must have planted something incriminating on her computer. Still, unless the authorities searched her home computer—extensively—which they had no reason to do, this wouldn't help them. So there must be more to their plan.

Anna lifted her phone to call a computer expert she had worked with many times, who could get to the bottom of what had been done, when her ringtone came to life. She examined the screen. The caller wasn't anyone she knew, but she doubted it was a solicitor. Even telemarketers had the good sense not to call at eight-thirty at night.

"Hello," she said, taking the call.

"Detective Anna Abbott?" said a male voice.

"Who is this?"

"My name is Jimmy Jessup."

She frowned. The name didn't ring any bells. "What do you want?"

"I work for a drug dealer here in town, Detective. I won't name names over the phone, but it's a name I'm sure you know. He's a major player, and I'm one of his primary lieutenants."

"I'll bet your mother is very proud."

The caller laughed. "Good one."

"I'll ask again, what do you want?"

"I've heard through the grapevine that you've got your panties in a bundle over a new drug that's just hitting the streets. One called Foria."

Her eyes narrowed. "And?"

"And I'm calling to offer my services. As an informant. More to the point, as a *paid* informant. *Highly* paid. Assuming you care enough about stopping this drug to spend all of your allowance in one place."

"And why would you inform on your boss?" asked Anna. "Even if I bust my budget on you, you won't exactly be able to retire to Maui."

"I'm making this offer because I'm a survivor, Detective. And I'm smart. It's clear that this new drug has hit your radar in a big way. And you've developed a bit of a rep. Word on the street is that you always get your man. So I'd like to stay out of your crosshairs. Give me a payday, and immunity from prosecution, and I'll help you nail my boss."

"I always get my man, Jimmy, remember? So why do I need your help?"

There was a long pause, as this question must have caught Anna's would-be informant off guard. "The launch of Foria is starting slowly," he replied finally, "but it will spread like wildfire. I can help you stop it *now*, rather than later. I gotta believe that's worth throwing a small fish like me back into the ocean."

"Maybe," said Anna, noncommittally. If he really was a primary lieutenant for a major player in town, he wasn't exactly a *small fish*, but she decided not to argue the point.

"If you're interested, meet me in thirty minutes at the back parking lot of Salem Hills High School to iron this out. If you don't show, my offer disappears forever."

"Why does it have to be tonight?"

"I'm smart, but so is my boss. And ruthless. If he finds out I'm doing this, it's my ass. If we agree on a deal, I can give you enough evidence to take him down within a few days. Which limits my exposure. So this is a one-time offer, Detective. Be at Salem Hills High in thirty minutes, or miss out. Your choice."

"No way I can make it in thirty minutes," said Anna. "It'd take me forty-five to get there if I left this second," she lied. "And I just stepped out of the shower, dripping wet. Give me an hour and a half."

There was a long pause. "An hour and fifteen," replied Jimmy. "Not a minute more."

"Understood."

"I'll see you soon, Detective. But know this, if I smell anyone else within five miles of you, the deal is off."

"Don't worry," said Anna evenly. "I'll come alone."

7

The detective ended the connection with Jimmy Jessup, and her mind began to race.

She relied on her subconscious to help her, yes, but like the Almighty, the subconscious helped those who helped themselves. Headquarters still needed to contribute the lion's share of planning in situations like these.

The meeting was a trap. This required no intuition at all. The most clueless civilian could have figured that out, provided they knew that her place was broken into, and her computer hacked, just prior to Jimmy's call.

Both happening at once was too much of a coincidence.

And given the level of skill and care exhibited by whoever had broken into her condo, the trap could well be elaborate, and heavily manned.

She had bought herself some precious minutes, but she had no time to waste. She slid into her black mesh office chair and pounded away at the computer, bringing up a bird's-eye view of Salem Hills High on her monitor, and conducting a virtual flyover of the school.

The grounds were more extensive than she had imagined, with endless places for hostiles to hide. A large concrete parking lot snaked around a multi-armed one-story building, which seemed to have expanded almost haphazardly over the decades as the student population had grown. There were a dozen or more cars spread out around the sprawling but mostly empty lot, either inoperable or left for unknown reasons. While the footage was archival, she suspected that a smattering of cars were always present.

The flyover revealed any number of towering trees, some looking wide enough to hide a tank, along with rising and falling knolls, football and baseball fields with dugouts and stands, eight tennis courts, and various stand-alone buildings. There were three small, self-contained concrete bathrooms with metal toilet seats spread around the grounds, like the kind found at public beaches, and two storage sheds for sports or landscaping equipment.

Satisfied, Anna quickly stripped out of her dress and donned black jeans and a bulletproof vest, which she concealed with a black sweatshirt. She armed herself with her police-issued Glock, and shoved a spare handgun between her waistband and the small of her back, slipping a switchblade knife into her front pocket for good measure.

She then went to work filling a blue canvas duffel bag with various weapons, including a third handgun, with a silencer attachment, a tactical flashlight, a pair of IR binoculars, plastic zip-ties, a roll of duct tape, and a comprehensive first aid kit.

She removed a padded case from a desk drawer and carefully placed it inside the large duffel, as well. The case housed two sophisticated octocopter drones, one the diameter of a dinner plate, and one the size of a dragonfly, duplicates of the ones she kept at her office. Finally, she added a small tablet computer that could control the drones and display the video footage they captured, and rushed to her car, duffel bag in tow.

The larger drone had served her well on many occasions, and she had no doubt it would do the same on this night. She had never anticipated a situation like this, but she had become an expert drone operator over the past two years, insisting on taking a bird's-eye video of every crime scene she could.

She continued to acquire more and more sophisticated drones as new technology became available, and this latest employed the best noise-canceling technology money could buy, along with the best night-vision lenses. The smaller version of the drone had the same technological bells and whistles as its larger twin sister, but was tiny enough to fit comfortably in the palm of her hand, giving it a more limited range and largely relegating it to indoor use.

Anna raced to the school in record time, sometimes streaking along side streets at twice the posted speed limit, and using her police remote to ensure that all traffic lights she encountered were green. She parked well out of sight of the school, lowered her window, and sent the larger drone into the sky. It leaped straight up, effortlessly, paused briefly when it reached its flying altitude of eighty feet, and then darted toward Salem Hills High.

Anna had no doubt there were any number of cameras active in the area, but it must have been child's play for those who were after her to temporarily disable them.

She watched the drone's feed on the small tablet computer, which was also controlling its flight, and could soon make out a figure down below, in the center of the back parking lot.

"Hello, Jimmy," she whispered out loud.

The man she had come to meet was standing near a towering parking lot light, which, although dim, was one of the few that was at least *working*. She guessed that whoever was behind this had seen to it that most of the other lights around the grounds—in the parking lot or otherwise—were turned off. Even so, the IR capabilities of the drone were state of the art, and it had no trouble capturing clear images of the terrain below despite the limited ambient light.

She flew the drone in ever-widening circles, and soon discovered that whoever had set this up had prepared even more of an ambush than she had expected.

Four additional hostiles were spread out around the grounds, each quite distant from Jimmy Jessup and out of his view. Two were on the move, patrolling to the east and west of the man she had come to meet, guns in hand, staying low or hugging buildings to remain unseen.

One other, nearest to where Anna was parked, was dressed in black, and was pressed against one wall of a corner of a building, using the building to stay screened from both Jimmy and the approach Anna would most likely take. This man was on his knees, with one eye glued to the scope of a sniper rifle, which was being held steady by a tripod.

Which left one additional hostile, fifty yards to Jimmy's south, who also had a sniper tripod in place, although he was standing, rather than kneeling, and was concealed behind a mighty tree, with only the tip of the muzzle peeking around the edge of the trunk.

Anna's gut was insisting that trying to turn the tables now was sheer suicide. That even *she* couldn't overcome odds this bad. But for once she ignored these signals.

She had to learn who was behind this, what they had done, and why they had done it. With this much of a concerted effort against her, she could run from the pending encounter, but she couldn't avoid it. And the longer she remained in the dark, the more vulnerable she would be. Right now they assumed she was a sheep being led to the slaughter, which gave her the upper hand she needed. But if she left now, the element of surprise would be gone, and they'd be bringing the party to *her*, which would be even more dangerous.

She double-timed it to the northernmost edge of the grounds, keeping one eye trained on the drone's feed. These men could well be communicating through a comm system. Even if not, she couldn't let them cry out. Which meant she had to take them out one at a time. And she had to do so with such speed, stealth, and precision that none of them would be able to sound an alarm.

Perfect, she thought miserably. She liked a challenge as much as the next gal, but come on . . . . She was a detective, not a commando.

Anna allowed herself a brief flicker of a smile at this thought. She might not be a commando, but she wasn't helpless, either. She had read books on martial arts, both consciously and for her subconscious, and had practiced for years. She wasn't anything special if she tried to direct her own moves. But whenever she let herself go, let her hidden mind read her opponent and make the moves *for* her, she was nearly unbeatable.

The night was cool and unnaturally still. Anna took a deep breath and then blew it out. *Here goes nothing*, she thought, and then began to creep quietly around the side of the building, approaching the position of the sniper nearest to her.

When she was a few feet from the corner of the building, she imagined she could hear the sniper breathing just around its edge, but knew that this was only the product of an overactive imagination. She knelt low and used the tablet computer to guide the drone closer to the sniper's position. Finally, she lowered the drone behind him, its noise-canceling technology so advanced that she made sure it hit the back of his leg on the way down so he would react the way she wanted.

An instant before the drone hit him, Anna placed the tablet on the ground and readied herself for action. As the drone deflected off the sniper's leg, he gasped and swiveled around to look behind him, still on his knees.

"What the hell?" he muttered to himself. As he lowered his eyes to inspect the drone, Anna darted around the corner of the building and savagely kicked his head as if she were an NFL punter. The man instantly jackknifed backwards and onto the ground, groaning in pain.

Remarkably, he somehow managed to shake off a blow that would have left most men in a coma, and rolled toward Anna, pulling a lethal combat knife from a sheath and slashing at her legs with catlike agility. She dodged this effort, skipping backwards with exceptional speed, as the hostile took this chance to jump up to his feet.

Anna's gut anticipated this move seconds before *she* did, and sent her right leg and body into motion before the man had even landed, such that she swept his legs out from under him the moment he was standing, giving him no chance to block or avoid the blow. He went down hard again, and Anna followed him to the ground, hammering the butt of her pistol into his forehead with enough force to crack a walnut.

The light in his eyes went out instantly, and this time he stayed down. Anna checked for a pulse, which was faint, but present. She quickly hogtied him with zip-ties, a detective turned rodeo star, and sealed his mouth with duct tape.

Anna blew out a long, relieved breath, and waited a few seconds for the deafening pounding of her heart to subside. When it did, she looked through the rifle's telescopic scope, being careful not to move it. As expected, it was aimed squarely toward Jimmy's general vicinity, but not directly at him. The sniper had most likely been awaiting *her* arrival, at which point he would adjust his aim to place the crosshairs on the middle of her forehead.

Still, something was eating at her. Something was wrong.

She didn't recognize the make and model of the rifle.

But why should *that* matter? After all, she wasn't a sniper. She wouldn't recognize *most* rifles.

Still, this was only one in a long list of wild suggestions her gut had made that had turned out to be important. So somehow it *must* matter. She took a quick photo of the weapon and had Google compare it with images it had in stock. Within seconds Google had found a match. The rifle was a Kester 8500.

It was a sniper rifle all right, one with an invisible laser site and night vision enhancement. But it didn't shoot bullets. It shot tiny *tranquilizer darts.*

Tranquilizer darts?

She wasn't aware that there *was* such a thing as a tranquilizer dart sniper rifle. At least not consciously. But the brilliant stranger in her mind had known.

And now the true picture slammed into focus all at once. The answer to why there were two snipers instead of only one. Why both were out of view of Jimmy. And why both were almost certainly shooting darts.

She had been stubbornly clinging to the idea that whoever was behind this had planned for Jimmy to shoot her during their meeting, and that his four colleagues were hanging around as possible backup—just in case.

But of course that wasn't right. The truth was that they were planning to sacrifice Jimmy along with her. They would make it look like she and this criminal had had a falling out, and had shot each other, nearly simultaneously.

They were framing her, and this frame would be all the more compelling if they were willing to sacrifice one of their own. When her body was found in a dark high school parking lot near the body of a known felon, this would certainly get the ball rolling.

They just hadn't told Jimmy.

If the snipers took either of them out with actual bullets, the ballistics would be *way* off. Their neat little story would pop like a balloon as it became almost instantly clear that one, or both, had been shot from afar.

Instead, while she was meeting with Jimmy, they would knock them both unconscious, simultaneously, no doubt using a very short-acting tranquilizer dart, probably to the neck. Then they could stage the double homicide at their leisure. They would use gloves and put Jimmy's gun in his hand, shooting her in the neck to cover up the puncture mark made by the dart. Then they would do the same in the other direction. Finally, they would plant evidence on her, so it would look like she had been on the take.

And this was only the beginning, because this incident would be more than enough to warrant an investigation into her past, leading authorities to her home computer, which they had doctored.

Very nice. She was as impressed as she was horrified.

Anna ejected a dart from the rifle and examined it, impressed by how far these darts had come since she had last seen one. This one was tiny, sleek, aerodynamic, and perfectly balanced, ensuring it would fly as true as a bullet. She shoved the tiny dart into a small, zippered compartment on the outside of the duffel.

This completed, Anna carefully adjusted the sniper rifle so that it was aimed precisely to the south, at the second sniper hidden behind a tree, and then commanded the drone to rise into the pitch-dark of the night sky once again.

She flew the octocopter carefully behind the second sniper, and then directed it to accelerate straight into his back, removing the noise-canceling feature at the last moment to increase the element of fear.

The instant this was done she returned her attention to the rifle, knowing she would need to aim and shoot within a second or two, and giving herself over to pure instinct.

The drone slammed into the second sniper's back and he reflexively moved a few steps forward, as Anna had known he would, temporarily bringing him into her line of sight. The detective adjusted the rifle and pulled the trigger in one smooth motion, taking her conscious mind out of the equation, and wasn't surprised when the man clutched at his neck and dropped to the grass like a felled tree.

She quickly located the last two men patrolling the area and used the sniper rifle to put them down as well, before finally doing the same to Jimmy, watching in satisfaction as he crumpled onto the surface of the concrete parking lot.

Anna gave the rifle a grateful nod. If the company ever needed a spokesperson to tout their product, she'd be first in line to volunteer.

The detective rushed to each of the three men who had been surrounding Jimmy and made sure they were each hogtied and gagged as she had done with the first. She collected her drone, returned it to its padded case, and placed it once again inside her blue duffel bag. While it had crashed into a man's back, she knew from experience that it was sturdily built, and could withstand more abuse than this before it stopped being operable.

Finally, she double-timed it to the parking lot and to the man she had come to meet, using her tactical flashlight to cut through the darkness.

She zip-tied Jimmy's wrists and ankles together, but in front of him rather than behind his back, and left him free to speak. Satisfied, she stood over her sleeping prisoner, now sprawled out on his back on the concrete lot, and waited for him to come to.

Finally, fifteen minutes later, his eyes fluttered open, and he eyed her in confusion, still punch drunk from the drug.

"Hello, *Jimmy*," she said firmly. "You and I need to have a little talk."

8

Jimmy Jessup blinked rapidly, as if to clear his head, and Anna could see comprehension return to his eyes. "What the *hell*?" he barked, rising to a seated position on the ground.

"I *know*," said Anna pleasantly, "I'm a little bit early. Sorry about that."

"What are you *doing*?" he demanded. "Is this the way you treat your informants?"

"Really?" said Anna in disbelief. "Still sticking with *that* tall tale? You were going to kill me, Jimmy. Just admit it."

"I was going to *help* you," he insisted.

Anna shook her head. "Your people are trying very hard to frame me. And they've decided that they can't leave me alive to refute their planted evidence. I'm sure they've done a very tight job, but they know how good I am. The question is, if they were going to kill me anyway, why go to all the trouble to frame me?"

Jimmy remained silent.

"Don't worry, I'm pretty sure I've guessed the answer. But I do need you to fill in the gaps."

"I'm not going to tell you shit!"

"Yes you are," said Anna evenly. "You're going to tell me everything you know." She shook her head condescendingly, as though she was dealing with an adorable yet obstinate toddler. "After all, your buddies just did," she lied, raising her eyebrows.

"*What* buddies?" he bellowed into the night.

The detective grinned. "Thanks for confirming that you're as clueless as I thought."

She held her phone out and showed him images of the men she had recently hogtied and gagged. "Recognize anyone?" she said, enjoying the confused expression on his face. "And if you don't like photos, how's this?" She directed her tactical flashlight to the west, where the high-powered beam was just able to illuminate one of the men she had incapacitated, on his stomach, his arms and legs bound behind his back, tiny in the distance.

"What's the matter?" she taunted. "You don't look happy. Upset that your boss didn't trust you to get the job done all by yourself?"

He glared at her, not responding, but it was clear that she had hit the nail on the head.

Anna smiled. "Well I've got bad news for you, Jimmy," she said in contempt. "It's actually a lot worse than that."

"What are you talking about?"

"They weren't here to babysit you, *genius*. They were here to *kill* you. Both of us were slated to die. That sniper rifle in one of the photos I just showed you was pointed at your head. Apparently, you aren't part of your boss's employee retention program. But he wasn't going to *fire* you. He was going to fire *at* you."

Jimmy Jessup whitened, and looked like he might vomit.

Anna held up a note she had found in his pocket, along with a packed brown paper bag she had found nearby. "Typed instructions for me to carry out," she said in disgust, waving the note, "to make it look like I'm on the take. Not leaving a lot to the imagination, are we? And a brown-paper bag filled with hundreds? Talk about *cliché*. Why not bring a sack shaped like a bowling ball, with dollar signs painted on the outside?"

She shook her head once more. "So you were assigned to lure me here, kill me, and then plant these items on me. But what you didn't know is that your boss had an even better idea. He thought it would be even *more* incriminating if we appeared to have shot each other during our transaction. And do you know what? He's probably right. You have to admire his attention to detail."

Anna paused. "I know your people planted incriminating evidence on my home computer. And no doubt elsewhere. And you're going to tell me all about it."

"I can't," said Jimmy. "Because my boss didn't tell *me*."

"My gut tells me you're lying," said Anna. "That you're the *only* one your boss told the full story to. You probably thought it was because you were important. Special. But really it's because you're expendable. Dead men don't tell secrets."

The detective shot him a look of disgust. "So why protect your boss now?" she asked. "He marked you for death. And even though his plan failed, you won't be getting a reprieve. After all, he can't risk that you figured out he was planning to kill you. He can't chance that you'll, ah . . . harbor a grudge against him."

Jimmy glared at her for several long seconds. "*Okay*," he spat bitterly. "I'll tell you everything I know. But I want immunity."

"How about you tell me what you know, and I won't put a bullet in your head."

"You're not going to kill me," he said dismissively.

"Aren't I? If I don't get answers, I'm as good as dead anyway, with my reputation poisoned. So what do I have to lose?"

"Go ahead then," said Jimmy, unconcerned. "Kill me."

Anna sighed. She had doubted this bluff would work, but it was worth a try.

"I didn't think so," he said smugly after several seconds had passed.

"Okay," said the detective. "I'll agree to your terms. But I can't *guarantee* immunity. All I can do is promise to do my absolute best to see to it that you walk."

Jimmy nodded. "It's a deal," he said. "Now, can I at least stand up?"

"Not a chance in hell," replied Anna immediately.

Jimmy stared up at the detective, as if deciding if he should argue further, but her tone and the resolve in her face made it clear he'd be wasting his breath. "All right," he said. "Ask your questions."

"Who is your boss?" said Anna

"Neil Marshall."

Anna considered. She wasn't surprised that this man was involved. He was smart, careful, and ruthless, which explained this elaborate plan.

There were other drug lords almost as powerful in the region, but Marshall now reigned supreme, controlling much of the territory as far south as San Diego, as far north as Monterey, and as far east as the outer edge of San Bernardino. While this control was not uncontested, he continued to slowly make inroads into enemy territory, slowly squeezing out any competition like a California-sized python.

"And where is this Foria coming from?"

"Unclear. Neil's supplier is a man named Shane Frey. I've never met him. For that matter, neither has Neil. But this guy claims to have invented the drug."

Anna's eyes widened. Now they were getting somewhere.

She had gotten wind of Foria recently, and while others in the department thought of it as just another illicit drug, with a better high and fewer side effects than most, she had seen it differently. Her intuition told her this would be a game changer, and not in a good way.

In addition, three cases had cropped up recently of men and women committing crimes and taking actions that had been totally uncharacteristic of them, including depositing fortunes in unknown bank accounts. Actions that made little sense no matter how they were viewed.

Anna's gut had told her there might be a connection between these cases and Foria, even though none of the perpetrators were even aware that the drug existed. Even so, her hidden mind continued to insist that she explore this possibility.

Either way, her instincts demanded that she raise red flags to her superiors, which she did with more persistence and urgency than ever before. She warned that LA was only the beginning, and that there was more to this drug than anyone thought. That if it wasn't torn out by its roots while this was still possible, it would sweep across the nation in a blink of an eye. She requested a national FBI task force be established to investigate immediately, since there were already rumors of the drug having surfaced in New York and Chicago.

If she were anyone else, her captain, a twenty-six-year veteran named Donovan Perez, would have laughed her out of his office. But she had a track record that couldn't be ignored, and her hunches had a funny way of paying off. So Perez had gone to bat for her, making it clear to those many levels above him that she had an uncanny knack for being right. If she was this adamant that Foria would herald a game-changing crisis, they needed to take her very seriously.

And Captain Perez had assured her recently that they were doing just that. The task force the FBI was considering would be much
smaller in size and scope than the one Anna had recommended, but
it would be *something*. And, in what the captain considered to be
a minor miracle, he thought that approval of the project had now
become likely.

Likely, that is, unless Anna Abbott was totally discredited as a
detective. The FBI was only humoring her because of her sterling
reputation, after all. She was on the verge of creating a tiny ember,
which she hoped to nurse into a raging fire, but the slightest taint on
her reputation would snuff out the ember before it was born.

Naturally, Neil Marshall and Shane Frey would want to prevent
the creation of this initiative at any cost, ensuring that their law enforcement opposition wasn't nationalized, and no dots were ever
connected. But they couldn't just *kill* her. If they did, her warnings
would become all the more credible, as it would look like someone
had taken her out because she was getting close to something big.

Which is why they needed to *frame* her at the same time.

Anna turned her attention back to her prisoner. "So what did they
do to my computer?" she demanded.

"They planted hidden files, supposedly created by you. Ledgers
detailing the bribes you've taken from a handful of criminals around
the city. To look the other way. Or to falsely pin their crimes on others. They also included records of how you planted and tainted evidence to make this happen."

Jimmy shrugged. "All of these files are buried, hidden, and password protected. But not so well hidden and protected that experts
wouldn't be able to eventually find them and crack them open."

"And has your boss also planted *physical* evidence of this supposed evidence tampering, to go along with the computer records?"

"Of course. He never does anything half-assed," said Jimmy. "He's
left breadcrumbs for the cops to follow to lead them to a storage
vault, rented in your name. Containing just enough physical evidence
to corroborate a few of the entries on your computer. Which will
make the cops believe that they're all true."

Anna felt sick to her stomach. She found this scheme to be unspeakably horrifying. If she hadn't turned the tables, she'd be dead about now, her reputation would be savaged, and the Foria task force would never come into being.

And she had no doubt the plan would have worked. Many in her precinct, in addition to being jealous, were suspicious of her success. They'd be quick to believe the picture that Marshall and Frey were painting, that the reason she always got her man was that she *cheated*. In addition to not caring if the person she sent to jail was guilty or not.

And most despicable of all, any number of criminals she had put behind bars would go free, as the chain of custody of the evidence against them, and even the evidence itself, could no longer be trusted. Had this plan succeeded, not only would she be dead, but her reputation would be destroyed, and much of her legacy undone.

"They also set up a numbered bank account for you," continued Jimmy, "with almost two million dollars inside. This and the price of your condo will cement the evidence that you're on the take. Clean cops don't tend to be rich. Dirty cops, on the other hand . . ."

Anna frowned. Ironically, since she already had a hidden account with many times this amount of money inside, the truth would make her look guiltier than the fabrication. But what was stunning was that they were willing to burn millions of dollars to further bolster their narrative.

"Anything else?" she whispered in horror, needing to remind herself that she had caught this in time, so she could unravel what they were attempting. Which is the very reason they needed her dead in the first place.

"They found and hacked your juvie records," replied Jimmy, "which were apparently sealed. They put them on your hard drive. Again, well hidden, so it will take some doing, even by experts, to find the file. But they will. You racked up quite a criminal record of your own as a teen," he added, raising his eyebrows. "This will shock your department, and show that being a dirty cop isn't as much out of character for you as they might have thought. The icing on the cake. Not that this particular cake *needed* any icing."

"Anything else?" said Anna, continuing to be stunned by how flawless the trap really was.

"No," said Jimmy, shaking his head. "But it's more than enough, don't you think?"

In lieu of a response, Anna removed a roll of duct tape from her duffel and sealed Jimmy's mouth closed over his protests. It was time to give Jimmy's voice a rest and call this in.

The cops on the graveyard shift would respond immediately. She would also call Captain Perez in on this, as well, despite the hour. After Jimmy spilled what he knew, Neil Marshall's grand plan would go down in flames.

Still, she'd be having nightmares about this for years to come. Talk about dodging a bullet.

As she pulled her phone from her pocket to call the station, a sick, panicked feeling swept over her. Her hand darted toward her gun of its own volition, her hidden mind reacting to a threat that her conscious mind had yet to even detect.

"Freeze!" shouted one of two men just emerging from the darkness. Both were dressed in black, and both had their guns drawn and extended in her direction.

Anna's subconscious yanked her hand away from her gun at the last instant, having calculated that she was sure to lose any exchange.

"Hands in the air!" demanded the shorter of the two men. "Now!"

9

Anna raised her hands over her head and considered the two men coming toward her. Both looked trim and formidable.

"Jesus, Jimmy!" said the taller man in amusement, looking down at his colleague still seated on the pavement. "How embarrassing for you. She's turned you into her *bitch*, hasn't she?" He grinned. "And taping your mouth shut is a nice touch. Someone should have done that a long time ago."

"But don't feel too bad, Jimmy," said the shorter of the two men, "Neil had four other men out here tonight, and she took *them* out too. The boss chose these guys over me and Cam," he added, nodding at his tall partner. A smile flickered over his face. "I guess the out-of-town talent wasn't as good as Neil thought. So we're going to leave these guys hogtied for a long time. While we do their job *for* them."

"Good thing we decided to check up on you losers when we did," added his partner, apparently named Cam. He approached Anna, but wisely remained out of her reach. "Kick your gun over to me!" he demanded. "Pull it out of its holster, upside down, using two fingers through the trigger. Carefully!"

Anna did as he asked, her intuition telling her that with two guns trained on her and without the element of surprise, trying to use the Glock would be suicide.

"Now toss me your phone," said Cam.

Anna lowered her right arm and underhanded the phone to him. He caught it and slid it into his pocket, his gun never wavering. He glanced at her duffel bag on the pavement fifteen feet away from her, but apparently decided it was enough out of her reach to disregard.

Anna cursed under her breath. Since she wasn't even scheduled to arrive at the school until about now, she would have bet her life that no one, other than the five men already here, would show up for at least twenty more minutes.

Her frown deepened. She *had* bet her life.

And she had lost.

Her intuition had let her down in a big way, reminding her that it wasn't perfect, and that she had to be careful not to become too dependent on it. A lesson that she had apparently learned too late.

"Get your right hand back up!" shouted Cam, unhappy that she had kept it near her side after tossing him her phone.

Anna raised her arm up into the air once again, slowly backing away from the tall gunman until she was just a few feet in front of Jimmy on the ground. "I don't feel well," she said, doing her best to paste a nauseated look on her face. "I need to sit," she added, crouching down and then dropping the remaining distance to the pavement onto her butt, nearly landing on Jimmy in the process, and blocking him from view.

"Feel free to puke," said Cam with a smile. "Just don't try anything stupid," he added. "Hector's gonna keep you in his sights while I call the boss and get instructions."

"I'm burning up," croaked Anna, looking like she might pass out. "I need to take off this sweatshirt," she added, lowering her arms to begin to pull it over her head.

"Freeze!" shouted Hector. "I don't care if you boil to death, get your hands away from your shirt."

She did as he requested, but only after she had yanked the sweatshirt up past her navel. Hector immediately noticed the bulletproof vest that was now exposed. "Well done," he said wryly. "Now that I know you have a vest, I'll be sure to shoot you between the eyes."

Anna shook her head in disgust. *What was Jimmy waiting for? Did he need a neon sign?*

She had pulled up her sweatshirt to uncover the gun hidden in the small of her back, which should now be exposed and facing Jimmy, inches away from his bound hands. She waited several more seconds, but when she didn't feel the gun slipping quietly from her waistband, as expected, she realized she needed to do more. How could anyone possibly be *this* stupid?

She faced Hector, her eyes now burning. "Jimmy is a lot smarter than you think!" she said defiantly, the sickly voice she had faked now gone. "He figured out that your boss wants him *dead*." Anna paused for just a moment. If this didn't wake up the idiot behind her, *nothing* would.

"Do you think Jimmy's just going to let your partner call Neil Marshall?" she continued. "So Marshall can order you to kill him? Jimmy brought a team of his own here, and they have guns trained on you *right now*. So drop your weapons!"

Both men broke out into laughter. "Are you kidding?" said Cam. He lowered his phone, deciding that the call to his boss could wait a few more seconds. "That's the dumbest bluff *ever*. And here I thought you were supposed to be impressive," he added derisively.

Adrenaline coursed through Anna's body as she felt Jimmy pulling the gun from the waistband of her pants.

Finally!

"If Jimmy brought his own muscle," continued the tall killer, "he wouldn't be bound and gagged right now, would he?"

"*Now!*" shouted Anna, throwing herself flat on the ground from her seated position so the unlikely ally behind her would have a clear view of his former comrades. Jimmy began firing the moment her body was out of his way, while she continued rolling away from him as quickly as she could.

Jimmy's first shot hit Cam in the forehead, turning his brain into soup.

Without wasting an instant, Jimmy turned his gun on Hector and got off three more rounds, but the man was already diving to the ground. One shot missed, one hit Hector's right shoulder, and one hit his left leg as he flew to the pavement. But before Jimmy could take another shot, Hector came out of his roll and fired, planting a slug deep into Jimmy's heart, killing him instantly.

Anna scampered to her feet as Hector turned to fire on her. The adrenaline in his body allowed him to aim true, despite a shattered shoulder, but she subconsciously jerked this way and that, somehow dodging his first two bullets. He tried to deliver another, but he was forced to lower his arm as blood continued to gush from his two wounds, and the pain in his shoulder became too great for him to bear.

Anna scooped up her duffel and raced from the scene, tucking her head low as she ran, knowing that she could survive a shot to the body, but that a head shot would be fatal.

Through sheer force of will, Hector managed to lift his arm and take one final shot at the detective, who was seconds away from vanishing into the night. The round slammed into her left upper back before she even heard the crack of the gun. Anna's body armor was next generation, lighter than ever and better able to dissipate force, but even so the strike was a sledgehammer blow to her back. She screamed in agony and stumbled to the pavement.

Pain exploded through her torso, and her lungs refused to operate. For a few moments she was convinced that her heart had stopped as well as her breathing, but after what seemed an eternity, her body finally sorted itself out and began functioning properly once again.

Anna lifted herself from the ground and continued running, ignoring the pain from an upper back that was now surely stained by a hideous purple-and-black bruise.

Despite having to absorb such a powerful blow, she knew things could have been much worse. And should have been. She was lucky to be alive, and she was now engulfed in darkness. Hector's injured leg ensured he wouldn't pursue her.

Anna put some additional distance between herself and Hector and then paused to remove the handgun she had packed in her duffel. She held it at the ready, slipping its silencer attachment into her pocket.

She considered returning to finish Hector off, but she could hear him barking into his phone in the distance, and decided against it. He was no longer a threat, and there was no telling how soon the reinforcements he had just called for might arrive.

Anna reached her car and gunned the engine, screaming away from the school even faster than she had arrived.

But now what?

Should she return home and destroy her computer? She shook her head the instant this occurred to her. This would be a big mistake.

She needed to get ahead of the planned frame, but Neil Marshall was bound to anticipate this move and have additional men waiting for her.

She considered becoming a human Ouija board, allowing her subconscious to turn the steering wheel and decide the route she would take, but her intuition abruptly decided to help in a more obvious way.

In a burst of inspiration, she knew exactly where she needed to go.

10

Anna Abbott parked at the main bus terminal in downtown LA and then hoofed it to the Camden International Hotel a mile and a half away, frustrated that she no longer had a phone, which would have enabled her to get a ride in a matter of minutes.

She assumed Neil Marshall and his associates would be tracking her car, so it would make sense to them that she'd abandon it as soon as possible in favor of a bus—to put distance between her and those trying to kill her, and to buy herself time to regroup. Hopefully, by parking where she had, they would be chasing buses all night like a pack of border collies and lose her scent entirely.

She strode into the hotel's magnificent lobby, still carrying the duffel, and spotted a white house-phone discreetly attached to a wall in a small foyer. Good. That was lucky. She could have forced the manager to give her Vega's room number by flashing her badge, but she had become understandably paranoid, and preferred to get it by less memorable methods. If this worked, great. If not, her badge was always there to use.

She lifted the phone and dialed 04 for room service. "Hi," she said cheerfully when it was answered on the second ring. "I'm calling from the hotel lobby. I'd like to surprise my husband with some champagne. Can you send your most expensive bottle up to our room in about thirty minutes."

"It will be our pleasure."

"Thanks!" she said, as if this would be her last word before hanging up.

"Wait!" said the attendant. "I'm sorry, ma'am, but since you're calling from the lobby, your room number doesn't show on my computer."

"Right. Of course." She paused for several seconds. "You know," she said, as if mildly embarrassed, "I'm not sure I'm even remembering it right. The room is in my husband's name: Tom Vega."

There was a brief pause. "Room 925?"

"That sounds right," said Anna. "Thanks!"

She waited almost a full minute and then dialed 04 once again. "I just ordered champagne to be delivered to room 925 thirty minutes from now. But this might not be ideal timing, after all. Go ahead and cancel the order and I'll call again when I've figured this out. Sorry about that."

"Not at all," came the reply. "But I should remind you that room service is only available until eleven."

"Thanks," said Anna. "I'll keep that in mind."

The detective rode the showy, mirrored elevator to the ninth floor, stood before Vega's door, and took a deep breath. She made sure no one was in the hall and screwed the silencer onto the end of her gun—in the off chance that she would be forced to use it. The unmistakable thunder of gunfire within the corridors of a bustling high-end hotel would create panic, and would bring hotel security and cops swarming.

She concealed her weapon beneath the folds of her sweatshirt, took a deep breath, and rapped loudly on the door three times in quick succession. "Room service," she said, trying to disguise her voice as much as possible, well aware of just how cliché this approach really was, and also that it was likely to work.

After a brief silence she heard Vega's voice calling through the door. "You must have the wrong room," he said. "I didn't order anything."

Anna didn't respond. A few seconds later she heard the sharp clack of a deadbolt turning and braced herself for action. As the door began to swing inward, the detective stepped inside before Vega could even see who she was and shoved him backwards with considerable force, allowing her momentum to carry her farther into the room.

"Don't move!" she commanded, pointing the gun at Vega's head and kicking the door closed behind her. She dropped the duffel to the floor and held her gun on him with both hands.

"Anna?" said Vega questioningly. He shook his head in what seemed like utter confusion. "What's going on?"

"You're hiding something from me! That's what's going on! And now you're going to tell me what!"

Vega's eyes narrowed and he nodded toward the gun. "I thought we decided that I mean you no harm."

Anna considered. Her instincts on this hadn't changed, she realized. Still, they weren't always right, and sometimes her conscious mind had to pull rank, as she had done at the high school after her gut had tried to discourage her from wading into the fray.

"You're working for Neil Marshall!" she barked. "Admit it!"

"What? I don't even know a Neil Marshall."

"Then you're working for Shane Frey."

"I've never heard of him either. Anna, what's going on?"

She hadn't taken her eyes from him since she entered, and she strained to pick up any signals coming from her subconscious. Nothing. Could he really be telling the truth? It still seemed unlikely, despite what her instincts were telling her.

She hadn't forgotten the lesson she had learned the hard way, just that night. Her hidden mind wasn't omniscient. Vega seemed to be genuinely shocked, and genuinely clueless, but she was determined to probe further.

"Dangerous people are trying to frame me," she hissed through clenched teeth. "They're making it look like I'm on the take. And they just tried to kill me. But you already know that, don't you? Because you're in on it!"

"Of course I'm not," insisted Vega. "But are you okay?" he added in horror, his eyes hurriedly scanning her body for possible injury. "Are you out of danger?"

Vega looked sincerely concerned. *More* than concerned. Alarmed. Petrified. If he was an actor, he was a great one, able to fool her conscious and subconscious both.

Still, she had to press further, one last time, to be certain. "Don't pretend to be worried about me!" she barked. "I know you're involved somehow! While I was at the restaurant with you, my place was broken into, and evidence against me was planted on my computer. Then I was lured to what was supposed to be my death."

Anna scowled. "You expect me to believe that this was all a co-incidence?" she added, shaking her head. "Well I don't *believe* in coincidences."

"I get why you think I'm part of this," said Vega. "But the timing of this really is a coincidence. Believe me, I would *never* hurt you. Just the opposite. I'd take a *bullet* to protect you."

Anna's eyes narrowed. He'd take a *bullet* for her? Where did *that* come from? She didn't need instinct to know that this last statement was beyond suspicious, unless it came out of the mouth of a Secret Service agent or a loved one.

"You aren't really a professor, are you?" she said. "I guessed this was a possibility at dinner, and I was *right*. And you aren't writing a paper on me."

Vega sighed. "No, I'm not a professor," he said softly. "I lied about that. But I'm *not* lying when I say that I'd do *anything* to protect you. To help you in any way I can. What do your instincts say about *that*?"

"Who are you?" she repeated.

"My name really is Tom Vega. I'm good with computers, and hacked Stanford's website to set up a fake bio there. I'm a scientist, but not affiliated with any university."

"What kind of scientist?"

He winced. "The kind that a lot of scientists don't respect," he admitted. "Even though I know more about physics and cosmology than most physicists and cosmologists. But over the years I've ex-panded my horizons. I've begun to poke around on what you might call the fringes of accepted science."

"Fringes?" repeated Anna. She thought about this for several long seconds. "So what are you saying," she continued, "that you're a—I don't know—a *paranormalist*?"

"That's as good a word for it as any, I suppose."

Anna shook her head in disgust. Her gut had been strongly suspi-cious of him, and had known he was hiding major things, but *this*? She hadn't pegged him for a lunatic. "So you already knew almost everything I told you tonight, didn't you?" she said. "That paper I wrote for the psychology blog before I joined the force, on intuition and the subconscious, you already read that, didn't you? That's why you pried into my background and my record on the force before you called me. You posed as a research criminologist to get me to go to dinner with you. To gain my trust. So you could study my abilities further."

Vega sighed. "You're right, of course," he said. "But I planned to come clean very soon. Do you think I didn't know you'd figure it out? If I really thought I could fool you for long, you wouldn't be the person I've been looking for. You knew something was wrong about me from the start. But I had to chance lying to you."

He frowned. "Come on, Anna," he added, "would you really have met with me if I had told you I was a paranormalist?"

"Not a chance."

"*Exactly*," said Vega. "So I arranged the meeting under false pretenses. But I planned to tell you the truth after our lunch tomorrow."

Vega stared deeply into her eyes. "Look, Anna, I've spent my *entire life* searching for someone like you. You have to believe me. I'm *certain* that you're the real deal. And while your intuition is quite special, that's not all. You have abilities that *you* aren't even aware of."

"That's ridiculous," said Anna. "My hunches can be truly remarkable, I agree. And they *can* seem like magic. But they're readily explainable by *normal* science. As opposed to *para*-normal science. I'm certain I don't have any paranormal abilities, because I had myself tested once. To see for myself if maybe I could . . . well, if I could read minds. I thought maybe I was doing this sometimes, barely, on a fuzzy, superficial level, and misinterpreting it as pure intuition. So I volunteered for one of those playing card studies. The tester looked at a series of twenty cards, and I had to guess the suit each time." She shook her head. "I didn't do any better than random chance would account for."

"That's because you *can't* read minds," said Vega. "I already knew that."

"So what paranormal abilities do you think I have?"

Vega hesitated, and then sighed. "Remember when you said you didn't like the word, *premonition*? You said it implied that you could see the future, which isn't true."

She nodded.

"Well it *is* true," said Vega simply. "You *can* see the future."

Anna stared at him for several seconds. "You're out of your mind."

"I'm not. You can see the future. I'm convinced of it. Not very much, and not very clearly. You aren't even aware that you're doing it. And the information does flow through your subconscious to become part of the data your intuition uses to tip you off. But you're precognitive. Clairvoyant."

"That's ridiculous."

"I can prove it to you," insisted Vega. "And I can give you a scientific explanation for how you do it, too."

"Which is what you planned to do at lunch tomorrow."

"That's right."

Anna lowered her weapon. Her every instinct continued to tell her that Vega meant her well, and this discussion had convinced both of her minds that he wasn't a threat. It explained why he looked at her with such awe, and why his ridiculous claim that he would protect her with his life actually rang true.

She was his white whale. His Holy Grail. The culmination of his life's work.

He was sorely mistaken about her, but she was convinced that *he* believed every word he was saying.

Still, she couldn't shake the feeling that she was continuing to miss something. As big, or even bigger than, what she had just uncovered. But an exploration of what this might be would have to wait.

"I don't have time for this right now," she said. "I need to call my captain and alert him to what happened tonight. I need to explain that Neil Marshall and Shane Frey have just spent inordinate money and resources trying to frame me. If I don't get ahead of this, and quickly, I could still get steamrolled by it."

Vega nodded. "I understand."

The detective frowned. "My phone didn't make it. Can I borrow yours?"

"Of course," he said cheerfully. "I'll help you in any way I can. All you have to do is ask."

11

Eldamir Kor sat as surreptitiously as he could in the lobby of the Camden International Hotel, pretending to be absorbed in his cell phone, unable to keep his skin from crawling. He could never get used to the low lighting on this planet, no matter how much experience he had with it, and it creeped him out. Every time.

He desperately wanted to activate the implants in his eyes to amplify the light, but there was no hiding their operation. He cursed the home scientists. How much effort would it have taken to eliminate this ridiculous side effect, so they could use this feature inconspicuously?

Even without gleaming eyes, he stood out like a supernova, tall, thick, and intimidating. His features were harsh by human standards, even threatening. Like all of his kind.

He passed the time by fantasizing about killing Shanifrey and Tiparax both. Shanifrey had been responsible for forcing them to carry out, in person, what could have been a simple remote surveillance mission. And Tiparax had chosen him for this miserable hotel lobby duty, while he remained upstairs with both Fanimore and Mezzitorp, relaxed, comfortable, and making full use of their implants to provide enough light to suit their needs.

Tiparax was the second-highest ranked member of their Earth contingent, just over sixty members strong, so Eldamir didn't blame him for staying in the room. Rank did have its privileges, after all. But Eldamir was third-in-command, while Mezzitorp and Fanimore were so low down the food chain they didn't rate any consideration whatsoever. Even so, Tiparax had chosen to let these peons stay with him in comfort, while sending Eldamir off to suffer alone.

It was infuriating. Eldamir imagined skinning Shanifrey alive, taking his time to picture every last cut and scream, and then imagined carving a protest letter into Tiparax's body with a sharp knife.

The third-in-command was so lost in thought that he almost missed a development of paramount importance, only realizing what he was seeing when it was almost too late. Even then he did a double-take, first thinking he must be mistaken since he was so poor at differentiating between human beings. But he was quickly able to confirm his suspicions using the facial recognition program he and his comrades had installed on their phones.

This was truly a stunning development.

He quickly reached out to Shanifrey Doe with his comm, conferencing in his three comrades in the room upstairs at the same time.

"*What?*" shouted Shanifrey after accepting the call. His tone was nothing short of furious. "You seriously have the nerve to bother me right now?" he barked. "I'm in the middle of something *important.*"

Eldamir had fully expected this level of ferocity. He desperately wanted to say, "What's the matter, Commander, did you misplace your detective?" but knew that the human expression, *poking the bear*, wouldn't begin to cover how big of a mistake uttering this particular sentence would be.

"I'm confident you'll find this worth the interruption," he reported subvocally instead. "We tracked our target to the Camden International Hotel," he added, speaking as quickly as he could to reach the punchline of the report before Shanifrey's head exploded, "where he checked in for the night. Tiparax, Mezzitorp, and Fanimore are in the room next to his, and I'm watching the lobby. Just minutes ago Detective Anna Abbott arrived here, and is now in an elevator, presumably heading to his room."

"Are you *certain?*" said Shanifrey, suddenly as alert as if he had been struck with a cattle prod, his tone no longer dismissive of Eldamir, or his wisdom in arranging for the call.

"I am. She's changed her clothing from the restaurant. But I've confirmed it's her beyond any doubt."

"How can that be, Commander?" said Tiparax from the hotel room upstairs. He rose from the bed on which he had been seated and came to full attention, carefully avoiding the bodies of a married couple whose throats they had slit when they had helped themselves to the room, and two expansive pools of crimson blood that were slowly soaking into the beige carpeting. "I thought she was slated to be killed after she left the restaurant?"

"She was!" snapped Shanifrey angrily. "But I made the mistake of leaving the operation to a group of humans. And they had a temporary . . . setback."

He paused. "But here's the good news. Because of your last call, which alerted me that she's much more important than I had known, I've upped our game. Significantly. In light of what we now know, perhaps it isn't entirely surprising that she managed to survive the attempt on her life. But after she did, I ordered that extreme measures be taken to see to it that her reputation is destroyed, *despite* our setback. Measures that I never would have considered had I not known about her dinner meeting tonight."

His second-in-command frowned. This was as close to a *thanks* or a *well done* as Shanifrey was likely to ever give him. "Glad to be of service," said Tiparax. "Do you have any idea why she would come straight here after she survived your ambush?"

"Not really, no. They must have developed more of a bond than I expected during their dinner meeting. But this works in our favor. She's put herself back on our radar."

"What would you like us to do?" asked Tiparax.

"First," said the commander, "I need to know what's happening in the room next to you. Use your comm to amplify the sound and transmit it to all of us."

"Understood," said Tiparax.

The voices of the man they had been following and Anna Abbott came though their comms almost immediately, loud and clear. They listened intently for several minutes before Shanifrey interrupted the feed. "I've heard enough," he said.

"Does that mean you have new orders for us?" asked Tiparax.

"It does," replied his commander. "I'm done playing games. I need you to kill them both. Attract as little attention as you can. But no matter what, I want them dead. As soon as possible. Understood?"

"Perfectly," said Tiparax enthusiastically. "I thought you'd never ask."

* * *

"Captain Perez," said the detective into Tom Vega's phone, "it's Anna Abbott. Sorry to bother you on a Friday night, sir, but it's important."

"Go ahead," said the gravelly voice of her captain. Anna sensed that something was off about him, although she wasn't certain what. In addition, her hidden mind seemed troubled that he hadn't bothered to ask her why her call was coming in from a phone that didn't register on his Caller ID, although he probably just didn't want to hold her up when she clearly had urgent matters to discuss.

Anna's head jerked upwards and she strained to hear an inaudible sound or see an invisible threat, like an alert gazelle having detected a stalking lioness through some sixth sense.

She gasped, and then, based on nothing but instinct and impulse alone, launched herself toward Tom Vega, executing a perfect tackle and driving both of them onto the bed, just as several muffled shots screamed through the wall of the room, missing Vega by inches. One of the bullets hit her instead, but luckily it only managed to crease her upper arm, creating an inch-long groove of blood but only superficial damage.

The moment they landed, Anna rolled off the side of the bed farthest from the shooting, pulling Vega with her, as several more slugs penetrated the wall, clearly coming from a silenced gun being wielded from the room next door.

Two table lamps and the plasma TV monitor on the wall exploded into shards as Anna attempted to roll under the bed, but was blocked by a solid wood platform under the frame that was resting on the carpeting.

The detective pulled Vega as close to the bottom of the bed as she could, while struggling to assimilate the situation and determine her next move.

Vega began to speak but Anna slammed an open hand over his mouth, muffling his words. She put a finger to her lips, indicating she wanted total silence. Let whoever was aiming for them believe they had succeeded. Besides, the shots had been fired with pinpoint accuracy, leading her to believe that the shooter had some means of getting precise telemetry based on their voices alone.

"*Anna!*" came the shouted voice of Captain Perez through Vega's phone. "*Anna, are you there?*" Only then did the detective realize she had kept her grip on the phone until she had hit the floor below the bed, and that it was now lying on the carpet, a foot away. "*What's going on!*" he demanded, his voice booming.

Three more bullets streaked through the wall and embedded themselves into the mattress and dresser, aimed with uncanny accuracy right where the captain's shouts had emanated from the phone. Only their position on the floor behind the bed had saved them.

Anna stabbed at Vega's phone with such urgency it looked like her hand was spasming, and managed to end the call before her captain could advertise their position, and that they remained alive, yet again. This done, she pulled her silenced gun from its holster and held it at the ready.

An eerie quiet settled over the room, which now looked like a war zone. No more shots were being fired, at least for the moment, and Anna's mind raced. She had to predict what would happen next to have any chance of survival. She strained to try to see the future, just in case Vega was right about her being clairvoyant, but she saw nothing.

Of course she saw nothing. The idea of precognition was ludicrous.

She needed to put herself in the head of the hostile in the room over, she realized, to predict his next move. What was he doing? What was he thinking?

Whoever he was, he would eventually need eyes on his targets. Shooting blindly through a wall had the benefit of surprise, but no matter how much confidence he might have in the accuracy of his shots, the only way to be certain the targets were dead was to be certain the targets were dead. The shooter would need to enter Vega's room to confirm the kills. Conduct a visual inspection. Check for breathing or a pulse.

If Anna were in the shooter's place, she would assume the targets were still alive, at least at first. She would stand at the ready in the hall outside their door. If they *were* alive, they'd have little interest in remaining fish in a barrel, and would bolt from the room to safety shortly after the shooting stopped. If they didn't exit the room after five or ten minutes, only then would she enter to confirm the kills.

She became convinced that this is exactly what the shooter was doing now.

Anna put her finger across her lips once again and motioned for Vega to maintain his position on the floor.

She slowly crawled away from the bed, soundlessly, avoiding the many shards of glass and splinters of wood scattered on the carpeting and throughout the room. As she neared the door, she realized that someone *was* waiting in the hall outside, just as she had predicted, although as was common with her, she had no idea *how* she knew.

She took a deep, silent breath, raised her gun, and fired four times through the door as quickly as she could pull the trigger. She adjusted the height of her aim each time, starting at what she hoped was head height, just in case the hostile beyond was wearing body armor.

The instant she stopped firing she heard the sound of what could only be a body completing a fall and slamming into the floor. A part of her was horrified by the need to kill, but she had no time for regrets, and it wasn't as though she had started this—or that there had been any real choice.

As she unlocked the door and pulled it open, her instincts commanded her to drop to the floor, just as several shots screamed through the air where she had been an instant earlier. A second hostile was standing behind the body of the man she had killed, firing a silenced gun of his own.

She rolled to her right and fired upward, hitting the second gunman in the forehead with an uncannily accurate shot, calculated by her savant subconscious. Part of her thought she had seen the man's eyes on fire, but she must have been hallucinating.

Anna sprang to her feet and rushed outside of the room, surveying the corridor in both directions. No other shooters were in sight. Miraculously, no hotel guests were about, either, although even silenced guns couldn't prevent other telltale sounds of the battle from making themselves known, and she was certain that guests nearby were even now phoning the lobby to report an altercation.

"Tom, help me move these bodies," she said urgently, and both bent to the task of sliding the corpses inside the room. Anna quickly closed the door and bent down to inspect the two hostiles for the first time.

She shrank back in horror.

She hadn't been hallucinating, after all. Both men, even dead, had eyes so red they were each miniature infernos, blazing with an otherworldly, sinister red fire.

And that wasn't all. Anna's breath stuck in her throat as she realized something at least as disturbing: both men were bleeding profusely, although she now knew that the term "men" was less than accurate. Because their eyes may have been red, but their blood was decidedly not.

Instead, the liquid that was still streaming from the two hostiles was unnaturally thick, and black as night.

12

Eldamir Kor strained to hear something. *Anything.* But his comm was now eerily silent. "Tiparax!" he yelled subvocally. "Respond!"

Eldamir paused for a brief moment. "Mezzitorp!" he called out again. "Respond immediately!"

Fanimore, who had also been conferenced in, pushed open a door and entered an underground parking structure. "I'm afraid they're probably dead," he said.

"Impossible."

"Tiparax didn't think so," noted Fanimore, "or else he wouldn't have sent me to watch the parking garage before he launched his attack. He said you and I were his insurance policy in case anything went wrong."

Eldamir fumed. He had his beef with his direct superior, but it couldn't be said that Tiparax was anything but a brilliant soldier. His training and reflexes were extraordinary. And while Mezzitorp might be low-ranked, he was a fierce commando in his own right.

How had their surprise attack possibly been thwarted by the unimpressive specimens in the room next door?

It was *unthinkable.* But it was time that Eldamir accepted that it was also very likely to be true. Eldamir may have passed the time by imagining horrible deaths for some of his comrades, but he knew what was at stake, and how important each and every one of them really were.

He wouldn't wish their actual deaths for the world.

And now they had lost *three* of their people on Earth, and all quite recently. Their first casualty had occurred not much more than two weeks earlier. Isiah Schaeffer, the New York drug lord that Shanifrey had wanted to work with, had insisted on an in-person meeting, if not with Shane Frey himself, then at least with a key lieutenant.

So Shanifrey had sent Paritor in his place, who was in command of their New York contingent, and fifth-in-command overall. But Paritor had never arrived. They had later learned that he had been hit by a car, of all things, while crossing West Thirty-fourth street. Truly a humiliating end to an elite agent. An accident that had likely only occurred because of Earth's dim lighting, and Paritor's inability to use his implants in a city forever packed with native beings.

Three men down! It was devastating. They had precious few people here on Earth as it was, and they wouldn't be getting additional reinforcements for an indefinite period, maybe never. They couldn't afford to lose too many more.

All of this flashed across Eldamir's mind in seconds as he hurriedly put in a call to Shanifrey through his comm.

"I asked *Tiparax* to report," spat the commander upon answering. "Not you!"

"Tiparax and Mezzitorp failed in their mission. I believe they were killed less than a minute ago. Fanimore is watching the hotel parking garage, per Tiparax's instructions. What are your orders?"

Shanifrey screamed an agonized curse upon hearing this news. "*How should I know?*" he shouted sharply. "*You're* the one on the ground. And you're now my number two. I'm giving you a battlefield promotion. So what are your recommendations?"

Eldamir paused to gather his thoughts. "I recommend that you send backup as quickly as possible," he began. "In the meantime, I expect our targets to be fleeing at this very moment. There are only two ways out of this hotel. Through the lobby, or out of the parking garage. I recommend that Fanimore and I maintain our positions at each point of possible egress, until it's clear which one they've chosen. Then we can regroup and take them out."

"How?"

"I can't say. We can't predict the exact situation we'll encounter. We'll have to play it by ear."

"Do it," said Shanifrey immediately. "I'll call for reinforcements as you suggest. I paid Neil Marshall a considerable sum to be able to put five of his best men under my temporary command in an emergency. I'll invoke that now.

"In the meantime," continued the commander, "if you think you can take them out, take them out. But if you aren't absolutely certain, abort the attempt. In that case, continue to follow them until reinforcements arrive."

"Understood," said Eldamir.

13

Anna Abbott was temporarily paralyzed, unable to look away from the two bodies on the floor beneath her. She searched her intuition for answers but got nothing in return. This wasn't something an audiobook on plant-based poisons, subconsciously remembered, was going to help her solve.

Finally, she pulled her eyes away and faced Vega. "What the hell *are* these things?" she whispered. And while he looked as horrified as she did, he didn't look confused. He knew exactly what they were, she was sure of it.

"I'll explain later," he said, at least not trying to deny he knew. "We have even bigger problems than before. Now we have one group after you, and another after me. Perfect."

"You think they were here to kill *you*?" said the detective in shock, having been sure that *she* had been the target.

"Initially," he replied. "You were probably just a nice bonus for them. But since it seems like there isn't anyone in LA who *doesn't* want us dead, let's get out of here."

Anna picked Vega's phone up off the carpet and quickly snapped a number of photos of the men who had attacked them, although the term *men* was unlikely to be accurate.

"Take my duffel bag," she ordered him, "and follow me."

She reloaded her gun, held it hidden between her black sweatshirt and body armor, and cracked open the door, looking both ways down the hall.

Nothing. No one was stirring.

"We'll take the stairs," she whispered to Vega. "I'll watch for activity on my way there, and you watch for activity behind us."

"Got it," he whispered back.

They made it to the exit they were looking for without encountering any nasty surprises, and cautiously made their way down the switchback staircase, the hotel elevator's embarrassing cousin, hidden away from view within a self-contained, vertical concrete chamber. Anna held her gun at the ready, no longer concerned about hiding it. The chance that they might encounter an innocent hotel guest taking the stairs when the elevators were in perfect working order was remote.

Anna quickly weighed a number of options. Whatever she was going to do, she needed to do it quickly. The bodies upstairs would soon be discovered, and all hell would break loose. She would call the shootings in herself once she was away from here, but not while she and Vega were vulnerable to additional attackers who might be on site.

Anna called a temporary halt when they reached the third-floor landing. "You have a car here, right?" she whispered to Vega.

"A rental," he replied softly. "It's in the parking garage the hotel shares with the apartment complex next door."

The detective nodded. She hated the idea of leaving in his car, knowing that those trying to kill him might be able to track it, but it was a chance they needed to take. With any luck, they'd be under police protection before it mattered. She'd keep her antenna up, and if more inferno-eyed hostiles were following, she'd count on her intuition to alert her before it was too late.

"Do you have any objections to me driving?"

"I'd prefer it," he replied, reaching into his pocket and handing her a small key fob. "And I spent extra for one that's capable of self-driving."

Anna nodded as she took the key. This guy really hated driving, even relatively short distances. "How do you get in and out of the garage?" she asked.

Vega reached into his pocket a second time and removed a credit-card-sized piece of molded plastic. "Just wave a room key in front of the reader and the arm will go up."

She nodded and took the proffered key card.

"Do you remember where you parked?" she asked.

"Three floors below the lobby," replied Vega. "Spot C128."

Anna nodded and continued down the stairs, acutely aware that time was not their friend. She needed to arrive at a plan for reaching his car, immediately, knowing that additional hostiles might be watching it and lying in wait. She had a stack of hundred-dollar bills in her bag. She could pay a hotel worker to get Vega's car for them.

She frowned deeply. There was no way she could put an innocent in danger in this way.

No. If an ambush was awaiting them in the parking garage, it was up to them to face it.

Her eyes widened as she had a sudden inspiration, obvious in retrospect.

They had to face whatever might be waiting for them in the garage, yes. But that didn't mean they had to face it blindly.

They continued their descent down the stairs until they reached the second parking level below the ground floor, and Anna called another halt, pausing beside the door into the garage. She took the duffel from her companion and set it on the floor. She reached inside, opened the drone case, and freed the tinier of the two octocopters from its padded resting place, gently palming the nearly insect-sized vehicle while also removing the tablet computer that controlled it.

"Don't move," she whispered to Vega as she shoved a bar on the steel door to open it, set the drone on the floor, and allowed the door to slam shut on its own. Anna quickly bent to the tablet computer, lifting the drone into the air inside the parking garage, making sure that it was in full noise-canceling mode and hovered just below ceiling height.

Anna maneuvered the tiny craft down the ramp to the floor Vega's car was on and expertly flew it in concentric circles. An older couple had just returned from an outing and were walking toward the elevator back to the lobby, and a Mercedes was driving up sharply angled ramps to reach the exit, but other than this the floor was quiet.

But as the drone got closer to parking spot C128, it revealed a man lying in wait with a gun drawn, twenty feet away from Vega's car, a blue Honda sedan. He was crouching low between a pillar on one side and a large SUV on the other, and his eyes were blazing red.

"*Son of a bitch*," she muttered, showing Tom the feed.

The hostile was in the perfect spot for an ambush. He'd be out of their sight no matter how they approached Vega's rental, and even the light from his gleaming eyes would be blocked from reaching them and giving away his location.

At least this man—this *thing*—was alone. It could have been a lot worse.

"Follow me," she whispered to her companion, opening the door and entering the garage. She made her way to where a driving ramp led down to the third level below the lobby and concealed herself behind a wide concrete pillar. Vega crouched behind her.

"Walk to the elevator," she whispered, "and take it down to three. Wait three minutes and then walk toward your car."

Vega nodded his understanding.

"When you get to here," she continued, pointing at a spot on the tablet computer where the drone's video feed showed a sharp turn that would put him in the line of sight of the would-be assassin, "pause and look behind you. Toward the elevator. Call out for me, loudly, like you can't imagine there's any danger. Implore me to hurry up. You're anxious and in a hurry, but act like a clueless sheep rushing off to the slaughter."

Vega nodded. "Got it."

"I'll walk down this ramp and circle around behind him. But I'll have to do it slowly and deliberately. So, like I said, give me three minutes to be sure I'm in place. He'll think I'm still near the elevator, about to join you—since you're looking that way and calling my name—so he won't be watching his back."

"So I'm your diversion?"

"Exactly."

"And you're certain he won't just shoot me?"

Anna nodded. "Positive. He'll think I'm about to join you, so why warn me off? Why not wait a few seconds and kill us both?"

"Good enough for me," said Vega. "I have absolute faith in your judgment."

Anna winced. She just hoped his faith was justified.

She flew the drone back to her and repacked the tiny aircraft and tablet computer into the duffel, which she handed to Vega. "Go!" she said.

She rushed down the ramp and onto the third parking level and then took a hard right to get well behind her target, who was hidden thirty-five yards away. She slowly, stealthily made her way toward her destination, gauging the time so she could be in place when Vega distracted her quarry.

Anna heard the faintest whisper of sound twenty feet behind her and suddenly jerked to her right, a move made without her conscious volition, just as a silenced bullet passed through the spot where her neck had been an instant before, piercing her upper left arm instead. The shot traveled clean through her arm, leaving a wound that began to gush blood.

Ignoring the searing pain, Anna dropped to the concrete and rolled under a car and to the other side. She repeated this maneuver, rolling under a second car, adding distance and angle from the shooter while leaving a slick red trail behind her like a giant snail.

Shit! she screamed on the inside.

The shooter had to have heard the drone, had to have known she was coming. But how? The noise-canceling tech, especially in the diminutive version, was nothing short of perfect. Then again, she realized, these fire-eyed men had been able to pinpoint the exact location of speech coming from a cell phone, through a wall, without the phone being in speaker mode. They either had top-of-the-line acoustic equipment, or top-of-the-line hearing.

The gunman had also correctly guessed that she would sneak up on him, and her exact approach. She couldn't help but be impressed. She should have left her drone deployed while she advanced, just to be sure, but hindsight was twenty-twenty.

Anna continued sliding across the ground as silenced shots zipped over her head, making their presence known when they burst through car doors or shattered nearby windows.

She was in a game of whack-a-mole, playing the part of the *mole*. The moment she raised her head above car level, she was dead. And she couldn't drag herself away from the shooter forever.

"*Anna!*" screamed Vega in panic from forty feet away, in position but off script after hearing and seeing a number of windows exploding in the distance. "Anna, are you okay!" he bellowed, almost hysterically.

In a burst of instinct, Anna rose, spun around, and fired, squeezing the trigger before she even saw where she was aiming, her subconscious having concluded instantly that the gunman, knowing he had Anna dead to rights, wouldn't be able to resist taking his attention away from her for the fraction of a second needed to kill Vega.

Anna's shot tore through the hostile's neck just as he was squeezing off a shot to take down Vega, deflecting his aim just enough to miss his target. A windshield behind Vega shattered and he dived to the ground, but the danger had passed. There would be no second attempt.

Anna rushed over to her unlikely companion, who gasped when he saw the blood leaking from her arm.

"We're clear," she told him as he rose from the pavement. "And I'll be fine," she reassured him as they headed toward his car. "The shot was through and through. Nothing vital hit. Just a lot of blood." She winced. "And pain."

He was somewhat relieved, but not entirely, probably unsure if she was telling the truth or telling him what he wanted to hear.

"Let's go," she said as they arrived at the blue Honda and she unlocked the doors. "I'm still driving."

"Are you sure that's wise?"

"No, but it's still happening." Anna started the car and screamed backwards, adrenaline and urgency combining to turn her into a daredevil driver.

She screeched to a halt in front of the thing she had just shot and popped the car's trunk. "We're taking it with us," she said to Vega. "Can't leave it out in the open like this. And I want to take a closer look at the body when we have time."

Vega knew better than to argue. He managed to hoist the dead body up and into the trunk on his own, refusing to allow Anna to assist in her injured condition. Less than a minute later, they were on their way again.

The detective remained in considerable pain, and was annoyed that things hadn't gone nearly as well as she would have liked. Still, she took solace from the fact that she and Vega were now on the move, not to mention still *alive*.

Which was something that their three recent adversaries certainly couldn't say.

14

Anna exited the parking garage and forced herself to limit her speed to inconspicuous levels, pulling into the first alley she came to. "There's a first aid kit in the duffel," she said to Vega.

He brought the bag from the floor to his lap and rummaged through it. "We'll have to change positions so I can reach your left arm," he said as he produced the kit.

She shook her head. "I can do this myself."

She had never been shot, or even badly injured, but she had taken several classes on how to apply a field dressing, even to herself.

Vega opened his mouth to argue, but the expression on her face made him change his mind. He opened the kit and left her to her own devices.

She cleaned her wound, sprayed it with a mesh foam that would staunch the flow of blood until she could see a physician, and wrapped it firmly with a bandage, finishing off with a copious helping of pain killers.

"Where to?" she said, relieved that her remaining blood supply, reduced as it was, would now be staying on the inside of her body. "We need to put distance between us and the Camden International Hotel. And I need you to keep watch on the rearview mirror in case someone tries to follow. Remember, we have two groups of killers after us now."

Vega manipulated his phone and studied a map. "Can you get on I-15 North?"

"I can," she replied, putting the car in drive. "The 101 can get us there, and there's an onramp about three minutes away."

Anna exited the alleyway, leaving the Honda in manual mode. Self-driving mode was nice, but it would be useless if another car were chasing them, or if they got into a gunfight—both now possibilities.

Even if an automated system could be programmed to handle these scenarios, Anna would bet on her own instincts every time.

"Why I-15 North?" she asked as she raced up the freeway onramp onto the 101, having been too preoccupied assessing her instincts for trouble to have engaged in conversation until this point. "What destination do you have in mind?"

"Before I tell you, we need to have a long conversation."

"I'll have to take a rain check on that," she said. "I need to make a call, and I need to do it *yesterday*."

As anxious as she was to learn who—or *what*—had tried to kill them at Vega's hotel, she had even more urgent matters to attend to. She had to speak with her captain and then jettison the phone immediately afterwards.

"I'll put it through the car's speaker," she said, "but I need for you to stay silent. As soon as I merge onto the I-15 I'm going to accelerate to as close to a hundred as I can get. If anyone is tailing us, this will flush them out. And I want to get far away from LA as quickly as possible. So your job is to scan the road for followers and speed traps, got it? Both would be very bad."

"Understood," said Vega, while she placed the call. Anna sensed he was uncomfortable in the car, almost sick, and wasn't eager to play lookout, but she appreciated his immediate compliance.

"Anna?" said Captain Donovan Perez upon answering. "What happened? I heard loud noises and then glass shattering. My phone didn't show your number, so I couldn't call back. Are you all right?"

"For now," said Anna. "But dangerous men are after me," she added, not bothering to mention the dangerous hostiles after Tom Vega, whatever the hell these fire-eyed, black-blooded bastards turned out to be.

"*Who*, Anna? Who is after you?"

"Neil Marshall," she replied immediately. "And associates."

"The drug lord, Neil Marshall?"

"That's the one," confirmed Anna, gradually increasing her speed to eighty miles an hour while her partner looked for trouble. "I've also learned who is supplying Foria. A man named Shane Frey. They planned to frame me tonight. And kill me."

"That makes no sense," said the captain. "If they planned to *kill* you, why bother to *frame* you?"

"Because their endgame is to make sure the Foria task force we've been trying to establish is never born. Killing me, alone, doesn't do that. But killing me and destroying my reputation at the same time does the trick nicely."

There was a long pause. "So they *already* tried to kill you?" said Perez. "Is that what you're saying? *Tonight?*"

"Yes!" said Anna adamantly. "And I'm sure they're *still* trying. One of them called me and offered to be an informant. But when I met with him, it was an ambush. I barely escaped. If you send detectives to the Salem Hills High School grounds, they'll find evidence of a gunfight, and blood that should match several bad guys in the database. They've had time to scrub the scene, so look closely in the back parking lot, near the only lamp that's giving off any light."

"I'll get some people over there right away," said Captain Perez. "But in the meantime, let's meet in person, and you can tell me more about your night. Fill in the details. And I can arrange security for you until we get to the bottom of this and we can be sure you're safe. Where are you now?"

Anna opened her mouth to reply, but thought better of it. "Why is that important?" she asked instead.

"I want to propose a meeting location," said the captain. "If it turns out that you're calling from Hawaii," he added wryly, "I'd want to factor that in."

"Right," said Anna, streaking past a white Tesla as if it were standing still. "Sorry. I know I'm paranoid, but it's been a long night. I'm not too far away. Why don't we meet at the station."

"Perfect," said Captain Perez. "Be there as soon as you can, so we can get to the bottom of this."

"Sounds like a plan," said Anna. "See you soon," she added, ending the connection.

15

"Report!" said Shanifrey.

"I'm afraid I have news you're not going to like," replied Eldamir, and in this case, the phrase, *I'm afraid*, wasn't just a figure of speech.

"Tell me!" bellowed his boss.

Eldamir swallowed hard. "Fanimore was watching the parking garage and had them in his sights," he began. "I then heard extensive gunfire from silenced guns through his comm, along with shattering glass, and then he was silent. I wasn't able to get him to respond to me afterwards."

"What does that mean? Is he dead?"

"I assume so, but I didn't have time to check. I had a car parked on the street in front of the hotel. In order to follow them, I needed to rush to it so I could catch them leaving the garage."

Shanifrey screamed a guttural curse, harsh even by the standards of *his* language. "Are you telling me we've lost *three* of our people tonight?" he thundered. "Three! In addition to Paritor!"

"I can't be certain," replied Eldamir, striving to stay as calm as possible, "but this is my best guess, yes."

Eldamir could understand the commander's fury. Things had gotten well out of hand. And in a hurry. Earlier that evening everything had been going their way. Their surveillance was going well, and Shanifrey was on the verge of rendering an irritating detective impotent, nipping a potential future problem in the bud.

And now *this*. Hard to imagine how so many things could go this wrong in such a short period.

"Where is the detective and her friend now?" demanded Shanifrey.

"Unknown," replied Eldamir, wishing he could give some other answer—*any* other answer. "I lost them on the I-15. Anna Abbott was driving. She accelerated to speeds that had to be a hundred or more, and weaved through traffic, which caught me off guard. If I had done the same, it would be obvious I was following. I tried anyway, but she had a significant head start, and I'm new to driving, so she was able to increase the distance between us until she was out of sight. I tried for a few minutes longer, but decided it would be futile to continue. So I exited and called you."

"How can you be so incompetent!" screamed Shanifrey. "You can detect them up to twenty miles away. Are you telling me they gained twenty miles on you in just a few minutes?"

"Our team only had the one detector," replied Eldamir hurriedly, "and Tiparax had it in the hotel room. I didn't have time to retrieve it. Hotel security had already gone to the ninth floor to investigate, so I made the decision to follow their car without it."

Eldamir braced himself for a flurry of invective, but this never arrived. Apparently, as angry as the commander was, and as poorly as this had turned out, he agreed with his subordinate's decision.

"Which direction did they go on the 15?" asked Shanifrey.

"North."

The commander paused in thought. "The reinforcements I mentioned earlier are already on their way to your location," he said. "A five-man human team. Not elite soldiers, which I'd prefer, but well trained and dangerous in their own right. So they'll do—at least for now. I was going to have them meet up with you, and place them under your command. But not anymore. I'll order these men to travel slowly up the 15, assuming the detective remained on this freeway after she lost you. Then I'll try to locate our targets in other ways. If I'm able to find them again, our human team won't have as much ground to cover to catch up."

"Assuming the detective continues on the 15," noted Eldamir. "Wouldn't it be better to send each of the five men in a different direction?"

"No. I'm beginning to think that just one of Marshall's men, alone, won't have a chance against Anna Abbott. I want all five of them taking her on at the same time."

"I should join them," said Eldamir.

"Yes you should. But you won't. We can't risk losing anyone else on our team. Marshall's men are expendable. We can decide what to do if, and when, they button things down."

"Button things down?" said Eldamir. "Won't they have orders to kill?"

"I've decided I want the targets captured and interrogated after all. The information we can gain is potentially too valuable to pass up. So the team will be ordered to take them alive if they're certain they can do it—kill them if not. If they do take them alive, they can lock them down until we can get there with an even more impressive force. I've been in discussions with a group of highly trained mercenaries, and I'll activate them now."

"When do you think these mercs can get here?" asked Eldamir.

"Unclear."

"And you really think human mercenaries are necessary?"

"I do now," said Shanifrey, his voice grim. "I've underestimated the dangers here on Earth," he admitted, "and I won't risk any further casualties. Not until I'm sure we're fielding an overwhelming force."

"Understood," said Eldamir.

"Now it just comes down to finding the car that you lost," said the commander pointedly. "There's a hacker I used last year who is extremely good. I'll get him on the job immediately. We know the license number of the Honda. He can try to hack street and freeway cams, as well as the car itself. There are no guarantees, and I have no idea on the timing, but I'm confident we'll eventually find them."

"They just killed all three of my comrades on this operation," said Eldamir. "So when we find them, and after they've been fully interrogated, I request permission to slit their throats myself."

There was a brief pause. "Permission granted," said Shanifrey.

16

Tom Vega turned to the detective the moment she was off the phone, highly agitated. "Before you go to the station to meet with your captain," he said, "give me the chance to convince you to stay with me, instead."

When she didn't respond immediately he continued. "Please!" he implored her. "Let me protect you. I know it doesn't seem like it at the moment, but there are more important things going on here than what happened to you at that high school."

"More important than a group of men trying to ruin my career and end my life?" she said in dismay.

"Give me twenty to thirty minutes to explain. Please!"

Anna digested this unexpected plea, and while she was dying to learn more about the things that had attacked them, and hear Vega out, she couldn't spare the time. She was taking a big risk with the phone as it was. "I want to hear you out," she replied rapidly, "I do. But first, you should know that I'm not—necessarily—meeting the captain anywhere."

"But you just told him you were."

"I *know* what I told him! But my intuition is smelling something fishy."

"What?"

"I have no idea, but something is wrong. Very wrong. So I need to make another call, and *quickly*. We need to ditch this phone so no one can use it to track us."

"Hurry, then," said Vega.

Anna thought for a moment, but the next call was obvious. There was only one other detective she worked with whom she considered a friend, Lieutenant Cole Boyer, Perez's number two man. The fact that her friends-and-family list only contained a single name was pathetic, and largely her own fault. She thought of herself as kind and loyal, with a good sense of humor to boot, so she believed she could be relatively popular if she made any kind of effort.

But she never had. She wasn't entirely sure why. Perhaps she felt she wasn't *deserving* of any friends. Or perhaps the loss of her parents when she was seven, and then Isabella, had soured her on forming any real attachments, stripping her of the courage required to leave herself open to emotional devastation yet again.

Add in departmental jealousies, her interest in keeping her personal life closely guarded, and her relentless focus on the job, and her lack of friends wasn't a mystery.

But she never had any regrets. Not really. She was still only twenty-eight, after entering the police academy at nineteen, becoming a uniform at twenty, and acing her detective exam at twenty-four. She had always assumed she'd have plenty of time for social entanglements, romantic or otherwise, which she had vowed to pursue before she reached thirty.

But now she wasn't sure if she'd even *live* to thirty. Hell, at this point, she wasn't sure if she'd live out the *night*.

She placed the call to Cole Boyer and held her breath. If he failed to answer, she was all out of ideas.

"Lieutenant Boyer," he announced.

"Thank God!" she whispered under her breath, at the same time hearing several voices near the lieutenant, making it clear that he wasn't alone.

"Cole, it's Anna," she said out loud. "I need your help. I'm in big trouble."

"Yeah, no shit," he replied, almost inaudibly. Then, more loudly, he said, "Hang on a second, Hailey, I'm having trouble hearing you."

Anna knew he was rushing off to seek privacy, but the fact that he felt the need to pretend the call had come from his wife, Hailey, was a very bad omen.

Almost fifteen seconds passed before his voice returned. "Anna, where the hell are you?" he whispered hoarsely. "And what in the hell is going on?"

"You're with Perez and others at the station, aren't you?" she said. "If I come in, it's a trap, isn't it?"

"Don't be ridiculous," said the lieutenant. "The captain has me here to help you. Make sure you're safe."

"Okay, now that you've issued the party line, you can come clean. Don't worry, you didn't do anything to tip me off. I wasn't coming in even before I called you, despite what I told the captain. So given that Perez's hook has no chance of reeling me in, I'd appreciate the truth. Neil Marshall and Shane Frey have somehow done something to convince him that I'm guilty already, haven't they? Despite the fact that I told the captain I was being framed."

"*Are* you guilty, Anna?"

"Come on, Cole! You know better than that. You *know* me. I have no life. I solve crimes and go home. I'm as straight as a ruler. As spotless as a fricking clean room. I'm being set up! You have to believe me."

"I'd like to," he replied. "I really would. But it's looking very bad."

"How bad?"

"A call came into the precinct about a shooting at Salem Hills High. A few uniforms were dispatched. Any idea what they found?"

"Yes. Because I already told the captain to go there, myself. This high school was where they tried to set me up. It was an ambush. I'm sure they've scrubbed the scene, but the uniforms probably found some blood evidence and shell casings. Pretty much what I told Perez they would find."

"Guess again," said Cole grimly. "How about *six dead bodies*?"

Anna's eyes widened in horror.

"If that's your idea of a scrubbed crime scene," continued the lieutenant, "then we have very different definitions of that phrase."

Anna suddenly found it very difficult to breathe. "*Six* bodies?" she repeated numbly.

"That's right. Six. But it gets a lot worse. Four of them were hog-tied, and had been shot in the forehead at point-blank range. With bullets fired from *your* gun, Anna. A gun that was also found at the scene. Along with your phone."

Bile rose in Anna's throat. This was all but checkmate. No wonder the captain hadn't asked why she wasn't using her phone when she had called. He knew she didn't have it. Her subconscious had been right to raise alarms.

"You claim that you walked into an ambush," continued Cole when she didn't reply. "But if that were the case, how, exactly, did you walk back *out* again? Are you suggesting that six men failed to ambush one lone detective? That you were forced to kill *four* of them *gangland* style?"

"Come on, Lieutenant!" snapped Anna. "You know I'm not that stupid. I told Perez to check out the high school, myself. Why would I do that if I had left such an obvious mess behind? The captain should have told me what he found and heard me out *before* he primed a trap to arrest me. I did incapacitate and hogtie four men at the scene, this much is true. But they were very much alive when I left. And we both know the other two weren't killed by my gun. Which calls your simple narrative into question. Marshall and Frey slaughtered their own people to make me look as guilty as possible. *Too* guilty, don't you think?"

Cole sighed. "The truth is that I do," he said. "Impossible to imagine a detective with your skill being so sloppy or obvious. Nothing about this rings true. But there's more that you don't know about. Rick Bunson came to me and the captain late this afternoon, just after you left for the day. He said he had overheard several suspicious conversations you've had recently. He heard enough to make him think you might be on the take. Wanted to recommend a quiet investigation."

Anna's stomach clenched. "He never heard any suspicious conversations," she insisted, "because I never *had* any."

"He also said that in one of the conversations," continued the lieutenant, ignoring Anna's denial, "you said that if things went south, if something arose that made you look dirty, you had a plan. You would claim that a drug dealer named Neil Marshall was trying to frame you."

Anna wanted to reply but the words were stuck in her throat, which felt as if it was constricting. And why not? The brilliantly fashioned noose she was now wearing, made of razor blades, could hardly be pulled any tighter.

"The captain and I both told Rick that he must have misinterpreted your conversations. We refused to begin an investigation unless he could supply hard evidence. We had your back."

"Until now," whispered Anna.

"I'm sorry."

"No. I get it. Who can blame you for changing your mind? The weight of evidence against me is crushing. My gun was involved in multiple killings. And Rick predicted I would try to blame Neil Marshall, which is exactly what I did. They had contingencies for their contingencies. Damn they're good. I busted up their plan and stayed alive, but they managed to turn my very success into an even *more* ironclad frame."

She paused. "What I don't understand is how they got to Rick. We were never close, but my gut says there's no way he would do this. Not for all the money in the world. I get a cop taking money to look the other way. But I can't imagine Rick would sell out a fellow detective like this."

"Look, I still believe that you're innocent," said Cole. "I *do* know you. And all of this is too convenient. You're right, if not for Rick Bunson, we'd believe every word you're saying. *Despite* how it looks. Or maybe *because* of it. So why don't you come in? I'll talk to the captain. Convince him not to arrest you until we've had the chance to pull at some threads and clear you."

Anna sighed. "Thanks, Cole. You're a good man. But it won't work. They've done too good a job. Based on everything he knows, the captain will have to arrest me. I would. *Anyone* would. And what you've seen tonight is only phase one. By now, the captain's obtained a search warrant for my home, hasn't he?"

Cole's lack of response spoke volumes.

"What he finds there will make me look even worse. Marshall's people broke in tonight, and planted files on my computer. When these come to light, no one will believe me. *I* wouldn't even believe me."

"Do you know what's on the files?"

"Yes, one of his lieutenants, a guy named Jimmy Jessup, told me during their attempted ambush. They planted records showing that I'm on the take. Other records that indicate I tamper with evidence to get convictions. Two million in a secret bank account. And a copy of my sealed juvie record, when I was a giant mess. Sure to make great reading."

"Jesus, Anna, I had no idea you even had a juvie record."

"No shit, Cole. That's what *sealed* means."

"That's enough evidence to choke a whale," he replied, ignoring her barb. "I am so sorry, Anna," he added sincerely. "I still think you're innocent, like I said. If not for Rick's allegations, I'd be certain of it. But if you are innocent, this frame of theirs is the tightest, most elaborate one I've ever even heard of."

"I know it is, Cole. They spent a fortune on this. And not just money. I'm stunned they were willing to sacrifice the four men I hog-tied. Especially since I was told that all four were hired from the outside. They really, really want Foria to be treated as just a run-of-the-mill new drug. Which makes me more certain than ever that it is anything but. So I'm begging you, Cole, as a personal favor to me, no matter what happens, don't let up on this. Redouble the department's efforts to get to the bottom of Foria and Shane Frey. Find a way to get the FBI in, and soon."

"I will," said the lieutenant solemnly. "And I'll do everything I can to prove that you were framed."

"You're a good friend, Cole. And I promise you that your belief in me isn't misguided. Somehow, I'm going to find a way to clear my name, even if you can't. You can bet on it."

"I'd never bet against the great Anna Abbott," he said wistfully. "If anyone can stay ahead of the coming manhunt long enough to clear her name, it's you."

"Thanks. This is the first time I'll be rooting for one of the department's manhunts to *fail*," she said wryly.

The lieutenant sighed. "Good luck, Anna. Hopefully we'll be on the same side very soon."

"Thanks, Cole," she replied. "From your mouth to God's ear," she added, ending the call.

Several tears came to the corners of Anna's eyes and slid down her cheek. She wiped them away with the back of her hand and her features hardened once again. No time to go soft now. She needed to be her strongest to have any hope of extricating herself from the mother of all traps. Once this was over, she could show as much emotion as she wanted.

She blew out a long breath, lowered the window in Vega's car, and unceremoniously flung the phone as far as she could into the night.

"That didn't go well," said Vega.

Anna laughed. This was an understatement of epic proportions. Besides, it hurt too much to cry.

When her laughter subsided, she turned to Vega and tried to look optimistic, without success. "Look on the bright side, Tom," she said, hoping to cheer at least one of them up, "you wanted a test of my intuition. Well it looks like you got it. Marshall and Frey are no doubt still trying to kill me. Whatever was back there is trying to kill you. And very shortly, every cop in America will be hunting me down, convinced that I'm a dirty cop and a mass murderer."

"We'll find a way to get through this," said Vega. "We have to."

"Because I can see the future?" she said, rolling her eyes.

"Among other things, yes," he replied.

"Well, Tom, I've got bad news for you. The only future I foresaw after I left the restaurant tonight was a bath and a good night's sleep. So you're betting on the wrong pony."

"It isn't just me who'll be betting on you, Anna. You just might be the most important person who ever lived."

Anna couldn't help but laugh once again. This was the most ludicrous statement she had ever heard. *The most important person who ever lived?* Had he really said that? "Yeah, I get that a lot," she said wryly. "But usually not until I've slept with a guy."

She shook her head and sighed. "You are completely, totally, out of your mind, do you know that?"

"Maybe," said Vega softly. "But I have a feeling that we're going to find out."

PART 2

"Intuition comes very close to clairvoyance; it appears to be the extrasensory perception of reality."

—Alexis Carrell (Nobel Laureate, Physiology and Medicine)

17

Colonel Stephen Leroy Redford threw up an image on the large plasma screen affixed to his office wall and couldn't help but feel like a little kid again.

He still couldn't believe he was looking at an alien being.

An honest-to-goodness, unmistakable, *no way he was born on this planet*, alien.

UFO sightings had been increasing dramatically in recent years, and many were convinced that a shadow government was hiding extraterrestrials from the public, and even the president and US government. But as far as Redford knew, this wasn't the case. As far as he knew, he had just obtained the first definitive proof in human history that extraterrestrials actually existed, and he was in charge of the team responsible for investigating this visitation. An investigation sure to be as extensive as any ever conducted.

Redford was living proof that childhood dreams really could come true. Even impossible dreams of landing the best government job in the world. One giving him absolute responsibility for finding and studying alien life on Earth, and even representing humanity during any first contact situations that took place in America.

And this *was* a first contact situation. True, technically, *first contact* required both sides to be alive when it happened, and the lone representative of this unearthly new species, whose image now appeared on Redford's monitor, was decidedly deceased. But why split hairs?

A living alien would have been better, but nothing could dampen the colonel's excitement. This was an event so extraordinary, so consequential, that Redford felt like he was floating in midair.

The colonel had been enamored by the concept of alien beings since before he could remember, and as a kid had sucked up superhero comic books, science fiction novels, and science fiction movies like a blue whale eating krill. Most kids loved the idea of aliens, but Redford had taken this to the *next level*, vowing to some-day join a *Men-in-Black*-like governmental agency, or to *start one* if one didn't exist.

And he had methodically set out to do just this. He had earned two masters, one in space science and one in the biology of adaptive natural selection, all before the age of twenty-two. He had joined the military as an officer and worked his way up the ranks. Along the way he had penned dozens of white papers focused on extrater-restrials, including first contact scenarios and strategies to fend off possible alien attack. Most importantly, he had been instrumental in the launch of a military version of SETI, which he had long insisted was of paramount importance.

Finally, Redford had landed in the Air Force Space Command at Peterson Air Force Base in Colorado, which had long been respon-sible for monitoring the solar system, overseeing and guarding criti-cal communications, spy, and GPS satellites, and any number of other undisclosed functions.

Redford had been at Peterson for three years, and had pushed hard for the formation of a hypervigilant new Black Ops group that would monitor America for any possible alien visitations. A group that would combine leading edge science, sensor technology, and in-vestigative techniques to carry out this mission in ways that Project Blue Book and others of old couldn't even begin to imagine.

And then, four years earlier, he had been given the green light to proceed. He became the commander of this new Black Ops unit that didn't officially exist, one designated EVI, for Extraterrestrial Visitor Investigations, pronounced like the girl's name, *Evie*, and soon spelled this way also.

Just like that, what he had strived for all his life was suddenly a reality. At the tender age of thirty-one his meteoric rise was complete. He was the founding member and commander of what was basically his very own *Men in Black* organization.

The only problem was that Evie was Men in Black *without* the aliens. The equivalent of a BLT sandwich without the bacon. Still, he was determined to turn over every last stone to find the missing ingredient. If extraterrestrials ever did visit Earth, Redford vowed he would find them.

He had set up shop in a secret underground facility five miles from Luke Air Force Base in Arizona. Aboveground it was made to look like a nuclear waste processing plant, and it had its own large helipad, although this was positioned a mile away so the helipad and facility wouldn't seem connected to each other.

Underground, the facility was remarkably spacious, with living quarters, quarantine capabilities, advanced computer and communication systems, medical and surgical suites, state-of-the-art laboratories, and even inescapable interrogation rooms and holding cells— just in case.

He had filled the facility with the best men and women he could find, scientists and soldiers alike. Each was put through an examination of their past so thorough it would make the most seasoned proctologist blush. In addition, each had undergone a large battery of psychological testing, ensuring Redford's largely unaccountable department was a megalomania-free zone.

And then the colonel had gotten down to the business of finding aliens. First he had tied Evie into the most advanced supercomputer ever developed, at the NSA's headquarters in Fort Meade, Maryland. This supercomputer also housed the most advanced AI ever developed, nicknamed Nessie, which could be used like a Siri or Alexa— times a thousand. Nessie also had access to nearly every past and present computer record, phone conversation, email, text, and internet posting, making it seem practically *omniscient*.

And while Nessie churned away, monitoring nearly all telephone and electronic communications, Redford's department had programmed in an algorithm of its own, ensuring the system was forever checking for key words and concepts of possible interest. If it caught the faintest whiff of anything that might possibly be otherworldly, this would be communicated to low-level people in Redford's group, and would be investigated further.

In this way, Extraterrestrial Visitor Investigations was like Project Blue Book, but with a much vaster array of potential inputs, and not limited to the investigation of UFO sightings. Redford worried that none of these tenuous possibilities would ever bear fruit, but he followed up on them anyway. He reasoned that if an advanced alien didn't want to be discovered, it wouldn't leave a single clue. And if it did, it wouldn't be coy about it. It would just announce itself, or ask to see a leader, or maybe even introduce itself with a killer *Instagram* post.

What he never would have guessed is that it might get hit and killed by a car in Manhattan while crossing the street. Which is exactly what *had* happened, about two weeks earlier. Exactly on his thirty-fifth birthday. A present from the universe.

The accident victim's body had been abnormal enough to end up with a forensic pathologist, Dr. Lanny Neff, in New York-Presbyterian hospital. Nessie had alerted the colonel to a call Dr. Neff had made to a colleague, asking her to come by immediately to help examine a corpse that couldn't possibly be human. Neff claimed that the body he was examining contained viscous black blood, and had organs of all the wrong kind, in all the wrong places. Not to mention a distinctive odor that Neff had never experienced before.

Redford was sure this was a hoax or a practical joke, but had his men intervene immediately, anyway.

And it had turned out to be anything but a joke. His people had clamped down hard on the pathologists who were on the call, and the cops who had discovered the body, making sure they kept what they had seen to themselves. They then found and deleted all related photos, so that if the witnesses did breach confidentiality, no one would believe them. Finally, the corpse was brought back to Evie's home base under the Arizona desert, where it was put in a refrigerated room and studied more extensively than any corpse in history.

Finally, indisputable proof of life on other planets. And not just life, but *intelligence*.

This was arguably the most momentous event in human history. And Colonel Stephen Leroy Redford was at the very epicenter of it all.

Evie's charter could not have been more lopsided. Until overwhelming evidence of a current alien visitation to Earth was revealed,

Redford had access to any computer, black site laboratory, or classified military equipment he wanted. But other than this he wielded less military power than the *crossing guard* at his niece's elementary school.

But if overwhelming, incontrovertible evidence did present itself, the entire military was his oyster, and he suddenly had more power than *God*.

And that switch had just been flipped. He now had access to an unlimited black budget and command codes that enabled him to control billions of dollars of military equipment and deploy veritable armies at his command.

But Redford couldn't care any less about his newfound powers, which he prayed would never need to be used.

This wasn't about power. It was about discovery. And history. And the future of humanity.

He was now giving the president daily updates, and key divisions of the military, focused on space, had been brought to full alert. Space-based and terrestrial telescopes had been diverted from their missions to scour space within a few light-weeks of home, looking for anything unusual. And a discussion had already begun among a very select group of military and government officials about the advisability of disclosing this event to the world.

Redford was dying to do just that, but even he knew that now was not the time. To paraphrase an old saying, a bird in the bush usually had a friend in there with him. This would be true for an *alien* in the bush as well.

The colonel couldn't imagine that a lone alien had arrived on Earth just to sightsee in the Big Apple. There had to be others. Before the world was told about this alien species, he needed to find a representative with a pulse—assuming they had pulses. He had to learn why they were here, how they had managed the journey, and their future intentions. And he was even curious if they smelled bad while alive, or if this odor only came to the fore after death.

Redford sighed. He needed to push these musings from his mind and get down to the task at hand. He needed to read the latest update from his medical and scientific staff, which was almost seventy pages long. The report detailed the latest analysis of the alien's DNA—similar but not identical to terrestrial DNA—along with its cell structure, physiology, the likely conditions on its home planet, and so on.

It was getting very late, but he was determined to work deep into the night, until he passed out at his desk. If this case didn't warrant round-the-clock attention, nothing ever would.

But before he began reading, the colonel couldn't help but stare at the image on his monitor one last time. The alien could pass for a man, but his size and features would give most humans the creeps. Redford had named this new species "the Travelers," which had already been abbreviated to *Travs*.

"Colonel Redford," said the pleasant female voice of the NSA's supercomputer, interrupting his reverie, "Nessie here. I have a priority one alpha alert. Do I have your permission to deliver it verbally?"

"Granted," said the colonel.

"I just intercepted a call to the police from a Nia Curtis, manager of the Camden International Hotel on Wilshire Boulevard in Los Angeles. She spoke with a Sergeant Darnell Rice to report a double homicide. Miss Curtis had received complaints from guests about a potential disturbance in room 925, and when she checked up on it, she found two dead bodies inside. Both appeared to have been gunned down. Both were described as having thick black blood."

Redford gasped. This was astonishing. Two additional Travs discovered on Earth, and so *quickly*. How many Travs *were* there? And why did they seem to have so much trouble staying *alive*?

"From Nia Curtis's physical description of the bodies," continued Nessie, "they both fall well within the parameters of what might be expected for a Trav, based on the appearance of Trav One. Both sets of their eyes were glowing, almost as if on fire, until they died out a few minutes after Miss Curtis arrived at the scene. This red luminescence is consistent with what your scientists identified when they activated the dormant implants found within Trav One's eyes."

There was a brief pause. "Shall I continue?"

"*Immediately*," snapped Redford impatiently.

"After ending the call with Miss Curtis seconds ago, Sergeant Rice just called his captain, Donovan Perez, and is speaking with him now.

I'm monitoring the call, and expect that Captain Perez will be sending his people to the crime scene momentarily."

"Break into their call," snapped the colonel. "Now!"

Nothing said *creepy power* and *Big Brother* more profoundly than when a third party suddenly materialized into the middle of a private phone conversation.

"Impersonate Perez's direct superior," said Redford, knowing that Nessie could access and analyze recorded calls made by the captain's boss in an instant. "Using his voice, tell the captain that he's off this case. Impress upon him that no one on the force is to go near that hotel, or discuss what the manager reported in any way. Ground him and don't answer any of his questions, including how you broke in on the call. Threaten his job if he pushes back too hard. Then kill any calls he tries to make.

"Assuming DHS agent Ed Rosiland is still in LA," continued Redford, "use my command codes to order him to call Captain Perez, followed by an emergency visit. Instruct Rosiland to tell Perez that the scene at the hotel involves soldiers with classified enhancements, which include synthetic black blood with higher oxygen-carrying capacity. Then, have him force the captain to sign a non-disclosure agreement in the name of national security. Got it?"

"Carrying out your orders now," said Nessie.

"Good. Now contact the hotel manager," he added, knowing that Nessie could comfortably hold many thousands of conversations at once. "Use Captain Perez's voice and title. Instruct her to close off room 925 and let no one in, under any circumstances, until the authorities arrive. Then have him introduce me as a consulting detective who will be in charge of the case. And tell her to keep everything she's seen confidential until I've had the chance to speak with her."

"Calling now," announced Nessie.

"Scramble our fastest jet to get me and Agent Royce Milne to Los Angeles Air Force Base at best possible speed."

"Are you aware that no military aircraft are stationed at this base?"

"Of course," said Redford. "It houses Space and Missile Systems." Nessie was amazing in many ways, but she had real trouble thinking outside the box. "But they put in a single runway last year, which should be just long enough for us to land on."

"It is," said Nessie.

"Good," said the colonel. "So contact Milne now and tell him wheels up in ten minutes. Have an exfil team meet us in room 925 as soon as possible with two refrigeration units to transport the bodies. Milne will be in charge of overseeing the transport back to Evie headquarters for further study."

"Implementing your orders now," said Nessie.

"One last thing. Have two of our pilots each fly an NG 225 helicopter to LA Air Force Base as well, and have these aircraft gassed up and ready to go in case I need them."

"I'll see to it," said the AI. "Would you also like me to contact and brief the president on your behalf?"

"No. I'll do that from the air. But I would like you in on the call."

Redford ended the conversation and rushed out of his office to prepare for his imminent flight.

The colonel was tall, solid, and had a rugged, outdoorsy appearance. But while he may not have looked like a stereotypical geek on the outside, he remained a geek through and through. Even so, while the hardcore geek inside of him still believed that any species capable of visiting Earth would be peaceful, these Travs hadn't exactly died while releasing doves or planting daffodils.

Alien beings gunned down in a hotel room was troubling, to say the least.

Steve Redford wasn't the type to jump to conclusions, but his enthusiasm was beginning to morph into trepidation.

What, exactly, was going on here?

18

Detective Anna Abbott kept a heavy foot on the gas pedal and the blue Honda hurtled up the I-15, piercing the night sky. It had only been thirty minutes, but she had already put almost fifty miles behind them, weaving through the light traffic whenever she had to.

They drove in silence for several minutes, each alone with their thoughts. Anna struggled to digest just how much had changed, and how quickly. She had gone from a star in her department to its most-wanted fugitive in hours.

Before today, she had never killed *anyone.* Now, she had spilled blood repeatedly, even if most of it was colored black—which was beyond surreal. She had also been responsible for spilling *red blood,* even if only indirectly. While she hadn't pulled the trigger, she had made sure Jimmy had a gun to do so, and had known what he would do with it.

Self-defense, no doubt, but still a heavy burden.

Worse, her life had been ripped away, only to be replaced by . . . what? She had no idea.

Yesterday her life had meaning. She was helping to put bad people behind bars, so they couldn't hurt others, the way those closest to her had been hurt. Now she was doing nothing but trying to stay alive and out of jail. The only person she had a chance of helping was herself, and even that had grown increasingly unlikely.

Anna clenched her jaw. *Enough!* she screamed at herself. It was time to stop thinking about how everything had gone wrong, and start thinking about how to make it *right.*

"Okay, Tom," she said with a fierce, no-nonsense demeanor, "let's talk. Start by telling me what destination you have in mind."

"Huntington, Utah. According to my phone, it's about a nine-hour drive, almost all of it on the 15. I have a colleague there who has a safe house. I can tell you all about her, and why this is an important destination, but I'd rather wait. There's a lot you need to know first."

Anna thought about this, keeping her eyes on the road. "Understood," she said finally. "I'll keep heading toward Huntington while you fill me in. It's as good a destination as any, I guess."

Anna paused. She had killed three men-like things with laser eyes and black blood, and even had one in the trunk. She was dying to know what the hell was going on. But her instincts insisted she first follow up on the preposterous statement Vega had just made.

"But before you begin," she said, "I need you to convince me you aren't stark, raving mad. You just told me that I might be the most important person who ever lived. I tried to laugh it off, but my gut tells me that you *believe it*. This isn't just hyperbole for you, is it?"

Vega shook his head. "No. Anything but."

"Come on, Tom, what am I supposed to do with *that*? Most important person *ever*? I mean, you've heard of Plato, Moses, and Jesus Christ, right? Or scientists like Darwin, Newton, and Einstein?" Anna shook her head vigorously. "Hell, I'm not even the most important person in my *yoga class*."

"You don't take a yoga class," said Vega evenly.

"See! How do you know that? You've studied me a lot more than you've let on. No way you'd be this convinced that I'm clairvoyant otherwise. No way you'd think I'm so important based only on my solve rate and an hour or so of conversation. So what do you know about me?"

He sighed. "Everything I could possibly learn. Which is a lot, given my expertise with computers. Your past was critical for me to explore. To really understand what you're made of. And I was certain that proof of your abilities didn't just manifest itself the moment you became a detective. I knew there had to be additional evidence in your background."

"You hacked my juvie records, didn't you?" said Anna, her intuition now sure this was the case.

"Sorry," he said, and looked genuinely apologetic. "I sealed them back up. And I had nothing to do with putting them on your home computer. But yes."

Anna shook her head and frowned, but didn't say anything. She was long past being surprised about anything.

"Do you want to talk about what's in them?" said Vega.

"Talk about *what*? I was a mess when my parents died. And then I bounced around foster homes for years, resenting the world. So I lashed out. I was the ultimate juvenile delinquent. I abused drugs, and alcohol, and sex, and did anything else I could do to drown my sorrows—before I was even fourteen. I broke the law. Repeatedly. I skipped school, and stole cars and robbed homes. I was wild and untamable and angry."

"And yet you were still studying what you could about the subconscious and intuition, even then."

"Yes."

"Which is why nothing ever really stuck to you. Not like others your same age, with your same record. Tell me that had nothing to do with your abilities."

She blew out a long breath. "You're right. I was able to use my intuition to minimize the trouble I got into. Read cops and judges. Predict the right things to say. I always found a way out of every mess. And let me tell you, I got into some *epic* messes."

"And you used the money you stole as seed money to amass a small fortune by the time you were sixteen."

Anna raised her eyebrows. "Very good," she said. "That's not even in the juvie records. As far as I know, you're the first to discover it. But yes, I falsified an identity so I could trade stocks online. And I made millions."

"Just lucky, huh."

"Not clairvoyance, that's for sure. I told you the subconscious is the best pattern-recognizing machine ever created. I read every book I could get my hands on having to do with economics, foreign currencies, trade, worldwide trends, and so on. I understood almost none of it."

"But you were loading up your subconscious."

"That's right. And it worked. My intuition was able to see correlations, opportunities, that my conscious mind could not. I only traded in the riskiest instruments, futures and options, which could see huge swings in value in a very short time. And I only traded when I came across a bet that my instincts screamed at me to take."

"So with no experience," said Vega, "as a kid, you turned peanuts into millions. All the while pulling off one Houdini act after another to get yourself out of trouble. And you still wonder why I'm convinced you can see the future."

"My success is fully explainable by the known abilities of the subconscious. Along with my much better than average ability to cultivate it, and my willingness to listen. No superpowers needed."

Vega eyed her with just the hint of a smile, but didn't respond.

"So I'm sure you know the rest, also," said Anna. "How my closest and only friend at the boarding school, Isabella Gutierrez, was found dead, after having been raped and murdered. I had finally let someone in, and once again they were taken from me. So I had my second Bruce Wayne moment, at the age of sixteen."

"I knew she had been killed, but very little else about what happened."

"The detective assigned to the case interviewed me, of course," said Anna. "Interviewed *everyone* who had known Izzy. But he got nowhere. I thought he was pathetic and incompetent. So I conducted my own investigation."

"And caught the killer, I'm sure."

"Yes. But the idiot detective wouldn't believe me," said Anna in disgust. "So I set a trap for the asshole who did it, and got him to reveal incriminating evidence. Then I negotiated a deal with authorities. In exchange for delivering this monster on a silver platter, I got my juvie record sealed away forever. As if none of it ever happened. A slate clean enough to eat off of." She shook her head. "Or so I thought. Now I'm wondering if there's *anyone* who hasn't hacked it."

"So after you found Isabella's killer," guessed Vega, "you turned your life around."

"Yes. I had never killed anyone, but I was guilty of just about everything else. And I was done lashing out. I could generate all the money I wanted at any time, so I didn't need to break any laws. I had a clean slate. And I was so tired of criminals destroying my life. It was time I started destroying *theirs*. So I turned over a new leaf and vowed to become a detective."

Vega shook his head and smiled. "Without your future department ever knowing you had closed your friend's case as a teen," he said. "So your solve rate is even better than I thought."

"Look," said Anna, suddenly becoming irritated, "this isn't supposed to be a trip down memory lane. The bottom line is that I was right. You've been invading my privacy in a big way, and have told me nothing but lies about what you've been up to."

She took her eyes off the road and stared at him intently. "So what do you say, Tom? Are you ready to tell me the *truth* for a change?"

19

"I'll tell you what's really going on," said Vega. "But I warn you, it's going to be a lot to digest."

"What a nice change of pace," said Anna sarcastically. "Because it's been a really boring, uneventful day *so far*."

Vega actually smiled at this, a rarity.

But Anna was frowning deeply. She was exhausted. What the day had really been was *never-ending*. She had worked a long shift even *before* her dinner with Vega, and that seemed like ages ago. Adrenaline was pushing her through her blood loss and fatigue, but this would not be true forever. And she wanted to give her full attention to the man beside her.

She glanced at the car's touchscreen, which read, "Hello, my name is Daisy" at the top in small letters. "Give me just another minute, and you can begin," she told Vega.

Anna lowered her speed from a hundred to the posted speed limit of sixty-five for the first time. LA was now seventy miles behind them, which had taken well under an hour to accomplish.

"Daisy," she called out.

"I'm listening," said the voice of the car's computer.

"Go to full self-driving mode now, always at maximum allowable speed."

"Understood," said the car. "What is my destination?"

"Huntington, Utah."

"Self-driving mode engaged. Following route to Huntington, Utah now."

"As you're proceeding," said Anna, "check your maps program for a cheap motel within a mile of a used car lot. If you find such a motel within twenty miles of our route, this will be your new destination. Understood?"

"Define *cheap motel*," said the pleasant, feminine voice of the car.

Anna realized the qualifier, *cheap*, was needlessly ambiguous. "Change 'cheap motel' to the following," she said after a moment's thought. "A one- or two-story motel at which guests can park in front of their rooms."

"Understood," said Daisy.

"Good. Please return to dormancy."

"Going dormant now," announced the car.

Anna tilted her body and head to face Vega now that she didn't need to drive.

Her fellow passenger looked confused. "I get that you want to find a good spot to stop for the night," he said. "And I get why you want to switch to a used car, so we can't be tracked. But how are we going to pay for it?"

Anna smiled wearily. "That brown paper bag in my duffel, which I'm sure you've seen, is filled with hundred-dollar bills."

Vega raised his eyebrows. "Okay, then. Cash it is."

"Now that that's settled," said Anna, "let's get on with it. What are those things that I killed back there?"

Vega took a deep breath and let it out. "Alien beings from a planet named Tartar," he said simply, "located in the central region of the galaxy. This Shane Frey is likely to be one of them, as well."

Anna couldn't help but roll her eyes, even though she knew she shouldn't. This was preposterous. On the other hand, given what she had seen, it was also strangely believable. The men she had killed weren't human, so this was an obvious explanation, as hard as she had tried to resist going there.

"A planet named Tartar?" she said. "Like in *tartar sauce*?"

"Close enough," said Vega.

"And how far away is the central region of the galaxy?" she asked. "I'm guessing we'd need to fill up the gas tank to get there," she added, trying to inject levity as she often did when things got too real. Or, in this case, when her brain was about to melt.

"Twenty-five thousand light-years, give or take."

Any number of questions popped into Anna's head at once. How had these aliens gotten here? What did they want? How could they pass as human? But one question seemed most pressing of all. "How can you possibly *know* all this?" she asked him.

Vega took a deep breath once again. "Because I'm from that region of the galaxy as well," he said evenly.

20

Anna gasped and gripped the car's center console for support. Once again, this statement was utterly preposterous, but her intuition knew that it was true.

Which explained why her instincts about the being calling himself Tom Vega had been so fuzzy. Because neither her conscious nor subconscious had any experience with non-humans. And there had always been something off about him. His face a little too young and androgynous. His skin a little too perfect and hairless. He was like a well-made facsimile of a man, with perfect English and expressions, but with eyes a little too big, and mannerisms that weren't quite right.

"I know how crazy this sounds," continued Vega, "but I can prove it to you in multiple ways. For example, if you press hard on my stomach, you'll feel several bony plates inside. Which humans *don't* have."

"Yeah, thanks for the anatomy lesson," said Anna sarcastically. "I'm pretty sure I knew that. But I'm going to pass. I believe you. And I have no interest in pressing on *any* part of your body."

Anna considered where to go from here. "Okay," she said finally, "my mind is officially blown. I have too many questions to even know where to begin. So I'll let you start at the beginning—wherever *that* is. Bring me up to speed in whatever way you think makes sense. I won't be shy about asking questions."

Vega nodded, and then paused in thought. As he did, Anna scanned the road behind them to ensure they didn't have a tail, something she intended to do periodically no matter how engrossing the conversation might become. Not that her prolonged speeding hadn't ruled out any followers long ago.

"I'm from a planet we call Vor," said the alien in the passenger's seat, "and my real name isn't Tom Vega. Since no human can pronounce my actual name, let's stick with that one."

"Any other alien species here that you want to tell me about?"

"Not to my knowledge. Just a small group of Tartarians, and a small group of Vorians."

Anna made a face. "Tartarians and Vorians?" she repeated, finding these words clumsy. She paused for a moment in thought. "How about we call them Tarts and Vors?"

Vega shrugged. "Whatever you prefer," he replied.

"Okay, so you were saying . . ."

"There are twenty-eight known intelligent species in the galaxy," he continued, "counting humans. But your species seems to be unique among all twenty-eight in a way that I'll tell you about later. And you're the only one of the twenty-eight civilizations to emerge on a planet located way out in the boonies of the galaxy."

Anna raised her eyebrows. Earth was considered a backwater planet? Who knew?

Regardless, she was impressed by Vega's use of the word *boonies*. He seemed to have a solid command of English dialect. "I didn't know that the galaxy *had* a boondocks," she said, vaguely aware of an ambulance wailing in the distance, far from the freeway.

He nodded. "The other twenty-seven known species all live at the center of the galaxy. Within a few dozen light-years of where we and the, ah . . . *Tarts* live."

"Why would that be?" asked Anna. "Is there something troubling about the outskirts of the galaxy I don't know about?"

"Not at all. It's just that the vast majority of stars reside in the center, which means that so do the vast majority of planets. The galactic center is *teeming* with suns, and in many systems they are binary, meaning two stars revolve around each other. Vor is in a binary star system—really almost a trinary—and so is Tartar. But the temperatures on both planets are similar to Earth's, since they're much farther away from their suns than you are to Sol."

Vega paused to let this sink in.

"On Vor," he continued, "night is a rare occurrence. When it does happen, though, the night sky is spectacular beyond words. Thicker with stars than you can possibly imagine, and anything but dark. Earth's nearest stellar neighbor is 4.3 light-years away. In my neighborhood, almost *four hundred thousand* stars are within this distance of us."

Anna nodded. "Now it makes sense," she said. "Why do you rob banks? Because that's where all the money is."

Vega looked confused. "I don't get it."

"I'm saying that you've made your point. I never thought about our stellar neighborhood as sparsely populated, but I guess it is. And I guess the odds of intelligence sprouting up are very low, so this makes sense. It's like sampling a square mile on Earth looking to find a human being. Take a square mile sample around Times Square and you're sure to find one. Take a square mile sample in the mountains of Wyoming and . . . not so much."

"Exactly."

Anna took a moment to imagine how glorious the night sky must be for these alien civilizations, each living on the galactic equivalent of the Las Vegas Strip. "But wouldn't you and the Tarts find our planet awfully dim, even during the day? And find darkness terrifying?"

"Yes on both counts," replied Vega. "Even after many years of training in these conditions, darkness is highly . . . unsettling. But both species also have technology we can have surgically implanted in our eyes to amplify light."

"Which must be why the Tarts' eyes glow red like they do."

"Exactly."

"So why don't yours?" asked the detective.

"Our scientists worked hard over many decades to perfect a version that we could use without being detected," said Vega. "This wasn't nearly as important to the Tarts for reasons I'll get to later. Mine are in constant use, even now. *Especially* now," he added anxiously, glancing out at the darkness that was enveloping the road.

Anna considered. "Okay," she said thoughtfully, "so there are twenty-eight species, and twenty-seven of them are fairly near to each other geographically, at least on a cosmic scale. So how did you find us way out here? You've obviously figured out how to travel faster than light."

"*We* didn't," he corrected. "But, yes, faster-than-light technology is known to all twenty-seven intelligent species."

"I can't help but notice that you left one species out of your little tech party," said Anna pointedly.

"Not really our choice," he replied.

"Whose?

"I'll get to that part soon enough. But the reason that Earth isn't part of this galactic community is because no one can reach you— not without help. Not that you'd want to be part of our . . . *party*, anyway."

Anna raised her eyebrows, but her gut told her not to digress to explore this statement further. "Why do you need help to reach us?" she asked instead.

"Because the maximum speed of our starships—anyone's star-ships—is only about fifty times the speed of light. Which is approximately nine million of your miles a second. Or more than thirty-three trillion miles an hour."

"*Only* about fifty times the speed of light?" said Anna in disbelief. "*Only* nine million miles a second? Are you kidding? That's what we on Earth call *ludicrous* speed."

"Maybe so," replied Vega, "but even travelling this fast, a twenty-five thousand light-year journey to Earth would take *five hundred* years to complete."

Anna raised her eyebrows. "That *is* quite the road trip," she said wryly. "But on the bright side," she added with a smile, "I have to believe you'd earn enough frequent flier miles to get free travel for the rest of eternity."

"I don't understand?"

Anna's smile grew. Just because humor wasn't Vega's strong suit, and just because, as impressively prepared as he was, any number of pop culture references were sure to elude him, didn't mean she still couldn't amuse *herself*.

"We considered trying to make the trip, anyway," continued Vega, "but a five hundred year journey is beyond even our capabilities.

Starships can be large, but not as large as we'd need. Not big enough for a good generational ship, or big enough to carry the equipment we would require to make our own fuel."

"Right," said Anna. "So, as you said, you needed help to get here."

"Exactly."

"So just what kind of help are we talking about?"

"In addition to starships," said Vega, "there are portals on each world that connect them to various other worlds. You can step through and travel impossible distances in the blink of an eye. In this case twenty-five thousand light-years. One moment I was on Vor, and the next I was here."

Anna's eyes widened. It was too incredible for words. *Instantaneous* really did put a mere nine million miles a second to shame. "That's amazing," she said. "Beyond amazing. But I still don't see why you needed *help*."

"Because the portals are random. In number, location, destination, and so on. And those that lead to Earth are all but nonexistent."

"Why would they be random?" asked Anna. "Who installed them?

"I only wish I could tell you. I wish anyone could tell you. This is the biggest mystery in the known cosmos. One even you wouldn't be able to solve, Detective."

Vega pursed his lips and then continued. "There are all kinds of theories," he said. "Some say it's just a natural phenomenon. Seems impossible, because the portals are so perfect, so flawless in construction. But some say that just because something is *natural*, doesn't mean its properties can't be perfect and brilliantly organized—like crystals, or better yet, stars. Some say the universe, in its entirety, is an intelligent organism, and creates the portals and chooses where to place them. But the vast majority believe a superintelligence, one not comprised of the entire universe, is responsible."

Anna paused to consider this. She had passed *surreal* and *mind-blowing* so long ago she might as well be Alice in Wonderland. "How do the portals work?" she asked.

"Again, unknown," replied the alien.

It occurred to Anna that they were sitting in a car that was driving itself to Utah. Something that might have been nearly as mind-blowing to her ancestors as a portal was to her. This was even truer when it came to computers, jets, microwave ovens, and televisions.

"We have endless theories to explain their operation," continued Vega, "but no direct knowledge. All we know is that we know nothing. The portals are impervious to our attempts to analyze them, and they have a mind of their own. The portal that brought me to Earth has now disappeared again. It was open between our two worlds for a thirty-year period once—twenty-eight hundred years ago—and then it disappeared. And three of your years ago it reopened for a brief period and then disappeared again. After only sixty-four of us had made it through."

"Did all sixty-four come through at once?"

"No. This portal is too small for that. They vary. Some are large enough that hundreds can go through at once. Some only allow single-file travel. They're fickle in every way. In addition to opening and closing whenever they feel like it, most of our technology won't go through, for unknown reasons."

Anna stifled a yawn. Fatigue continued to knock at the door, and while she was staying sharp and fending it off, this wouldn't be possible forever. "Apparently, the implants in your eyes made it through," she pointed out.

"Yes, *thankfully*," replied Vega. "And a comm system we have implanted internally as well, which allows us to communicate subvocally. The Tartarians—the Tarts—have a similar system. And thousands of years ago, when we first began coming here, and before we had the ocular implants, we were able to get wearable external light devices through."

Anna suddenly snapped out of her relative stupor to let the enormity of what was being revealed to her sink in, beyond the nuts and bolts of the portals. Yes, the portals were a miracle, but the big picture was that Earth had been visited by the Vors in its ancient past. It was yet another stunning revelation. What might this imply? Had the Vors helped to shape human history?

And if so, how?

21

A flood of additional questions came to Anna's mind all at once as the blue Honda named Daisy continued its journey, having no idea of the epic nature of what was being said within its confines. Anna could have spent eons asking follow-up questions on the topics Vega had *already* introduced, and the alien didn't seem anywhere near the finish line.

"How many of you came here originally?" she asked Vega, forcing herself to narrow her questioning. "Did they stay? Have they and their offspring been sharing the Earth with us all these years without us knowing it?"

Anna paused and her eyes narrowed. "Was Jesus a Vor?" she added. "Or Buddha? Or Muhammad?"

"Almost twelve hundred of my people arrived on Earth all those years ago," replied Vega. "At that time, the Vors were the only one of the twenty-seven intelligent species here. And all were stranded when the portal disappeared. Just like my fellow Vors and I are stranded here now. But they and their offspring only survived for five to six hundred years before dying out. I'm guessing that this was before any of these historical figures you mention came on the scene."

He paused. "Not that any of my ancestors would have attracted this kind of attention to themselves, anyway. They stayed out of the limelight. Also, apparently, they had their hands full with other matters—but more about that later."

Anna nodded. He was putting off numerous subjects, but her gut told her he was only doing so to avoid putting too many carts before too many horses.

"So why are you here now?" she asked him. "What is your intent?"

Vega paused to consider the best way to answer this question. "Let me back up," he replied finally. "This will take some explaining."

The alien took a deep breath and forged ahead. "All twenty-seven intelligent species are at the same basic level scientifically and technologically. Give or take. There are minor differences. Vors excel at optics, genetic engineering, and computer modeling, for example. And the Tarts are better at chemistry. And so on."

"But you're all more advanced than we are, aren't you?" said Anna. "Which means humans are the slow learners in the bunch."

Vega actually smiled. "Just the opposite," he assured her. "Your species is among the fastest learners of any of us. And also, unfortunately, one of the most aggressive and ruthless. Along with the Tarts. But humanity will reach the same level as all of the others soon enough."

Anna's gut suddenly insisted that she probe something that her conscious mind would have ignored. "Let me back up to something you said just a moment ago," she said. "That all twenty-seven intelligences are at the same level of scientific advancement. How is that even possible?"

"Great question," said Vega. "It *isn't* possible. Or at least it shouldn't be. Even though it's often true in human science fiction."

"So you don't know about frequent flier miles, but you know about our science fiction?"

Vega nodded. "I've studied it extensively. It can reveal a lot about how you might react to the knowledge of extraterrestrial civilizations. And also how you imagine the future to be. Both are important for me to be aware of."

"That makes sense," admitted Anna.

"In *Star Trek*," continued the alien, "there are any number of different species, but all are more or less at the same state of technological development. The same with *Star Wars*. There are exceptions in *Star Trek*, of course, including the Q and the Borg, among others, but most species are in the same tech lane."

Anna whistled. This alien really knew his *Star Trek*. "But you're saying this shouldn't be the case."

"No, it shouldn't. Not for these shows, and not in reality. The reality is that each of the twenty-seven species were all climbing the scientific learning curve at different rates, at different times. Yet all of us eventually reached our current level and slammed into an impenetrable wall. The *same* wall. Something we now call the *Omega Point*. And none of us were able to progress any further.

"Sure," continued Vega, "we all continue to make marginal improvements and advances, but nothing game changing. The Vors were on the plodding side. It took us thousands of your years to go from taming electricity to reaching the Omega Point. You'll achieve this in a fraction of that time. Your progress has been as fast as any of the twenty-seven known intelligences. But make no mistake, you will hit this same wall. And you will not go beyond it."

Anna's eyes narrowed. "How can you be so sure?" she said.

"We believe that whoever is supplying the portals is actively making certain of this. Actively retarding scientific progress once any of us reach the Omega Point. Even though this shouldn't be anywhere near the *real* Omega Point. We're convinced it's an artificial barrier."

"Maybe," said Anna. "But isn't it possible that a civilization just reaches a certain level of knowledge, beyond which there just aren't any more secrets to discover, or magic to wring from the universe?"

Vega shook his head. "That's not how it works," he insisted. "Einstein said he stood on the shoulders of giants, and he was right. And the more advanced a species becomes, the more shoulders of greats from the past there are to stand on. Or, said without the metaphor, the more science and tech you've discovered, the easier it is to advance even further.

"Your species is seeing this now in ways that couldn't be any clearer. The progress of your technology has been exponential. And the *exponent* itself has been growing. This applies to communications capabilities, computer speeds, speed of DNA sequencing, and so on."

Vega paused. "And exponential growth has a funny way of sneaking up on you," he continued. "At first, it's barely noticeable. Start with a dollar and double your money every day. At first, when you're only increasing your wealth from one to two dollars, or from two to four, it's hardly meaningful. But on day twenty-one you have a million dollars. And when you double this, it's an impressive jump—another million. Nine days later you've got *five hundred* million. Now you're taking gargantuan steps. Which is where humanity is now. Science and tech advancements are happening so fast you can barely keep up. More has changed on this front in the past twenty years than in the entirety of human history before this, combined. The world your grandparents lived in seems positively primitive."

Anna thought about this. It was impossible to disagree. Advances were coming at a dizzying pace. Too fast for most of humanity to truly absorb.

"Getting back to the money example," said Vega, "if you continued to double your money each day, in far less than a year you'd have more dollars than there are atoms in the known universe. *That's* the power of exponential growth."

Anna sighed. "This is undeniably impressive," she said. "But it hardly makes your point. If you, or whoever agreed to double your money each day, runs out when you get to a thousand dollars—*that's it*. Stick a fork in it. The *fun with exponents* game stops."

She raised her eyebrows. "My point is that science and technology can't stay on an exponential path forever. At some point, Moore's Law stops working."

"Very good," said Vega in admiration. "I guess I shouldn't be surprised that you have great insight into areas that you aren't expert in."

"Right," said Anna. "Because my hidden mind is expert in a lot of areas that I'm not. Believe me, any insights I appear to have are just coming to me, forged in this cauldron." She grinned. "For that matter, the phrase *forged in this cauldron* must have come from the same place, because it sure doesn't sound like the conscious me speaking."

Vega actually returned her smile. "Getting back to your point," he said, "you are right, of course. Exponential growth can't go on forever. There is sure to be a true Omega Point. But all twenty-seven species, and yours as well, are certain that we aren't even *close* to that point.

"To use your Moore's Law example," continued the alien, "our computers are much more advanced than yours—but not nearly as much as they *should* be. Theoretically, progress in computer science shouldn't stop until we have computers billions of times more powerful than what we have now. It shouldn't stop until we have systems that calculate using atoms and electrons themselves, and thus can pack more computing power into the head of a pin than all the computing power that has ever been used in the history of your planet."

Vega paused to give Anna time to ponder this point. "This is true for computer systems *and* biological systems," he added. "Both should reach a stage of runaway evolution, during which they rapidly evolve into transcendent species. Species that are so advanced they have as much in common with us as we do with *bacteria*.

"That isn't to say that we'd expect both types of super-species to exist in all cases. Whichever form is first to achieve transcendence, biological or computer, might destroy the other. Perhaps like in your Terminator movies. Or, more likely, a hybrid of the two might emerge. Regardless, one or both should self-evolve, reaching what your scientists have called a singularity event."

Anna considered. "So you're saying that the twenty-seven intelligences should have self-evolved into a nearly omniscient state a long time ago. But didn't somehow."

"Exactly. All twenty-seven are certain of this. Twenty-eight, counting you, because even your scientists see this as inevitable. Provided you don't self-destruct first."

"Just because twenty-eight intelligences agree on something," noted Anna, "doesn't mean it has to be right."

Vega nodded. "This is true," he said. "But this is just one example among many of unexplainable phenomena. I'll give you another. The twenty-eight known civilizations all arose within thirty thousand years of one another. That is stunningly improbable. The Milky Way is over thirteen billion years old. Civilization ought to be separated, not only by trillions of miles, but by eons of time.

"Some civilizations should have arisen billions of years ago. Others millions of years ago. And some should be even younger than you are. And yet we still all, independently, reached sentience and the Omega Point over a span of less than thirty thousand years. That would be far less probable than if twenty-eight patients in a coma, who could each wake up at any time during an entire year, all just happened to awaken *within the same fraction of a second*."

"And none of you have come up with any explanation?" said Anna.

"A number of explanations," replied the alien. "We just have no idea which of them, if any, are right. The most popular theory is that one species did achieve transcendence. Call it Godhood. Hundreds of thousands, million, or even billions of years ago. Maybe they wiped out all other emerging intelligences at the time. Maybe intelligences wiped themselves out. We've landed our starships on several planets to find nothing but the ruins of great civilizations that warred themselves into extinction. So we know this isn't rare.

"Regardless," continued Vega, "it seems fairly clear that this super-species arranged for our current situation. Arranged to stall out our progress."

Vega shook his head miserably. "Why?" he continued. "Good question. For their own amusement? For entertainment? Or just *maybe* because they don't want any other species to achieve transcendence."

"These are all fairly petty reasons," said Anna.

"Maybe so. I offered these up because they're the easiest to understand. There are many others that are more complicated. But the bottom line is that we believe they set things up so that all the intelligent species we know of emerged at about the same time. And ended up with about the same technology. Some of us believe that they seeded what would become intelligent life on all twenty-eight home planets at once, making us all related in a sense. Some of us have theorized that they manipulated time itself to ensure that our civilizations are all approximately the same age. Regardless, they also set up some sort of regulator valve to ensure that no matter how sophisticated our computers become, they never turn sentient, never achieve runaway evolution.

"And the same goes for runaway biological evolution. Whenever one of the twenty-seven nears the point at which they're sure runaway evolution will occur, the attempt fails. Every time. Most of us believe that this is because it is *sabotaged* to fail. Most of us can think of no other reasonable explanation as to why all intelligences have slammed into the same wall, which none of us have been able to punch through after thousands of years of effort."

Anna struggled once again to absorb the enormity of everything Vega was saying. But there was no way anyone could. The alien had used the words *transcendent* and *Godhood*—but these were mere words. But as he had run through a litany of the unimaginable power of these beings, who could well be orchestrating the galaxy-wide manipulation of dozens of civilizations, these words took on a much deeper meaning.

She issued a sizable yawn as the car changed lanes to give room to a semi rolling slowly up an onramp ahead. She knew that if she closed her eyes and let herself drift for even five to ten seconds, she wouldn't be able to open them again. But now was not the time to give in to fatigue. She shook her head vigorously, forcing her mind to full wakefulness, ensuring that she was as sharp as possible for this vital discussion.

"Is there any other evidence that points to a grand manipulator?" she said.

"Plenty of it. For example, all twenty-eight species hail from worlds with similar, breathable atmospheres. Some have more oxygen than others, and so on, but they are close enough that all species can survive on all planets, with varying degrees of comfort. All planets have very similar gravities. All species are roughly humanoid in appearance."

The alien paused. "There *is* such a thing as convergent evolution," he added. "Which explains how a useful body plan can evolve over and over again. But all twenty-eight? This is the actual galaxy, not the set of the first *Star Trek* television show where aliens had to appear humanoid to save on the special effects budget."

"But this might make some sense if the seeding hypothesis were true," noted Anna. "All the planets are similar, and the species are all humanoid, because this superintelligence selected planets to seed life on based on narrow criteria."

"This is a possibility, yes," said Vega. "And, as you might expect, there are other theories to explain it as well. Some believe that this superintelligence is grouping civilizations according to their environmental needs and evolutionary convergence. That our grouping isn't the only one. They believe that somewhere else in the galaxy there are other collections of sentient species. Other groups also linked by a network of portals and starships, who are all methane breathers, or who all live under water, or who are all insectoid in nature."

Anna couldn't help but be caught up in the mystery of it all. If what Vega believed was true, the transcendent species he described was as alarming as it was majestic. Even those Westerners who were deeply religious believed that God had largely left humanity alone since biblical times. They believed that this omniscient, omnipotent being was indeed watching over humanity, but only to help. Never to actively, maliciously suppress human achievement.

"So if this theory of yours is correct," said Anna, "this super species of yours has been *busy*. Not only manipulating dozens of intelligences on dozens of worlds, but even manipulating their evolutionary development. Like so many chess pieces."

"Yes, we think so," said Vega. "We call this theoretical species the *Gatekeepers*," he added. "For obvious reasons. We can reach the gate to transcendence, but we aren't allowed to pass through."

"I can only imagine how maddening this must be. Is that why you suggested earlier that Earth might not want to be part of the galactic group of civilizations? To protect us from the knowledge, for as long as possible, that we're about to hit a barrier that we'll never be able to breach?"

Vega shook his head. "Not at all," he replied. "Because this was just a partial backgrounder. The actual situation in the center of the galaxy is a lot worse."

"I get there are a lot of mysteries. And I get some kind of cosmic force is preventing you from further advancement. But you're all still pretty advanced, right? Not transcendent, but not without electricity, either. Or starships. So how bad could it possibly be?"

Vega sighed. "That's a great question," he said grimly. "But I'm sure that you're not going to like the answer."

22

Anna sniffed the air for several seconds and made a face. "What is that?" she asked her passenger.

Vega shook his head. "We can hear a lot better than you can," he said, "but you have the better sense of smell. What does it smell like?"

The detective frowned. "I'm not sure. But pretty awful. Maybe rotten eggs. I thought I smelled it in your hotel room also."

Vega nodded. "I'm told the Tarts give off a distinctive odor. Which increases slightly right after death. You're probably smelling the Tart body in the trunk."

"Lovely," said Anna, just as the self-driving sedan suddenly veered to the right and onto an off ramp. The two passengers exchanged questioning glances.

"Daisy, what is your destination?" said Anna.

"As ordered, I have changed it from Huntington, Utah, to the Rest Easy Motel, since this motel meets the specified parameters. It is fourteen miles from our route. It is a one-level structure with parking in front of its rooms. Finally, it is nine blocks away from Hastings Motors, a used car seller."

"Outstanding," said Anna. "What is our estimated time of arrival?"

Anna knew that if she were at the wheel, given the time of night, the fourteen miles would go by in record time. But Daisy wouldn't exceed the posted speed limit if they were the sole survivors of a worldwide apocalypse.

"Just under twenty-three minutes," replied the car.

"Thank you. Please return to dormancy."

"Going dormant now," said Daisy.

Anna took a long pause to study the road behind them. If anyone was still following—which was highly unlikely by now—this was another time when their presence would be most evident.

"So what is it that you aren't telling me, Tom?" said Anna warily when she was satisfied they hadn't grown a tail.

Vega frowned deeply. "Simply this," he replied. "The known intelligences have been at war with each other for almost twenty-two thousand of your years now."

Anna considered this powerful statement. It was a lot to take in. "All of them?" she asked.

"I'm afraid so. They have no other choice."

"What does *that* mean?"

"As I've said, there is virtual parity among all twenty-seven. No one is sure which species invented the star drive, but it first came on the scene after the last of the twenty-seven had reached the false Omega Point, and it quickly spread to all. Most suspect that *none* of the twenty-seven invented it, since none has been able to improve upon it, or even truly understand its operation."

"The Gatekeepers then?" said Anna.

"Yes. That's what most believe. My bet is that this superintelligence gave it to all sides simultaneously."

"Very democratic of them if they did," said Anna dryly.

"It also turns out that all twenty-seven have the same planetary energy shield technology," continued Vega, "which is all but impenetrable. Starships have to slow to about ten percent of light speed within star systems due to gravitational interference. But try to smash a starship, or a missile, or anything else into a planetary shield, even at that speed, and the projectile will evaporate the instant it hits. It's the ultimate bug zapper."

The alien paused. "And even though we all have them, we aren't sure how they work, or who first invented them. Which points to the mysterious Gatekeepers yet again."

"You have to give them credit for sharing protective technology, as well," said Anna.

"No doubt about it," agreed Vega. "Most species would now be extinct without it. Since space around a planet is vast, and starships are small, there is no way to build a defensive net dense enough to keep out every one. So any planet without a shield would be helpless, and would be annihilated almost immediately. Just one starship would be enough to do the trick. Either by crashing into the planet at one-tenth light speed, hitting it with a single antimatter bomb, or using any number of other tactics."

Anna swallowed hard. She hadn't really considered just how vulnerable Earth was to an attack, and humanity didn't seem to have one of these planetary energy shields handy. It was fortunate that Earth wasn't within starship range of the galactic center.

"You said the shields were *all but* impenetrable," she reminded him. "Why the qualifier?"

"Because it is possible to breach them," replied Vega, "but it takes an extraordinary effort. Hundreds of battleships working in concert, very near the planet, concentrating force on one small part of the shield. And this is something that solar system and planetary defenses, along with a modest force of defensive starships, can prevent. Unless the defending planet's fleet has been all but destroyed."

Anna nodded, doing her best to absorb it all.

"So the war has become a chess game," said Vega, "played out almost entirely on the outskirts of the home solar systems of the twenty-seven intelligences. Mighty fleets forge alliances, which evolve, grow, and collapse. Enemies collaborate on occasion from desperation, and friends have been known to stab each other in the back. Perhaps this is the way the Gatekeepers intended for things to be."

"Why?" said Anna in horror.

Vega shrugged. "Maybe they just have a cruel sense of humor," he said. "Or maybe this war is meant to keep us busy and content with our lot. Perhaps it's a measure to ensure that no single species evolves to superintelligence and wipes out all the rest. Or to ensure that the first species to develop star travel doesn't spread throughout the entire universe exponentially, like an unstoppable plague of locusts," he added. "A means of population control, if you will."

The alien shrugged. "Or perhaps they're bored, and this provides many hours of entertainment for them."

Anna didn't doubt this last. The war did sound like a galactic version of *Game of Thrones*, with chess moves and shifting alliances galore. "But why fight each other at all?" she asked. "What's the point?

Why not *join* forces? Try to ally and get to the bottom of what's happening? Force the Gatekeepers to show their hand."

"I couldn't agree more," said Vega. "And many of the twenty-seven do also."

A pained expression flashed across his face. "But there are those who don't. The reason for the endless war is complicated. Some species hit it off with each other like humans and dogs, becoming fast friends. But other pairings can't stand each other, their cultures and personalities clashing horribly, bringing out primitive primal hatreds."

The alien sighed. "But most importantly," he continued in disgust, "some believe that war is what the Gatekeepers *want*. The Gatekeepers have never done anything to suggest this, of course, assuming they even exist. For all we know, they may have wound this clock up and then left the universe. But some of the twenty-seven intelligent species are convinced that these theoretical Gatekeepers set all of us up at technological parity, wanting a winner-take-all war to break out."

"Parity to ensure a more interesting contest?" asked Anna.

"If you subscribe to the *war as entertainment* theory, yes," replied the alien. "But there are species who believe the parity was created to ensure a fair contest. To ensure the winner is truly worthy."

"Worthy of what?" asked Anna.

"Some believe this is forced Darwinism in action at the transcendent, galactic scale," he replied. "Some believe the winning species, having proven its superiority over the others, will be allowed to reach the technological singularity and join the Gatekeepers as gods. Some believe the winner will be awarded a separate, newly formed universe to manage on their own.

"No theory is too extreme. One species seems to be convinced that superintelligent species arise in *most* of the hundreds of billions of galaxies in our universe. They believe the Gatekeepers have arranged a contest among the twenty-seven intelligences to identify the most talented species to allow to evolve and join them. Why? To help them battle many billions of other gods, each claiming entire galaxies as their stomping grounds."

"But your people don't believe the Gatekeepers want war, correct?"

"Correct."

"Then what *do* you think they want?" she asked, shaking herself once again to keep the tendrils of sleep from finding the purchase they so desperately craved.

"We're unsure. But if they *are* testing intelligent species, we believe the way to *pass* the test is by working together—like you just suggested. Show the Gatekeepers that we can. Perhaps when this happens, when the twenty-seven have all shown maturity, sobriety, and open-mindedness—have finally eradicated the last vestiges of their warlike natures—we can *all* go forward."

Anna nodded thoughtfully. "Sounds like the galactic equivalent of being forced to wander the desert for forty years."

"I have no idea what that means."

"I shouldn't either," admitted Anna with a grin. "But I heard it on the radio once. It's from a Bible story. God freed the Jews, who were slaves in Egypt, and promised them a home in Israel. The distance between Egypt and Israel is less than four hundred miles. But the ex-slaves had bad habits. And they also failed to truly believe in God's might, despite repeated demonstrations. So God decided that only their *offspring* would enter what he called the Promised Land. To make this happen, he arranged for them to wander the desert for a full *forty years*—getting nowhere during all of that time." She raised her eyebrows. "I guess they really could have used a GPS."

Vega smiled.

"Anyway," continued Anna, "it just reminded me a little of your theory. The Gatekeepers are making you wander the *galactic* desert. It seems like you're stalled out forever, but as you suggest, they may just be waiting for you to shed bad habits."

"Fascinating," said Vega appreciatively. "If I ever return to Vor, I think our people will find this story quite interesting."

"Are there any other theories?" asked Anna.

"There are as many theories as there are intelligences," replied Vega. "*More*, since there are multiple schools of thought alive within each species." He shook his head grimly. "The problem is, if even a single species believes the Gatekeepers want them to prove themselves by destroying all the others, war is inevitable."

"Why?" said Anna. "You don't have to engage, right? You said yourself the planetary shields are all but impenetrable. So why not just *defend* your planet? Without any aggression on your part."

"Some have tried to do that," acknowledged Vega, "but they get sucked in. Because if your fleet gets decimated, as I said, a hostile fleet can destroy your planet. This isn't just a hypothetical. There used to be one additional intelligence in the galaxy," he added. "The Hangory. A species who tried what you suggest: defense only. But an alliance, led by the Tartarians, managed to achieve such an overwhelming fleet advantage that they were able to destroy the Hangory's home planet. They then rooted out the remnants of this species and drove them into extinction."

Anna shrank back in horror. Millions of humans had been slaughtered in human wars, and this was devastating enough to ponder, but to lose an entire species in all but an instant was *unthinkable*.

"So total passivity isn't an option," continued Vega after a brief pause to pay tribute to the Hangorys' passing. "War and aggression are necessary. Battles and shifting alliances are necessary. To ensure that no one species, or alliance of species, is allowed to reach such dominance that their fleet is unstoppable. We all learned this lesson the hard way from the Hangory about twenty-two thousand years ago."

He gave Anna time to digest this and then switched gears. "Most of the battles are in space, as I said. But when portals are open between worlds, each side tries to send soldiers and spies through to the other, to disrupt them from within. When the portals are stationary, the exits are well guarded. But new ones continue to arise randomly, allowing enemies to get through."

Anna couldn't help but be fascinated by this unfolding picture. It was the most immensely complicated situation she could imagine. Space battles, protective planetary shields, but also portals offering instantaneous travel between worlds. But fickle travel. Travel that was random, couldn't be counted on, and excluded most technology, including weapons, from making the trip.

Vega had likened the war to chess. But in Anna's opinion, this was a gross simplification. It was more like chess in *twenty-seven* dimensions.

"So how do *we* fit in?" asked Anna after a long silence. "Earth and humanity? And how do *I* fit in, specifically? You obviously didn't seek me out by accident."

Vega shook his head. "No, anything but by accident," he said. "And what I've been telling you is just the minimum background you'll need to make sense of my answer. So you can put what I say about humanity, and you, into the proper context."

"And do I have the proper context now?" said Anna.

"Ideally, I would want to wait until I've had the chance to explain the science behind your abilities," said Vega. "And demonstrate them to you."

The alien sighed. "But I guess there's no time like the present," he conceded. "And no one deserves a good answer more than you do."

23

Vega asked for a moment to gather his thoughts, and Anna waited in suspense while the sedan continued to cut through the night. Only a few seconds later he resumed.

"To understand how you fit in," he began, "it's best to go back about twenty-eight hundred of your years, to when the portal between us first opened. I'm sure it's hard for you to imagine, but nothing much has changed in the galactic center in all this time. Sure, there is an ebb and flow to the war, but in big-picture terms it has been maddeningly static."

"While here on Earth it's been the complete opposite."

"That's right. When the portal first appeared and opened long ago, we were eager to explore a planet so remarkably distant, and be the first to make contact with a new intelligence. We came through as I mentioned, and began to study your emerging civilization. We even brought back a number of volunteers so we could learn more about your species. Exchange students, if you will. We studied them. Did comprehensive brain scans, and used these to make perfect computer models of the human brain. We also studied physical specimens of human brains. Taken from those already dead," he hastened to add.

The corners of Anna's mouth turned up into the hint of a smile. "Good to know," she said, breaking into an unexpected yawn as she did.

"It was readily apparent to us that your conscious minds were inferior to those of the other known intelligences," continued Vega. "Vorian memory, for example, is orders of magnitude better than yours. I can memorize entire languages in days, and store a hundred different ones for easy conscious access. This is true for almost all twenty-seven species."

He raised his eyebrows. "At the same time," he continued, "our scientists came to realize that your *subconscious* minds more than made up for this conscious deficiency. Unlike every other sentient being we have yet studied, the vast majority of your calculations, analysis, and decision-making are hidden, even from yourselves. Something human science has come to appreciate more and more recently also, as you so eloquently explained over dinner."

Anna frowned, annoyed that she had spent an hour telling him what he had already known, but didn't interrupt. She understood why he had approached her in this way.

"After further study," continued Vega, "our scientists came to understand just how unique your hidden minds really are," he continued. "They came to believe that your subconscious has nearly unlimited potential, in fact."

"We saw some evidence of this even then. But now, it's abundantly clear. The subconscious minds of your greatest scientists—your Newtons, and Einsteins, and Feynmans—were able to grasp breathtaking concepts in one fell swoop, in ways that no conscious mind ever could. Catapulting you forward in bursts of inspiration that weren't possible for the rest of us, exactly as our brain modeling data predicted would happen."

Anna shook her head. "Where were you and your brain modeling data when I was writing that paper on intuition?" she said wryly.

Vega smiled. "I would have loved to be there for you," he replied. "If only I hadn't been trillions of miles away at the time."

"If I've heard that old excuse once," said Anna with a grin, "I've heard it a million times."

She paused, and her smile vanished. It was time to brace herself for what was to come. "My gut says you're about to get to where *I* come in," she said.

"Your gut is, of course, correct," said Vega. "Based on our analysis of the human brain, our scientists predicted with great confidence that a small fraction of humanity—their best guess was one in five million—would have slight mutations that would give them a conduit to their brilliant stranger. And I'm not talking about autistic savants—which they also predicted, by the way—but intuitives like you."

Anna kept her eyes glued to the alien, mesmerized by what he was saying, but also apprehensive.

"Our scientists also predicted that this trait, given certain structures they found in your brains that I'll get to later, would allow these precious few to see future events. A weak, murky clairvoyance, to be sure, that the few carriers of this trait wouldn't even know they possessed. Still, even weak precognition is quite powerful. And our scientists were also certain that the power of this future sight could be boosted considerably, given the right scientific techniques. Certain that this clairvoyance could be dramatically sharpened, and extended to reach further and further into the future."

"Which is why we're going to Huntington, Utah, isn't it?" said Anna. "Your colleague there is Vorian, and you want to try to amplify my abilities."

"You're right, of course. My colleague will also be able to explain the science behind clairvoyance, and how she proposes to improve yours. But that's a discussion for later. The point I'm trying to make is that it became clear to our scientists on Vor that if they were right about all of this, your species could be a game changer. Or, perhaps more accurately, individuals with this particular phenotype could be. Individuals like *you*, Anna. And I've come to believe that you'd stand out, even among fellow intuitives."

The detective shook her head. "You're exaggerating my abilities," she said, "and my importance. By about a million fold."

Vega sighed. "No," he said firmly. "I have little doubt that you could be a true game changer. You could break the deadlock, turn the tide in a twenty-two-thousand-year galactic war. We have reasons to believe that the Gatekeepers monitor *conscious* functioning, be it biological or computer, to keep us in our place. All attempts made by any of the twenty-seven to push conscious minds to higher levels, or to achieve what you would call paranormal abilities, fail."

He nodded slowly at Anna. "Which brings me to you," he continued. "The evidence is complicated, and beyond even my understanding, but I've been assured that *subconscious* minds are not monitored. They are much too wild, their workings hidden and largely unknowable. So when someone like you possesses extraordinary abilities stemming from their subconscious, this will fly below the Gatekeeper's radar. Which would allow you to operate unmolested. Or unsabotaged, in any case."

Anna looked unconvinced. "You aren't even sure that these mythical Gatekeepers really exist," she pointed out. "Yet you're certain of what will, and won't, escape their notice?"

Vega smiled, as if pleased with a prized student. "When Einstein came up with his theory of relativity," he said, "there was no direct evidence that it was correct. To use your word, it was as mythical as the hypothetical Gatekeepers. But if it *was* correct, relativity implied certain truisms about the universe."

"So there may not be Gatekeepers," said Anna, "but if they *do* exist, and act in the way you believe the evidence supports, theory predicts that my subconscious and I will fly under their radar."

"That's right," replied the alien. "But to continue, my people came to Earth all those years ago. And once our home scientists fully realized the potential of your species, the Vorians on Earth began searching for a clairvoyant. But it was a daunting challenge. The population of the entire planet was small and spread out. If you're looking for a one-in-five-million phenotype, you want the largest, most concentrated population you can find.

"Then, too," he continued, "life was exceedingly hard for most humans at the time. And meritocracies were few. If you were a peasant, poverty-stricken, or born into a lowly caste, you couldn't stand out, no matter how superior your intuition. Society was too stacked against you. Even the genius of Albert Einstein would have never come to light had he been born into absolute squalor."

"You really have a thing for Einstein, don't you?" said Anna with a smile.

Vega nodded. "Of all your historical figures," he admitted, "I find him and Richard Feynman the most fascinating. But the bottom line," he added, "is that we fully expected our search to take centuries. And also, once we did identify a candidate with abilities like yours, they had to be kind as opposed to evil. Compassionate as opposed to ruthless. They had to be someone we could put our faith in. Someone we could be confident would use their abilities for the good of all, rather than just for themselves."

Vega frowned deeply. "Then the portal disappeared," he said miserably. "And that was that. So much for any human game changers."

His voice took on a note of pride. "But we readied ourselves in case the portal ever opened again. We improved our tech so that rather than needing an external light source, we could use an undetectable internal one. We taught generations of selected recruits all about Earth. Recruits trained for the day the portal did open, with a mission that we believed might end the war."

Vega stared at his companion, almost in awe. "All of which has led us to you."

Anna considered this for several long seconds. "Even if I have the abilities you think I do," she said sadly, "which I don't, you still have the wrong person. I'm far from the saint you're looking for. I broke our laws repeatedly. And I was selfish. And sometimes cruel. All of which disqualify me."

"*Not at all*," insisted Vega. "So you acted out as a kid. So what? This makes your journey even more impressive. Despite being pushed into a dark place by fate, and succumbing temporarily, your innate altruism and optimism could not be smothered. I've been with you in the trenches now. I've seen how you handle yourself when your world is caving in, and people are trying to kill you. Throughout this discussion we've been having, your obvious decency, empathy, humility, and compassion have shined through."

Vega stared deeply into the detective's blue eyes. "You're *exactly* who we've been looking for, Anna Abbott," he added softly. "I'm sure of it."

Anna thought about this further. "Even if that *is* true," she said, shaking her head, "it doesn't matter. I can't even help you win a single skirmish. And you seriously think I can change the course of an entire war?"

"*Yes*," said Vega emphatically. "Not immediately, but yes."

Anna shook her head once more. "Not a chance. One human being against the galaxy? Are you kidding? This makes the other preposterous things you've said seem downright reasonable. Even if I'm a little bit clairvoyant, and even if you can amplify this so I can see a short time into the future—without the Gatekeepers knowing it—I was barely able to save myself tonight."

"What you say is true," acknowledged Vega. "You, alone, wouldn't move the needle a nanometer." He paused. "But you directing tens of thousands of warships could well turn the tide. You'd never lose a battle."

The alien paused to let this sink in. "I wasn't sent here to find a detective, Anna," he added evenly. "Or even a clairvoyant to make vague predictions of the future." He raised his eyebrows. "I was sent here to find the next admiral of the allied fleet."

PART 3

" . . . the goal was a mental flash, achieved somewhere below consciousness. In these ideal instants one did not strain toward an answer as much as relax toward it."

—Richard Feynman (Nobel Laureate, Physics)

"Once the future is foretold, that future becomes a living thing and it will fight very hard to bring itself about."

—Stephanie Garber

24

Anna couldn't help but laugh at this latest demonstration of Vega's ridiculous faith in her abilities. Admiral of the allied fleet? *Her*?

She was absolutely stunned. There was surreal, and then there was *this*.

She must not have heard right. Had Vega really suggested he wanted her to command tens of thousands of starships—*warships*—in a raging battle in the center of the galaxy against numerous advanced alien species?

It would make more sense to put a *fruit bat* in charge of the US Air Force, simply because it had its own built-in radar system.

She shook her head at the continued absurdity of it all. How had her vaunted intuition missed something as obvious as *this*? she thought to herself wryly. She should have known she'd be getting this offer when she had awoken that morning.

At least now the seemingly outlandish statements Vega had uttered earlier made sense. He *would* take a bullet for her. And he really did believe that she was the most important human in history.

But not based on what she could do for humanity, but what she could do for twenty-seven alien species.

As Anna thought about this further, she realized this wasn't technically true. Presumably, humanity was about to enter this desert, this fray, as a wanderer, along with the other twenty-seven. So if she really could do what they thought, her deeds could well be critical for the future of humanity as well.

Except that there would be no deeds. It all continued to be preposterous.

The Honda arrived at the chipped and weathered concrete parking lot of the Rest Easy Motel, which appeared to be mostly vacant. Anna resumed manual control and parked the car around the corner from the small, dingy office, just out of sight. Against her better judgment she turned the inside lights on for the benefit of her alien companion, who looked relieved by this mercy.

"I'm not going to be the admiral of *anyone's* fleet," she said to Vega firmly, making no move to leave the car. "Hell, I don't even want to be captain of my own department. But at least I could be successful in *that* role."

"Believe me, you could be successful commanding the allied fleet, as well," insisted Vega. "You just don't know it yet. But give me a chance to explain more about your abilities, and how we can enhance them, and I think you'll see the potential."

"I don't care how much you enhance my supposed clairvoyance, it's not going to happen. Me as an admiral? Commanding a fleet of ships that can travel nine million miles in less time than it takes me to say *nine million miles*? I'm a good detective, but I never even played chess or Risk as a kid. Or even one of those battle games online. And I don't even like to kill bugs if I can help it."

She winced. "It's true that I had to kill today—yesterday by now—but I had no other choice, and I feel awful about it. Beyond awful."

"Another example of why you're the right choice," said Vega softly. "As admiral, you'd be responsible for making choices that would result in countless deaths. I can't sugarcoat that. But that's the nature of war. You're killing people who want to kill you and yours. So you're saving as many lives as you take.

"But most importantly," he continued, "once we've annihilated all other fleets, giving us free rein, we wouldn't destroy planets and drive species to extinction. We would use our dominance to secure a lasting peace among all intelligences. Perhaps this will prove to the Gatekeepers that we're worthy of moving forward in our evolution. If not, we can work together to learn if there really are Gatekeepers, and if not, find other explanations for our stalled progress."

Anna put her hand over her mouth once again as yet another yawn refused to be denied. "Look, why don't we table this admiralty discussion for now," she said, still unable to believe that she was actually saying these words. "Let me finish assimilating the entire situation and we can come back to it. Not that it will do any good, but at least I'll hear you out."

Vega sighed. "Whatever you say," he replied. "So what else can I tell you to help bring you up to speed?"

She thought about this. "A lot," she said, pausing to attend to yet another yawn. "Beginning with how the Tarts fit in. And what they're doing on Earth."

Anna gestured in the direction of the small motel office. "But that will have to wait," she added. "As much as I want to continue, we have to get settled in. I've been fighting off sleep, but I won't last much longer. My brain is about to shut down."

Anna had managed to keep her growing exhaustion at bay, helped along by revelations so compelling they could have kept her on the edge of her seat if she were *dead*. Still, there was a limit to what even adrenaline could do, and if she didn't recharge, she was about to crash *hard*.

Her day had been endless, and she had lost blood, to boot. Besides, she had more to digest than ever before, and her subconscious seemed to consolidate information best during sleep. She owed it some downtime to further analyze what Vega had told her and begin to draw its own conclusions.

Anna drove the short distance to the lobby and again left the lights on inside the car. "Wait here," she told the alien. She pulled a single hundred from the paper bag inside her duffel and shook herself like a dog so she could remain alert a little longer.

Minutes later she returned with a room key, the old-fashioned kind. "We're in room forty-nine," she told Vega. "At the very south end of the motel. I asked for no guests on either side."

She put the car in drive, yawned, shook herself awake again, and parked in front of a poorly lit door with gaudy brass numbers nailed to the wood. Room forty-nine.

It was past midnight, and no guests could be seen on the entire property. They exited the car, with Vega carrying the duffel bag.

"Follow me," whispered Anna, veering off to her left and walking briskly but quietly to the north.

"Isn't *that* our room?" Vega whispered back, gesturing to a door with a brass four and nine affixed to it that was rapidly receding behind them.

"It is," said Anna in low tones, not slowing. The nearly non-existent lighting must be driving Vega mad, even with his implants, and she gave him credit for not whining about it. "But we'll be staying in an empty room at the far north end. Occupied rooms are almost sure to have a car in front. Unoccupied ones won't. Although we'll check first to be sure." She shrugged. "Then we'll break in."

"So you paid for room forty-nine, only to break into another one?"

"Sure," replied Anna with a weary smile. "Isn't that what *everyone* does?"

25

Anna found the room she wanted and removed her thick sweat-shirt, wrapping it around the door handle to muffle the sound to come. She pressed her gun just under the handle and squeezed off two silenced rounds in quick succession. The sound of the lock giving way to the point-blank shots was much less stealthy than she would have liked, but the motel was largely vacant, and she didn't think she had drawn enough attention to matter.

She flipped on the lights and entered the room. The inside was just as dingy as she expected. Tiny, with a single queen-sized bed sporting an orange floral bedspread, a fake-wood dresser, a small TV, and not much else, other than the hint of mildew in the air. She took a much-needed biological break, noting that the bathroom was in great need of repair, with cracked and dirty-looking white tiles, and faucets that only seemed to deliver ice-cold water.

"Give me a few minutes," she said to Vega when she exited the bathroom.

She proceeded to remove the drones from their cases, along with the tablet computer controller, and placed both drones outside. She quickly landed the larger of the two on the roof above their room, and the smaller on the roof above room forty-nine, making sure the drones' IR and audio features were enabled. Finally, she checked the tablet computer to be sure each had a wide view of anyone approaching.

Vega watched her as she worked, but remained silent.

"Turn around, Tom," she said when she had finished. When the alien complied, she removed her body armor vest and put her sweat-shirt back on, which now smelled of gunshot residue from when she had broken into the room. She had no idea why she felt any need for modesty around a member of a different *species*, but old habits died hard.

She dropped to her rear-end on the bed, feeling dizzy, and her eyes slammed shut of their own accord. "If anyone is on to us," she muttered almost drunkenly, holding on to consciousness by sheer force of will, "they'll bribe the clerk to tell them we're in forty-nine. Our car's there too. When they realize we aren't inside, they'll know they've been had, and leave the motel."

Anna laid down on her back, almost melting into the bed when her head hit the pillow.

"You don't think they'll guess we're in another room?" asked Vega.

"No way," she mumbled dreamily, her eyes still closed. "And once we get . . . used car . . . they won't find us . . . again."

She was rapidly winding down, but fought off sleep for just a few moments longer. "You take . . . first watch," she said, slurring her words. "I'll spell you in . . . few hours. Watch the . . . drone feed," she finished, trailing off.

"No need for you to take a turn," said Vega. "I don't require as much sleep as you do," he explained.

But this explanation fell on deaf ears, as Anna Abbott was already in the midst of a deep and dreamless sleep.

26

"Anna, wake up!" said Vega urgently, shaking her gently as he did so.

The detective's eyes slowly fluttered open. Her sleep had been deeper than any she had ever experienced, and she was disoriented for several seconds, not remembering who this stranger was, or why she was in a strange bed.

It was a wonder she even remembered who *she* was.

But suddenly, her sense of self returned with a rush.

"How long was I out?" she mumbled.

"About three hours. It's just after four in the morning."

Anna brought herself to a seated position and rubbed her eyes. Only three hours? Despite still being groggy, she felt like a new person. Three hours of pure, concentrated sleep had done wonders for her, as restorative as her usual six or seven.

Vega held a tablet computer in front of her, and upon seeing the drone feed from room forty-nine, all traces of sleep finally left her body.

Five men, all dressed in black, were creeping forward toward the room, and all had weapons drawn, two of them holding assault rifles. Despite the darkness and their black attire, the drone was so near to them that its impressive IR capabilities provided clear images.

Anna took the tablet from her alien friend and turned up the volume on the tiny drone's audio receiver as high as it would go.

"Look, DeShawn," whispered a hairy, heavily bearded man to the tallest and thickest of his comrades, "this is stupid! We stick out like dicks in a convent."

The words coming through the tablet computer were faint, but audible.

"The rest of you need to wait in the van," continued the human Yeti. "I've got this. The gas will knock them out just like everyone else."

"Kiss my ass, Wolfy," replied DeShawn. "Frey told us not to underestimate them—the girl especially—and to expect surprises."

"You think they're sleeping with gas masks on?" said Wolfy. "I've got this," he repeated.

"And yet Marshall put *me* in charge," said DeShawn, as the five men continued to near the room. "If Frey wants us to all go in at once, that's what we're doing. So shut up and get on with it."

Wolfy fumed, but didn't argue further. Instead, he lifted what looked like a flare gun, pointed it at a window, and pulled the trigger, sending a tube about twice the size of a roll of quarters crashing through the glass and the closed curtain inside. The noise this created was sharp, but it was four in the morning, and just as was the case when Anna had broken into her room, it was unlikely to draw any panicked reactions from the precious few guests on the property.

Anna manipulated the touchscreen controls on the tablet computer, sending the tiny drone through the jagged opening in the window, and watched as the canister released a thick cloud of gas, which soon spread to every square inch of the small room.

The detective's mind raced. She had learned much from the brief conversation she had overheard. Frey was behind this, but he didn't want them dead. At least not now. And these men were all human beings, which Anna found strangely comforting. Men who worked for Neil Marshall, but who were apparently being commanded by Shane Frey.

Anna bolted off the bed to a standing position as a signal from her subconscious made itself known, unlike any she had ever received. Sharper. Clearer. More certain.

A large steel structure near the woods flashed across her mind's eye, followed by a dozen rapid-fire but fuzzy images, followed finally by the voice of Captain Perez. Like a fleeting dream that darted between any number of wild settings, but only lasted an instant. It was a wild jumble, but it was clear to her that her subconscious had made sense of it all, and was calling her to action.

She gasped, suddenly certain of one astonishing fact.

She *was* glimpsing the future. Her intuition was certain of it.

And her subconscious wasn't operating as it always had before, focusing solely on her immediate situation. Instead, it seemed to be playing several moves ahead, a deeper game than she had thought was possible.

Vega was right! She *was* somewhat clairvoyant. Or at least her subconscious was.

In retrospect, her instincts told her that she should have always been more open to the alien's claims. She had dodged *bullets* the previous night, after all. *Literal bullets*. At both the high school and in Vega's hotel room.

Who could *do* that?

Yes, her hidden mind could pick up on sights, sounds, and smells that she could not. It was brilliant at pattern recognition. But could any of this really help her to dodge a bullet? At close range?

Of course not. She had known which way to jerk her body because her subconscious had seen the future. Maybe even more than *one* future.

Not even her subconscious had been aware that it was using precognition as one of many data inputs to help it reach conclusions. But clearly she hadn't been the only one listening to Vega and considering his wild claims. Her hidden mind had been busy while she slept, consolidating what the alien had told her, and conducting experiments of its own. For the first time making a concerted effort to tune into and tap an ability it had never guessed it had. Focusing on these strange signals rather than ignoring them.

Vega's confidence in her had been an inspiration, a catalyst, pushing her abilities forward, even prior to his much-heralded enhancements.

As usual, she had no idea how she knew this, just that she did.

And she knew what she had to do now, as well. It was counterintuitive, but the signal was so strong she didn't question it.

Anna glanced at the drone feed, which was now showing Frey's assault team streaming into the room she and Vega were supposed to have been in, all five men holding their breath in case the gas hadn't dissipated as quickly as advertised.

Anna removed her sweatshirt and donned her bulletproof vest once again, this time not instructing the alien to avert his eyes. Inside room forty-nine, confusion had broken out. And fury. They were realizing just how expertly they had been played.

"Your strategy is working *brilliantly*," said Vega in admiration. "We'll be home free as soon as we can buy a used car."

Anna shook her head. "Change of plans," she said. "We aren't going to buy a car. We're going to surrender, instead."

"Surrender?" said Vega in disbelief.

Anna nodded. "It's our best option."

"Better than escaping them entirely?"

"Yes. My instincts on this have never been stronger."

"You do realize that even though they plan to take us alive, that will only last until they've had a chance to interrogate us. Then they'll kill us without mercy."

"I do," replied Anna simply.

"Which means you must also know how crazy this sounds. Any idea what your instincts have in mind?"

"Not the slightest," admitted Anna. "But you just told me you were ready—eager—to trust me with your entire fleet. Are you saying you don't trust me now?"

"No. I'll do whatever you say. I'm just surprised that this is the right answer."

"You and me both," said Anna with a sigh, pulling a gauze bandage roll from the duffel bag and beginning to wrap it loosely around her left wrist, ignoring the much tighter bandage around her upper left arm where she had been shot.

"Okay, then," said Vega, swallowing hard. "We'd better get over there and give ourselves up. Before they leave."

"Give me just a few more seconds and we'll do just that," said Anna. She temporarily halted her efforts to wrap her wrist while she unzipped a side pocket of her duffel bag.

"What are you doing?" asked Vega.

"You'll see," she replied. "Something my gut is insisting is a very good idea."

Anna blew out a long breath. She would never take a leap of faith this titanic had the signals she was receiving not been so powerful. She just hoped that *powerful* was the same thing as *correct*.

Because if these signals were *wrong*, she would soon be signing her and Vega's death warrants.

27

DeShawn Young placed a call on his cell phone and waited for it to be answered. He was gratified that Neil Marshall had put him in command of this temporary five-man team, but outraged that he and his colleagues had been passed to a stranger like an STD in a whorehouse.

"Young here," he said when Shane Frey picked up.

"Report," said Frey, this time through a phone rather than a comm, and speaking English rather than his own language.

"We arrived at the Rest Easy Motel about twenty minutes ago," began Young. "The Honda was parked in front of room forty-nine, but we wanted to be sure. So we held a silenced gun to the night manager's head and had a little chat. He confirmed we had the right room. Then we made sure there were no witnesses and killed him."

"Did you hide the body?"

"Of course," replied Young, trying not to be offended by the question. "But here's where it gets a little . . . strange."

"Go on," prompted Frey.

"When we gassed the room and then entered, no one was there. Almost like they knew we were coming."

"So you lost them!"

"We didn't *lose* them," replied Young angrily. "They outsmarted us. *You* included. You told us they were staying at the motel, and the night manager confirmed it. Not our fault they weren't there."

"Unless they saw you coming?" snapped Frey. "Or saw you kill the clerk."

"They didn't!" insisted Young. "I'm sure of it."

"We'll never know," said Frey. "But can I assume you're at least searching for them as we speak? They left their car at the motel, right? So if they did see you coming, they're on foot. They couldn't have gotten too far."

"We thought the same thing," said Young. "But here's where the odd part comes in. Just as we were leaving to begin searching for them, they walked right up to us and *surrendered*."

"Say that again."

"You heard me. They surrendered. Just like that."

"It's a trap!" said Frey immediately. "It has to be. Tell me you searched them for weapons?" he said urgently.

"Yes! Of course. Thoroughly. Vega didn't have any, but the detective was a human armory. They had a large duffel bag with them, but nothing else. Now we have both of them in room forty-nine, bound and gagged."

"Watch the woman like a hawk. As I told you, she's the more dangerous of the two. Are you positive she's bound securely?"

"Positive! With plastic zip-ties. She's not going anywhere. And she's wounded. When we searched her for weapons we lifted up her sweatshirt. She's wearing body armor underneath, and we found she has a mass of bandages around both her upper left arm and left wrist. The one on the upper arm is pretty bloody. Maybe that's why she surrendered. Knew that she didn't have the strength to run anymore. Bottom line—she isn't a threat."

"Have you not heard anything I've been telling you?" barked Frey. "Of course she's a threat. Get them out of that room! Now! You shouldn't still be there. You killed the manager. And if she's truly allowed herself to be nullified, it probably just means that reinforcements are on their way. So it's still a trap for you. Or more likely, for *me*, when I take them off your hands."

"And when will that be?" asked DeShawn Young, ready to reach through the phone and choke this patronizing asshole to death with his bare hands.

"I'll let you know. Do you have a secure location you can take them to?"

"Yes. About thirty-five minutes away from here, a little closer to LA than we are now. A large steel warehouse. With woods on three sides, and only one road in. Isolated and private."

"Who would build a warehouse in a location like that?"

"No one would *now*. But it was built fifty years ago, when it was near a thriving supply line into the heart of California. It's been abandoned for more than thirty years. Neil Marshall bought it and the land around it. We use it for various purposes as our organization expands north and east of LA. As a high-level meeting place. For drug storage. For private chats and torture sessions with would-be rivals. That sort of thing. It's sealed with heavy padlocks, but we all have keys."

"Then get going. You can text me the location when you're on your way. Do you have another gas canister?"

"Yes."

"Good," said Frey. "Knock them both out right now."

"It's short-acting. They'll wake up soon after we arrive."

"So what? At least they won't be a threat until then, and won't have any idea where you took them."

"Consider it done."

"One last thing," said Frey. "Be *careful*. And vigilant. Even when they're out cold. Continue to expect surprises. When you arrive, make sure they're bound good and tight, and then lock them inside the warehouse. Alone. Don't you or any of your men stay in there with them. That would be asking for trouble."

"Understood," said Young as he ended the connection, even though he didn't understand at all. Why the need for this extreme level of caution?

Was this guy really serious? Why did the detective make Shane Frey so damn nervous? She was bound, injured, and not more than a hundred and twenty pounds dripping wet. Talk about your paranoid delusions of stupidity.

Still, he would do what Frey had asked. Because he couldn't help but be troubled by two things.

One, Anna Abbott had outsmarted them with apparent ease, which was impressive.

And two, instead of fleeing to safety, she and her companion had given themselves up—which made no sense at all.

It was true that Shane Frey was being overly cautious. But Young couldn't deny that there had to be more to these two prisoners than met the eye.

28

The detective awoke with a start. Three men surrounded her, each pointing an automatic weapon her way, while a fourth finished tying her legs to a heavy chair with thick plastic zip-ties. He then proceeded to zip-tie her wrists together on her lap before backing away to join his comrades.

Anna was still slightly befuddled, and only realized her mouth was sealed with duct tape when she tried, unsuccessfully, to speak.

She blinked several times and the world began to swim into better focus.

The alien known as Tom Vega was tied just as she was, right next to her, with their respective chairs actually touching, both in the center of a sea of concrete. He appeared to have been awake the entire time, which her gut suggested was, indeed, the case. An oversize steel banquet table stood twenty feet to her right, with nothing but her blue duffel bag on top, which she was happy to see.

She proceeded to take in the entirety of the large, steel warehouse surrounding them, which was dark, old, and largely empty, save for six wood pallets nearby, stacked high with canvas bags that she knew instantly contained cocaine.

Anna's eyes widened and a chill flashed up her spine. The inside of the warehouse was a perfect match to one of the fuzzy images she had seen in her vision.

Amazing.

She still had no idea how this surrender was helping her, but she would continue to play it by ear, and by instinct, and trust that her newly amped-up subconscious knew what it was doing.

The man aptly nicknamed Wolfy reached forward and tore the duct tape from her mouth, and then did the same to Vega before backing away.

"What color is your blood?" Anna whispered to her alien friend the moment she could speak, having no idea why.

"Green," he whispered back immediately, to his credit not wasting time asking questions.

"Stay silent, Tom," she said urgently, just as a fifth man entered the warehouse from outside. It was the thug named DeShawn Young, a towering tree of a man, even larger than he had appeared in the drone feed.

He walked over to the two prisoners and inspected them carefully. "Comfortable?" he said with a cruel smile. "I hope so. Because you'll be staying put for a while. There are people coming to see you."

"When?" asked Anna.

"Why don't we let that be a surprise. In the meantime, you're now inside a warehouse, which is all but soundproof. So if you'd like, feel free to scream your hearts out while you wait."

"Thanks, *DeShawn*," said Anna mockingly. "That's very thoughtful."

Young shrank back in surprise. "How do you know my name?"

Anna raised her eyebrows. "Why don't we let that be a surprise," she said, mirroring his earlier statement.

He shrugged. "It doesn't matter anyway," he said. "I'll never see either of you again. We're going to leave you two alone until your, ah . . . *company* arrives. In the meantime, if you need anything, be sure *not* to call. Because we really don't give a shit."

"You're just going to leave us unguarded?" said Anna. "What if we free ourselves?"

"You can't," replied Young. "But knock yourselves out. Neither of you have a phone or a weapon. Even if you do free yourselves, the doors are steel, and padlocked. And while none of us will be inside, each of the warehouse's three exits will be guarded by one of my men, who will be carrying a machine gun."

He gestured to the blue duffel bag on the table nearby. "And not to disappoint you," he added, "but I'll be taking your duffel outside, so you don't have access to the weapons we took from you. And I know Neil Marshall wants his bag of hundreds back."

"Why such a hurry to leave?"

"Because my current boss thinks you're too dangerous for us to stay within reach of you," replied Young. He shook his head and grinned. "Ridiculous, I know, but there you have it."

The detective almost gasped as a wave of inspiration washed over her, and she suddenly knew exactly how she needed to proceed, and why she had asked Vega the question she had when she had awakened.

"Leaving us is a very bad idea, DeShawn," she said. "Because here's the thing, I need to tell you something. Something vital. Urgent. Information that will save your life." She raised her eyebrows. "I promise you, you'll be thanking me."

"Good try," he replied. "But I'm not falling for any distractions."

"What am I *distracting* you from? Do you think I'm stalling until a tiny army hidden in my duffel bag has time to shoot themselves with a grow-ray?"

Young actually smiled. "You may have a point," he acknowledged. "Okay. So tell us about this urgent information of yours."

Anna shook her head. "Only *you*," she insisted. "You're the boss, DeShawn, so this is for your ears only. Have your comrades go outside and guard the exits until we're done. Which won't be for a while, since there's a lot I have to cover."

"Sorry," he replied, turning toward the nearest exit, "I don't have that much time to spare."

"Wait!" shouted Anna. "Give me three minutes. If I haven't convinced you that what I'm saying is worth a longer discussion, then you can run out of here like a scared little girl. You know, like you've been ordered to. But *trust me*," she added emphatically, "you're going to want to hear the rest."

Young turned back toward her and shrugged. "I think I'll take a pass," he said.

"Why?" demanded Anna. "Because Shane Frey put the idea in your head that I'm too dangerous to even be in a room with? Even bound, unarmed, and wounded? Really?"

The detective shook her head in disgust. "You have to admit that sounds bonkers," she said. "Have you considered that he's insane? I mean, *clinically* insane. The kind of insane that you and Neil

Marshall need to know about. What's more likely, that he doesn't want you near me because he's worried I'll overpower you? Or that he's desperately afraid for you to hear what I might tell you?"

She paused to let this sink in. "But it's your call, DeShawn. Just don't blame me when it all blows up in your face."

He frowned deeply. "Everybody out!" he ordered, reaching a decision. "I'm going to hear what she has to say. Guard the exits until further notice. I'll join you when I join you. Wolfy," he added, gesturing to his hairy second-in-command, "take the duffel bag with you on your way out."

Young walked closer to the prisoners as the rest of his team exited the warehouse. Anna glanced reassuringly at Vega beside her, who had dutifully remained silent as she had instructed.

"Okay, Detective Abbott," said the team's leader, "what have you got? You have three minutes to make your case."

"Shane Frey isn't who you think he is," began Anna immediately. "More importantly, he isn't even *what* you think he is." She gestured to Vega with her bound hands, and then returned them to her lap. "And neither is my fellow captive. Both are aliens from the center of our galaxy. Different *species* of alien."

DeShawn laughed. "And you're telling me that *Frey* is the crazy one," he said. He turned to leave them. "You can keep the rest of your three minutes."

"Wait!" said the detective. "Did your gas knock out my fellow captive?"

"What?"

"You heard me. You knocked *me* out. But my gut tells me the gas didn't work on him. Am I right?"

Young turned back toward her once again. "So what?"

"So *what*? Have you ever known this gas to fail? Ever even heard stories of it failing?"

Young didn't reply, but his expression spoke volumes.

"It failed *this* time because this guy isn't human. He has a different metabolism. Different a lot of things."

"There has to be another explanation," said Young.

"There isn't," replied Anna, "and I can prove it to you. And when I do, I'll tell you some things about Shane Frey you're going to want to know. This is bigger than all of us. Are you really going to trust the motives of an alien being?"

Young studied Tom Vega carefully. "This is ridiculous," he said. "He looks human enough. What's your proof?"

"Do you have a knife?"

Young nodded.

"Then cut his arm. Just a little. His blood will run green rather than red. If it doesn't, then turn us over to Frey, and I won't say another word."

Young's eyes narrowed as he continued to study Vega from head to toe. Finally, he removed a switchblade knife from his pocket and snapped the razor-sharp blade into place. "You're on," he said, slowing approaching the alien, who shrank back, clearly not ecstatic about the prospect of being cut.

When Young bent down with his knife to cut Vega's arm, Anna threw her bound hands to her right and drove a tranquilizer dart deep into Young's massive thigh.

Young jumped from surprise more than pain, pulling out the offending item and inspecting it carefully, his confusion turning to rage. "You bitch!" he shouted at Anna, raising the knife, but this time with Anna as the intended target. "I'm going to gut you like a fish!"

Saying this, the mighty oak that was DeShawn Young collapsed to the floor at her feet, unconscious, as though a light switch had been thrown from on to off.

Anna allowed herself a brief sigh of relief. Just before surrendering, she had retrieved the dart she had put in her duffel bag at the high school, and used the gauze she was wrapping on her left wrist to hold and conceal it. While she was speaking to Young, she had carefully worked the small, needle-nosed pellet free, keeping her hands in her lap, and keeping all but the needle hidden between the thumb and forefinger of her right hand.

Her heart continued to beat wildly in her chest as she tipped the chair over and slammed into the concrete floor. She ignored the jarring of her body and inched over to the fallen knife, less than a foot away.

When she had it, she carefully reversed it so the blade was pointing backwards and sawed at the tough plastic between her wrists. Finally, after several minutes of concerted effort, unable to wield the knife as effectively as she would have had her hands not been bound, she severed the last strand of plastic. Once her right hand could operate independently, she was able to free herself and her alien companion in only a few minutes more, while a relieved Vega sang her praises.

With this complete, Anna helped herself to the fallen thug's gun, and cracked the butt into his head, ensuring he wouldn't awaken, even after the short-acting tranquilizer had worn off.

"Now what?" said Vega, as sober reality returned. "Even with a gun, I don't see how we can breach these steel doors." He spied Young's automatic rifle leaning against one wall of the warehouse. "Even a machine gun won't do it."

"I have no intention of leaving just yet," said Anna. "And it just became clear to me why my subconscious wanted me to surrender. It saw deeper than ever before. Had we run, I'd be wanted by every cop in America. But this way, I'll have the chance to clear my name. Prove my innocence. Which will get one of many monkeys off my back, and give me more time to understand this intergalactic war thing—not to mention my clairvoyance."

Vega raised his eyebrows. "Did you just acknowledge being clairvoyant?" he said in delight. "Does that mean you've finally accepted that your subconscious can do more than mere pattern recognition?"

"*Yes*," said Anna. "You win. I seem to be weakly precognitive. And it does seem to be a handy trait to have."

Vega opened his mouth to speak, but Anna held up a forestalling hand. "We're in a major hurry here," she said, frisking Young's unconscious body as she did, removing a phone.

"The good news is that the clairvoyant part of my intuition is telling me that Frey and reinforcements won't be arriving for an hour or more."

She frowned. "The bad news is that the Cavalry won't be arriving for a while, either."

29

Anna glanced at her borrowed phone and noted that it was now five fifteen in the morning. It would still be pitch-black outside. She entered her captain's number and sent him a text message. *Captain Perez*, she wrote, *it's Anna. Pick up.*

She then called his cell and waited. The call ended after three rings, not unexpectedly.

She imagined the captain bleary-eyed and furious that a solicitor had awakened him from a deep sleep. He kept his phone on during the night in case of emergencies, but had let it be known in the precinct that no emergency was important enough to wake him unless LA was about to get hit with a nuke, and he was the only one who could stop it.

"Captain, this is Anna," she said to his voice mail. "Pick up."

She waited three minutes and dialed again. This time he answered on the first ring. "Anna! Is that you?"

"Sorry to wake you, but I'm surrendering, and I thought you might want to know."

"Is this a joke, Anna? Or do you seriously want to come in?"

"Not a joke. But I don't want to come in. I need you to come get me."

"What's going on?"

"I don't have a lot of time. I'm trapped inside a warehouse with six massive, stacked pallets of cocaine. I'll get the GPS coordinates from my phone in a minute and text them to you. Outside there are four of Neil Marshall's men with automatic weapons keeping me inside."

"So how—"

"I'm not finished," interrupted Anna. "I'm expecting an even larger hostile force to arrive here in an hour or two, so you need to haul ass. Put on your sirens and go a hundred and twenty, or get a few helicopters, but get your ass here! *Everyone's* ass. You'll need a big team. Bring an army of cops. Flash-bang grenades, bulletproof vests, the whole nine. I recommend SWAT if you're willing. Try to take one or more of Marshall's men alive, because they'll be able to tell you about the elaborate frame Marshall pulled off. But don't worry if you can't. I have one of them alive in here with me, unconscious. I know someone used my gun to kill those four out-of-towners who were as-sassinated at the high school. I'd bet good money that one of the guys here pulled the trigger."

"So this is about clearing your name?" said Perez.

"You're damn right it is. Plus, we get a haul of bad guys in the process, and enough cocaine to fill a truck. Win-win. But the clock is ticking. The warehouse is steel, and I'm padlocked inside, so bring some heavy-duty bolt cutters along with you. There are three doors, so if your men can get one of them open early, I can help. I have an innocent friend in here with me. We'll both need to be placed un-der police protection once we've been rescued. Which I'm sure you'll want to do anyway, until you've cleared my name. I'll send the GPS coordinates now."

"How do I know you're even there? How do I know this isn't an ambush?"

"Come on, Captain. I know it looks like I assassinated helpless men at Salem Hills High. But in your heart, you know I don't have that in me. And I'm not going to harm people I've worked with for years. You'll have an army with you, so how big of an ambush could it be? Send a drone in first to confirm the four armed men and the warehouse if you want. But *hurry!* You need to be here *yesterday.*"

There was no immediate reply.

"Come *on*, Captain!" she snapped. "Worst case, you activate a team and it's a hoax—which it isn't. But that's worst case. Even then, it serves as a great drill to see how quickly you can galvanize and move a large team in an emergency."

"All right, Anna," said the captain after a brief pause, "I'll bite. You're the best detective I've ever worked with, and seemingly the most honest. If that doesn't buy you my trust in this situation, nothing ever will. Send the coordinates."

"Roger that," said the detective. "Get here *soon*," she added, and then ended the connection.

"That seemed to go well," said Vega tentatively.

"I think so too," replied Anna. Then, with a frown, she added, "But this clairvoyance of mine is fickle. I really felt like it was clicking when you woke me up at the motel, but now I don't feel any different than usual. Or any better able to see the future."

"Not surprising. Your subconscious needs a lot of practice. Right now, I suspect that the higher the stakes, the more likely it is to perform. But until it's been enhanced, and until you can forge such a strong bridge to your future visions that you'll have much more of a conscious awareness of them, it will be spotty, at best."

Anna nodded. She suspected that the more she strained, the more she reached for the future, the less likely it was to appear. She had to just let it come to her when it so chose.

In the meantime, they would be trapped inside for thirty to forty-five minutes, at minimum, with nothing really to do. It was time to return to the discussion she had been having with Vega when the urgent need for sleep had interrupted. Once they were under police protection, there was no telling how long it might be before they had the proper privacy to continue.

"So after you proposed that I command your fleet," said Anna, "I asked for more background. You were going to tell me how the Tarts fit into all this. And what they're doing on Earth—other than trying to kill the two of us."

Vega looked around at their expansive steel prison, decorated with pallets of cocaine. "You want me to do that *now*? In *here*?"

Anna shrugged. "No time like the present," she replied. "Besides," she added with a grin, "since I can't leave, I'm what you might call a *captive* audience."

30

The alien named Tom Vega paused to gather his thoughts. "Thousands of years ago," he began, "as I've said, the portal between Earth and Vor disappeared, and cut off our people. But about eight years after that happened, another portal opened. This time a portal between Earth and Tartar. And the Tartarians came through, just as we had."

Anna's eyes narrowed. This was an unexpected wrinkle. She knew that the Tarts were here now, but he had led her to believe they weren't *then*.

"But the Tarts' motives were very different than ours," continued the alien. "They saw humanity as primitive, *worthless*, and decided this portal would give them a rare opportunity to expand their reach. Considerably. If they established a foothold here in the boonies, they'd be twenty-five thousand light-years removed from all the action. Untouchable except possibly through gates.

"On Tartar, expansion is all but impossible due to the war, and so many other intelligences straining to keep each other in check. There are gates between worlds, yes, but all are local. Nothing more than express lanes to where our starships could take us anyway."

"I see," said Anna thoughtfully. "So if they established a colony here, they could spread across this region of space unchecked."

"Exactly. They weren't big fans of Earth as a starting point, but they saw this as a chance too good to pass up."

"What didn't they like about Earth?" asked Anna.

"The same thing we Vorians don't like, to be honest. It's too dark during the day, and has a long night every single cycle. The sky is the wrong color. The atmosphere isn't optimal. That sort of thing."

He paused. "Still, this wasn't a deterrent to the Tarts. Technology could brighten their personal space, brighten the entire planet eventually, and transform its atmosphere more to their liking. Eventually, their descendants would adapt. They would just need to wipe the planet clean of human life and bring as many of their people here as the gate would allow."

Anna was horrified to hear these words, but her gut had known it was coming. "How do you even know this?" she asked. "You just said they didn't arrive until after Vor was cut off from Earth?"

"I *didn't* know it before I arrived here. In the twenty-eight hundred years since we were cut off, we on Vor had no idea the Tarts had been here too. I only learned of this three years ago.

"The Vor-Earth portal opens in a secluded forest in Albania, a hundred miles from its border with Greece. When I arrived, I went directly to an underground stronghold nearby, built by those of my kind who had visited thousands of years ago.

"The stronghold contained rudimentary equipment they were able to construct, which took many decades considering there were no advanced components to be found on the planet. And a storehouse of gold coins that were worth many millions of your dollars. After the portal vanished, those stranded here knew that those back on Vor were aware of the stronghold. They left as much gold as they could there in the hope that eventually the portal would reappear, and gold would still be of value if future Vorians ever came through."

Vega looked troubled. "But that wasn't all," he continued. "I also found historical records, detailing everything that had happened after they were cut off from the home planet."

"So what you just told me was part of this record," said Anna.

"Exactly. And much more. The Tarts wanted to wipe humanity from the Earth. But, as you already know, my people saw yours as a possible salvation, our only hope to end an endless stalemate. Not that we would have tolerated what the Tarts were trying to do under any circumstances," he added.

Anna studied him, but her instincts continued to suggest that he was being truthful. "So you and the Tarts had a minor . . . disagreement," she said. "They wanted to kill us all. And you were desperate to save us for your own ends."

"For *your* ends as well," said Vega defensively. "But, yes, the situation was untenable. Unsurprisingly, a war broke out between my people and the Tarts for supremacy here on Earth. Which wouldn't be assured until one side had wiped out the other. Fortunately, the Tartarian portal also disappeared after a number of years, leaving both sides more or less even, at about twelve hundred strong. But both sides had their people, and forces, spread out across the globe. All were well hidden, and well protected. Very difficult to root out.

"So a multigenerational chess game ensued, each side trying to identify and kill members of the other. Both sides setting traps. Both sides ranging across the globe, with the Tarts using humans as guinea pigs along the way, trying to discover the most efficient means of eradication. And the Vors doing whatever they could to stop them.

"Both sides also had offspring as quickly as they could," continued Vega, "to shore up their numbers. Offspring that would later join the battle as they came of age."

Anna was mesmerized by this tale of a history completely unknown to humankind.

"If not for my ancestors," said Vega, "I have no doubt that the Tarts would have eventually succeeded in driving your kind into extinction."

"Ah . . . thanks," said Anna tentatively. Somehow, this didn't seem to convey the proper level of appreciation. A smile crept across her face. "Thanks . . . *a lot*," she added in amusement, knowing this didn't cut it either. "So I assume this means that you won the war, right?"

"Yes. The entries I read made it clear. My ancestors were certain they had found and eliminated the very last of the Tarts. And along the way, they were also able to confirm our theory about the clairvoyant potential of the human subconscious."

"How?"

"They managed to find several human intuitives, precognitives, over the centuries, including a few women who became famous throughout the ancient world as so-called Oracles of Delphi."

"Amazing," whispered Anna in awe. The insights Vega continued to give her into ancient history were truly extraordinary. "So what happened after your people had finally eliminated the Tarts?"

"Not much. The war had taken too heavy of a toll on our side, as well. It lasted for almost five hundred years, and when it ended, only fifty-seven of my people were left alive. These managed to survive for a few generations, but the hardships of the planet took them faster than they could reproduce. Finally, about twenty-two hundred of your years ago, the last Vor on the planet made his last entry into the log in Albania."

"I'm so sorry," whispered Anna.

Vega nodded. "Thanks," he said. "It was a very long time ago. I'm just glad they left records behind, so their sacrifice will be remembered."

"But now you and the Tarts are here again," said Anna.

"Yes. The portals to Earth decided to reappear for both sides, within a few years of each other. And this, after thousands of years of dormancy."

"The Gatekeepers must have enjoyed the skirmishes between you and the Tarts enough to want a sequel," noted Anna. "Vors versus Tarts, part two."

"Apparently so," said Vega miserably. "Although I wasn't even aware the Tarts were here until the scene at my hotel. Seems too coincidental that both sides should converge on you, Anna. There must be a reason for it."

He paused in thought. "I know from my people's log entries that the Tarts of old had learned we were searching for a special human to be our salvation. Since our portal disappeared before theirs, they could still report back to their home planet for many years. So the Tarts here now must surely know how important we believe your species to be. But the logs also indicate they thought we were crazy, and had no interest in finding an Oracle of their own."

"They'd still want to stop *you* from finding one," pointed out Anna. "Just in case you were right, and they were wrong."

"Good point," acknowledged Vega.

"Hold on," said Anna, feeling like she suddenly had an itch she couldn't scratch. Her hidden mind was telling her she needed to pause and ponder all that had been said. It was too much to take in. One once-in-a-generation revelation after another.

She made her mind blank, so her conscious wouldn't interfere with her intuition. Suddenly, right on cue, a question popped into her mind, whispered to her by her subconscious, which had picked up on something that she had not.

"Do you have an image of the light-amplifying devices that your ancestors used here?" she asked Vega.

The alien looked understandably confused. "Why?"

"I have no idea," admitted Anna. "But I never argue with my instincts."

Vega nodded thoughtfully. "I've long since scanned the records I found in the stronghold into my phone," he said, "and then into the cloud. My people were never able to reinvent a computer or digital camera, but all of us are natural-born artists, able to faithfully recreate anything we see. And these external light generators were depicted in any number of records painted over the centuries. I'll call one up."

He manipulated DeShawn Young's phone to connect with his own account in the cloud, entered a password, and in less than a minute was able to find what Anna was asking for.

The detective took one look and gasped. "Holy shit!" she said in disbelief, now understanding just what it was that her subconscious had pieced together.

A chill shot up her spine. "You have to be kidding me!"

31

"What is it?" said Vega. "What are you seeing?"

Anna's eyes were as big as saucers and her mouth hung open. "Your illumination devices sat on Vor heads like a hat," she said excitedly. "But slightly elevated, shining a blindingly bright light around their faces and surroundings at all times."

"Correct," said Vega, having no idea where she was headed. "Powered by solar cells many times more powerful than you have yet developed. So well built they lasted the full five hundred years my predecessors were here. The Vorians stayed isolated, avoiding humans whenever possible. So they weren't worried about being seen with the device. If this happened, and they were attacked because of it, they could easily defend themselves. Their superior knowledge allowed them to forge weapons that were ahead of their time."

"That's great," said Anna dismissively. "But here's the thing. Your device is basically a glorified miner's hardhat with more lighting attached. A thoroughly unremarkable technology for a species with your capabilities. But to a human at this time, it would be *astonishing*. Nothing short of a *miracle*."

"Okay," said Vega. "And this caused you to get all excited because . . . ?"

"Because if you use your imagination," she said with a smile, "this device looks like something our ancestors might have given a very special name to." She paused for effect. "They might have called it a *halo*."

Vega paused for a moment before finally showing his first signs of comprehension. "I see," he said slowly. "And this is something from your Bible, isn't it?"

"I'm not sure it was actually mentioned in the Bible," said Anna. "I'm not an expert. But I know for sure it's something indelibly carved into the human historical consciousness. Into our mythology. Our very psyches."

The detective paused. "Any guess as to what else is part of our mythology?" she asked excitedly.

Vega shook his head no.

Anna arched an eyebrow. "Harsh-looking, scary men with shining red eyes and black blood. In fact, there's another very good way to describe these laser eyes of theirs."

"How?"

"A lot of us might call them *demon* eyes."

Vega continued to look more confused than enlightened.

"Don't you get it?" said Anna excitedly. "The Tarts and their less-than-stealthy implants must have been the genesis of demon legends thousands of years ago. Or, at the very least, solidified and defined legends that already existed at the time. And the Vors were the genesis of the *angel* legends. Unbelievable!" she finished.

Her eyes widened yet again. "And I just figured out what I was smelling at the hotel and in the car," she said in dismay. "Sulfur! Get it?"

Vega shook his head no.

"*Sulfur.* In ancient lore, this is the smell of a demon. It fits perfectly." She paused, her mood still electric. "Wait a minute!" she added, as another subconscious-inspired question came to her mind. "Hand me DeShawn's phone."

As soon as she had the device she called up a search bar and typed in *Tartar in Greek mythology*.

Her heart skipped a beat as she read from the first few results. "Nothing comes up with *Tartar*," she whispered to Vega. "It gets corrected to *Tartarus*. But can there be any doubt that Tartarus is a derivation of Tartar? Let me read an entry.

"In Greek mythology," she began. "Tartarus is both a deity and a place in the underworld. While better known Hades was the place of the dead, Zeus sentenced titans and other beings who were threats to the gods to Tartarus instead. Also known as the abyss, Tartarus was located well below Hades. As far below this region of the underworld as Earth was below Heaven. According to Plato's *Gorgias*, written in

400 BCE, 'Tartarus is the place where souls are judged after death and where the wicked received divine punishment.'"

Anna beamed. "It all hangs together," she said in wonder. "Your five-hundred-year war with the Tarts didn't go unnoticed. The Greeks somehow learned the name of the Tarts' place of origin and decided it was the ultimate hell, the ultimate home of the damned."

She paused. "Later, halos and red eyes would become part of human lore, as would an epic struggle between angels and demons. With the angels, on the whole, looking out for mankind. And the demons trying to destroy us."

Anna shook her head in disbelief. As though the existence of aliens wasn't a big enough reveal for one day. Or maybe a galaxy-wide war that was raging at the heart of the Milky Way. Or perhaps an enigmatic superintelligence, which might just be mythical, but which was likely to exist and possess cruel or incomprehensible motives.

And now this. An explanation for some of the most persistent and important mythology in human history.

"Why didn't the Tarts develop stealth implants?" asked Anna.

"When we were first trapped here, our . . . *halos* weren't exactly stealthy either. But because humanity was so important to us, we spent centuries improving this technology back on Vor, so we could blend in if the portal ever did reappear.

"The Tarts didn't care about blending in. They were here to destroy you anyway, so if someone did happen to notice their gleaming red eyes, they were only too happy to kill them. But they didn't count on how quickly your technology and population would grow since their last visit. So now they do have to be more careful. It was an important miscalculation on their part."

Anna's mind suddenly urged her to ask another question. Apparently, it wasn't finished making connections. "How did the Tarts plan to destroy humanity?" she said.

"They were working on super-virulent diseases," replied her alien companion. "We made disrupting this work our top priority. Fortunately, they were only moderately skilled at genetic engineering. Their real strength, as I mentioned, is chemistry. They were also able to create a drug that allowed them to turn a human being into their unwilling, unwitting puppet."

Anna felt her heart stop in its tracks. Her intuition had been right again.

Could what Vega had just described be anything other than actual demonic possession?

Could this really get any wilder?

Her mind had been utterly blown ten revelations ago. And now *this*. Demonic possession wasn't just a crazy myth, after all. Instead, it was *scary* real.

And these insidious aliens were doing it yet again.

"Tell me more about this drug," said Anna.

"In their language they called it Human Control Serum, or HCS. Our records indicate it was exceedingly difficult for them to make. And impossible to store. So they had to use it sparingly. I looked into the chemical composition of the drug myself a few years ago, and it appears to be a distant relative of your drug, scopolamine. Scopolamine is thought to make human beings *suggestible*. HCS makes them *programmable*. So they'll do whatever the Tarts tell them to do. Even to the point of ignoring self-preservation."

Anna nodded. This explained a lot. Why alarm bells had rung so loudly when it had come to Foria, and why her instincts had suspected this drug was also linked to people taking uncharacteristic, unexplainable actions. Seemingly against their will.

Because these actions *had* been against their will. They were marching to the Tarts' drummer.

"How easy would it be for them to improve this, ah, possession drug—HCS?" she asked Vega.

"In what way?"

"To make it easier to mass produce."

"Impossible. Not with the equipment available here. Probably not even with their own equipment. It's slow and painstaking to synthesize, and they can't change that."

Anna considered. Foria was a drug that *could* be mass produced. So Foria wasn't the possession drug. It was an animal of a different stripe.

But whatever Foria turned out to be, it was bound to be ugly. Her intuition and conscious minds both suggested that the Tarts had developed a mass producible, highly addictive drug that could be turned lethal in some way at the time of their choosing. A means to achieve their goal of the complete eradication of Earth's human population. Or at least a strong beginning, cutting the population down to size for additional attempts to come.

Anna quickly explained her thinking to Vega, including a suspicion that had come to her that the Tartarian creator of Foria, Shane Frey, had used some of his precious possession drug to get Detective Rick Bunson to help frame her.

She couldn't understand why Bunson would lie the way he had. Until now. The devil had made him do it. Almost literally.

"We're very lucky this Human Control Serum is so hard to make," said Anna. "We'd never have stood a chance."

"According to the records," said Vega, "despite a limited supply of HCS, the humans the Tarts did take control of caused my ancestors a lot of trouble during the war. But we were lucky again. HCS is nearly impossible to make, but the antidote is fairly straightforward if you have the right chemical ingredients. To be honest, if both of these things weren't the case, we wouldn't be standing here talking, because the Tarts would have won our war and driven humanity into extinction."

"Can the antidote be given *before* the HCS," asked Anna, "like a vaccine? To inoculate top people so they can never be susceptible?"

Vega shook his head. "I'm afraid not," he replied. "It has to be given after the HCS is present. It neutralizes the effects of the drug on the brain. And if another dose of HCS is given, even after a person is cured, he'll become the Tart's unwilling slave for a second time."

"But the cure is permanent unless someone is hit with HCS again."

"Yes."

Anna considered. "And did *your* kind come up with any drugs to mess with our minds?" she asked, knowing her subconscious had assisted with the question.

"We didn't during our first visit. But we have one now," he admitted. "We perfected it over many years on Vor once the portal disappeared. We still had precise computer simulations of your minds. It's a memory erasure drug. Fairly straightforward to make, and very precise. We thought it important to maintain our anonymity here on Earth."

"So if you were discovered, you could use the drug to excise human memories of this discovery?"

"Exactly."

"Have you used it yet?"

"No. We made a batch, just in case, but we haven't needed it yet."

Anna's intuition told her that he was telling the truth, so she decided to drop it for now. She made a mental note to consider the implications of this further when she had more time.

They continued their discussion for another ten minutes, and it became clear how events had unfolded as they had. Especially how Anna had become central to both alien species. It was still somewhat coincidental, but not nearly as much as they had thought before.

First, it wasn't all that surprising that representatives of both alien species had ended up in LA. It was one of the most famous cities of all, and the second largest city within what was still the predominate superpower in the world. If the Tarts wanted to initiate the spread of a highly addictive drug, LA was surely one of the cities they would choose to begin with.

As for the Vors, looking for their Oracle, Vega had explained why California had been one of their highest priority hunting grounds. China and India had greater populations, but the US, and especially California, had one of the broadest swaths of wealthy individuals in the world.

And where would a gifted intuitive be most likely to end up? Where they could most take advantage of their gifts. In Tokyo, Hong Kong, London, or New York. Or in California, which is where Vega had assigned himself, as the ranking Vor on the planet.

These cities were the best places for clairvoyants to succeed, and the best places for the Vors to identify them. The wealthier the country and the greater the meritocracy, the greater chance of an intuitive making it big. And also leaving an enormous footprint on the internet.

The more records that were computerized, the easier the search. Which is how Vega had found the detective in the first place, by rooting out her article on intuition and the subconscious with just a few keystrokes.

And when he had arrived in LA to continue researching her, two days before their meeting, the Tarts must have picked him up on sensors, which would have had limited range. They had known for thousands of years that the Vors had been on Earth, but the Vors hadn't known the reverse. So in the interim, while the Vors were perfecting stealthier light-amplifying lenses, the Tarts were probably developing sensors to detect Vors on Earth. Sensors that could be constructed from materials likely to be found here.

So the Tarts had identified Vega in LA, and had followed him.

At the same time, Anna had become a thorn in their side. In Vega's mind, this was *anything* but a surprise. She was an intuitive and a detective in the city they were trying to poison. And she was special, even among the run-of-the-mill, one-chance-in-five-million intuitives.

So Frey had pulled out all the stops to make sure she was killed and discredited. Having no idea the Vors were on Earth, until they had detected Tom Vega, or that she had been identified as an Oracle. Knowing simply that she was too clever by half, and was giving them a migraine headache.

So both sides had converged around the same young detective. The timing of the intersection had been a coincidence, but not the intersection itself.

In retrospect, it had almost been inevitable.

32

Anna eyed one of the wooden pallets nearby, stacked with eight-foot-high walls of canvas bags, and shook her head in disbelief. She was trapped inside a warehouse, filled with many millions of dollars of cocaine, waiting for a war to break out—and this was the *least* bizarre experience she had had lately.

"So now you know everything," said Vega after they had sorted out how events had likely unfolded. He blew out a long breath. "Well . . . almost. There are a few details I've left out," he added guiltily. "I would have liked to give you more time before I hit you with bad news, but we don't have this luxury. The situation is deteriorating, and it's more urgent than ever that we get you to Utah."

"Deteriorating how?" asked Anna, not sure she really wanted to know.

"I told you sixty-four of us had come through the portal. What I didn't tell you is that only fifty-nine remain. Over the past six months, five have been systematically eliminated."

"By the Tarts?" said Anna.

"I don't think so," replied the alien. "I didn't even know they were here until last night, but I see it as very unlikely. Who or what is behind this isn't clear, but they're able to somehow locate our people anywhere in the world with great precision. If the Tarts had this capability, they'd have destroyed us all months ago, even if they had to pay humans to help. It would have become their highest priority."

"Who else could it be?"

"Good question. Whoever it is, they've been able to breach security that should have been impenetrable."

"Anything these five Vors have in common?" asked Anna.

"They were the best among us at finding humans that fit our prescription. Intuitives who might also be clairvoyants."

"So there's a hostile out there who doesn't want you to find what you're looking for."

"Again, this is possible, but uncertain. Most of us have been engaged in hunting for the right candidate. While these five were having the most success, all the candidates who have looked promising have ended up disappointing, for various reasons. Which is why I can be so certain that you're the ideal candidate. Because I've studied and interviewed so many who are *not* ideal. None have scientifically and systematically developed their intuition like you have. And those whose intuition is sharp have most often used it for selfish reasons. Apparently, the intuitive group of humans is enriched for megalomania, narcissism, and sociopathy."

He paused. "In any case, the disappearance of my five colleagues is very troubling. We've never found any of them, so it wasn't accidental death or natural causes."

"Earlier you told me you weren't looking for a detective," said Anna. "You were looking for a fleet admiral, instead." She shrugged. "Looks like you could use both."

Vega nodded grimly. "I also have news that's even more troubling," he continued. "The records of my ancestors made it clear that the Tartarian portal opened in an isolated mesa in the foothills of the Balkan mountains in what is now Bulgaria. Thousands of years ago. Not all that far from our portal in Albania. Or from Greece, the preeminent civilization at the time.

"After our people arrived here three years ago, we had a lot to get done. We had to understand the current state of your civilization. Learn languages that had become important since we were last here. Determine how to convert gold into spendable currency.

"Once we were established and had our Earth-legs under us, and the wherewithal to do it, we installed a system of video monitors to surveil the last known location of the Tart portal in Bulgaria—just to be sure it didn't appear again. But it took us six months, and we were apparently too late to see Shane Frey and his fellow . . . demons come through."

"Unless their portal appeared in a different location this time."

"Also a possibility," said Vega, "although less likely. In any event," he continued, "by the time we managed to set up surveillance the portal wasn't there. This has been true for the past two and a half years. But this changed recently, when the their portal suddenly reappeared again."

"*How* recently?"

Vega hesitated. "While you and I were driving to the Rest Easy Motel last night," he replied finally. "And it was massive. Orders of magnitude larger than the one here before. It only stayed active for a few hours before disappearing, but the Tarts managed to get more than six hundred of their people through. And more females than males, to increase the reproductive potential of the group."

Anna swallowed hard. As if the smaller number of Tarts already here weren't a big enough threat. "I thought the Gatekeepers liked parity."

"Apparently not this time. Or perhaps our portal will reopen soon as well. But we can't count on it. So we don't have a second to waste in getting your abilities enhanced."

"You never did tell me the science behind clairvoyance," said Anna, "or how you plan to sharpen mine in Utah. Not to spoil your plans, but what if I don't like what I hear? What if I refuse your enhancement procedure?"

"We can't coerce you," said Vega. "If you're going to lead our fleet, you have to do it of your own free will. So if you don't like what you hear, there isn't anything we can do about it. But I'm not concerned about that. When I have the time to lay it out for you, I'm confident you'll agree."

Anna's eyes widened. "Wait a minute," she said. "Let's back up. You found out *last night* that the Tart portal in Bulgaria had opened up?"

"That's right."

"How?"

Vega hesitated, but only for a moment. "One of my Vorian underlings contacted me to tell me the bad news."

"*Contacted* you?" repeated Anna in dismay.

t all became clear. Vega had told her that the Vors and
d comm systems implanted in their ears and throats,
~~and that this~~ and their light-amplifying technologies had made it
through the portals. She had assumed that the comms only worked
over relatively short distances. But apparently this wasn't the case.

Anna didn't like the implications of this at all. "How many of
your people are assigned to California?" she asked. "How many are
in the region we're in now?"

"It's a high-priority state, so eight, including me."

"And you could have called them at any time?" she said in dismay.
"You could have asked them to meet us, send reinforcements, or help
in other ways? And you *didn't*?"

Vega sighed. "No, I didn't. I chose not to."

"*Why not?*" she demanded. "We've been fighting for our lives. If
you really believe that I'm the most important human who ever lived,
why didn't you pull out all the stops to protect me?"

"Because you *wouldn't* be the most important human who ever
lived if you needed me to. Since I'm in the same boat as you, I've been
betting my life that you can get us through this on your own."

"But you've been betting *my* life too," she hissed through clenched
teeth.

"It couldn't be helped. We both needed to see what you could do.
And my hope was that once I made it clear that your subconscious
could tap into the future, this knowledge, along with life-and-death
adversity, would awaken your abilities. Our computer models predicted that this might be the case."

"You son of a bitch! You callous, manipulative bastard!"

"I'm sorry," said Vega. "I truly am. But your clairvoyance *has* been
awakened. It worked! And the Vorians close enough to reach us were
unlikely to have made a difference anyway. Even if they had rushed
to our side, the Tarts can bring more than enough force to bear to kill
us all. It's possible that these reinforcements could have saved us. But
it's more likely that their presence would have done nothing but give
you a false sense of security, and ensure that you remained unaware
of your clairvoyance."

"Not your call to make!" snapped Anna.

"I am truly sorry," said the alien. "But I had every confidence that you could get us through this on your own. The risk I took with both of our lives was very small. But the reward is potentially *staggering*. It isn't an exaggeration to say that triggering your awareness of your precognitive abilities can have a dramatic impact on the fate of the entire galaxy, and, in the end, save many billions of intelligent lives."

Anna didn't reply. Vega may have been right about her clairvoyance, but he overestimated her value in this war of his by many orders of magnitude.

"I hope that you can bring yourself to understand my motivations," added the alien. "And to forgive me."

Anna glared at him, but didn't reply.

"And one last point," said Vega softly. "You know that I can't put anything over on *you*. As I've said before, if I could, you wouldn't be who I was looking for. You knew that we Vors had internal comms to communicate. So how is it that both your brilliant conscious mind, and your even more brilliant subconscious mind, both failed to consider that I might be able to call for Vor reinforcements? How could your intuition fail to see something this obvious?"

He paused to let this sink in.

"If you're being honest with yourself," he continued finally, "isn't it likely that your subconscious mind *was* aware of this? But it purposely kept it from you. Maybe even found a way to distract your conscious mind from this truth. Perhaps your hidden mind guessed that life-and-death adversity could spark it to greater heights, also— and was fully in favor."

Anna suddenly felt ill. Could the alien be *right* about this? Had her subconscious mind actively worked to keep her in the dark? This was a wrinkle she had never even considered.

Could she and her hidden mind work at cross purposes? As though they really were two different entities? Or did her subconscious purposely keep some of its grandmasterly chess moves hidden from her for her own good, fearing that she would fail to understand their depth and override them?

Either way, this just meant that things had gotten even *more* complicated. And given everything that had come before, Anna wouldn't have thought that this was possible.

33

Abel "Wolfy" Medina stood outside an impenetrable steel door holding a machine gun in the dim pre-dawn morning and stroked his wild beard. He continued to feel like an idiot. A *pissed-off* idiot. The goddamned Hulk couldn't get through this door, so why the hell was he *guarding* it?

He was a loyal soldier who had been with Neil Marshall from the beginning, and he deserved better. Better than being lent out to Shane Frey, who insulted their competence by insisting they treat Anna Abbott like she was twenty times the threat she really was. And better than having a relative newcomer like DeShawn Young placed in command of the team above him.

As he thought about Young, he wondered once again what their esteemed leader was doing inside the warehouse after all this time. Wolfy was certain that the girl was bluffing and didn't have any information worth knowing. But even if she had, there was no way it would take this long to spit it out.

Was Young thinking with his dick? Was he trying to force himself on the young detective? Was this the reason for the delay?

Wolfy couldn't entirely blame him if that was the case. She was pretty hot, even now, and that was saying something. She was wearing a bulky sweatshirt—over shape-compressing body armor—and she looked like she had been through hell, which couldn't have been far from the truth. If she could look this good under these circumstances, how good would she look when she was dressing up for a party? Or, better yet, naked?

Wolfy shook his head. He was letting his imagination get away from him. Even if Frey had never issued any warnings about how dangerous the detective was likely to be, she had already proven herself to be a bad-ass, having apparently slipped a noose at Salem Hills

High that should have been unslippable. Young would have better luck forcing himself on a giant scorpion than doing the same to Anna Abbott.

So what *was* he doing?

Wolfy heard a sound in the direction he was facing. What the hell? At first he thought it was a car, but that didn't seem quite right.

And then he realized the truth. It wasn't a *single* car—it was a *fleet* of them. A swarm of angry wasps bearing down on the concrete parking area in front of him with reckless speed.

He was on the east side of the warehouse, the only side completely out in the open. The other three sides faced a nearby woods, which could provide cover for a retreat. The woods were densest to the west, making that his best option.

He took off running, but before he reached the edge of the building the swarm of vehicles broke into view, and their headlights turned the approaching dawn into broad daylight. They screeched to a stop in the empty parking area, fanning out.

"This is the police!" boomed a deep voice through an electronic megaphone. "Surrender and you won't be harmed! Repeat, this is the police. You have no chance!"

Wolfy manipulated his phone as he ran, placing a call, which was picked up on the first ring. "We're under attack!" he shouted at Shane Frey. "Where are you?"

"Still ten minutes out."

"Hurry!" shouted Wolfy as he made it to the edge of the warehouse, unable to pay attention to Frey's response, as he half-expected to be cut down by gunfire at any moment.

As he emerged on the other side, he found that he had jumped from the frying pan into the fire. His three comrades had all tried to escape into the woods, as he was planning, but the cops had anticipated this move. They had planted teams in the woods before making a flashy entrance from the east. Now, all three of his teammates were retreating back to the west warehouse door, and multiple spotlights were locking onto them like they were Broadway stars.

Wolfy took in the scene all at once, realizing that his men had just unlocked the padlock on the door and were rushing inside as warning shots from the woods hit the warehouse, producing sparks and a symphony of steel-and-bullet percussion. Miraculously, all three made it inside, slamming the door closed behind them, and Wolfy realized this was his only chance as well. Inside they would be protected, and would have hostages, which would buy them the time they needed for reinforcements to arrive.

Wolfy sprinted for the door, laying down a steady burst of machine-gun fire directed toward the unseen enemy in the woods as he ran, which threw up bark and leaves like a wood chipper. But when he was only eight feet away from his destination, a bullet found his kneecap, shattering it, and sending him to the ground screaming in agony.

* * *

Lieutenant Carl Mendoza kept his eyes on the road as he and his five fellow mercenaries streaked toward the coordinates he had been given, which led to an isolated warehouse. They had been warned to come prepared for a war, just in case. But their actual mission simply involved locking down two prisoners who, based on everything they had been told, were *already* locked down beyond any possibility of escape.

Meanwhile, Shane Frey, their new boss, and a few of his friends were ten minutes behind, not wanting to be too close to any action until the mercenary muscle they had hired assured them that it was safe.

It was the strangest op Mendoza had ever been involved with, and that was really saying something.

The panicked voice of Shane Frey burst through Mendoza's comm, nearly rupturing his eardrum. "There's trouble at the warehouse!" thundered Frey. "My men there are under attack!"

"How many hostiles?" asked the mercenary.

"Uncertain," replied Frey, thankfully no longer shouting. "But it must be a large number to spook a five-man team armed with automatic weapons."

"Roger that," said Mendoza.

"Change of orders," said Frey. "I no longer want you and your team to secure the prisoners for our arrival. Instead, I want them *dead*. All of them. The new hostiles on the scene, and *especially* Anna Abbott. She's much too lucky for her own good. So no more playing with fire."

"You're aware that this will double our fee."

"Done," said Frey. "Can you wipe them out? Even if they have a force considerably larger than yours?"

"Uncertain. We have enough explosive power to turn the warehouse and vicinity into slag. But your men are right there, so we'll have to try something else."

"No, Lieutenant, do what you have to do. My men are expendable."

Mendoza's eyes narrowed and he glanced around him and in his rearview mirror to gauge the reaction of his comrades, whose comms were also picking up the call. If Frey was willing to waste the team already at the warehouse without a second thought, he wouldn't hesitate to do the same to them. It was certainly food for thought.

"Lieutenant?" repeated Frey. "Did you hear me?"

"I heard you loud and clear," replied Mendoza. He blew out a long breath. "And we'll do as you request. The area will be wiped clean of life within ten minutes."

* * *

Anna broke off the discussion with her alien companion as a war erupted outside. First there had been a police warning, amplified by a megaphone, which could barely be heard inside the warehouse. This had soon been followed by prolonged bursts of pistol and machine-gun fire all around, a horrifying cacophony that easily penetrated the thick steel walls.

She suddenly felt ill.

"What's wrong, Anna?" said Vega worriedly. "Isn't this the Cavalry?"

"Yes, but they're also my friends," she replied anxiously. "They should have enough of an advantage to come through this okay, but there's always a risk."

"What does your intuition say?"

"Absolutely *nothing*," she said unhappily. "No signal at all. Maybe I overtaxed it and it's decided to take a rest," she added with a weak smile.

Anna gasped as the west door suddenly burst open and three of DeShawn Young's comrades rushed inside. They slammed the door closed behind them and looked to where the prisoners had been tied to chairs, shocked to see nothing but the unconscious form of their boss instead.

Anna fired as the men dived for cover behind a pallet of stuffed canvas bags. She hit one hostile in the chest before he reached safety, but the other two made it unscathed.

The detective continued firing, purposely hitting several bags of cocaine, which exploded, belching huge clouds of white powder into the air, momentarily blocking the view of their adversaries. She continued shooting while leading Vega to the long banquet table nearby, pushing it over and dropping behind the newly formed steel wall for cover. But just before Vega ducked down behind this barricade, the man Anna had shot managed to squeeze the trigger on his machine gun, sending a poorly aimed curtain of fire their way with his last breath, and one stray bullet nicked the alien's lower forearm. A trickle of neon green blood began to seep from the superficial injury. Anna removed the loose gauze bandage from her wrist and handed it to the alien to use on his wound.

The detective cursed her precognition-fueled intuition for abandoning her completely. How had it failed to give her any warning of what had just happened? Talk about letting her down. Her newfound clairvoyance was as fickle as one of Vega's portals.

And she cursed herself, as well. She had already let this newfound power become a crutch. She should have known—consciously—that if the cops did their job, DeShawn's men would have nowhere to run but inside the warehouse. And no other option but to turn this into a hostage negotiation.

Another curtain of fire swept across the upended steel tabletop, which was now thoroughly decorated by pockmarks. "Cease fire!" screamed Anna as loudly as she could. "Your only chance is to take us hostage! Killing us doesn't help you!"

The firing tailed off and then stopped as these words registered. "Does that mean you're surrendering?" said a deep voice. "Good choice," he added. "That table won't save you forever."

"How about this," called out Anna, no longer needing to shout, "I won't press charges for kidnapping. I'll see to it that you walk. All I ask is that you tell my fellow officers how Neil Marshall framed me."

"No deal!" said the same man who had spoken earlier. "Marshall will skin us alive!"

Anna was about to say, "Not if he's in prison," but even her old-fashioned, non-clairvoyant intuition told her that this would fall on deaf ears.

She handed Vega the closed switchblade she had taken from DeShawn Young and put her lips to his ear. "The instant they tell me to drop my gun," she whispered hurriedly, "throw this ten feet to your right."

He nodded.

"Okay, okay," said Anna out loud. "I'll surrender. But you have to promise not to kill me when you're done using me as a hostage."

"Done."

Anna rose from behind the table with her hands in the air, still clutching the gun. The two men tentatively came out from behind the eight-foot wall of cocaine, machine guns pointing her way. They inched closer, never taking their eyes from her right hand.

"What about Vega?" asked the shorter of the two men.

"He's been hit. And you know he's harmless, anyway. But if he pops up from behind the table, kill him."

This seemed to satisfy the two hostiles. "Drop the gun, Detective!" barked the shorter of the two.

Upon hearing these words, Vega flung the switchblade to his right, as instructed. It crashed down onto the concrete floor about fifteen feet to the hostiles' left with a sharp crack, and both men reflexively turned toward the sound.

Anticipating this moment, Anna moved instantly, firing a bullet into each man's thigh in a blur of motion, and then ducking back down behind the table. Both men collapsed to the floor, moaning in pain.

"My offer still stands!" she shouted. "Testify, and I'll see to it that you walk."

Before they could answer, Donovan Perez rushed through the west door with four other armed policeman in tow. "Freeze!" he shouted at the two men, who were now trying to staunch the flow of blood from their matching wounds.

One of the uniformed cops disarmed them while Anna rose up from behind the table once again. She made a show of dropping her gun to the ground and raising her hands. "Hello, Captain Perez," she said cheerfully. "Glad you could make it."

He nodded and then turned to another man beside him. "Go outside and sound the all clear," he ordered. "Get a medic in here to attend to these two men, and call for an ambulance. Confirm that all teams are in place to ambush any possible incoming reinforcements."

Suddenly, Anna's intuition came to life once again, giving her its usual, vague instructions without explanation. It would have been nice if her gut had given her a warning when the three men had stormed their castle, but better late than never, she supposed.

"Captain Perez," she said urgently, "I need you to also have your men trigger the sirens on three of the cars. *Immediately.*"

"Why would I do that? If additional hostiles are on the way, as you suggested on the phone, why advertise our presence?"

"They'll know you're here, anyway," said Anna. "Please! You've trusted me this far. I'm asking you to trust me one last time."

34

"The explosives are primed and ready," reported Lieutenant Carl Mendoza. "We're using missiles and multiple drones. Each is loaded with C99, an experimental explosive we've gotten our hands on that is many times more powerful than C4. We've entered precise GPS coordinates that should ensure an even spread."

"Are you within sight of the warehouse?" asked Frey.

"Negative. We stopped about a hundred yards away, with a woods between us and the target. We don't want to chance being seen and tipping them off. Would you like us to launch now, or should we await your arrival?"

"Launch immediately!" insisted Frey.

"Roger that," said Mendoza. "Launching now." He reached for a launch button icon on his touchscreen computer and heard a faint wail off in the distance, coming from the direction of the warehouse. He jerked his hand away at the last second as he recognized the sound.

It was a siren. Multiple sirens.

Police sirens.

"I've paused the launch," he reported to Frey. "Why are we suddenly hearing police sirens at the site? Was it the *cops* who attacked your men?"

"I have no idea," snapped Frey. "What does it matter?"

"What does it *matter*?" repeated Mendoza in disbelief. "It matters a lot. I was under the impression that this was a turf war between drug lords. To use this kind of explosive power on US soil to kill rival criminal gangs is dodgy enough. But using it to kill *cops*? Are you out of your mind? This is where we draw the line. Besides, kill this many cops and no precinct in the state will rest until they have all of our heads on a spike."

"I'll triple your pay," said Frey.

Before Mendoza could answer, two stealth military helicopters streaked by overhead, eerily noiseless in operation, and began to settle down over the warehouse grounds.

"What the hell is going on at that warehouse?" demanded the mercenary leader. "Because the *military* just joined in on the fun. Probably Black Ops. What aren't you telling us, Shane?"

"I don't know why they're here," said Frey, "but cops will burn just like everyone else. And so will soldiers. Launch your explosives now, and I'll pay you and your men *six times* your normal rate."

Mendoza snorted, having no need to check with his team. "I'm afraid that's a negative," he said. "Not for all the money in the world. The police and military, both?" He shook his head in disbelief. "If only there were little kids on site, we could have pulled off a *no-way-in-hell* trifecta."

* * *

Shanifrey Doe screamed a curse, while the other three Tartarians in the car tried to blend into the woodwork so as not to become the focus of their boss's ire. "Turn the car around!" he ordered Eldamir Kor, now his second-in-command. "She did it *again*. She escaped what should have been certain death."

Eldamir banked to the right to take the next off ramp. "She's been good," he said, "but she's also been lucky. If our mercs hadn't happened to hear those police sirens at the last second, which she had nothing to do with, she'd be toast."

"But they *did* hear them," said Shanifrey in disgust. "Events seem to have a way of working out in her favor. Perhaps the Vorians are on to something with this Oracle nonsense. The empirical evidence is building, which means that she's more of a priority than ever."

The commander fumed. "And these mercenary hires turned out to be worthless. They seem to have a lot more lines they won't cross than was apparent during our negotiations."

Shanifrey thought about this further. Maybe it had been a mistake not to use their Human Control Serum on the mercenary leader. If they had, the site would be rubble by now, and Anna Abbott would be dead. But they were down to their last dose, and were too busy to devote the many hours needed to make more. They were saving this dose for a rainy day, for more important uses.

But even though the detective had eluded them again, Shanifrey forced himself to look on the bright side. Despite the repeated blows they had been dealt over the past twelve hours, things were looking up. He had received an important call on his internal comm from Bulgaria just the night before. Their portal had reappeared briefly, bigger than ever, and alert soldiers on Tartar had managed to send over six hundred of his people through. Soon, Shanifrey would have the resources he needed to make more HCS, as painstaking as this was.

And to accomplish so much more, as well.

They had suffered some severe reversals of late, but the Tartarian commander had no doubt that their long-term prospects were better than ever—Anna Abbott or no Anna Abbott.

35

Stephen Redford's pulse quickened as the helicopter he was in landed near an array of police sedans and SUVs spread out along a warehouse parking lot. Seconds later a matching helicopter set down beside his.

Dressed in civilian clothing, he had rushed to LA the night before to take over the Camden International Hotel case and do damage control. He had questioned hotel personnel, examined forensic evidence, and helped his people sneak two alien bodies back to Evie headquarters in refrigerated containers.

And he had found what he was looking for, a solid lead, one that he was desperate to follow up on. A lead by the name of Anna Abbott.

Footage had shown this woman calling down to room service and then riding the elevator to the ninth floor shortly before all hell had broken loose. But there was no footage of her riding the elevator back down, which meant she had likely taken the stairs.

The Camden International Hotel catered to a wealthy clientele who expected the utmost in privacy, and so cameras were relegated to the lobby and elevators, period. Redford would have given his last dollar for a room or hallway camera, but this was not to be.

Still, this woman's behavior was more than suspicious enough for him to do further digging. Redford had sent one of his people to wake the poor sap who had taken the room service call near the end of his shift, and he had recounted the conversation he had had with this suspect.

Apparently, she had tricked the young employee into revealing the room number of a man named Tom Vega. A man staying in room 925, the very room in which all the alien blood had been spilled. In the next room over, a married couple had been found with their throats slit, and numerous bullet holes had been punched through the wall between the two rooms.

Nessie had checked the footage until she found an image of Vega checking in, but even she hadn't been able to learn anything about him. Vega wasn't his real name, and he was a ghost, not leaving a single electronic fingerprint anywhere. There was off the grid, and there was *this*—so far off the grid that even the NSA's AI, the most impressive on Earth, couldn't find any evidence of his existence, despite having access to the most impressive collection of data in history. To Redford's knowledge, Nessie had never come up this empty before.

Redford hadn't arrived back at Los Angeles Air Force Base until almost two in the morning, and by that time he could barely keep his eyes open. So he had set an alarm that would give him five hours of sleep. He had then instructed Nessie to do three things: Prepare a comprehensive report on the life and times of Detective Anna Abbott for him to read in the morning. Scan through the footage of every street and store camera in a five-hundred-mile radius, looking for any sign of this detective or Tom Vega, and use any and all other methods at her disposal to find them. And finally, to awaken him if there were any events that she believed warranted his attention.

Sure enough, less than three and a half hours later, Nessie had awakened him with an alert. The detective had become the subject of an All-Points Bulletin, nationwide, and police captain Donovan Perez was rushing a veritable army to apprehend her at an abandoned warehouse a forty-minute drive away.

While Perez had a big head start and was moving fast, the colonel had seen to it that two NG 225 helicopters were on standby at the base, and managed to arrive at the warehouse only a few minutes after the police captain.

Redford exited the chopper and surveyed the warehouse and vicinity, which was a beehive of activity. He tried to concentrate, but police sirens were blaring all around him, penetrating his skull like a dentist's drill.

What idiots, he thought. What was the point of sirens? The site was secured, so why would they want to draw attention to themselves?

And how in the world had this crew found Anna Abbott before Nessie had?

Redford ordered the four commandos and two helo pilots who had arrived with him to stay where they were, marched to the warehouse, and entered. Inside there was a maelstrom of activity. Banks of lights had been brought in to make the large space bright as day. White powder had settled onto the floor and around a wood pallet containing a number of exploded canvas bags, no doubt filled with cocaine. Police were cataloging endless shell casings, and the body of a man, shot through the heart, was lying in his own blood.

The rest of the room was decorated by a pockmarked steel table, lying on its side, machine guns, an unopened switchblade, and at least a dozen people milling about.

And in the center of it all, Anna Abbott, in handcuffs. Along with the mysterious ghost known only as Thomas Vega, unrestrained. Captain Perez was to her left, along with a second man he didn't recognize.

"Nessie," he said subvocally, "who is the man next to Perez?"

The colonel had perfected this silent form of communication with Nessie, using sensors in his throat that converted subvocal impulses into words, which were then transmitted to the AI.

"Lieutenant Cole Boyer," said Nessie through the comm embedded in his ear. "Perez's number two man. Texts and calls between him and Detective Abbott suggest that they're friends, but not romantically involved."

Satisfied, the colonel made his way over to the foursome, which included the two people he most wanted to speak with in all the world.

"Can I help you?" said Perez irritably as Redford approached, clearly annoyed by his intrusion.

"I doubt it," snapped the colonel. "You've shown no ability to follow orders so far."

Perez did a double-take. "Look, asshole," he hissed, "I don't know who you are, but you'd better have a very good reason for being here."

"I'm Colonel Stephen Redford. I'm the one behind the order you got to back off the Camden International case. So what about that order didn't you understand?"

"What are you talking about?" said Perez. "I *didn't* go anywhere near that case. And none of my people did either."

"You issued an APB on Anna Abbott," said the colonel, "and mounted a military-style raid to get at her and Tom Vega. Is that what you consider not going anywhere near the case?" he added incredulously. "I'm going to have your job for this."

"Are you an imbecile?" snapped the captain. "This raid has nothing to do with the Camden case."

"It has *everything* to do with the Camden case," said the colonel.

Anna winced. "Let me clear this up for you, gentlemen," she said. "What we have here is a simple misunderstanding. Colonel, the captain isn't after me because of the double homicide at the Camden International. He has no idea that I was involved with that. He wants me for multiple murders at a high school last night."

"Jesus, Anna," said Perez in dismay. "Any murders lately that you *haven't* been a part of?"

Redford's eyes narrowed. This woman had been *busy*. How in the world did this all fit together? "Apologies, Captain," he said to Perez. "I guess you did follow orders, after all. Sorry that I jumped to the wrong conclusions. But the stakes here are very high, and while I hate to pull rank, I'm afraid I'm going to have to take custody of these two and ask you to leave us."

"These *two*?" said the captain. He gestured toward Vega. "This guy isn't even *in* our custody," he added. "Anna was about to tell us how he fits in when you interrupted. Are you saying he's involved in the Camden Hotel case?"

"Yes," said Redford. "So with all due respect," he added, "I need you to step away."

"Why do I have a bad feeling about you, Colonel?" said Lieutenant Boyer. "I'm not going anywhere until someone I trust can convince me that Anna will be well-treated and receive her due process rights."

"I admire your loyalty, Lieutenant," said Redford. "I do. But I'm not sure there is any way of reassuring you that my intentions are good, other than reassuring you that my intentions are good."

Boyer looked unconvinced.

"It's okay, Cole," said Anna softly. "I'll be fine. Please do as he says. You, too, Captain. I actually want to talk to him. And I no longer think additional hostiles are converging on us after all. Just be sure to interrogate the men you just captured and clear my name while I'm keeping the colonel company."

Captain Perez couldn't quite let it go. "You do know, Colonel, that I don't take orders from you, right?"

Redford sighed. "I know that, Captain. And I really am sorry about this. I hate to come across as the overbearing asshole you think I am. But trust me, if you challenge me on this, you'll just be getting angry calls from your superiors within the hour, telling you to do whatever I say."

The captain stared deep into Redford's eyes and decided not to test this assertion. He reluctantly handed him the key to Anna's handcuffs, and then he and Cole Boyer said their farewells to her, promising to do everything they could to absolve her of all charges.

"Thanks," she said to them both. "You busted your asses to get here and rescue me, and I'm grateful. And thanks for believing in me."

Redford waited until the police captain and lieutenant were out of earshot and opened his mouth to ask his first question, but then thought better of it. He could wait another minute or two until he was in a more private setting. "Let's go," he said to his two prisoners.

"Where to?" said Anna.

"We're taking a helicopter to a site very near Luke Air Force Base in Arizona," he replied. "And the three of us are going to have a nice little chat along the way."

36

Vega had remained silent for some time, but was growing increasingly agitated. "Anna, we can't get sidetracked in Arizona," he said as if Redford wasn't there. "Not now. As I said, it's more urgent than ever that we get to . . . our destination."

"What destination?" asked Redford.

Vega continued to ignore him. "Did you know this guy was coming?" he asked Anna.

She frowned and shook her head. "Not even a hint. I guess my crystal ball is broken. But don't worry, I have a good feeling about him."

"Do you have any idea what he wants?" said Vega.

"Every idea," she replied cheerfully.

She turned to Redford, who was beginning to think he was invisible. "Look, Colonel, you're in charge of investigating alien visitations, am I right?"

Redford studied her for several seconds. "What makes you think that?"

"Come on, Colonel, don't insult my intelligence. You swooped into LA to take over a case involving two dead aliens. And you have enough juice to push around the upper echelon of civilian law enforcement like they're your own personal playthings. Your role is obvious."

"How do you know the case involves aliens? Did you kill them?"

"I did," she admitted. "In self-defense. But I know a lot more than just that there were aliens in room 925," she added. Anna gestured to her companion. "Tom and I can tell you things that will blow your mind ten times over. But there are conditions." She arched an eyebrow. "Assuming you're interested, of course."

Redford smiled, despite himself. "I think it's fair to say that you've caught my attention."

"Good," said Anna. "First condition: We'll cooperate fully, tell you anything you want to know. But *only* you. At least for now."

"Why?"

"Because my gut tells me I can trust you."

"Your gut?" repeated Redford. "You seem to be putting a lot of faith in a hunch."

"Are you saying that I *can't* trust you?"

"If you couldn't, I'd lie to you and say you could. But the truth is that I'm a man of my word."

She smiled. "I believe you, Colonel. So, second condition: We'll tell you everything—but not if you force us to go to Arizona. Only if you take us to Huntington, Utah, instead. And you can't disclose our location or destination to anyone else."

"Why Huntington, Utah?"

"Short answer," said Anna, "to try to save the world. Because those demon-eyed, black-blooded bastards back at the Camden Hotel, and their entire species, are hell-bent on wiping us out. And by *us*, I mean the human race. And while there were only about sixty or seventy of them on Earth yesterday, over six hundred more just arrived."

The colonel's stomach tightened. "Arrived from where?" he asked.

"Take us to Utah," said Anna. "Just the three of us. And find out. Take us to Arizona, on the other hand, and we'll refuse to cooperate, even knowing that our species is moving closer to the brink with every passing second."

"So what's in Utah that's such a game changer?" asked Redford.

"*Who's* in Utah," corrected Anna. "It's a very long story, but it turns out I have certain . . . precognitive abilities. There's a scientist in Huntington who can help strengthen them. Apparently, that will make all the difference."

Redford snorted. "So now there's an alien invasion—*and* you're precognitive? I was beginning to get excited by what you might tell me. But now it seems that you're delusional. So I suppose you see yourself as some kind of savior, is that it?"

"*She* doesn't see herself that way," said Vega, leaping to her defense. "It's me and my species who do."

"Your *species*?" said Redford.

"I'm not from this part of the galaxy, either," said Vega. He removed the gauze bandage covering the wound on his forearm to reveal neon-green blood.

Redford's mouth dropped open and froze there. If this had happened prior to his discovery of the Traveler species, he would have been sure it was a hoax. But given the circumstances, he was equally sure it was real.

He was speaking with a living, breathing, extraterrestrial. *Incredible.*

A million questions raced through his mind, but he deemed it important to play out the current thread before moving on. "Does that mean you're responsible for trying to convince her that she's precognitive?" he said.

"Not trying," corrected Anna. "Succeeding."

Redford stared deeply into her arresting blue eyes. "How do you know you can trust him?" he asked. "He's convinced you of a coming invasion by a second alien species, and that you're clairvoyant. But how do you know that anything he says is true?"

"Long story," said Anna. "My intuition tells me to believe him, and it's almost never wrong. And these black-blooded aliens *have been* trying to kill us. Finally, when Tom told me I was clairvoyant, I thought he was crazy myself. But then I discovered he was right."

Redford blew out a long breath. "I've always believed in the possibility of extraterrestrials," he said. "Which recent evidence has confirmed. But I don't believe in the paranormal. Aliens are scientifically possible. Clairvoyance isn't."

"That's what I thought, too," replied Anna. "But what if I can *prove* that I'm clairvoyant? Will you take us to Utah?"

"Prove that you're clairvoyant and I'll take you *anywhere* you want."

"Good," said Anna. "Let's do this. Tom, what's a good demonstration?"

Vega sighed and turned to the colonel. "I need to point out that she's new to this," he said. "Her abilities are all over the place. Spotty. She can mostly see very near term, with the occasional vision, days, or even years in the future. Although *she's* not even aware of these more long-range abilities yet. And her clairvoyance takes place entirely in her subconscious, with her conscious mind able to perceive just the tiniest fraction of what her subconscious is able to see."

"What?" said Redford, blinking in confusion.

"Never mind," said Anna. "Let's get on with it."

"Okay, Colonel," began the alien. "We're going to go five rounds, since, as I've said, Anna's abilities aren't fully reliable. Think of a number. *Any* number. From one to a million. Anna will guess what it is. But here is the critical part. Right or wrong, you have to tell us what the number is right after she guesses. You have to say it out loud."

Redford considered. "I get it," he said, his eyes sparkling with an easy intelligence. "Because she won't be reading minds. She'll be seeing the future. If the number is never revealed to her in the future, she has no better chance than anyone else of getting it right."

"Exactly," said Vega, and in a rush Anna understood why the playing card experiment she had participated in had failed to reveal her abilities. She had never been told the right answers.

Redford thought of a number and nodded his readiness. Anna strained for some time, but her intuition was nowhere to be found. "I have no idea," she said finally, giving up. "Ninety-four?"

The colonel shook his head. "Not even close," he said. "Is there really a point of repeating this?" he said to Vega. "Or are you ready to tell me where you're from, and what you're doing on Earth? And what your *real* agenda is?"

Vega sighed. "So *you* ruin the experiment," he said, "and then blame us when it doesn't work. You agreed that you would say the number out loud right after her guess. Does that ring a bell?"

A smile slowly spread across the colonel's face. "Right you are," he said sheepishly. "Let's go again. This time, I vow to say the number out loud even if an earthquake swallows me whole."

"Good," said Vega as Redford thought of another number. Once again he nodded at Anna, indicating his readiness.

Anna's eyes widened. "I don't have any vision of you saying the number in the future," she said. "But I have this strange hunch that the number is 27,456."

Redford's breath stuck in his throat. To his credit, he did remember to say the number out loud, which matched her guess exactly, something that had been obvious from his stunned reaction.

"No need to go again," said the colonel, still in shock. "A one-in-a-million guess is good enough for me."

He tried to appear steady and in charge, but inside he was reeling. Was he really in the presence of a living extraterrestrial and a clairvoyant, both? He forced himself to breathe. He finally managed to snap out of his paralyzed state and unlocked Anna Abbott's handcuffs, dropping them to the concrete floor below.

"Can I get my gun back?" said Anna. "Well, it's actually Deshawn's gun, but why split hairs?"

"You'll get it back when I'm sure I can trust you completely," said Redford. "But for now, let's get the two of you to Utah."

The colonel grinned. "And after you've saved the world, we really need to play the lottery together. The cost of the ticket is on me," he added in amusement.

"Very generous of you," said Anna wryly.

And just for an instant her mind's eye held a picture of her sharing a passionate kiss with this man. But the image vanished so quickly, she wondered if it had just been her imagination.

PART 4

"It is a poor sort of memory that only works backwards."

—The White Queen, *Alice in Wonderland*

"Do I contradict myself?
Very well then I contradict myself,
(I am large, I contain multitudes.)"

—Walt Whitman, *Song of Myself*

37

Colonel Stephen Redford escorted his two guests to the helicopter, wanting to shake himself to be certain this was real. He had to be dreaming. Except that he *wasn't*.

There really were two extraterrestrial species visiting Earth. After the entire long history of the human race, absolute proof of alien visitation had finally been found, in the form of a body that had dropped onto his lap—or onto a busy street in New York City, to be more accurate—just weeks earlier.

And now this.

When it rained, it poured.

And if the detective was to be believed, he was about to get hit with an information storm so epic it would make the torrential rains that had flooded Earth in the time of Noah seem like a *drizzle*.

Was Anna Abbott really clairvoyant? It seemed to him that this was the only explanation for what he had witnessed. Redford decided that he would take everything she and the alien told him at face value, until it was proven otherwise. And Anna seemed confident that the alien calling himself Tom Vega could be trusted, which he found more comforting than he should.

But if what she had said about the black-blooded aliens was true, the first proven alien visitation had turned into something out of the worst nightmares of horror writers.

Redford found himself taken with the detective, a stronger first reaction than he had ever had to a woman. And why not? She was mysterious and possessed information he would die to know. Information he had been seeking his entire life.

But there was more to it than just this. She was also poised, smart, and competent. Not to mention having a down-to-earth personality and an obvious sense of humor. She had stood there in a plain black sweatshirt, handcuffed, knowing that aliens and drug lords were determined to kill her, and had exuded nothing but confidence and self-assurance.

Redford imagined her being surrounded by ten men with machine guns, and not only being unperturbed, but serenely telling them to get more men so it would be a fair contest.

Finally, not only was she extraordinarily accomplished at twenty-eight—the youngest and most successful detective on the force—she was undeniably attractive, with flawless skin, lively blue eyes, and a face that could well be at home on a Covergirl Clean Makeup advertisement.

Redford pulled himself from his reverie as they neared the helicopters and barked orders to his men. Moments later he and his two passengers were alone in one of the two aircraft, which could easily seat eight, waiting for takeoff. The helicopter possessed advanced stealth technology, making it completely invisible to radar and other sensors, although it still could be seen by the human eye at short distances.

They sat in silence for several minutes while the colonel issued silent instructions to Nessie.

Redford didn't know the first thing about flying a helicopter, but this model was a self-piloting prototype, which also sported other advanced technologies that were truly extraordinary. Even so, only a vanishingly small number of military personnel were authorized to fly it in self-flying mode. Crash avoidance was written into the system, so the aircraft could never be commandeered and used to ram buildings or stadiums full of people. In addition, the AI pilot had no access to weapon systems, as decades of science fiction had demonstrated the stupidity of this idea.

Redford had never flown without a pilot, but Anna's instructions had been quite clear about the need for urgency and privacy, both.

"Buckle up," he told his passengers. "I've instructed the helicopter to take us to Huntington. You can direct me further when we get close."

"You've instructed the *helicopter*?" repeated Anna. "Does that mean you're not a pilot?"

"I'm afraid not," said the colonel. "But the helicopter can pilot itself. So it will still be just the three of us going to Utah, as I agreed. And rest assured, no one can track us. I've had the transponder disabled, which only someone at a very high rank can make happen. I'm not boasting, just making it clear that I intend to live up to my part of the bargain."

"Thank you," said Anna.

"As an added insurance policy, to make sure we arrive safely, I've also ordered fighter aircraft to execute training drills from various bases all along our route. We'll be in full stealth mode, so they won't know we're there. But a fighter jet will always be within fifty miles of us throughout our journey. On my order, these fifty miles can be closed in less than two minutes."

"That's quite the protective detail," noted Anna, impressed.

"I trust that we won't need it," said the colonel. "But better to err on the side of paranoia. And speaking of paranoia," he added, "both of you should know that I still don't trust you entirely. Especially you, ah . . . Tom. No offense, but alien motivations are even less clear than human ones. So until I have proof of your goodwill, I don't intend to drop my guard."

"I don't blame you," said Vega.

"Me either," said Anna. "But help me out," she added uncertainly. "We've been with you this entire time, so when, exactly, did you issue all these complex orders?"

Redford grinned. "Fair question," he said. "I have electronic sensors in my throat, and I've practiced forming words subvocally that an AI friend of mine named Nessie can pick up. I hear her voice in a comm implanted in my ear."

"So you're one small step from having an AI in your head," said Anna.

"Essentially correct," replied the colonel.

"Interesting," said Vega. "This is basically identical to the system that we and the other extraterrestrial species on Earth are now using."

"Now that's something I wouldn't have guessed," said Redford.

"So when we were sitting here in silence," said Anna, "you were issuing orders to this Nessie?"

Redford nodded. "She's being kind enough to interface with the helicopter's AI to direct our trip to Huntington. She also issued the orders to scramble jets on practice runs along our route to ensure one is always relatively nearby. She's very good with logistics that way," he added with a smile.

"Then before we begin," said Anna, "you might want to have Nessie locate the Rest Easy Motel. I'm not exactly sure where it was, but we were there just prior to being brought here."

"She's found the address," said Redford almost immediately. "What about it?"

"You might want to send a few of your people there," replied Anna. "There's a blue Honda rental parked in front of room forty-nine. Inside the trunk is the body of yet another black-blooded alien."

"Of course there is," said Redford wryly. "Thanks for the tip. If I had to guess, I'd say this relates to the mess we found in the underground parking structure at the Camden International."

Anna smiled. "Good guess," she said. "I'll tell you all about what happened later. As I said, I don't plan to hold anything back."

Redford ordered Nessie to send his people to the Rest Easy Motel to retrieve the alien body as the detective had suggested, this time out loud.

"How long is the flight to Huntington?" asked Anna when he had finished.

"Nessie says about two and a half hours. I'm having her take off now. You can start bringing me up to speed once we're in the air. I can't begin to tell you how eager I am to hear what you have to say."

"Won't we need headphones?" asked Anna as the aircraft gently lifted from the ground and began to rise.

As the warehouse became a small dot and then vanished behind them, the answer to Anna's question became obvious, as the cabin remained almost perfectly quiet. "That's quite some noise-canceling technology you've got there," she said.

"Thanks," said the colonel. "It's the best there is." He paused. "Although I'm not sure why I said thanks," he added with a smile. "It's not like I invented it. Speaking of which, do you know how active noise-canceling systems work?"

Anna nodded. "I have it on a few surveillance drones I use. It's my understanding that these systems pick up ambient noise, analyze it, and generate counter sound waves—equal but opposite. Where the incoming wave has a high crest, the counter-wave will have an equally low trough, and vice versa. So the waves cancel each other out."

"Very good, Detective," said Redford. "The system this aircraft uses does exactly that, but better, faster, and more accurately than any other yet developed. And the counter-waves are stronger. It does calculations to ensure that the noise is zeroed out in front of each passenger's ears. Not only does it know not to cancel out our voices, it actually amplifies them a little."

"Impressive," said Anna. "If you close your eyes, you'd think you were in an executive conference room back on the ground."

"Nothing but the best for my clairvoyant friend and her alien emissary," he said with a smile. "So let me turn the stage over to the two of you. Ready to tell me what this is all about?"

"More than ready," said Anna. "But brace yourself," she added. "You've heard of drinking from a fire hose?"

Redford nodded.

"Well, this will be like drinking from a fire *hydrant*," she finished with no hint of exaggeration.

38

The two-and-a-half-hour flight seemed to be over in a flash, as their discussion was so engrossing they lost all sense of time. First Anna described what had happened at Salem Hills High and the Camden International, and how her instincts, which she had long honed, and her willingness to give herself over to her subconscious when necessary, could transform her martial arts and sharpshooting skills to rarefied levels.

When it came to extraterrestrials and the state of the galaxy, Redford was able to come up to speed even more quickly than Anna had managed. He had spent his entire career thinking and writing on the subject of extraterrestrials, and he was able to see certain implications of what he was being told without needing them spelled out.

Vega ended the discussion with the last bit of information he had shared with Anna. He told Redford how several Vorians had been eliminated, and provided additional background on what Anna had already told the colonel, that over six hundred additional Tarts had just arrived on Earth. Finally, Vega disclosed how he had refused to call for possible Vorian reinforcements when he and Anna were running for their lives, and the reasoning behind this decision.

This completed, Anna added her insights into the angel/demon nature of the historic conflict between the Vors and Tarts, and the colonel was just as astonished and intrigued as she had been. Anna could tell that if Redford died at that moment, he would die happy, knowing that he finally had answers to questions that had plagued him his entire life, as well as answers to questions he would have never even thought to ask.

Anna liked the colonel from the first moment they had met, and the positive signals she continued to receive from her hidden mind could not be stronger. He insisted that she and Vega call him Steve, to remove any barrier of formality between them, and the more they spoke, the more she trusted him.

And the more attracted to him she became.

But was she attracted to him simply because of her vision of them kissing? And if this was the case, and if this preview ultimately *led* to the embrace she had seen, had her vision of the future actually *caused* this future to come into being?

After she had told Redford about Foria, and that the Tarts were behind it, he had paused to issue a flurry of orders, scrambling US intelligence and military assets to LA, Chicago, and New York to find anyone involved and stamp out this drug with a vengeance. The force that he ordered to be assembled was authorized to use whatever resources were necessary, and do whatever it took, including invoking martial law, to destroy every last atom of Foria and anyone involved with its distribution. Handpicked members of Redford's own team would lead the charge, and would take over whenever the trail led to a Tartarian.

Finally, the colonel ordered any and all samples of the drug to be brought for analysis to the most advanced Black Laboratories in the country, where it would be treated with the respect, caution, and menace it deserved.

Anna had been fighting to get an FBI task force to investigate Foria, but Redford's powers seemed limitless, and what he was setting up would make her vaunted FBI task force look feeble. She had been alarmed by this drug, and wanted it weeded out, and now the might and resources of the US military were being pressed into doing just that.

Given everything she had learned, this development messed with her head in a big way. Had she just been lucky? Or was her subconscious mind as powerful as Vega thought, orchestrating events to achieve this remarkable result?

She still couldn't believe this was the case—her powers were much too weak—but it was definitely food for thought.

They finally made it to their destination, not having encountered a whiff of trouble along the way, and landed in the middle of a barren stretch of desert that turned out to be nothing of the sort. Once they exited the helicopter, they found themselves on a compound spread out over ten acres of desert, with four expansive ranch houses in close proximity, two serving as living quarters, and two as offices and labs. The entire compound had been absolutely invisible until Vega had pressed a button, and then it had materialized in an instant.

Vega also let it be known that they had constructed a single long runway two miles distant, also invisible, and a small hangar containing several private jets capable of international travel, and a number of helicopters. He and most of his fellow Vorians had become licensed to fly both types of aircraft.

Their alien host led them to the closest ranch house, where they took bathroom breaks, and where he fed them a much-needed brunch from a surprisingly well-stocked refrigerator and cupboard. Finally, with their bladders emptied and food in their stomachs, their alien friend introduced them to two of the four Vorians stationed there.

Tom Vega was a jack of all trades, a leader and problem solver. He had been the first of the current Vors to go through the portal, and was in charge of the entire Vorian contingent. All four of his underlings at the facility, on the other hand, were scientists. And while none of them were soldiers, each had undergone extensive military training on Vor prior to the mission.

Two other Vors were absent, currently visiting Silicon Valley, where they were buying experimental technology they could use to construct an array of specialized transmitters. These transmitters would provide protection if the Tarts ever found the Vorian base. The devices would be spread out about a quarter mile away from the central ranch house, surrounding the compound with a twenty-foot-thick ribbon of sound, like an invisible fence used by a dog owner. The frequencies it produced would be inaudible to both humans and Vors, but would be agonizing, debilitating, to any Tart who tried to cross the threshold. And it would even thwart any noise-canceling technology that the Tarts might use, generating a tangential wave that could actually counter the counter-wave, keeping the original sound pure and at full intensity.

The two Vors they did meet were both females, with features similar to human females, at least while clothed. Both looked as if they could have been Vega's sisters. Baby-faced and slender, with flawless complexions, hairless arms and legs, and eyes that were slightly too big.

The first introduced herself as Lisa Moore, and the second as Kaitlyn O'Connor. They explained that their names had been chosen using a random name generator, as had Vega's. Kaitlyn was the Vor's chief scientist on Earth, and Lisa was their expert in genetic engineering. Both also served as medics, having been trained in human and Vorian physiology alike before arriving on Earth. Kaitlyn had been overseas until just the night before, when she had rushed to Utah in the hope of meeting Anna.

After the introductions were out of the way, the three Vors gave Anna and the colonel a quick tour of their labs and facilities, which were top of the line. Anna was particularly interested in the chemistry labs.

"So is this where you store the cure for the Tarts' demonic possession drug?" she asked.

"It will be soon," said Vega. "We weren't aware there were any Tarts on the planet until just last night, as you know. Now that we are, we'll be sure to have the antidote on hand. But I'm told our lab is short one of the needed ingredients, methyl-chloro-hexadiene. We're having some delivered to a PO Box in town, which is scheduled to arrive in a few days. After that, we'll be able to whip up a batch in no time."

"What about your memory erasure drug?" asked Redford. This was one he was particularly interested in. He had been working with a Black Laboratory trying to perfect such a drug, but so far the project had been a total failure.

Vega gestured to a wall of cupboards at the far end of the lab. "We have about twenty of these pills in a bottle in the first cupboard. As I said earlier, we haven't used any yet. Now that our presence here has been discovered, I doubt we'll ever have the need."

"How do they work?" asked Redford. "Do you need complicated computer and medical equipment to actually excise the memories after the pill is taken?"

"Not at all," said Vega. "Once taken, the subject is in what you might call a hypnotic state for several minutes. During this time, you just have to have a subject recall certain specific memories, and then order them to forget them forever."

"Sounds a lot like the Tarts' zombie drug," said Anna disapprovingly.

"Not at all," said Vega. "Yes, you can direct an unwitting human subject, but only during the few minutes the hypnotic state lasts, and only when it comes to memory erasure. If you tried to direct someone to do your bidding after the drug wore off, it wouldn't work."

Anna nodded, but she was still troubled by the concept of memory erasure. Once again, she filed this away to revisit at another time.

They finished the tour and returned to one of the ranch homes that served as a residence, ending up in a magnificent library, complete with actual, physical books, and a sizable conference table. The library, like the entire house it was in, had been designed to be as comfortable to a human being as possible, so that it could become the residence of the eventual winner of the Vors' Oracle lottery.

The two humans sat on one side of the table, and the three Vorians on the other, with Vega in the middle, Lisa Moore to his right, and Kaitlyn O'Connor to his left. A pitcher of ice water was in the center of the table, and Vega poured them each a glass as if he were hosting a tea party rather than one of the most important meetings in the history of both species.

"Your facilities are impressive," said Redford when they began. "How did you do it?"

"I don't understand," said Vega.

"You've only been on Earth three years, right?" said the colonel. "You came knowing nothing about our current society. And you possessed nothing, other than gold. You had to learn our languages, technology, customs, and so on. So how did you get from there," he added, gesturing all around him to encompass the entire compound, "to *here*, so quickly?"

"Our conscious IQs are very high, and our conscious minds are much more adept at soaking up information than yours. So learning what we needed to learn took us a fraction of the time it would have taken you. Also, we spent many years back on Vor training and planning our steps once we arrived here. And our minds were . . . programmed, if you will, to convert Vorian expressions into human ones, since they don't match. We can switch this programming on and off at will."

"Thanks, Tom, but you already touched on all of these points in the helicopter."

"Right," said Vega. "Given the limitations of your conscious memory, I thought you might have forgotten."

The colonel laughed. "Trust me, I might forget the name of the street a friend lives on. But I'll never forget a word of my first conversation with an extraterrestrial."

Redford paused. "Let me ask the question a different way," he said. "The construction of this compound, alone, must have taken enormous amounts of money and resources. I mean, hell, you have your own private jets here, which run ten to twenty million dollars apiece. And you're also financing other facilities and activities around the globe. So how did you possibly manage it?"

"Now I see what you're asking," said Vega. "The answer is that since we're more advanced than you technologically, we're able to raise money very quickly. Almost a hundred million dollars so far. A dozen of our people began selling scientific advances to corporations around the world as soon as they got their Earth-legs under them."

A disturbed look flashed over Redford's face. "Please tell me you didn't sell the tech that makes this facility invisible."

Vega shook his head. "Not a chance," he replied emphatically. "Only things like improvements in manufacturing and logistics. Or mathematical advances only useful to software engineers. Or cheaper optical processing. That sort of thing. Nothing that would make the papers. Nothing flashy."

Redford exhaled loudly. "That's a relief," he said. "Because your invisibility tech makes what we have look primitive. We can't afford it getting into enemy hands. And our own military would *kill* for it."

"I trust you're using the word *kill* metaphorically," said Vega.

"Yeah. Sure," said the colonel, in such a way that suggested even he didn't know just how literal this statement might be. "But not to worry," he added. "No one will hear about the tech from me."

"As an interesting aside," said Vega, "we developed the invisibility technology on Vor for our use here if the portal ever reopened. And assuming you had enough sophisticated technology for us to build it when we arrived. Not even the Tarts have anything this advanced," he added. "Not that it gives us any real advantage in the war effort back home, since it can't be used to cloak a starship."

"So just how far ahead of us are you tech and science-wise?" asked Redford. "How long until we're completely stalled out like the other twenty-seven intelligences?"

Vega nodded to the Vor named Kaitlyn O'Connor to reply

"Well," said the Vorian chief scientist, "none of us are *completely* stalled out, as I'm sure Tom has told you. We continue to make progress, as evidenced by our light-amplifying and invisibility tech. But this progress is relatively minor. Evolutionary, not revolutionary.

"But to answer your question," she continued, "I'd estimate that humanity will hit the externally imposed Omega Point in about fifty of your years. Maybe less. The Gatekeepers—or if you don't believe in them, the laws of nature, our own incompetence, what have you—seem to keep the tightest leash on advanced genetic engineering, neuronal engineering, runaway computer evolution, and nanotechnology. So you'll catch up even faster in these areas."

"Why would they rein in nanotech?" asked Anna.

"If I were to guess," replied Kaitlyn, frowning, "it's because by now we should be able to perform miracles in this area. I suppose the Gatekeepers believe that if we become adept at building anything we want in the material realm, one atom at a time, we could become invincible, immortal. We could build artificial constructs to beam our consciousness inside, and so on, and eventually bypass their control."

Redford opened his mouth to ask another question, but Vega interrupted. "I'm going to have to ask that we table further discussion on these topics. For now. Sorry for cutting you off so abruptly like this, but in the interest of time, I'd like to begin the discussion I brought Anna here to have. The scientific rationale for clairvoyance. And how we propose to enhance her abilities."

Anna nodded. "Okay," she said uneasily, visibly bracing herself. "Let's do this. I'm all ears."

39

"I'll ask Kaitlyn to lead the clairvoyance discussion as well," said Vega.

Both humans nodded and turned to the most accomplished scientist in the room.

Kaitlyn paused to decide the best way to begin, and Anna used these few seconds to check her gut. Although she wasn't picking up any clairvoyant signals, her non-clairvoyant instincts told her that Redford was placing considerable faith in her. In both her good intentions and her intuition. He would be loyal to the cause and trust Vega until he was given reason to do otherwise, although he hadn't forgotten he and Anna were vulnerable and were putting their lives in the Vorians' hands.

If the aliens turned on them, they were unlikely to survive, and then Earth would go back to being blissfully unaware of all that was extraterrestrial on the planet. A disastrous outcome. Yet, despite the colonel's instinct for caution, he was willing to trust Anna's call on this.

It was obvious even to her conscious mind that Steve Redford was in heaven. Getting the chance to have a face-to-face meeting with actual extraterrestrials was something he had dreamed of his entire life. It was a powerful, almost religious experience for him, and he could barely contain his enthusiasm.

And when it came to enthusiasm, Anna's intuition also indicated that he was falling for her as much as she was falling for him. A chemical reaction that she was more certain than ever would result in the embrace she had foreseen. This certainty of his interest was driven by signals picked up by her subconscious alone, since it wasn't as if he had the time for flirtation, or to deliver other overt signs.

As expected, Anna's intuition wasn't able to get a particularly clean read on the aliens calling themselves Lisa Moore and Kaitlyn O'Connor, since her hidden mind had almost no experience with their species. Still, as was the case with Vega, she sensed they had good intentions.

"How much do the two of you know about consciousness?" began the Vorian chief scientist finally. "About what makes us sentient? What separates us from computers?"

"I've studied this subject fairly thoroughly," said Redford.

Anna smiled. "And I know surprisingly little about it," she admitted. "I've mostly focused on the subconscious."

Kaitlyn nodded. "Your scientists call it the *hard problem* of consciousness," she said. "And in that, they are correct. What makes a squishy three-pound lump of insensate matter suddenly become self-aware? Suddenly have hopes, and dreams, and imagination, and inspiration? Suddenly have an appreciation for the color red, or for the scent of cinnamon?"

She paused to let the humans consider these questions for a moment. "All biological intelligences across the galaxy are conscious," she continued. "But why aren't super sophisticated computers? Many years ago humanity created an artificial intelligence that could beat the best human players in a TV gameshow called *Jeopardy*. But this AI certainly wasn't conscious. It could win, but it couldn't understand what it meant to win, or care in any way. It couldn't feel pride, or joy, or a sense of accomplishment. It couldn't feel embarrassment that a human occasionally was able to beat it to the buzzer. Or boredom when it wasn't engaged. Or excitement when it was working on a challenging problem.

"Computers can be built to pass the Turing test," continued Kaitlyn. "To produce responses in conversation that can fool a sentient being into believing that *it's* sentient. Like a parrot, mouthing words without comprehension. Following a fixed set of instructions from which it can't really deviate.

"But consciousness *can* deviate. It *can* be unpredictable, go off script. Respond a different way to the same stimulus. A computer will always respond to the same input with the same output. And yes,

those as sophisticated as the colonel here will know this last statement isn't precisely accurate, but for the sake of our discussion, it's
accurate enough. But it's safe to say that no computer can marvel at a
sunset, have an epiphany, dream of a better future, or regret an action
taken in the past."

"You've framed the question well," said Redford. "So can we assume you're going to give us the answer? Tell us the magic ingredient
the brain has that a computer doesn't?"

"Yes," said Kaitlyn. "I will in just a moment. But I should tell
you that a few of your scientists have figured out the answer on
their own. Although it's an answer that has yet to be accepted by the
mainstream."

The Vorian chief scientist took a long drink of water, and Anna
took the chance to do the same. "What do the two of you know
about the quantum realm?" she asked, changing subjects.

"A fair amount," said Redford. "I've read four or five books on
the subject."

"Nobody likes a showoff, Steve," said Anna with a broad grin.

The colonel laughed.

"I've played audiobooks on quantum physics while I was sleeping," said Anna. "So my subconscious probably knows all about it. I,
on the other hand, know almost nothing. All I know is that when you
want something to sound mysterious, and science-fictiony, you just
throw the word *quantum* in front of it."

"That's not too far off," said Kaitlyn in amusement. "Actually, humanity has learned quite a lot about quantum reality, but is still only
scratching the surface. Basically, this field involves the inconceivably
small. Much that goes on in the quantum realm is completely counterintuitive to how you've come to see reality, but even your scientists
have proven these bizarre phenomena beyond the shadow of a doubt.
You don't understand the *why* of it, or how it could possibly be like
this. But you have used quantum theory in your computer industry
and elsewhere to revolutionize your world."

The chief scientist paused. "I'll just give you a brief overview
of some of the quantum craziness I'm talking about," she said.
"Electromagnetic radiation and other submicroscopic particles in the

quantum realm travel as waves of probability. While this is happening, they don't exist at any given place. In fact, they exist at all places at once. Until a conscious observer takes a look, observes a particle, and then it collapses to a discrete location. Most important for our discussion is the random nature of the quantum realm. Particles mostly collapse to where you'd expect them to be, but they're all probabilistic, so they could appear *anywhere*. In fact, particles are constantly popping into existence like magic, and then back out again, like infinite fireflies blinking on and off inside the vacuum of the empty void."

She paused to let this sink in. "And this activity is totally random. Strangest of all, when two particles are born, or interact in certain ways, they become what is called *entangled*. In this state, if one lands heads, the other always lands tails. No matter how far apart they are."

Anna blinked in confusion. "I get that heads and tails are just a metaphor for opposite properties," she said, "but I'm still not following."

"I'll give you a better explanation," said Kaitlyn. "But even after I do, you won't be able to wrap your head around it. Einstein never could. Or any of your scientists, for that matter. Your scientists know the truth of it, just not the how or why of it."

She paused in thought. "Imagine you entangle two coins and set them spinning. While they're still spinning you separate them by the length of the entire universe. Then you force one of them to land. Well, if it lands heads, the other will instantly collapse and show tails. And if the first lands tails, the other will collapse and show heads. *Instantly*. Despite being separated by many billions of light-years. They're connected somehow across this vast distance, and this connection makes itself known at basically infinite speed."

Anna smiled. "Of course it does," she said sarcastically. "How could Einstein possibly be confused by something as obvious as *that*?" The detective shook her head. "Look, I think I've heard enough quantum science that I'll never understand. Why does this have anything to do with consciousness?"

"Because consciousness is a quantum phenomenon," whispered Redford, almost to himself. "It operates in the quantum realm, which is what introduces randomness into the works. Creates free will, unpredictability. Allows sentient minds to go off script."

"Right you are, Colonel," said Kaitlyn cheerfully. "Consciousness makes use of quantum phenomena that biological systems are uniquely evolved to tap into. But which electronic systems are not. Even quantum computers can't make use of quantum properties in the same way that biological systems can. This quantum weirdness, as your people have so often called it, is what ultimately allows sentient minds to become self-aware. And your scientists will eventually learn that the quantum world is much weirder even than they think it is."

"Okay," said Anna. "I understand very little of what you've been saying, but this makes some sense to me."

"Good," said Kaitlyn. "It makes sense to many of your scientists, also—in theory. But only a few think that it's possible. Your physicists have only been able to create the quantum effects consciousness would require in the lab, under very complicated and restrictive conditions. These conditions include ultra-cold temperatures and sophisticated shielding to protect against even the slightest interference. Until very recently, none of your physicists could conceive of the necessary quantum phenomena taking place in such a warm, wet, and noisy environment as the brain."

Redford's eyes widened. "Are you saying the Penrose-Hameroff model is right?" he said in awe. "Do you know this for certain?"

"You really are quite impressive," said Kaitlyn with a smile. "For a human being," she added, attempting her first joke. "But for Anna's benefit, let's back up."

She turned to the detective. "Colonel Redford is referencing a theory introduced by Stuart Hameroff, an anesthesiologist, several decades ago, and Sir Roger Penrose, a legendary mathematical physicist. Hameroff was always fascinated by the hard problem of consciousness, and took up anesthesiology to pursue this further."

"Why anesthesiology?" asked Anna.

"The brain of a human patient under anesthesia is basically normal in every way," replied the chief scientist, "with one notable exception. It isn't conscious. Neurons fire, pain signals travel normally, and so on. But the pain never registers. Somehow, everything works just fine, all except subjective experiences, which are eliminated."

Anna nodded thoughtfully. "Very interesting," she said. "So what theory did he come up with?"

"Like others, Hameroff thought it made sense that consciousness was a quantum effect," replied Kaitlyn. "But neurons were too large to make use of these effects. So he theorized that structures called microtubules were the actual engine of the brain. These tiny, sub-microscopic structures are like the Legos of the biological world, found in every plant and animal cell on Earth. They're very versatile. They act as structural elements in the cell, pull chromosomes apart during cell division, form into cilia and flagella to allow for cellular movement, and so on.

"Hameroff concluded that these microtubules were *the* key structures in the brain, even more so than neurons, after studying paramecia."

Anna rolled her eyes. "Of course he did," she said. "Because when you think about human consciousness, you think about paramecia."

Redford laughed again as Kaitlyn continued, her expression unchanged. "Paramecia are single-celled, freshwater animals," she explained, "that have no central nervous system, no brain, and no neurons. Still, they're able to swim, find food, find mates, and avoid danger. These are rudimentary responses. Still, Hameroff came to believe that these responses required a form of crude cognition, which he concluded had to take place in microtubules, the paramecium's only internal structure."

"This is fascinating," said Anna, "but just to fast-forward, are you saying that Hameroff was right? Is that what you're getting at?"

"Yes," replied Kaitlyn simply. "Microtubules are the key ingredient for human consciousness, and are able to exhibit quantum effects. Even in the warm, wet, and noisy environment of the brain."

"I'll be damned," said Redford. "Even though Hameroff teamed up with Penrose, who had a stellar reputation, their theory has been ridiculed for decades."

"This is true," said Kaitlyn. "But your scientists are beginning to generate evidence that supports it. I estimate that in another seven to ten years, it will be hailed as the breakthrough that it is."

"What evidence?" said Redford.

"For one thing," replied Kaitlyn, "your scientists are coming to believe that photosynthesis relies on quantum effects. That it couldn't be as efficient as it is without them. And if quantum effects can take place in plants, why can't they take place in the brain?"

She paused. "Other recent experiments speak directly to microtubules in the brain. Anesthetic drugs have been shown to destabilize them. If you protect the microtubules from this effect, the drugs no longer work. This leaves little doubt that microtubules play some role in consciousness. And if you apply a current to microtubules inside axons, this can cause neurons to fire, or to stop firing. In fact, it's been found that these microtubules can resonate like guitar strings, firing thousands of times faster than neurons. Not only that, but when specific charges of alternating currents are applied, the microtubules take on the electrical properties of a semiconductor, which is truly a stunning result."

"Fascinating," said the colonel.

"I'm not trying to diminish the importance of what you're telling us," said Anna. "But even if microtubules are the magic ingredient leading to consciousness, what does this have to do with clairvoyance?"

"Everything," said Kaitlyn simply. "All twenty-eight known intelligent species have a form of these structures in their brains. They're all different, but they largely serve the same purpose. But *human* microtubules, and *human* minds, are unique. First, your microtubules are much more active in the subconscious than in the conscious. And unlike the rest of the known intelligences, human microtubules are able to receive quantum signals from the future—which are continuously being broadcast back."

Anna's eyes narrowed. "Continuously being broadcast back?" she repeated. "What in the hell does *that* mean?"

"Time travel is impossible," said Kaitlyn. "This much is true. But in the quantum realm, future events affect the present. Your scientists are only now beginning to appreciate this. You call it retrocausality. Cause and effect in reverse. What you eat tomorrow gives you a stomachache today. Your fall tomorrow causes a bruise today. Like that, but in the quantum realm."

"That sounds ridiculous," said Anna.

"I know it does," said Kaitlyn. "But the ridiculous is par for the course in the quantum world. It's well known, even to humans, that the laws of physics work perfectly well in either time direction: forward *or* backward. Richard Feynman showed that anti-matter is identical, mathematically, to ordinary matter traveling backward in time. He used this insight to develop a tool, called Feynman diagrams, that revolutionized nearly every aspect of theoretical physics. So much so that he was awarded the Nobel Prize for this work."

Kaitlyn paused. "There are experiments that even your scientists have done that hint at retrocausality, but they're much too complicated to describe, and require knowledge of advanced mathematics. Some involve the entanglement phenomenon, which suggest that the instantaneous signaling between two particles separated by staggering distances can only be explained by communication through time. It's also known to your science that if you take two radioactive atoms, absolutely identical in every conceivable way, they will decay randomly. The first might decay immediately, while the second doesn't do the same for an hour or more. Why the difference? After all, they're identical. Scientists have never found any way to explain it, or predict when this decay will occur. But evidence is slowly emerging, even here on Earth, that this is because the information that controls the fate of these particles doesn't come from the past or present. It comes from the future. Cause and effect in reverse."

The colonel looked mesmerized. "So let me get this right," he began. "You're saying that not only can Anna's microtubules read these quantum signals from the future, but her mind can actually make sense of them."

"Exactly," replied Kaitlyn. "Yours can too. All human minds can. But this takes place solely in the subconscious, so only one in five million of you has any chance of becoming aware of it. We believe this ability to see the future is so rare because it was weeded out by natural selection. The conscious minds of your primitive ancestors had more than enough information to sort through in their *present*, without becoming befuddled by an avalanche of sometimes opaque information coming from their future. Perhaps those who became engrossed in these future visions neglected the present, with disastrous consequences. Cause and effect, and immediacy, provide simple rules for survival. A maelstrom of threats coming from an indeterminate time in the future would slow reaction times and attention. Potentially lethal in primitive times, when humanity faced a constant battle for survival."

"So you're suggesting that natural selection led to a firm barrier between the subconscious and the conscious," said Redford.

"Possibly, yes," said the chief scientist. "Those whose conscious minds could easily pick up clairvoyant visions from their subconscious minds were weeded out—in favor of those whose conscious minds were blissfully unburdened by future signals." She shrugged. "But this is just speculation."

Redford nodded thoughtfully, soaking it all in. "Getting back to the topic," he said, "you've told us that all other intelligences have versions of microtubules, which lead to consciousness. But none of these lead to clairvoyance. So what's different about ours?"

"Yours are able to somehow vibrate at the right frequency to pick up these future quantum signals," said Kaitlyn. "Like a tuning fork. And while we've tried to modify ours using genetic engineering to match yours, this alone isn't enough. It's not just the microtubules, but their interactions with your neuronal structures and the architecture of your brains. It's a perfect storm that we believe none of the other twenty-seven intelligences can duplicate, even given genetic engineering. And even if we could, we believe that this capability in a conscious mind would draw unwanted attention from the Gatekeepers."

"Which is where Anna comes in," said Redford.

"Which is where Anna comes in," agreed the alien known as Tom Vega.

40

There was a long silence in the library as the two humans considered everything that had been said. Anna could tell that Redford had been won over by Kaitlyn's presentation. He had been so sure there could never be a scientific justification for clairvoyance, but the Vors had turned him into a believer.

Anna sighed. "If you did enhance my abilities," she asked, "wouldn't I be overwhelmed by future visions? The very reason you speculate that people like me are practically extinct?"

"Not at all," said Kaitlyn. "Our computers modeled this possibility also. As you just said, this theory of ours is only speculation. But even if it is true, you'll still be fine. The early hominids who tapped into the future, whom we believe natural selection may have weeded out, were not like you. Our theory supposes that the clairvoyant channel between *their* subconscious and conscious minds was wide open. Full throttle. But yours is mostly closed, allowing only a trickle of the visions your subconscious mind receives to get to you. So you'll have the best of both worlds. You aren't inundated with a maelstrom of visions, but you can get them when they're desperately needed. And we have reason to believe you'll ultimately be able to exert a reasonable level of control over the process."

Anna thought about this. It did make sense. She had recently had visions, which were disconcerting, but this was her first experience with them, and she was still quite able to focus on the present.

"And if I were to agree to have my clairvoyance augmented," she said, "how would you do it?"

"I'll ask Lisa to field that one," said Vega.

Anna studied the Vorian medic and genetic engineer, but her intuition continued to draw a blank.

"The genetic material for all twenty-eight species differs in a number of ways," began the Vor named Lisa. "But there are also considerable similarities. And processes like mitosis, meiosis, protein synthesis, energy production, and so on are even more similar. I studied human DNA and the human genome for many years on Vor, using knowledge and computers beyond what you have here. I was able to design gene therapy constructs that can alter microtubule production and location in your brains. Since I've been here, I've been able to acquire the proper human equipment to make these constructs, and to encapsulate them in pill form."

"So I just have to take a pill?" said Anna dubiously. "That's it? And then my genes suddenly begin spitting out superior microtubules?"

Lisa nodded. "More or less, yes," she replied. "Once the gene cocktail in the pill activates the proper genes in the proper way, they should stay on. Our modeling has suggested that just a minor tweak in your microtubules will dramatically improve their ability to resonate with quantum signals from the future. Right now they work, but it's like receiving music on the very edge of a radio band, which comes in mostly as static. This will be like tuning in to the dead center of the signal, with no static whatsoever. Exquisitely sensitive."

"But even so," Vega hastened to add, "the partition between your two brains will still only allow a trickle of these visions through. And only on certain occasions. Your hidden mind was only getting a faint signal, and you were only receiving a fraction of *that*. After your microtubules are enhanced, what does make it through to your conscious mind will contain more meaningful information."

"It all sounds fascinating," said Anna. "But I don't love the idea of having my brain screwed with. Won't this alter my consciousness? Or worse? How do we even know it won't kill me? It's great that your advanced computers are satisfied that it's safe, but I'm not about to trust my life to your modeling."

"We never would either," insisted Vega. "We've been looking for you for thousands of years. Do you really think we'd take any risk, whatsoever, with your life?"

He shook his head. "We've given this pill to dozens of well-paid human volunteers, although we lied to them about its purpose. And we studied them extensively, before and after. They didn't experience the slightest change in intelligence, personality, or behavior. We followed up for over a year, and they still have the same spouses, friends, jobs, and so on, and are as well-adjusted after the pill as they ever were before."

"Did it improve their clairvoyance?" said Redford.

"We think it did, yes," replied Lisa. "But unlike Anna, who has a certain porosity between her two minds, they weren't able to receive any signals from their subconscious. So there is no way to be sure. The bottom line is that it didn't affect their health or welfare in any way. And no group of people has ever been more thoroughly examined."

"So you did this to be sure you wouldn't put your precious Oracle at risk," said Anna, "whoever that turned out to be. But you didn't care about putting your guinea pigs at risk, did you?

Vega frowned. "We did have concerns, yes. Especially with the first few we tried it on. But our computers indicated that the risks were exceedingly small. And we had to know. I'm sorry, Anna, but my conscience is clear. We're talking fate of the galaxy here."

Anna sighed. "Funny," she said, "that doesn't sound nearly as preposterous as it did last night. Still preposterous, I'm not going to lie. But gaining ground."

Vega smiled. "Good. Aren't you glad you agreed to dinner last night?"

"Worst decision of my life," replied Anna in amusement. "And how in the world is it still only Friday?" she added.

"There's no question that much has happened since the restaurant," allowed Vega, uttering what might be the biggest understatement in history. He leaned forward intently. "So what do you think, Anna? Should we proceed?"

"How long will the process take?" asked the detective. "And what am I likely to experience?"

"Not long," said Lisa. "When you take the pill, we'll also give you a sedative. While you're sleeping, your genes will flood your subconscious brain with improved microtubules, and your subconscious will have full rein of your mind to begin to adjust to its enhanced capabilities. We believe that you'll already begin noticing an improvement in precognition upon awakening. Greater clarity and range. But your abilities will continue to grow after that. We can't be sure how quickly, but your subconscious will continue to hone its mastery of these skills through practice and trial and error."

Lisa paused. "We also believe that you'll eventually develop a greater conscious control of this ability than you have now. It won't be perfect control, but it will be much better. You'll be able to focus on the futures that you want to see, and not on those you don't."

The room became silent, and all eyes turned toward the detective as she decided what to do.

Anna knew she was contemplating the unknown. A scary unknown, since she was considering altering the structure of her own brain. And once she stepped off this cliff, there was no returning. She was also putting an extraordinary level of trust into these aliens. Into their veracity, their motives, their computer models, and their judgment.

Still, her gut continued to urge her on, telling her that the waters were safe. Not only safe, but inviting. She just hoped that her hidden mind, and she, weren't at cross purposes this time.

Regardless, she decided that she had to take this leap of faith. This was her chance to rise above. To matter. She was the lottery winner who happened to have the right brain structure, and who had trained herself to take advantage of it.

Maybe she *could* prove decisive in an endless galactic war. She was still skeptical, but would she have believed *any* of this the day before?

Not a chance in hell.

And if there was any possibility that the Vors were right, how could she refuse to do what she could to help? Even if they were wrong, the Tarts were a looming crisis, and her intuition and clairvoyance could certainly help in this regard.

Anna blew out a long breath. "I'm in," she said finally. "When do we start?"

41

Anna's eyes fluttered open and she found herself on a king-sized mattress so thick that a bagful of doorknobs underneath wouldn't have impinged upon her sleep in the slightest. The wound on her upper arm was almost completely healed, presumably by some magic process known to the Vors, and she was showered and dressed in fresh jeans and a T-shirt, provided to her the day before by her benefactors.

She felt fantastic. She glanced at a digital clock on an end table, which read 7:00 a.m. She had slept for more than seventeen hours, and all the events since her dinner with Tom Vega came rushing back to her. After two never-ending days, punctuated by only a few hours' sleep, and after fighting off both human and alien adversaries, her body and mind had been more desperate for sleep than she had realized.

The last thing she remembered was the colonel contacting his people to tell them that he was on a secret mission, which he couldn't disclose, and to be ready to carry out an avalanche of orders at a moment's notice. And then she had taken the magic pill, along with a sedative.

The detective freshened up in the bathroom and then wandered into the main house, where the four other current residents quickly assembled as if they were part of a military drill, having eagerly awaited her emergence.

A lavish buffet breakfast had been laid out on the vast quartzite island in the kitchen, and Anna realized she was starving. Tom Vega checked her vital signs, reflexes, and other simple measures of health in between breakfast courses, and deemed the results to be good.

The group engaged in small talk while she ate, but once breakfast was over, Vega asked that they retire once again to the library, and to the conference table, which now contained a deck of cards and a digital timer.

"Having any visions?" Vega asked her while they all took their seats as before, with the exception that Redford was now seated across from her, with the cards in front of him.

The detective shook her head. "None that I'm aware of," she replied. "I don't feel any different."

Anna smiled. "Well, that isn't quite true," she amended. "I feel spectacular. Like a new woman. But that's just the sleep talking."

"Still very nice to hear," said Kaitlyn. "So let me tell you why you're seated here," she continued. "We'd like to get a baseline read on your abilities. Get a sense of just where you are on the clairvoyance scale."

"Didn't know there was such a thing," said Anna.

"There isn't," said Vega with a smile. "But we're trying to create one."

"What did you have in mind?" she asked.

"The four of us had lengthy discussions while you were asleep," replied Vega, "about how best to test you. And about possible aspects of your abilities we wanted to explore. Colonel Redford—Steve," he corrected, as the colonel had continued to insist that he be addressed informally, "was quite helpful. He only has a human conscious mind, but it's very sharp, and very well trained."

"Thanks," said Redford. "I think," he added in amusement, and then quickly returned his affectionate eyes to Anna's face, where they seemed to enjoy dwelling.

"Okay, Anna," began the alien leader. "We'd like to do a few different types of tests. I'll tell you about each as we get to them. First, we'll ask you to tell us the card on top of the deck. After ten seconds, Steve will turn the card up for all of us to see. When we've run through all the tests, we'll come back to this one and repeat it many times, each time with a longer delay before revealing the cards."

Anna confirmed her understanding and signaled her readiness, and less than five minutes later they had run the first test ten times. She had guessed the right card correctly in all cases. For eight of the trials the card's identity had come to her as a hunch, while for the other two, she had actually flashed on an image of Redford turning it up. She had no doubt her clairvoyant abilities had already seen a dramatic boost, as Lisa Moore had predicted.

The entire group was delighted by these results.

"There is one thing I don't understand," said Anna when they had finished the first round. "I was right for all ten cards. But I'm not receiving any subconscious signals as to what others in the room might *say*, the words that they're about to speak. Why would that be?"

There was a long silence in the room as everyone considered this question, and everyone was equally stumped.

"This is a tough one," said Kaitlyn finally. "If I had to guess, I'd say it's because the card task is a lot easier. It's very well defined. Your subconscious has been told exactly what will happen, and exactly when. And the identity of the card won't change based on subtle things you do. But the response of a sentient being with a quantum consciousness might. So perhaps when you're interacting with another consciousness, their future responses are harder for you to see, since there are an infinite number of ways you can unknowingly impact them by your own actions."

Anna thought about this. "You may be right," she said. "But as I listened to you, I realized there's another good reason I wasn't able to *see* what your answer would be just now. It was very complex, and my hidden mind is a poor communicator. It's relatively easy for my subconscious to implant a hunch in my conscious mind that the next card will be the king of diamonds. A lot harder to communicate what you just said," she added with a smile.

Kaitlyn nodded. "You make an excellent point."

"I guess I'm ready to move on to the next test," said Anna.

"Okay then," said Vega. "This test will be the same as the first one, with the following exception. When you have a *vision* of Steve turning the card up—and not just a hunch—tell us. And then tell us the identity of the card, as usual."

Anna nodded her understanding and the test began. During the third trial she let the group know that she had seen an image of the colonel turning over the five of clubs.

Redford eyed the Vorians anxiously. "Okay then," he said. "Let's see if we can change the future." Anna noted that he was clenching his teeth, as if lightning might come out of nowhere and strike him dead for having the audacity to even suggest such a thing.

"Time!" said Vega, as he had done on twelve previous occasions when the timer hit zero.

But this time, instead of turning the card face up to reveal it to Anna, Redford shoved it into the middle of the deck.

Anna raised her eyebrows. "I assume you discussed this test and this possible outcome while I was sleeping," she said.

"We did," said Vega.

"So can one of you walk me through the significance of what just happened?"

"Gladly," said the colonel. "When you first tried to demonstrate your clairvoyance to me at the warehouse, you had no idea what number I had in my head. That must have been because there was no future in which I remembered to actually *tell it to you* in a timely manner. But here, I had every intention of showing you the card on time. I vowed to deviate from this plan only if I received new information from you. Namely, that you had actually *seen* me turn over the card in the future."

Anna paused in thought. "So there *was* a future in which you showed me the card," she said. "The future I saw. But you were able to change things so that future never came about."

"Exactly," said Lisa excitedly.

"Now let's do a variation of this experiment," said Vega, handing her a notepad and pen. "This time I'd like you to write the numbers one through ten on the pad. Then we'll begin. For each trial, if your subconscious provides you with the identity of the card, write a Y next to the trial number. If it doesn't, write an N. But put the pad below the table so Steve can't see what you're writing."

"Are you going to tell me why?"

"We will when we're through," said Vega. "Ready?"

Anna indicated that she was, and minutes later the experiment was complete, accompanied by broad grins all around. For the first five trials, after Anna had written a Y or an N each time, Redford had randomly decided whether to go through with showing her the card, or not. Some he showed her at ten seconds, as planned, and some he buried. For the second set of five trials, after Anna had written a Y or an N, Redford had flipped a coin, showing her the card if it landed heads, and burying it if it landed tails.

The results were conclusive. Anna's clairvoyance had known the identity of every card Redford had ended up turning over. And it had not known the identity of every card he had ended up burying.

"Okay," said Anna, "so what does *this* mean?"

"It means that your clairvoyance can't be fooled," said Vega excitedly. "It means that only you have any free will when it comes to the future. Whatever future Steve chose, using his free will or a random coin, was the future that you had *already* seen come into being."

"But he *was* able to change the future in the previous experiment," said Anna. "He was able to bury a card after I had seen it in an alternate future."

Redford nodded. "Yes, but only because in that experiment," he said, "you provided *information* about the future. Before I made my choice. You told me you saw me turn the card up in the future, so I could then choose to bury it, instead. That's the only way we mortals can alter what you see coming. Otherwise, anyone who'd like to change the future you see will fail every time."

Anna pondered this while the group waited patiently for her to reach the proper conclusions. "I think I understand," she began tentatively, clearly straining to keep the logic straight. "When I told you I had seen you turn up the five of clubs, you had the free will to bury it instead. And this changed the future. But when you weren't sure which future I saw, you and the coin always acted in a way to bring this exact future about. It was cemented in, no matter how you tried to alter it."

"Exactly," said Redford. "Tom thought this would be the case, but the implications are profound. It's impossible for a non-clairvoyant being to cheat the universe. We have no ability to change anything that you see coming. Only *you* can. Period. By seeing a future, you can take steps to change it. Or you can provide information to others, giving them the free will, the *option*, of changing it."

Anna nodded. "Go on."

"But if you *don't* provide information," continued the colonel, "and don't do anything, yourself, to change the future, every other being in the universe is on an unchangeable path to whatever destiny you foresee. Since we don't know for sure what our futures will bring, we blindly go down the path that leads to the future you see every time, even if we think we're making random choices to avoid this. So even our random choices are already baked in. Again, you're the only intelligence we know of with the power to *avoid* a future that you see."

"Well said, Steve," added Vega. He sighed and faced Anna. "It's going to take some time for the full implications to really sink in. For all of us. But these results suggest that if anyone can turn the tide of a war, it's you. It appears that there are two levels of free will. We mortals, as Steve described us, can exercise free will to create a future, but we can't then change our minds. But *you* can. You can decide to take a future action, look ahead to see if you like the result, and then change your mind if you don't. You can force the universe into a do over. In that sense you aren't just a mere human being. You're more like a *god.*"

Redford nodded his agreement, mesmerized. *Hottest god ever*, he said to himself, not even moving his lips.

"Did you just say, 'hottest god ever'?" asked Vega.

The colonel looked horrified. "Of course not," he said. "You Vors have pretty wild imaginations."

"No. Our hearing is many times sharper than that of humans," persisted Vega. "I'm sure that's what I heard."

Redford shook his head. "Jesus, Tom!" he snapped in exasperation. "Thanks so much for clearing that up."

The colonel turned back to the woman across from him and winced. "I'm so sorry, Anna," he began. "I thought I only said that in my head. And I know the word *hot* sounds lustful, but that's not how I meant it. The truth is that what's, um . . . *hot* about you is your poise and competence. Not that you aren't very attractive also," he added awkwardly. Redford grimaced as he realized he was just making things worse. "I'll shut up now."

A smile spread across Anna's face. "Don't worry, Steve. I know better than anyone that the subconscious sometimes has a mind of its own." Her blue eyes sparkled impishly. "And just so you know," she added, "I've already had a vision of us sharing a passionate kiss. I don't know how far ahead I was seeing, but this happened in the warehouse, when my powers were far weaker, so this vision must have been a pretty important one."

The colonel's mouth dropped open. "Really?"

"I wouldn't lie about that," said Anna. "After all, the vision was pretty . . . *hot*."

Redford laughed. "Then in that case," he said, "this is one future that I hope like hell you don't plan to change."

Anna smiled. "I wouldn't have brought it up if I did," she admitted. She arched an eyebrow. "But not in front of the extraterrestrials," she added wryly.

"Let me understand," said Vega. "You've just learned that you're the only known sentient being in the galaxy with the power to change the future. For all we know, *you're* what the Gatekeepers have always been after. Perhaps they orchestrated events over many thousands of years to bring about the right conditions for the emergence of a woman like you, who can go on to become a god. Maybe they'll let you achieve transcendence so you can lead them. All of these possibilities, and more, are now on the table. Yet given everything, the first thought that comes to your mind is about *copulation*?"

"Not the *first* thought," said Anna in amusement. "And a kiss isn't exactly copulation. Either way, suggesting I'm some kind of god who can mold the universe is ridiculous. It's so over the top it isn't even worthy of a response. But even if you *are* right, don't gods need affection too?"

Vega shook his head. "*Humans*," he said in mock exasperation. "The fact that you're the only species who can end the galactic war means only one thing for certain: The Gatekeepers have the most demented sense of humor in the cosmos."

42

Stephen Redford was on his back on the thick mattress, naked, with his arm around Anna Abbott lying beside him, her head resting on his chest.

Could this be real? he thought for the dozenth time.

Perhaps he had been kidnapped and plugged into the Matrix. Or perhaps this was the longest, most vivid, most improbable dream he had ever had.

He had imagined meeting intelligent aliens. He had imagined finding a woman he could become head-over-heels enamored with almost at first sight, and then making love to this very same woman. He had even imagined transcendent beings, galactic wars, extraterrestrials bent on worldwide conquest, starships, and interstellar portals.

But all of these at once? Not even in his most insane fever dreams.

Then throw in that the woman he'd become enamored with was clairvoyant, and that their lovemaking would take place at a ranch house in Utah, owned by aliens, which could be made absolutely invisible—and it couldn't possibly be real.

Except that it *had* to be. Because even if he were to experience a total psychotic break, his delusional mind could never be *this* imaginative—or insane.

Anna Abbott was even more amazing than he had guessed. They had retired early and made love as if this was their last day on Earth. And they had been in total sync. Caring, wild, compassionate, and generous. Like him, he learned that she hadn't had sex in quite some time, but that wasn't what made this experience so transcendent. It was that their personalities, for whatever reason, genuinely clicked, and their mutual admiration for each other exerted an irresistible magnetic pull. As they made love repeatedly, talking for hours in between, their attraction to each other only grew.

Redford told her about his geeky childhood, his obsession to learn what was out there, to expand his horizons, and to be present when humanity learned it wasn't alone in the universe.

And she told him everything. About her parents' murder. About her troubled, delinquent childhood, in far more depth than she had told Vega. And about her friend Isabella, and how her death had cemented Anna's resistance to letting anyone get close to her.

Until now.

"So what do you make of the Vors who have mysteriously disappeared?" he asked her, stroking her hair gently. He decided that they had covered their pasts thoroughly enough for now, and it was time to return to pressing questions in their surreal present.

"Hard to say," she replied. "But I'm not thrilled that it happened to Vors who were especially good at finding people like me."

"According to Vega, there *are* no people like you. Hell, according to *me* there aren't. I've only known you a few days, and I'm sure of it. There may be fellow one-in-five-millions, but none of them systematically honed their intuitions like you did. None of them fed their subconscious a Library of Congress worth of audiobooks. And as Vega told us in the helicopter, most of them were selfish, or arrogant, or were unfit to serve for any number of other reasons. You took an ability that could have made you rich and powerful and became a public servant instead. Risking your life to make the world a better place."

"That's kind of you to say, but it's not like I'm Mother Teresa."

"Thank God," he said with a grin. "Because I'm pretty sure you wouldn't be having sex with me now if you were." He cringed. "And I'm *absolutely* sure I wouldn't be having sex with you."

She laughed.

"You aren't a saint, no," he continued on a more serious note. "But you've been in the trenches and come out stronger. And yet retained decency and compassion. You're truly the Goldilocks candidate, Anna. Or maybe the Mary Poppins candidate: practically perfect in every way."

"Wow. Did you just reference Goldilocks *and* Mary Poppins in the same breath? Is that the kind of tough, macho talk that helped you rise to the top of a Black Ops unit in your early thirties?"

"I had to sprinkle in some references to Smurfs, as well," he said, trying to keep a straight face. "But that's just the kind of bad-ass I am."

Anna laughed.

"But getting back on topic," said Redford, serious once again, "I'm worried about the Vors who disappeared also. It suggests that some faction doesn't want them to find their Oracle. Now that they have, it seems to me that this faction will be coming after you."

"They'll have to get in line," said Anna dismissively. "Maybe all the factions who are after me will battle each other for the honor. But I'm actually not too worried. We're on guard anyway."

"If some unknown party did want to take you out," said Redford, "the time to do it would have been before your clairvoyance was enhanced. If it keeps getting stronger, like the Vors think it will, it'll be harder and harder to surprise you. Especially since life-and-death stakes are more likely to bring out your precognition than anything else."

Further testing the day before had revealed that Anna's ability to see a card ten seconds into the future was absolute, but became less than a hundred percent at three minutes, and vanished completely at over fifty minutes. But Vega was convinced that she could see *much* further than this already, either randomly or because of the importance of the vision. Her vision of kissing Redford was proof. That vision, as it turned out, had been more than a day into the future.

"So right now," said Anna, "everyone here thinks I'm the only sentient who can change the future. But what if the Vors find and enhance other humans? Then there will be any number of us who can. What then?"

Redford considered. "I guess it depends," he said. "If your futures never intersect, I guess it doesn't matter how many clairvoyants there are. You see yourself stubbing your toe in the bathroom in five minutes, and choose not to go into the bathroom to avoid this. The future universe is changed, but very little. At the same time, a decision by a clairvoyant in Japan to slam on the brakes to avoid a future crash has no impact on you, or anyone but a few people in Japan."

"And when the futures of two or more clairvoyants *do* intersect?" she asked.

Redford nodded thoughtfully. "In that case," he said, "things could get pretty wild. Dueling future changers. Imagine two clairvoyants on opposite sides of a battle. Each one sorting through multiple possible futures, their heads wrapped up almost entirely in what might be, rather than what is. At the same time having to lapse back into the present to try to force the outcome they want. But both sides doing this at the same time. Talk about complex. Talk about Wild West." He shuddered.

Anna blew out a long breath. "Tom said that now that they've found me, the Vors will no longer be hunting for other possible intuitives. If this is true, I guess we'll never have to worry about more than one clairvoyant operating at the same time."

They laid together in silence for several minutes, basking in the affection and intimacy that had long been absent from both of their lives. "Speaking of your clairvoyance," said Redford, "I'm forever in its debt for sending you the vision of us that it did. But you didn't happen to see anything else about us in the future recently, did you?"

Anna rolled off his chest and onto her side, facing him. "I didn't," she said. "And I don't want to. I think we have a real shot at something that will last." The detective raised her eyebrows. "And I know you feel the same way," she added, "because you're going to tell me so in about eight minutes."

"You are joking, right?" said the colonel, making a face.

"Of course," replied Anna, grinning. "But my intuition does have a good feeling about you."

"Yeah, mine does too," said Redford. "But I do worry that your clairvoyance might make a relationship a little . . . unusual."

Anna laughed. "You think?" she said playfully. "*A lot* unusual. But I plan to learn to control it, and if this relationship does continue, I won't ever use it to spy on us."

"Can't imagine that you won't be tempted."

She shook her head. "Not as much as you'd think. For the most part, I want to live in the present. Being inside my own head to see future visions can come in handy, but a cell phone is distracting enough for anyone wanting to live one's life in the moment. So I plan to use my clairvoyance judiciously. What fun is life if you always know what's coming? Every time you read a book or watch a taped show, you have the power to look ahead and see the ending. But you don't. You'd never even think of it. Because you know it would ruin the experience."

"You make some great points," said Redford.

"Thanks," said Anna with a grin. "And I'll try to pretend that I didn't know you were going to say that."

"Okay," said Redford. "I know you're kidding, but you really have to cut that out."

"Sorry," said Anna sheepishly. "I guess I'm letting the absurdity of this new ability get in my head, and it's coming out as attempted humor."

"My instincts tell me you're a kind, decent human being," said Redford. "And while I know they aren't as good as your instincts, I'm pretty sure I'm right. Which means that you'll soon have the power to do a lot of good in the world. Although I guess I should say, in the galaxy."

Anna blew out a long breath. "Maybe," she said. "I certainly intend to *try*. But good intentions can be a tricky thing. Have you ever heard the parable of the Zen Master, the boy, and the horse?"

Redford shook his head no.

"A boy in a small village gets a beautiful horse on his sixteenth birthday," she began, "and everyone in the village says, 'What a lucky boy.'

"To which the Zen Master replies, 'We'll see.'

"The next day, while riding his horse, the boy is thrown off and breaks his leg. Everyone in the village says, 'How horrible for the poor boy.'

"To which the Zen Master replies, 'We'll see.'

"The next day a war breaks out. All men sixteen and older are pressed into battle against an unbeatable foe, which will mean almost certain death for each of them. But the boy is exempt from the fighting because of his broken leg. Everyone in the village says, 'What a lucky boy.'

"To which the Zen Master replies, 'We'll see.'"

She paused and raised her eyebrows.

"Wow!" said Redford. "That's a lot more profound than I was expecting."

"It's one of my favorite parables," said Anna. "And never has it been more disconcerting than in the context of clairvoyance. Because what if I saw the happy future when the boy got the horse as a gift, and was even lucky enough to see the future beyond that, when he broke his leg? But I didn't see the war. So I change the future so he doesn't break his leg, and he gets killed. Good intentions. Acting on solid information. Yet with disastrous consequences. And who knows how many other layers of the onion there are going forward that I'm not seeing."

Redford grinned.

"What are you smiling about," she said. "You don't think this is relevant?"

"No, it's very relevant. And I admire you even more for considering it. I was smiling because I realized that I'm even more smitten with you than I thought. This parable and your analysis is so thoughtful, so insightful, and so beautifully presented. You are, by far, and in so many ways, the most impressive woman I've ever met."

"You're going to have to do a lot better than that," said Anna playfully. "In the past few days I've been called the most important person who ever lived. The galaxy's only hope. And a god. By comparison, calling me the most impressive woman you've ever met is like an insult."

Redford laughed. "Do you see any future where you get such a big head that it won't fit through a door?"

"Come on, Steve, would the most impressive woman you've ever met let herself get a big ego?"

"Good point," said Redford.

"Seriously, though," said Anna, "how do I ever know the decisions I make are really for the best? How do I know I have a long enough perspective?"

"The answer is that you don't. Unless you truly are a god. Maybe an actual god has the kind of perspective to know to let the boy break his leg."

Anna nodded. "True believers say that God works in mysterious ways," she said. "That things happen for a reason—or for the best. And all of this speaks to having the right perspective, and a view of the entire future, rather than just one part of it. If there is a god, he or she lets horrible, despicable things happen. Wars that kill tens of millions of people. The holocaust and other attempted genocides. Earthquakes and volcanoes and hurricanes.

"Atheists insist this is proof that God doesn't exist," she continued. "But believers think we just aren't seeing the big picture. That God is playing eight moves ahead. The boy breaks his leg, and we can't see that God's endgame is to save the boy's life."

"It's certainly a lot to think about," said Redford. "As if we don't have enough on our minds already," he mused.

"No doubt," agreed Anna. "And this line of thought provides a slightly different perspective on the Gatekeepers' motivations. The twenty-seven intelligences have scores of theories as to what the Gatekeepers might be up to, but most of these see their interference in a negative light. But maybe what they're doing is necessary and compassionate, if only we could see the big picture."

"It's impossible to say," replied the colonel. "But as for you—as for any of us—I think we have to live our lives and make the best, most compassionate decisions we can with what we know. Yes, maybe some will be wrong. But what other choice do we have? We can only decide based on what we know. If we think about this any other way we'd be paralyzed. We have to be ants, striving to build, striving to be the best ants we can be, putting on blinders to the fact that at any moment a boot can descend from above and wipe us out. We can't live fearing the boot, fearing wrong decisions, or giving up on life because of uncertainty."

Anna grinned.

"What?" said Redford. "I'm serious"

"I know you are. I'm just smiling because I love how you put that. You may just be the most impressive man I've ever met."

Redford smiled and drew her into his arms, and soon they were making love yet again, finding reserves of energy neither knew they had. When they finished, they agreed they needed to get four or five hours of shut-eye. They were scheduled to fly back to Evie headquarters in the morning, and it was sure to be another eventful day.

"Before we go to sleep," said Redford, "if the Vorian portal does reappear, which Tom thinks is now more likely since the Tart portal just did, will you agree to become their admiral? Have you thought about it?"

"I have," said Anna. "And the answer is absolutely not. Maybe in ten years or so. Maybe. But not before then. I have too much to do here, and too much to learn."

"I think that's a wise choice," said Redford. "On the other hand," he added wryly, "I've always dreamed of sleeping with the admiral in command of a fleet of starships."

"You have, huh?"

"Absolutely."

Anna laughed. "Well, sorry to crush your dream, Steve," she replied. "But maybe you can sleep with whoever—or *whatever*—is in command of the allied fleet right now. You never know," she finished, raising her eyebrows, "you just might have a shot."

PART 5

"Physics is the only profession in which prophecy is not only accurate but routine."

—Neil deGrasse Tyson

43

The self-piloting Black Ops helicopter flew to Hill Air Force Base to refuel, and then began its flight to Evie headquarters in Arizona in full stealth mode. The mighty aircraft carried only three passengers: Colonel Stephen Redford, Detective Anna Abbott, and Vorian Chief Scientist Kaitlyn O'Connor.

Vega's compound had a large selection of firearms, and each of the Vors were trained on how to use them, so both of Redford's companions armed themselves for the trip—Kaitlyn, out of an abundance of caution, and the detective because she felt naked without a firearm.

While Anna trusted the colonel implicitly, she wasn't willing to trust anyone else in his organization. Not until she had the chance to meet with them and size them up. For this reason, Redford had agreed to take but a single Vorian to his headquarters to meet the family, while promising not to give away the location of Vega and his invisible compound in Utah.

The colonel planned to learn what progress his team had made on the Foria front, and in their analysis of the Tartarian corpses they continued to examine, and then determine the best way to ease his people, and his superiors, into the true situation. Assuming they passed his Anna Abbott litmus test.

But none of this would happen right away. First Redford wanted to get the lay of the land and plan out just what he would disclose, and how he would disclose it, which might take several days. He had now spent considerable time in discussions with the Vors, and he wasn't about to be overruled on decisions that could well impact the fate of humanity by someone with a shadow of his knowledge and experience, or who was innately paranoid of extraterrestrials.

Once he did bring everyone up to speed, he felt that Kaitlyn would be the ideal Vor for them to meet. A scientist who could dazzle his people in any number of fields, and who would come across as un-threatening. And someone many of them could get to know first, before Redford revealed that she was an extraterrestrial.

The three passengers were ninety minutes into their flight to Arizona when a call came in from Tom Vega, which Redford channeled through the aircraft's speaker system for all to hear.

"Our portal just reappeared!" began Vega ecstatically. "I just got word."

"Outstanding," said Anna. But in the back of her mind, the nagging Zen Master parable wouldn't go away. Maybe this *was* wonderful news. It sure seemed that way. But maybe not. The only thing she knew for sure was that she hadn't experienced a dull moment since her dinner on Thursday.

"Is it as large as the recent Tart portal was?" asked Redford.

"No. The opposite. It can only transport two at a time. Since the fluctuation pattern is identical to what it was before, we'll only be able to send people through every forty hours or so. We have no idea why the sizes of the recent Tart portal and this one are so asymmetrical."

"But then again," noted Anna, "you have no idea why they'd be symmetrical, either."

"This is also true," admitted Vega. "The Tart portal vanished right after their horde came through. I'm hopeful that while ours is smaller, it will stay active for longer. But even that isn't critical. Because we now have the opportunity we've been working toward for thousands of years."

The alien paused for what seemed like forever. "So what do you say, Anna?" he continued finally, and it was clear that he was extremely nervous. "Will you go through the portal with me? Will you become our fleet admiral?"

Anna considered how best to let the poor alien down, but before she could utter her first word she was hit in the stomach with the most powerful intuitive signal she had ever received. She fought to even breathe.

There could be no doubt what response her subconscious insisted that she make. She considered ignoring it for a moment. She was so tired of being controlled by a cryptic hidden Oracle, so tired of following orders whose rationale she didn't understand. But in the end she knew that she had to obey and hope that her hidden mind knew what it was doing.

"Yes," she replied. " I'll go through with you, Tom. And I'll lead the allied fleet as you've requested."

"What?" barked Redford beside her, looking as though she had betrayed him. And she had. This was a complete reversal from what she had told him just the night before.

"Thank you!" said Vega, whose relief couldn't be more palpable. "You won't regret this, Anna," he gushed. "You're going to change the galaxy."

Anna gasped and held her head with both hands as two visions entered her mind in quick succession. And while each vision lasted only a few seconds, both were seared into her mind's eye like a cattle brand.

In the first vision she and Tom Vega were approaching the Vorian portal in Albania, with Steve Redford looking on, a melancholy expression on his face. The portal loomed in front of her, a shimmering, mesmerizing hole in the fabric of the cosmos, which hurt her mind to look at. It was something that human eyes had never been evolved to see, so it appeared to be made up of every possible color, and no color, all at the same time. Its perimeter continuously changed shape, like a hyperactive amoeba, and its center, large enough to walk through, pulsed and throbbed as if alive. The movement of the hole was fluid, like cascading water, but water with a million facets, as if made of five-dimensional diamonds rather than H2O.

It was magnificent, spectacular. But more than anything else, it radiated such unimaginable power that it was terrifying on a visceral level, like an approaching wall of water during a tsunami, a hundred feet high, or the inside of an active volcano.

Anna took one last glance around her at the Earth she was leaving. The woods were as peaceful as they could be, and other than Steve Redford, not a single soul was in sight. And then she and Tom Vega stepped through, and the vision was over.

The second vision was at the same approximate location but was an absolute horror show, a bloody skirmish so ferocious and vast it could have been ripped from a *Lord of the Rings* battle scene. Anna somehow knew without looking that nearly every Vor and every Tart on Earth was congregated near the portal, either to help her reach it or prevent her from doing the same.

The surrounding forest had become the ultimate killing field. Gruesome tattered bodies, many in pieces, were strewn about the ground like so many autumn leaves, and intestines and brain matter were dripping from branches like Christmas ornaments. At least five hundred combatants were already dead, most of them Tarts, since despite having far greater numbers, Anna's clairvoyance had almost balanced the scales.

Almost.

Anna somehow knew the battle's history, even though she was only seeing a brief slice of it, although she didn't know if Redford was in the forest, or still back in the States. US special forces commandos had been helping the Tarts, and their involvement had tipped the scales in the Tarts' favor. There were well over a hundred of these American troops swarming the woods, and they were ruthlessly efficient.

And then the unthinkable happened. A Tart with a machine gun emerged from behind a tree, right next to a Navy SEAL, and they both began to fire. Even Anna's precognition was helpless against the onslaught of bullets, which she couldn't prevent from turning her body into bloody Swiss cheese.

She inhaled loudly as the vision ceased, as abruptly as it had begun, and she had to steady herself, even seated in the helo.

Anna was vaguely aware of Redford's panicked voice, seemingly a hundred miles distant and under water, calling her name worriedly.

She was finally able to reply, to assure him that she was okay, and then launched into a description of what she had seen in great detail, while her fellow passengers and Tom Vega listened in dismay.

"I don't know what to make of this," said the alien leader despondently when she had finished. "Your description of the portal and its surroundings are exactly right. Even though these are details I've never shared with you. So there is no doubt these visions were real.

But I don't understand why you'd have two different visions of what seems like the same event: your attempted trip through the portal."

"Is it possible that both futures are balanced on a razor's edge?" said the colonel. "Each equally probable?"

"No," said Kaitlyn bluntly. "Anna sees one future, and this future comes to pass. No probability about it. True, after seeing this future, she can tell others about it, who now have the power to change it, or she can change it herself. But if she doesn't do either of these, this one *single* future is cemented in. Remember?"

The chief scientist paused in thought. "After seeing the first vision just now, Anna did nothing in the instant before the second vision came about that could have possibly changed this initial future. Especially not something that could have changed it so dramatically. Changed it into the absolute carnage she saw next."

"We've spent a single day doing experiments," said Redford. "*One*. That's it. So we can't say *anything* with certainty."

"I agree," said Anna. "We're up against the unknown here. Maybe we'll understand how this happened at some point. Maybe not. But for now, let's just make sure my first vision comes to pass."

The detective paused. "Just to double-check, Tom," she continued, "the Tarts don't know the location of your portal, right?"

"Right," said Vega through the helicopter's speaker system. "We found theirs thousands of years ago. But they never found ours. Because by the time they arrived it had already disappeared. Same thing this time."

Redford was shaking his head and looked utterly horrified. "What disturbs me the most about this second vision," he said, "is that US special forces were helping the Tarts. How can that be? Who deployed them in a foreign country? And why would they ever turn on the Vors, who are our allies? Worse, why would they help the Tarts kill Anna? It makes no sense, and it's highly troubling."

There was a long silence in the helicopter as everyone mulled this over. Redford was right, and there were no good explanations.

Anna sighed. "Here's what I'd like to do," she said finally. "We'll stay at Steve's facility for a few days, meet his people, and introduce them to Kaitlyn, as planned. Hopefully, during this time, I'll get additional visions that will clarify the situation. If so, we can act accordingly. If not, we'll travel to the Vorian portal. Just me, Steve, and Tom. We'll make sure no other Vorians are there. This will ensure that my first vision is the true one, since the second requires a large contingent of Vors."

"Now that you've had these visions with so much time to spare," said Vega, "I can't imagine that either one will take place exactly the way you saw it."

"We can't make that assumption," said Anna. "I still want to be proactive in making sure the second one never comes to pass."

"I agree," said Kaitlyn. "We know there's a serious flaw in our understanding of how this works, or Anna wouldn't have had a dual vision in the first place."

"You're right," said Vega. "Which is why Anna's plan sounds sensible to me. If we rush her to the portal before we know what's going on, we risk everything. Hopefully, she'll gain more clarity on this situation soon. Just don't wait *too* long, Anna. Because if the portal disappears before we get to it, we'll never forgive ourselves."

"Understood," said the detective.

"In the meantime," added Vega, "the next time the portal is active, I'll send a messenger through alerting Vor not to send anyone this direction until the last minute that it's active. Until further notice. That way, during the vast majority of its period of activity, it will be earmarked for your use only, until I get you to Vor."

"I don't understand how these portals work," said Anna. "How is it that you can only send two people through every forty hours?"

"When the Albanian portal is present," said the alien leader, "it most often appears as a perfectly spherical mirror, reflecting its surroundings. This is its inactive form. And when it disappears, which it has now done twice, there is no evidence it was ever there. But when it *is* present, every forty or so hours, it changes from reflective to the appearance that you saw in your vision. For about two hours. During this time, it's active and ready to transport. At any time during this period, two beings can go through. Two can go from Vor to Earth, or two can go from Earth to Vor. Or one can go to Earth, and another to

Vor. But after two have gone through, the portal immediately reverts to inactivity, and the forty-hour clock starts again."

"And you have no idea why they work this way?" said Redford.

"None," replied Vega. "And they all vary. Some are active almost always. Some less than once per year. And as we've seen, their sizes vary. Basically, they play by their own rules. We're in the same boat your ancient scientists were when it came to celestial mechanics. They could track heavenly bodies across the sky, but they had no idea of the underlying physics that dictated these movements. Like them, we can observe the periodicity of the portals easily enough, but we have no idea of the physics that might dictate this periodicity."

Redford shook his head. "That's assuming that physical laws are dictating the portals' properties," he said. "Which may not be true. They may just be set based on the Gatekeepers' whims."

"This is probably the case," said Vega. "But the important point for now is that we won't waste an active portal on anyone but Anna. No one will go through until the last minute, until they're sure she isn't coming to Vor during that round of activity."

"Then I guess we're all set," said the clairvoyant detective, swallowing hard.

Vega nodded. "Good luck at Evie headquarters, Anna," he said, his tone pained. He exhaled loudly. "And please contact me immediately if you have another vision."

"Will do," replied Anna as Redford ended the connection.

Anna felt sorry for the alien leader. He was at the height of ecstasy after she had agreed to become his fleet admiral. But just seconds later, after her two visions, he was forced to consider a future that could not have been more horrific.

Not that Anna was thrilled about this possible future, either. Seeing machine gun fire tearing into her body wasn't her idea of fun.

She only wished she could be certain that the steps she was taking to ensure this vision never came to pass weren't the very steps that led to it happening in the first place.

44

The helicopter landed at Evie's helipad and a civilian SUV was waiting, with one of Redford's low-level functionaries driving. As they drove away from the helipad, another of Redford's underlings pulled up to the aircraft with a fuel truck to top off its tank. Redford had issued a standing order long before that all incoming helicopters should be refueled as soon as possible so they were always at maximum readiness.

They drove for a mile before reaching a fenced-in industrial building, surrounded by a parking lot large enough to accommodate hundreds of cars.

Metal signs were attached to the fence at frequent intervals, which read, "Nuclear waste processing plant. Employees with radiation badges, only, allowed beyond this point."

The guard manning the gate recognized the driver and the facility's commander, and they were quickly waved through.

"Nuclear waste processing, huh?" said Anna, arching an eyebrow. "Nice touch."

"Thanks," said the colonel. "I figured this would deter potential snoopers better than just about anything else."

The building was a large, ugly, single-story structure with no windows, as inviting as a morgue—as one might expect for a nuclear waste processing facility. But its true purpose was to house dual elevators the size of three-car garages, which brought passengers to the actual Evie facility five stories below ground.

The driver left to park the SUV, and Redford escorted his two guests inside. But before they got close to one of the two elevators, a looming giant of a man, in his fifties, with gray hair and what seemed to be a permanent scowl on his broad face, was waiting for them. He was surrounded by five uniformed soldiers, each gripping an assault rifle with two hands, although all were pointed down at the floor. The soldiers were hyper-alert, as if they were behind enemy lines, and gave off an aura of menace.

Anna's eyes widened as she recognized the gray-haired man. She didn't keep up with politics, but she had seen his face on television a number of times. He was Wilson Stinnett, America's secretary of defense and Redford's boss—although Redford had told her he had only met with the man on one occasion during his entire tenure as head of Evie.

Before becoming the secretary of defense, Stinnett had been a military strategist who had long consulted with the Pentagon. And even though he was a civilian, it was widely known that he had earned black belts in three different martial arts disciplines, and was thought to be a hard-ass.

When Anna had shared a bed with Redford the night before, the colonel had explained exactly how he and Evie fit into the scheme of things. The secretary of defense had command of the entire US military, second only to the president, and in normal times, Redford was so far down the chain of command he didn't even register. But if proof of an ongoing alien visitation was obtained, he would suddenly become second only to Secretary Stinnett and the president, which is how he was able to galvanize a Foria task force so quickly, and with no questions asked.

"Colonel Redford," said Stinnett by way of greeting, his tone disapproving. He extended a hand in a way that was anything but friendly.

"Mr. Secretary," said Redford, shaking his hand. He then quickly introduced the secretary of defense to Kaitlyn and Anna.

"Nice to meet you, sir," said Anna uncomfortably. She had never met anyone in this rarefied position of power before, and she wasn't sure of the proper protocols. Redford hadn't even saluted, which she guessed was either because Stinnett was a civilian, or because neither man was in uniform.

Stinnett barely deigned to grunt back at her before turning back to Redford. "What a nice surprise to see you here, Colonel," he said icily, his words dripping with sarcasm. "Nessie mentioned that you had finally decided to grace us with your presence. So I thought I'd be the welcome wagon."

Redford's lip curled up into a snarl, but only for an instant. "Thank you, sir," he said in clipped tones. "Can I ask why you have a Special Operations team with you?"

Stinnett looked as if he had almost forgotten that the five commandos were there. He issued orders and they retreated to the elevators, out of earshot, but maintained a clear state of alertness, never taking their eyes from the group.

"Why the Special Operations team?" repeated Stinnett derisively. "Well, maybe you haven't heard, Colonel Redford, but alien bodies have been stacking up around here like *cordwood*. And it's my understanding that the small armies you sent to Chicago, LA, and New York have been kicking up quite the hornets' nest. Based on my conversations with Nessie, I've come to believe there might be any number of what you're calling *Travelers* here on Earth—and that they could well be hostile to the human race. Is any of this ringing a bell, Colonel?"

"Yes it is, Mr. Secretary."

"*Good*," said Stinnett. "So these Spec Ops soldiers are serving as bodyguards. I command the most potent military force on Earth. So it's occurred to me that I might be a target of these black-blooded Travelers. Not that I've heard word one about any of this from the man in charge of investigating alien visitations."

"Yes, sir," said Redford. "Apologies, sir. I was just coming back to give you and the president a full report."

Stinnett raised his eyebrows. "Really, Colonel? I wasn't sure you remembered that you *had* superiors." He shook his head angrily. "We've just experienced the most consequential event in the history of humanity, and you decide to go dark! For almost two days! Where were you? Did you have a golf outing you couldn't cancel?"

"I can explain, sir. I was—"

"I know you can!" spat Stinnett, interrupting. "I know you *will*. So let's go down below so you can give me a thorough briefing. Unless you have a croquet game you need to flitter off to. I mean, as long as it's convenient for *you*."

"Sorry, sir. I realize that my radio silence may have seemed inappropriate. But there were any number of vital things happening that required my full attention. And I wouldn't have been able to gather the critical information that I've gathered if not for a promise I made not to report any of this until now. Once I brief you, I believe that you'll understand, and will agree with the decisions I've made."

"You had better be right, Colonel, or I'll have your head on a platter. You and I have a holographic vid-call scheduled with President McNally in four hours. So I'm giving you three hours to deliver your report to me. A dress rehearsal for the president, whose briefing will need to be shorter."

The gray-haired secretary of defense gestured toward Anna and Kaitlyn. "You can begin by telling me who the hell these two are, and what they're doing at a Black Site."

"I'll tell you all about them, Mr. Secretary, but let's take this to a private, secure room down below. I doubt your security detail over there can hear us, but I would like to keep this for your ears only. I'm sure you understand. And I'd like to have these two women with me when I report, as they'll have a lot to add."

Stinnett grunted his agreement, and the four of them approached the elevators and the five commandos. The soldiers all wore body armor, and all had the lean musculature and intensity of jaguars stalking their prey, coiled and ready to strike.

"Lieutenant Russo," said the secretary, addressing the man who headed the security team. "Please frisk these two women for weapons. Gently. They're friends until proven otherwise."

"That isn't necessary, Mr. Secretary," said Redford immediately. "I can vouch for them both."

"*You* can vouch for them?" said Stinnett in mocking tones. "The man who's been MIA for two days. Who then shows up to his secret facility with two unknown women who don't have any clearances. And you can vouch for *them*?"

The secretary shook his head. "Who can vouch for *you*, Colonel? Maybe you only think they're trustworthy. Maybe they have you fooled. How would I know, since you haven't briefed me on *anything*."

While the secretary was speaking, the lieutenant completed his task, removing a gun from both women, and a knife from Anna.

"Are *you* armed, Colonel?" asked Stinnett.

"You can't be serious," replied Redford.

"Until I get a report and learn where the hell you were, Colonel, I'm not prepared to trust anyone. Especially since you want me alone in a room with two strangers. I'm not armed, either, if that makes you feel any better. Your lady friends will get their guns back when they leave. And you will when you convince me I can trust you."

Redford scowled but carefully surrendered his weapon to Stinnett's bodyguards, and then all nine present entered the oversize elevator and rode it down to Evie's underground headquarters in silence.

"Nessie," said Redford subvocally as the elevator descended, "why didn't you tell me that Stinnett was waiting for me?"

"You didn't ask," said the AI into his comm.

Redford shook his head in disgust. As amazing as Nessie could be, even the most incompetent human assistant would know to volunteer this information.

The elevator door opened into an expansive reception area, and Anna was struck by how bright and cheerful the facility was, how roomy and unclaustrophobic. It was bright, colorful, and well decorated, and had ceilings higher than most aboveground structures. Other than the lack of windows, they could have been in the main headquarters building of a Fortune 500 technology company.

Anna doubted this bright, inviting ambiance was accidental. Steve Redford must have insisted on an optimal work environment for his people.

"Conference Room A is the closest," said Redford as they exited the elevator. "But I recommend D, which offers absolute privacy. It has no windows and is fully soundproofed. And I mean fully. There are active noise-canceling systems just beyond the room, so no one can eavesdrop, even using advanced sound amplification tech. It's also in a section that is all but sealed off from the others, only housing Conference Room D, surgical suites for alien autopsies, and containment cells."

"You mean prisons," said Stinnett.

Redford nodded. "Which we hope to never use," he said. "But to continue, D also has a holographic projector system for virtual face-to-face meetings, which we can use when we're briefing the president. I'll have Nessie disable it for now, just to be sure no one can use it to surveil us."

"Are you usually this paranoid, Colonel?" said the secretary of defense.

A chilly smile flashed across Redford's face. "These are unusual times, Mr. Secretary," he replied. "And I'm not the one with a Spec Ops team with full-on assault gear guarding me in a friendly facility."

"Fair point, Colonel," replied Stinnett. He gestured toward the corridor. "Lead on."

They worked their way past dozens of labs, rooms, and offices to the sector farthest from the elevator and only came across three Evie personnel, who quickly made themselves scarce upon seeing the approaching entourage. Stinnett had probably ordered Redford's people to go home, take breaks, or leave the corridors empty, so his escorts carrying automatic weapons wouldn't make them nervous.

They entered Conference Room D, and Stinnett ordered the five commandos to wait outside and remain alert. A lustrous cherrywood table was positioned in one half of the large room, surrounded by eight black-mesh chairs, but the entire group stood in the empty half, making no move to sit.

"Okay, Colonel Redford," said the secretary of defense. "You have the floor. Please begin."

"Before he does, Mr. Secretary," said Anna, moving closer to him, "I want to tell you what an honor it is to meet you, sir."

Stinnett gave her a look of disdain and opened his mouth to speak. But not a single syllable slipped from his tongue. Instead, Anna's stiffened right hand shot out with the velocity of a striking rattlesnake and knifed into the secretary's Adam's apple. She connected dead center, but even though he was moments away from toppling to the floor, she executed a roundhouse kick that slammed into his jaw with bone-jarring force, ensuring he would be rendered unconscious for a good long time.

Anna's instinct-driven speed and accuracy were astonishing, and her kick propelled Stinnett right into Redford's arms before the colonel had even processed that she had moved. Even so, Redford managed to hold onto the incoming secretary of defense and lower him gently and quietly to the conference room floor.

45

Redford blew out a long breath, and even though he knew the guards couldn't possibly have heard anything coming from the sound-proofed room, he instinctively checked the closed door to make sure they weren't storming inside. Kaitlyn looked horrified, but remained silent.

The colonel could hardly believe what he had seen. Anna had told him that when she gave herself over to her instincts her fighting speed and effectiveness were dramatically increased. But nothing could have prepared him for the blur of precision strikes he had witnessed. Stinnett's martial arts prowess was well known, yet the detective had dispatched him as if he were a clumsy grade-schooler.

"Okay, Anna," he said, surprisingly calm. "Do you want to tell me about it? I mean, Stinnett is a bit of a dick, but I'd like to think you did this for other reasons."

"The Tarts got to him," said Anna. "They must have hit him with HCS, their possession drug."

"How do you know that?"

"I had a vision of him shooting you in the head at point-blank range while you were bound to a chair."

Redford swallowed hard. "Well, that would have . . . *sucked*," he whispered.

"He wouldn't kill a helpless man if he wasn't possessed, right?" said Anna.

"Absolutely," agreed Redford. "He isn't *that* big of a dick."

The colonel paused. "Let's see what Stinnett's been up to," he said. "Nessie," he continued, still out loud, "list all orders issued by Secretary Stinnett during the past forty-eight hours."

There was no response.

"Nessie," he said again. "Respond immediately."

A shriek issued through the colonel's internal comm, sending searing pain into his temple. He collapsed to the floor and held his ears, but just when he thought his head would explode the sound ceased.

Anna knelt on the floor next to him and held his head as his eyes fluttered open. "What happened, Steve?" she asked anxiously.

"Nessie sent a signal through my comm intending to knock me out," he replied, still reeling from the pain.

"Why didn't it work?" asked Anna.

"The comm has a fail-safe. It's surgically implanted in my cochlea, so I made sure I'd never be vulnerable to this kind of attack. It possesses a rudimentary computer intelligence. If the comm detects a signal meant to be lethal or debilitating, it shorts itself out."

The process had only taken a few seconds, and even in this short time Redford felt as if he had been repeatedly stabbed in the brain.

The colonel rose to a standing position. "Only two people in the world have the ability to order Nessie to ignore me, or actively try to take me out."

"But Nessie followed your order to disable the holographic vid system in this room," said Anna.

Redford frowned. "I don't think so," he replied. "I think she only pretended to. Stinnett must not have wanted me to know anything was amiss."

"Which means we probably *are* being listened to right now," whispered Anna, assimilating the situation with remarkable speed. "Shane Frey," she called out. "It's time to show yourself. We know you're there."

A perfect holographic image of a humanoid figure shot from hidden projectors and materialized on the floor eight feet away from where the three conscious inhabitants of the room were standing, as if he were there in person. An image of a being who was unmistakably Tartarian, tall and intimidating, with severe features and blazing red eyes.

Kaitlyn gasped and shrank back in horror.

"Shane Frey?" said Anna.

"In your language, yes," replied the alien.

"It was a good effort, Frey," said the detective. She gestured to the fallen secretary of defense. "But as you can see, your plan has failed."

"My plan has *failed*?" repeated the alien in contempt. "Really, Detective? Why don't you let Colonel Redford tell you what's wrong with that statement. Go ahead, Colonel," he added mockingly. "I'll wait."

Anna and Kaitlyn both turned to Redford.

The colonel frowned miserably. "The only way Frey could be doing this," he began, "is if he controls Nessie himself. Stinnett is unconscious, so *he* can't be doing it. The secretary must have given Frey access to the AI equal to his own. So now Frey can have Nessie issue orders using the secretary of defense's command codes, giving him nearly absolute power over the US military. He doesn't really need Stinnett anymore."

"Very good," said Frey.

It suddenly hit Redford that this explained how the US special forces must have ended up in the forest in Anna's vision. Because the Tart leader now had the command authority to make this happen. An element of her vision that had seemed impossible suddenly didn't any longer, making her vision all the more chilling.

"But that makes no sense!" insisted Anna. "How can any command and control system allow something like this to happen?"

"It can't," said Redford. "Not under normal circumstances. Nessie will only allow transfer of these command prerogatives if it's done by Stinnett himself. And only after putting the secretary through a sophisticated battery of tests, to ensure he's sane, healthy, not under duress, not being drugged, emotionally stable, and so on. The Tarts' possession drug must not have affected him on any of these dimensions, fooling Nessie into believing it was a valid transfer. One made by a fully rational secretary of defense of his own free will."

"Right again, Colonel," said Frey.

"How did you even know to do all this?" Redford asked the menacing, fire-eyed hologram.

"Why not have your clairvoyant friend tell you what I'm going to say? Then I don't have to waste my breath."

"Because I'm not seeing your responses," said Anna. "Any of them."

"Really?" said Frey. "Can't even see what I'll say less than a minute into the future? How unimpressive. And the poor Vorian idiots think you can change the course of an entire war."

"She's made it this far, hasn't she?" barked Redford. "She's escaped *your* traps."

"I'm not saying that clairvoyance isn't a handy skill to have," said Frey. "But it's sketchy, isn't it? Temperamental. Unreliable. And even if she can see a myriad of futures, all you have to do to kill her is make sure there isn't a single future in which she lives. Put her in such an ironclad box that nothing she can do can change her inevitable fate. Like locking her in a conference room surrounded by special forces commandos," he added pointedly, "who Nessie will ensure will follow my every order."

"Are you going to answer the colonel's question?" said Anna. "How did you manage all this?"

"I'm more than happy to tell you," said the demon known as Shane Frey. "It's time you understood just how outclassed you really are. Humanity never stood a chance, despite your feeble efforts. Your conscious minds are pathetic. Vorian minds are better, but still not as sharp as ours."

"And yet they managed to wipe out *your* sorry asses on Earth thousands of years ago," taunted Anna. "You talk a good game, but how special are you really?"

If anything, Frey's eyes blazed even brighter, and his fury was evident. "The Vorians got *lucky!*" he hissed. "But their luck has run out! And so has yours!"

Frey took a deep breath, and, after a brief pause, managed to compose himself again. "It was easy to outmaneuver you," he continued in more measured tones. "I was nearing the warehouse to collect you and the Vorian named Vega when I learned that Black Ops helicopters were approaching. There is only one reason that these could possibly have joined the fray: a secret military group must have learned of our presence on Earth. A group tasked with investigating alien visitation. I knew that the ranking military officer in these two helicopters would end up in possession of Vega and his clairvoyant detective."

Redford frowned as it all became clear. "And you realized that the secretary of defense was one of the few people in the world who would know who was in charge of this secret group," he said.

"I'm glad you're able to catch on after I spell it out for you, Colonel. But yes, you are correct. So we stalked him and waited for an opportunity to drug him with Human Control Serum. Which we finally managed to do last night. Then, when he was fully compliant, I gave him detailed instructions on what I needed him to do. I'm sure Vega has told you all about this drug. Under its influence, Stinnett was only too glad to tell me everything he knows. Your identity as head of Extraterrestrial Visitor Investigations, the location of your headquarters here, and how he could transfer power to me. Everything."

"So why the charade with Stinnett?" asked Kaitlyn.

"Frey wanted me to be fully cooperative," replied Redford. "He was hoping I'd give a thorough report to the secretary of my own free will, while he listened in. So he could know everything the Vors had told me before he had Stinnett kill us."

"Right again," said Frey. "And I made sure this place only had a skeleton crew when you arrived. To reduce uncertainty as much as possible."

"How many of my people are here?" asked Redford.

"About ten percent. I had my puppet Stinnett order the rest of them home."

"If he's your puppet," said Anna, "how do you control him?"

"After we drugged him we established a dedicated channel through the comm already implanted in his inner ear. The one he uses to communicate with Nessie. But we modified the comm so that it's now booby-trapped. If any of your surgeons attempt to remove it, he dies. He's primed to respond to my voice. Whatever I tell him, he does. Without question."

"Too bad he's unconscious," taunted Anna.

Frey shrugged. "It's worse for you than it is for me," he said. "If you hadn't caught on, I'd have obtained the information I'm after the easy way. Now it looks like I'll have to beat it out of you. Not optimal, because you tend to get less reliable information that way."

"Why not use your HCS drug?" asked Anna.

"I used our last dose on Stinnett," said Frey. "It's not easy to make. But don't worry about us. Our numbers on Earth have just seen a major increase, so we'll have enough hands to make plenty more. And to do a lot of other things that you won't like."

"Why didn't you just drug Stinnett or our president when you first arrived?" asked Redford. He knew that Frey would happily answer his every question, since the alien was certain they wouldn't live to repeat what he was telling them.

"Because it would have been more trouble than it was worth," said the demon-eyed alien. "Better to work in the shadows. These men are too high profile. Even just getting close enough to drug them would pose a considerable risk. And we'd continue to risk being exposed while we were pulling their strings. Dramatic, uncharacteristic changes in behavior by such high-profile people don't go unnoticed."

"But once you realized that you were already exposed," said the colonel, "this was no longer a concern."

"Exactly. But back to your question, we also had little interest in wielding your military. We could kill most of you using your nuclear arsenal, but this would render your planet uninhabitable. Since Earth will soon be our base to expand into this region of space, we'd prefer to kill you off while keeping your planet pristine."

"Which is where Foria comes in," said Anna. "So what does it do?"

"It heightens human senses," said Frey. "It floods human brains with so much pleasure that the feeling of ecstasy is like a migraine headache by comparison. Like a dozen of your orgasms at once. But with no side effects."

"Except when it kills us," said Anna.

Frey smiled. "Well, there is that. It acts like a time-delayed computer virus. After just one use it modifies a host's DNA in a way that will prove to be lethal, but won't give away even a hint of this lethality for almost three years."

"Which gives the drug time to spread to every corner of the world before anyone realizes they've swallowed a time bomb," said Redford.

"Yes. We don't expect it to kill everyone on Earth, but it will be a good start. And if you and the Vorians hadn't caught on, no one would have ever guessed that a non-human species was responsible. But now, given our increased numbers, we won't even need Foria. We'll be able to construct weapons of mass destruction that you've never dreamed of. And use other Tartarian technology that will make us invincible."

"You're delusional," said Anna. "Invincible? How'd that work out for your fallen ancestors?"

"This time it's very different," said Frey. "Back then, human science was primitive. There were no manufacturing techniques, materials, or technological building blocks our people could use to recreate our technology. A thousand of your greatest tech wizards couldn't create a modern cell phone if they were stranded on a desert island. But now you have the tech we need to recreate Tartarian advances that you won't have for decades. And we also brought a library here with us. The equivalent of tens of millions of pages worth of specifications. A detailed compendium of all of our technology. And given the more advanced state of your technology, we'll actually be able to use it."

Anna knew that Frey was right. It would have been impossible in ancient times to construct anything meaningfully advanced from the materials available at the time. But the Vors had already demonstrated that this was no longer true. They had sold scientific advances to technology companies, and had developed jaw-dropping invisibility tech to protect their compound. So the Tarts probably could do exactly what Frey was threatening.

"This has been fun," continued the holographic alien dryly. "But I'm almost out of time."

Frey gestured to Redford. "But just so you don't think you've made any inroads against us, Colonel," he added, "my first act upon gaining control of your secretary of defense was to have him reverse your every order. The few Foria-related prisoners already taken were released, as were all samples of Foria. And as of this morning, you're wanted as a traitor and enemy of the state. Your closest friends and allies will now turn their backs on you as if you were a *disease*."

Anna scowled at the alien commander. "You're very pleased with yourself," she said in disgust. "But I pity you. Because you have no idea what you're up against."

Frey laughed. "Starting to believe your own press, Detective?" he said in disdain. "How pathetic. I'm truly embarrassed for you. The truth is, you're going to tell me what I want to know, and then you're going to die. Very soon. You're the most overrated sentient being who ever lived, Anna Abbott.

"I know all about the Vorians' theories. About microtubules resonating with time-reversed quantum signals. My people looked into this thousands of years ago on Tartar. We couldn't get your microtubules to work with our brain architecture. But our modeling suggested that even if the Vorians succeeded in finding a clairvoyant and optimizing their abilities, this would be of marginal value in the broad scheme of things. At best.

"You've been lucky so far, Anna, but face it, you don't even understand what you see most of the time. You have no idea what any of your hunches really mean. No military ever succeeded by taking cryptic orders from someone who doesn't even know the reason for her own orders. You're a clairvoyant, not a magician, and easy to nullify. And even if you manage to see a few pieces of the jigsaw puzzle clearly, you'll never see enough of it to matter. Like in the old human parable—you're a blind woman feeling an elephant's trunk and mistaking it for a snake."

This last hit Anna hard. Frey had restated her biggest fear, that her clairvoyance could mislead her just as much as it could show her the truth.

But she also knew that this was the least of their problems right now. Because if they didn't manage to find a way out of this, they'd have an eternity to ponder this issue in the afterlife.

46

Shanifrey Doe surveyed the two humans and one Vorian from the vantage point of his holographic avatar projected into the conference room in Arizona. "As I mentioned earlier," he said, "I need to sign off. These are busy times. But you'll see me again soon, when I fly out to handle your interrogation personally." He shot them a menacing scowl. "And I know tortures you humans can't even *imagine*."

"I'm afraid we'll be gone before you arrive," said Anna defiantly.

The Tartarian commander laughed. "Your bluster is cute, Detective, but misguided. One of Evie's holding cells is being prepared for you now. The colonel knows that these are impossible to escape from, since he approved the final design. So sit tight, and try not to miss me. It won't be long before the commandos outside come to collect you."

He paused. "And just so you know," he continued, "the conference room door has been locked tight from the outside. Try to leave and it won't go well for you."

With that, Shanifrey ended the connection, and his holographic image disappeared from the conference room. He had Nessie kill the audio while he watched the three inhabitants stewing in the room on a video feed, and finally clicked it off entirely.

"I'm ordering Nessie to have the commandos gas the room," he said to his second, Eldamir Kor. "Using the same type of canisters Neil Marshall's men used at the Rest Easy Motel. But this time using a gas that will also be effective against a Vorian. I like the idea of them being unconscious while they're being taken to a secure holding area."

"You had Stinnett strip them of their weapons," said Eldamir. "You don't think five elite human commandos can handle them?"

"I never take chances when I don't have to," replied Shanifrey.

He paused to issue orders through Nessie and then returned his attention to his second-in-command. "The holding cell will be ready in eight minutes," he reported. "They'll gas them a few minutes before that time."

Shanifrey then called for silence so he could consider recent events. Anna's realization that the secretary of defense was under his control had been unfortunate. If not for this, they would have already learned the location of the Vorian portal, the most prized, decisive piece of intelligence of all.

He cursed inwardly. If only they had been able to turn Stinnett sooner things might have played out differently. But they had only managed to gain control of him the night before. And they hadn't been able to turn Nessie into an expensive bug until even later that night, just in time to hear the vomit-inducing noises of Redford and the clairvoyant in the act of copulation. Even worse, if worse could be imagined, was their syrupy sweet pillow talk afterward, their gushing, fawning declarations of affection for each other, which made him want to stab at his ears with a knife.

Most discouraging of all, Nessie had caught the tail end of what he guessed from context had been a very long and interesting conversation between them. As it was, after overhearing a single session of mating and before the two had fallen asleep, all Shanifrey had learned was that Anna was unwilling to become the admiral of the Vorian allied fleet.

Yet this unwillingness had been short-lived, as she had reversed herself only the next morning, for inexplicable reasons, as they were flying to Evie headquarters. Until that point, very little of interest had been gained by Shanifrey's audio surveillance. But this had quickly changed. First came Vega's revelation that the Vorian portal had reopened, a vital piece of intel. This was followed by Anna's agreement to command the fleet, after all. And finally, the detective had experienced two very intriguing visions, which she had quickly shared.

Shanifrey turned his thoughts to these possible glimpses into the future when his second-in-command broke the long silence. "I find the first vision the detective had in the helicopter troubling," he said, demonstrating that he and his commander had been thinking along the same lines.

"That's because it *is* troubling," said Shanifrey. "We can't let her get to Vor, even if she's one-tenth of what the Vorians think she is."

"Then why don't we kill her immediately?" asked his second. "Making sure this vision never comes to pass."

"Patience, Eldamir. She's the bait we need to round up every Vorian on Earth. While we have the might of the entire American military at our disposal."

"What if she escapes?"

"She won't."

"What if she does?" persisted Eldamir.

"Don't believe the Vorians' hype. What I told her is true. Her abilities are sketchy and grossly overrated. But let's imagine for a moment a miracle happens and they do escape. We'll just have to make sure her second vision comes into being."

"But in the helicopter, they never mentioned the location of their portal. And we have no idea where it is."

"Thanks!" snapped Shanifrey sarcastically. "I wasn't aware!"

"My apologies, Commander," said Eldamir immediately. "It's just that I fear her first vision is the more likely of the two to come true. They also mentioned in the helicopter that they believe that once a future has been announced, anyone who knows about it can change it. After she described these visions, I have no doubt that she and the Vorians will take actions to ensure her second vision never comes to pass."

"Unless actions taken to change this future are the ones that actually bring it about," said Shanifrey.

"I think this would only work if you didn't know the details of the future," said his second. "But if you see a future in which you die in Paris, you can change this for sure. Just never go to Paris."

"It might not be that simple," pointed out Shanifrey. "What if your vision was incomplete? What if you failed to see that you would be kidnapped and brought to Paris against your will?"

The Tartarian leader shook his head. "Look," he added, "we can debate this forever. But there is one takeaway from her visions that

I find heartening. In her second one, we *do* discover the location of their portal. Which means that we must be very close. Given that so many more of our comrades are now on the case, maybe one of them is on the brink of discovering its whereabouts. But even if not, I'll get this information from Redford anyway. If I can't break him—which is hard to imagine—we'll have another dose of HCS ready in a day or two. Then he'll have no choice but to tell us where it is."

He paused. "And then we'll use the detective as the lure to wipe out all the Vorians here on Earth."

"And if the impossible *does* happen," said Eldamir, "and she escapes? What then?"

"I'll order massive Tartarian forces to converge on the Vorian portal, to make her second vision come to life."

"But if what she saw does comes true," said Eldamir, "this would be a disaster for *us*, as well. We'll kill her in the woods, yes. But not before losing a majority of our comrades. And our portal may *never* reappear to replenish our ranks."

"If she really can escape from Redford's headquarters," said Shanifrey, "against all odds, then we won't have a choice. If she can manage *that*, then she just might be the potent force the Vorians think she is. So even if we have to take heavy losses to kill her, it's worth it. With her gone, and given that we'll be able to patrol the Vorian entrance to Earth, there will be little to stop us from carrying out our plans."

Shanifrey noted that his second-in-command still didn't look convinced. "Cheer up, Eldamir," he said. "Remember, this is just a hypothetical discussion. The Gatekeepers are more likely to turn themselves into a school of *fish* than Anna Abbott is to escape. Besides, even if she did, I'd keep sixty of us behind, forty women and twenty men, all of the highest rank. Including the two of us. If the rest get wiped out near the Vorian portal, so be it. That's what pawns are for."

Eldamir was about to reply when his commander held up a forestalling hand. Nessie was reporting that the commandos at the Evie facility were seconds away from gassing the conference room.

Shanifrey turned on the feed once again, just in time to see the door suddenly open and a tiny canister roll into the center of the room. The feed was soon blocked by a thick haze of gas, but less than a minute later this had dissipated just enough to reveal a Vorian woman and two humans collapsed on the floor.

Shanifrey Doe switched off the feed contentedly. In another minute, when the gas had fully cleared, the five commandos would rush into the room. But the alien leader had no need to watch further. Not even a clairvoyant could resist capture while unconscious.

Besides, it was time to begin planning for his upcoming journey to Arizona.

47

After Frey had signed off, the three inhabitants of Conference Room D struggled to come up with an escape plan, but it was an exercise in futility. The room was now silent as each of the three furiously searched their minds for Hail Mary options they might have overlooked.

Anna suddenly bolted upright. "The door's about to open," she blurted out with great urgency. "They'll be gassing us."

"A vision?" said Redford.

"No. A strong hunch. And another says that if we hold our breath when the door opens, and fall to the floor, we won't be knocked out."

"Right," said the Vorian chief scientist, "because gas rises."

"When your face is on the floor," said Redford hurriedly, "encircle your head with your arms to create a tiny pocket of breathable air."

"What's the plan if we do stay awake?" asked Kaitlyn.

Redford was about to respond when the door was thrown open a crack and a gas canister was tossed inside, right on cue.

Anna gulped in a giant breath of fresh air and fell to the floor as the door slammed shut, happy to note that the colonel and Kaitlyn were doing the same. She held her breath until her lungs were on fire, and then held it longer, pushing off panic and the irresistible primal need to inhale. Finally, when she couldn't fight it any longer, she sucked in a breath from the tiny pocket of unpolluted air she had made and held her breath again.

But this time, the agony returned almost immediately.

***

Lieutenant Antonio Russo slammed the conference-room door closed and checked the time. In two minutes the gas would disperse enough through vents in the room that they could enter without masks. Russo had been on many dozens of missions with his fellow SEALs in hellholes around the world, and he had thought he had seen everything.

But he had been wrong.

There had never been a mission like *this* one. Not ever. Commanding a team tasked with protecting the secretary of defense, himself, was wild enough. But Russo had been told they'd be protecting him from possible *extraterrestrials*.

It seemed so insane.

But at the same time he felt as if he had won a lottery. Those SEALs who had brought down bin Laden had been the previous lottery winners. Nothing could top that. What could be more professionally gratifying? And there were no better bragging rights in all the world.

Until now. Until a team had been formed to protect the secretary of defense from being killed by aliens intent on invasion. Now this was truly *incomparable*.

"Weapons up," commanded Russo to the men behind him. He had been told that the gas would work on those inside the room, but he wasn't about to take any chances. "We're going in single file on my mark. Three. Two. One . . .

"*Mark!*" barked Russo as he threw open the door and rushed inside, being sure to continue moving to leave room for his comrades behind him.

Russo's mouth dropped open, unable to believe what he was seeing. The two women were standing along the left wall of the room, very much awake and alert. Colonel Stephen Redford was sitting on the floor with his back against the back wall, and Secretary Stinnett was unconscious on top of him, facing outward. It was as though Stinnett was using Redford as a chaise lounge. Only the colonel's arms were visible. His right arm was wedged under the secretary's neck, and his left arm and hand encircled Stinnett's head like a python.

"Lieutenant Russo!" barked Redford from beneath the unconscious secretary of defense. "Make one false move and I'll snap his neck."

Russo's mind raced. "Let him go!" he demanded. "Or we'll kill your two friends. You have five seconds!" He turned and pointed his automatic rifle at Anna and Kaitlyn. "Four. Three—"

"Don't try to bluff me, Lieutenant!" shouted Redford. "We both know you have orders not to hurt us. Nice try, but I'm not biting."

Russo sighed and lowered his weapon.

"Good choice, Lieutenant," said Redford. "You do know that I'm a colonel and in command of this facility, correct?"

Russo didn't reply.

"Who ordered you to breach this room?" demanded Redford.

"I don't answer the questions of enemies of the state," said the lieutenant.

Redford began applying pressure to Stinnett's head, twisting it so hard it seemed a miracle that Stinnett's neck didn't snap, but he stopped just short of the breaking point and held it there. "Do you really want to explain to President McNally how you watched his secretary of defense die just because you were too stubborn to stop it?"

"Okay!" shouted Russo hurriedly. "The order to breach came from Admiral Gerald Simms, US Special Operations Commander."

Redford released some of the pressure on Stinnett's neck. "That's better, Lieutenant. But the order didn't come from Simms. It came from an AI system housed within the NSA that we call Nessie. Which is under hostile control."

Russo shook his head. "It was Admiral Simms," he insisted. "I'm positive. It was a 2D video call. I know what the admiral looks like, and I know his voice."

"Trust me," said Redford, "perfect impersonations are child's play for Nessie. Call Admiral Simms and confirm the order. Do it!"

"What you're trying to do won't work," said Russo. "We aren't letting you escape, even if it costs the secretary his life. He told us before you arrived not to trust anything you said, or even our own eyes. He said that you're an alien and a threat to humanity, and had to be contained no matter how many lives were lost. Including his own."

"I'm an *alien*?" said the colonel incredulously. "Really? It's true that I'm wearing Stinnett like a suit so you won't shoot me, but trust me, if you got a good look at me, you'd know that I'm fully human."

"The secretary told us that all three of you were aliens. Extremely dangerous. That you could reach into our minds and distort how we see you. So that you appear human, even though you aren't."

"There *is* an alien threat to humanity," said Redford, "but we're not it. You and I are on the same side, Lieutenant. The aliens who are responsible have a drug that compels human beings to do whatever they say. Stinnett was under its influence."

"Nice try," said Russo. "But I'm not buying it. So release the secretary and give yourself up. Like I said, this will only end one way, with you contained, no matter what the collateral damage."

"Come on, Lieutenant," said Anna. "Use your head. Suppose aliens really can fool you the way you've been told. What's more likely, that Stinnett is under alien control and we had to take him out like we said? Or that *all three* of us are aliens? Including the man in charge of finding and investigating extraterrestrials on Earth?"

She paused to let Russo mull this over. "And if we really did have the power to reach into your minds and make you see us as human, why wouldn't we just make it so you couldn't see us *at all*? Or cause you to see phantom monsters behind you? Or cause you and your men to see each *other* as horrifying aliens about to attack, so you'd all be shooting at members of your own team?"

Russo blinked in confusion. She made some good points.

"And why did we keep Stinnett alive?" added Anna. "Why would we willingly come to the very government agency best able to see through us?"

Russo's mind was spinning. What if they were telling the truth? What if Stinnett *was* under extraterrestrial control, such that everything he had told Russo and his men was a lie before any of this had even begun. How could he tell for sure?

The answer was that he couldn't. With stakes this high, he could only do one thing. Contain everyone in the room, including Stinnett. Lock them all up in the inescapable prisons installed in the facility. Until he could be sure of what he was dealing with here, he couldn't let *anyone* go free, no matter what the cost.

"Steve!" said Anna suddenly. "Let Stinnett go! Do it! Russo can't be persuaded."

Redford hesitated, staring into her eyes.

"Trust me!" she demanded, nodding slowly. "Give yourself up. Now!"

The colonel rolled Stinnett off his body and rose to a standing position.

"Jackson and Wenzel," commanded the lieutenant, "bind his wrists and ankles with zip-ties. Norwood and Fry, do the same to the two women."

As Norwood and Fry approached to carry out their orders, Anna pulled off a series of martial arts moves that were as rapid as they were mesmerizing, and in seconds both men were on the floor, unconscious.

Russo couldn't believe his eyes. She moved as if Norwood and Fry were in slow motion, as if avoiding their attempted rapid-fire blows was effortless. When she had come at the two men, they had thought they could defend themselves and take her down without firing, but they hadn't been able to lay a glove on her. Whatever part of her they attempted to strike was no longer there when their blows arrived, devastatingly quick though they had been. It wasn't her speed, which was impressive, it was her *anticipation*. It was as if she knew their next move before *they* did.

The being calling himself Redford attempted to fight off Jackson and Wenzel as the woman had done, but he was incapacitated almost immediately by a rain of blows. Once the two commandos had ensured he was no longer a threat, they spun around to face Anna and their two fallen comrades.

"Finish tying him up!" shouted Russo, raising his automatic rifle and pointing it at Anna. "I've got this handled."

Russo set his rifle to semi-automatic. He had seen enough to know this woman outclassed him in hand-to-hand, which was really saying something, since he was elite in this discipline, even among his fellow SEALs. He might be under orders to take her alive, but that didn't mean she had to be perfectly intact.

Russo aimed for her leg and pulled the trigger. After missing with the first shot, he pulled the trigger again and again, squeezing off several shots per second. But he continued to miss each time while she raced closer, distorting her body like a herky-jerky ballet dancer to somehow dodge the bullets. At this range, he should have been able to hit her every time, yet he might as well have been shooting at a phantom.

The lieutenant finally stopped firing and assumed a defensive stance, but she breached his defenses as if they weren't there, knocking him to the floor, groggy and barely hanging on to consciousness.

Not wasting a moment, the berserker woman raced over to Jackson and Wenzel, who had just finished ratcheting the zip-ties tight, and after she put on yet another impossibly choreographed display of fighting brilliance, they joined the others on the floor.

Russo regained just enough of his senses to reach and grip his rifle. But just as he finished setting it to fully automatic, the heel of a shoe descended from above and slammed into his head like a hammer, knocking him into oblivion.

48

Redford stood while Anna cut his restraints with a knife she had taken from a fallen commando, his cheek and lip bleeding from his feeble attempt at resistance. He couldn't help but feel slightly emasculated, no matter how much he tried to fight it. He was crazy about this woman, and he felt as if he should be rescuing her, not the other way around.

Even so, he had nothing to be embarrassed about. He had been up against two men who were combat specialists, while he was a geeky desk jockey at heart. And even though the script hadn't played out the way he might fantasize it would, it made him even more in awe of the LA detective.

She was extraordinary in every way. And not just because of her intuition and precognition. Even without these gifts, she was a force of nature, composed, tough, and uncannily smart and quick on the uptake.

The moment he was free, he and his two companions began rifling through the pockets and vests of the fallen commandos, taking handguns to re-arm themselves. Redford found two additional items he was searching for, a backup canister of gas and a handful of zip-ties, which he shoved into his pocket. He held up the canister for the two women to see. "Let's get out of here," he said.

As they exited the room, Redford pulled the pin from the canister and sent it back inside to ensure the men didn't regain consciousness too early.

Redford scanned his surroundings, relieved to note that the hallway was still uninhabited. "We'll give the gas a few minutes to dissipate," he told his companions, "and then go back in for Stinnett."

He turned to the detective and shook his head in awe. "Jesus, Anna. You made that look *easy*."

"I *know*," she replied, grinning in delight. "I was amazed myself. I really didn't think I had a chance."

"Did you have visions of where the men would be?" he asked. "How they would move?"

"I must have. But not any that hit my conscious mind. I wouldn't have had time to sort it all out if they had. My hidden mind is a *genius*. I went blank and let it control everything. I was just along for the ride." She shook her head in amazement. "But *what* a ride."

"If this whole admiral thing doesn't work out," said Redford, "you might consider a career on the mixed martial arts circuit."

Anna smiled. "Do you think anyone heard the gunfire?" she asked as her smile vanished.

"No. The room's soundproofing system contained most of the noise. Not all, because no system is *that* good, but a healthy percentage. Enough of it must have been blocked so that it didn't make it through to the adjoining sector. If it had, this corridor would be swarming by now, even if only ten percent of my people are here."

Redford decided he had waited long enough and reentered the room. He rushed over to Stinnett, lifted him, and draped him across his shoulders in a fireman's carry, not without considerable exertion, as the secretary of defense was a looming hulk of a man.

"Kaitlyn, under no circumstances is anyone to be killed while we try to get out of here," he said, assuming that Anna was already aware of this. "These people are our friends. It isn't their fault they've been turned against us."

"I understand," said the alien chief scientist.

"Follow me," he said to his companions. "I have a plan." He shot them a pained expression, and not just because he had a sequoia tree draped over his shoulders. "A really, really poor one," he admitted. "But I figure, with Anna on our side, anything is possible."

"Way to not put too much pressure on me," said Anna wryly as he began leading them away from the conference room.

"You do realize that the Vors expect you to *literally* save the galaxy, right? And you're complaining that *I'm* putting too much pressure on you?"

Anna winced. "You just might have a point there," she allowed as Redford reached his destination nearby, a large, well-stocked infirmary.

They entered the room and closed the double doors behind them, and the colonel lowered the secretary of defense carefully onto one of two stainless steel gurneys. "I'll be back in a few minutes," he said. "Gather wound-healing spray and a bunch of bandages."

Redford made his way to a surgical suite nearby, procured two scalpels and a medical bag, and then rushed back to the infirmary. When he entered he collected the items that Anna and Kaitlyn had gathered and put them in the bag.

He then picked up one of the two scalpels and walked over to the secretary of defense, explaining his intentions to the two fellow inhabitants of the infirmary. He pulled Stinnett's shirt up past his navel, blew out a long breath, and then carefully made a long incision across the secretary of defense's stomach, too shallow to cause any lasting damage, but deep enough to bleed profusely. He quickly lowered the secretary's shirt back down so it would become soaked in blood, and then covered him from head to toe with a lightweight bedsheet.

"My turn," he said, sitting on an identical stainless steel gurney and lying down on his back. "Anna, I'd like you to do the honors."

Anna gritted her teeth and shook her head.

"Anna, we can't afford for you to be squeamish right now. And we need to get moving."

She nodded and lifted the second scalpel, which was unused. "You're right," she said unhappily.

"I want you to cut the side of my neck," he said. "But very, very carefully."

Anna swallowed hard. "Of course," she said weakly. "Although I'm usually not the kind of girl to sleep with a man and then stab him in the neck the next morning."

"Quit stalling, Anna," he said, bracing himself. "And no one said anything about *stabbing*," he added, forcing a smile.

"I was wondering if you would catch that," she said, returning a forced smile of her own.

She paused for a moment to muster up her resolve, and then reluctantly put the scalpel to his neck, doing as he asked, although she looked to be in far more pain than he did. When she had finished, more than enough blood had leaked from the cut to make both his and Stinnett's act properly convincing—as long as no one inspected their wounds too closely.

Anna covered the colonel with a bedsheet, and she and Kaitlyn began rolling the gurneys to the facility's entrance.

When they reached more populated sections of the facility, Anna whispered instructions to Kaitlyn, which had been provided to the detective in the form of hunches by her clairvoyance-aided subconscious mind. She would order the alien to halt abruptly, speed up, or duck into empty rooms and offices. They made it almost all the way to the entrance without coming across a single soul, but Anna's expression as they approached the finish line made it clear that their luck had run out.

"My gut says there's no future in which we get into an elevator without being seen," she told them.

Redford nodded grimly. "Amazing we got this far," he said. "And we knew we'd have to bluff our way out at some point." He forced a confident smile. "So let's do this," he added, pulling the sheet over his face and closing his eyes once again.

Anna took a deep breath, nodded at Kaitlyn, and proceeded to the lobby. The moment they entered, four men pointed guns at their heads. "Freeze!" shouted one of the four.

Anna and Kaitlyn raised their hands, while another of the four searched the medical bag hanging from the gurney, finding nothing but bandages and wound-healing spray inside. Two others frisked the two women, removing the handguns they had just taken from the commandos.

Easy come, easy go, thought Anna miserably.

"I'm Captain Ed Coleman," said the man who had spoken previously. "We have orders not to let anyone leave here."

Anna drew back a sheet to reveal Wilson Stinnett. "The secretary of defense has been shot in the stomach!" she said, doing her best to sound panicked—which wasn't hard, since her heart was racing—but she wasn't able to tear up as she had hoped. She pulled the sheet below Stinnett's midriff to reveal his blood-drenched shirt. "We have to medevac him to a proper hospital *immediately*! There's no time to waste!"

Coleman winced. "I'm sorry," he said, "but Secretary Stinnett phoned ahead of his arrival with strict orders. He told us that after he and his party entered the main facility, no one was to leave until he cleared it himself. *No one.* "

"And you don't see a problem with that?" thundered Anna. "How's he going to clear us to leave *now*? And since he'll die in an hour or so if we don't get him to a hospital, does that mean that no one can ever leave again? Unless he clears them from the fricking *grave*? Are you a complete moron, Captain?"

Coleman didn't respond, but he wasn't put off by Anna's insults, as if he knew he deserved them. "Who's on the other gurney?" he asked instead.

Anna pulled the sheet down to reveal Coleman's boss, still playing dead.

The captain's eyes widened.

"Colonel Redford's been stabbed in the neck," she said. "He'll die also if we don't medevac him out of here."

Coleman sighed. "The colonel is a traitor and an enemy of the state," he said.

"Yeah, don't believe everything you hear," said Anna. "But even if this is true, let him be court martialed. Don't let him and the secretary of defense die because of your stupidity."

"Who did this to them?" asked Coleman.

"Several of the secretary's bodyguards turned on him. All five are now unconscious in Conference Room D. It's a long story, and I won't spend time telling it while the lives of these good men slip away."

"Who are you, anyway?" asked the captain.

"We came in with Secretary Stinnett. Kaitlyn here is one of his personal assistants, and I'm his personal physician. Although he needs care well beyond my skill level."

Coleman's eyes narrowed. "Why would he bring his personal physician along?" he asked.

"I have no idea!" barked Anna. "I thought it was strange myself. How about we ask him *after* we save his life?"

"You think I'm happy about this?" said Coleman, his frustration finally bursting out. "Of course I'm not. Every fiber of my being says we need to let these men get to a hospital. But the secretary made the stakes very clear to us. He told us that *no one* was to leave. Period. Even if it cost him his own life. He specifically said that."

Anna nodded. "I'm glad you told me that, Captain. I'm sure you're a good man. And I get why you're torn. So here's what's going to happen." She gestured to one of the two massive elevators behind him and his three comrades. "My colleague and I are going to wheel these gurneys into that elevator and then medevac these men to a hospital. I'm sure you know that your helicopters are capable of flying themselves, and Secretary Stinnett gave the self-piloting system the authorization needed to let me control it.

"So you and your men have a choice. You can shoot two innocent women in cold blood, because of an order that has been rendered ridiculous. Or you can escort us to the hospital and watch us like hawks. You can let us save the lives of two good men while you satisfy yourself that the world's not going to end because of it."

Coleman blew out a long breath. "Okay," he said, reaching a decision. He turned to his three colleagues. "Wade, you and Tristan stay here. Make sure that no one else leaves until you get word from me. Travis and I will fly with these women to the hospital."

"Thank you, Captain!" said Anna in relief. "Can you have someone pull up a vehicle large enough to fit these gurneys into for the trip to the helipad?"

He nodded. "Wade, call Rodrigo at the gate and have him pull the *Reaper* around front. Tell him we need it yesterday."

"Roger that," replied the man named Wade.

Anna and Kaitlyn pulled the two gurneys into the elevator, and the captain and a man named Travis escorted them inside. "How did you know we even had such a vehicle here?" asked Coleman as the elevator began to rise.

"You're set up to retrieve alien bodies if any are ever found. You'd need a vehicle spacious enough to transport them from the helipad to here, presumably in refrigerated caskets. Which I assume is why you call this vehicle of yours the *Reaper*."

Coleman looked deeply into Anna's blue eyes. "Whoever you are," he said, "you're very impressive."

Anna laughed. "Thanks, Captain," she replied. "That's very nice of you to say. But I'm intent on staying humble, and talk like that really isn't helping," she added in amusement, giddy that they were actually now leaving Evie headquarters alive.

49

Anna watched the shrinking, unconscious forms of Captain Ed Coleman and the man named Travis as the helicopter rose in the sky. She had been as gentle as possible while knocking them out on the helipad, and tried to shake off her guilt. Yes, she had now rendered eight of the good guys unconscious, but she had managed to escape without doing permanent damage to any of them, a remarkable achievement by any measure.

"Great news," said Redford excitedly beside her. "The transponder is still off-line."

"So we still can't be tracked?"

"Not while flying in full stealth mode," he replied cheerfully.

Anna bent to the task of patching up Redford and Secretary Stinnett. After cleaning their wounds and using the wound-healing spray and bandages that the colonel had included in the medical bag, she was confident that they would suffer no lasting damage. The colonel then produced the zip-ties he had taken from the commandos and bound the unconscious secretary of defense to one of the seats so that his arms and legs couldn't move more than a few inches.

"Brilliant job of escaping, by the way," said Redford to the detective. "From now on I'll know to expect miracles from you. Well done."

"Are you kidding?" replied Anna with a grin. "Well done *yourself*. You were so convincing. If there were ever an Oscar for most convincing bleeding in a life-and-death situation, I have to believe you'd take home the statue."

"That means a lot to me, Anna," said the colonel in amusement. "I've always dreamed of winning an award for bleeding from the neck. It's second only to my dream of sleeping with an admiral of an interstellar fleet."

"You do dream big," mused the detective.

Now that they were safely hidden in the clouds, Kaitlyn got Vega on her comm and put him on speaker. The group quickly brought the alien leader up to speed.

"At least you're all okay," said Vega somberly when they had finished. "It could have been worse. Much worse."

"Glad to see you're a glass half-full kind of . . . alien," said Anna. "And I guess I really am moving up in the world."

"How so?" asked Vega.

"Two days ago," replied the detective, "I was being hunted by every cop in America." She shrugged. "Now, the entire US military is trying to hunt me down. Definitely an upgrade."

Redford smiled. "You should be very proud," he said wryly. "But to get serious for a moment," he continued, "Tom, can you tell us more about this possession drug? Frey said they modified Stinnett's comm to give them a private channel to control him. And also to kill him if we try to remove it."

"We can determine if it's been booby-trapped or not when Stinnett arrives here," said Vega, "but I suspect it's true. Historically, according to the log entries of my people thousands of years ago, the Tarts relied on face-to-face voice instructions to program their victims. But proper technology didn't exist at the time for them to do otherwise. Now that it does, it wouldn't surprise me if they were able to modify the secretary's comm as Frey specified. As for the booby trap, they most likely altered his comm to release some kind of poison into Stinnett's bloodstream if removed."

"However they pulled it off," said Redford grimly, "I don't think it was a bluff. Frey had no reason to lie. He expected we'd be taking whatever he told us to the grave."

"The good news is that we can nullify Frey's control without removing the comm," said Vega. "Your helicopter uses stealth technology, right Colonel?"

"Right," said Redford.

"Which I'm guessing means that you can also choose to block Wi-Fi and other EM signals coming in. If I'm right, do this the moment we're finished so the Tarts can't use Stinnett's comm to locate you."

"Good call," said Redford. "I will. Regardless, we have the secretary bound, and we'll keep him unconscious."

"We have a signal dampener at our compound as well," said Vega. "So we can make sure that Frey can't influence the secretary while he's here. And in a day or two, when we get the chemical ingredient we need to complete our HCS cure, Stinnett will be free, comm or no comm."

"The question is, what will he be like when he awakens?" asked Anna.

"The log entries I've read make that clear," said Vega. "If he receives no further instructions, he'll continue to try to carry out the previous ones. But other than that, he'll be himself. From what you told me, it sounds as if he was given a fairly basic set of instructions. Continue acting like he's your boss, and do whatever he can to get you to willingly give him a comprehensive briefing."

Redford nodded thoughtfully. "In that case," he said, "he's going to be a very happy puppet. Because right after we land, I need to contact and brief our president, with the secretary in attendance. So he'll get the briefing that Frey programmed him to want, after all. Only Frey won't be able to hear it." The colonel paused. "Do you have a room with a secure vid-conference system, by any chance?"

"I do," said the alien leader. "I'll have it ready to go when you land."

"And by secure, I mean *absolutely* secure."

"It's more secure than any human technology can make it," replied Vega. "Your conversation with the president will be private, I assure you."

"Thank you," said Redford. "We'll expect to see you in a few hours."

"Understood," said Vega. "And just so you know, I plan to have thirty more of my people fly in today and tomorrow, including a number of our warrior class. We'll all be protecting Anna with our lives. Not that she'll need our protection," he hastened to add.

"Of course not," said Redford in amusement. "Why would she? She's *only* up against the entire US military and almost seven hundred very pissed-off extraterrestrial demons."

"You're right," said Vega, not catching the sarcasm. "Nothing she can't handle herself. But I still like the idea of having extra bodies. After all, you can never be too careful."

50

At forty-four, Quinn McNally was the third youngest US president ever to serve, but after only two years in office he felt as if he had aged decades. The job was even more demanding than he had thought it would be. He wondered how presidents in their sixties and seventies had managed to survive even a week in office, since there were weeks when he thought *he* couldn't, and he was the picture of health and endurance, having run marathons into his thirties.

McNally was pale, as dictated by his Irish ancestry, but his jet-black hair served as a nice contrast to his skin tone. He was considered handsome, but this worked against him as much as it worked for him, with his political and media opponents suggesting that due to his looks and youth, he seemed more of an actor playing the role of president than someone with enough knowledge and experience to be effective in the job.

McNally tried to stay focused on Keisha Aaron, his secretary of agriculture, but his mind kept wandering. "And while Senator Fontenot is pushing hard for increases in corn subsidies," she was saying, "my own view is that he doesn't care about these at all. His popularity has slipped, and he's worried about his reelection. My guess is that if you promised to campaign for him a few times, he'd drop these demands like a flaming bag of . . . leaves."

The president nodded, but didn't reply.

"So what do you think, sir? Should I tell him you'll hold a few rallies for him in exchange for backing off this folly? His demands don't make economic sense. The corn farmers in his state are doing very well right now."

There was a rap on the door to the oval office. "Mr. President," said Sophia Salazar, his chief of staff, letting herself in. "I need to interrupt."

McNally blew out a relieved breath. He welcomed any excuse not to continue the discussion he was having with his agriculture secretary. Sophia Salazar approached his desk and asked Keisha Aaron to step outside for a moment.

"Secretary Stinnett just called," reported the chief of staff the moment she and the president were alone.

McNally's eyes widened. *Thank God*. He had feared that his secretary of defense was dead. Three hours earlier, reports had come in that Stinnett had sustained a nearly fatal gunshot wound to the gut, and was last seen flying away from Evie headquarters, unconscious, in the control of two women, one of whom apparently had the combat skills of a ninja.

"How did he sound?" asked the president.

"Great. Strong, aware, and articulate. He said the reported injuries were exaggerated, and that he just sustained a superficial wound. And he is very eager to brief you, sir."

"Where is he?"

"He didn't say," replied his chief of staff. "And the call was untraceable. All he told me was that it was an emergency, and it was urgent that you receive a full briefing. He asked for you to clear your schedule for the next three hours. He'll be calling again in fifteen minutes. He says the briefing is vital, but for your ears only. At least for the time being."

McNally nodded. "Please close the door behind you," he said. "I'll take Stinnett's call in here. And clear my schedule as he asked." He paused. "Also, please tell Secretary Aaron on your way out that we'll have to reschedule our meeting for the near future. And apologize for me."

"Of course, Mr. President," said Sophia Salazar. "Right away, sir."

* * *

Anna sat on one side of an elongated oval table, along with Colonel Steve Redford, Secretary of Defense Wilson Stinnett, and two Vors calling themselves Tom Vega and Kaitlyn O'Connor. Although Anna tried not to, she realized she was staring at the man who had popped into existence on the other side of the table with her mouth open.

President Quinn McNally. In the flesh. Or at least a perfect holographic representation.

"Welcome, Mr. President," said the secretary of defense.

McNally squinted in disbelief. "Are you bound to that chair, Wilson?"

"I'm afraid so," replied Stinnett. "But for good reasons, which we'll get to later. You're familiar with Colonel Stephen Redford, head of Evie," he added, gesturing to the man in question. "He'll introduce you to the three others in the room in a moment. The colonel plans to give you a lengthy briefing. But first, he has an urgent request."

The president's avatar turned to face Redford. "I'm listening, Colonel."

"Thank you, Mr. President. As you know, we've found incontrovertible evidence of an alien species on Earth, which we called the Travelers. We've since learned that they call themselves the Tartarians, and we call them Tarts for short. It turns out that these Tarts are a hostile species who would like to wipe us out. We can bring you fully up to speed. But before we do, I can tell you that they have a drug that can turn a human being into their puppet. They used this drug on Secretary Stinnett."

McNally nodded slowly. "Which is why he's tied up."

"Yes," said Redford.

"But he doesn't seem to be under anyone's influence right now."

"That is correct, sir," replied the colonel. "He isn't. But we wanted to incapacitate him anyway, as a precaution, and he agreed. He still has no choice but to follow previous instructions—programming, really—that the Tarts established. He was ordered primarily to get me to provide a full briefing, which I will soon be doing. Since setting up this meeting isn't in conflict with his programming—in fact is in perfect alignment—he was free to do so as himself. And to participate. But what I'll ask you to do now is in conflict with previous instructions he's been given, which is why the request has to come from me."

The president eyed Redford suspiciously. "You are aware that early this morning," he said, "the secretary branded you a traitor. He told me he had absolute proof that you're working with extraterrestrials against US interests. Against the interests of humanity itself."

Redford nodded. "I'm aware," he replied. "He did this because he was under Tart control at the time."

The president paused in thought. "How do I know that you don't have him under *your* control right now?" he asked. "How do I know that you *aren't* a traitor?"

"You don't, sir," said Redford. "But if you bear with me, I'll prove that my version of events is true. Which brings me to my urgent request. Under the influence of the Tartarians' drug, Secretary Stinnett gave the Tart leader command authority equal to his own. A Tart named Shane Frey. If you check with Nessie, she'll confirm this.

"As commander-in-chief," continued the colonel, "you're the only one who outranks the secretary, so you're the only one who can get Nessie to confirm what happened. So I would ask that you put us on hold and check this out. If Nessie confirms what I'm telling you, you have to admit that the only way this could happen is if Secretary Stinnett was under alien influence. And you'll need to reverse Frey's authority immediately. We can't have a hostile extraterrestrial leader in a position to control our military."

"Yeah, thanks for that insight," snapped the president sarcastically.

Stinnett was growing more agitated by the second, pulling against his restraints, unable to fight off the compulsions HCS had created in his brain. Vega had warned them that this would happen when anything that Stinnett had accomplished at Frey's command was in jeopardy of being undone.

"But what you say *can't* be true," continued the president, so lost in thought that he didn't notice Stinnett's behavior. "Nessie was programmed to allow me or the secretary of defense to transfer powers to trusted underlings in times of crises. *Military* underlings. Which is how *you* quickly gained extraordinary powers when the Travelers—*Tarts*—were discovered. But the transfer was supposed to be to military leaders already extremely high up in the chain of command. Not random strangers. And only under very special circumstances."

"That may be true, sir," said the colonel, "but either the programmers forgot to tell Nessie that these powers could only go to a narrow group of recipients, or Frey figured out a way around it. Either way, it happened."

McNally frowned deeply. "I'll check this out immediately," he said. "I'm putting you on hold, Colonel," he added as his perfect likeness, and that of the chair he was in, evaporated from the room.

Anna considered the initial exchange while the group waited for McNally's return. It should have been surreal for her to be in a meeting with the actual President of the United States. But after all that she had been through in the past seventy-two hours, it was one of the *least* unusual events she had experienced.

A holographic Quinn McNally, seated in his holographic chair, materialized once again less than ten minutes later. The president looked shaken to his core. "You were right, Colonel," he said. "The secretary did transfer command authority to a stranger named Frey. *Unbelievable*. That authority has now been fully rescinded. I've also taken the liberty of restoring your good name, Colonel, and your emergency powers. Nessie will make it clear to all concerned that you were framed, remain the head of Evie, and are as loyal to our country as ever."

"Thank you, sir," said Redford, and while he maintained a stoic expression, Anna could tell how much this meant to him. Of course it did. He had spent his entire career building a sterling reputation and earning the passionate loyalty of his subordinates. And that had been wiped out in an instant. Anna had recently been the victim of false accusations herself, so she knew better than anyone just how painful this could be.

The president's cancellation of Frey's powers also ensured that Anna's second vision would never come true, since the Tart leader could no longer send special forces commandos into the woods of Albania. All of those in the Vorian conference room were well aware of how significant this really was.

"After I restored your powers, Colonel Redford," continued the president, "I made sure that Nessie could never transfer power in this way again."

Stinnett was now fighting against his restraints like a feral animal. "Mr. Secretary," said Redford in his most soothing voice, "I'm going to begin the briefing now. Are you ready?"

Stinnett instantly stopped struggling and blew out a long breath. "I am," he said calmly, now that Redford had aligned reality with his programming. "And *thank you*," he added. He shook his head in horror. "This is a nightmare. I'm at the mercy of the instructions Frey fed me. When they're triggered, positively or negatively, I have no control of my own actions. It's maddening."

"I'm truly sorry about that," said Vega. "Had we known the Tarts were on Earth earlier, we'd have had a supply of the antidote ready. But it won't be too much longer."

The president stared at Vega and raised his eyebrows.

"Allow me to make introductions before I begin the briefing," said Redford. "But I'll ask you to brace yourself, Mr. President. There's a hell of a lot going on here, and most of it will seem impossible. Or at least preposterous. But I'm hoping you can humor us while we lay it out."

McNally nodded. "I'll try to keep an open mind."

"Thank you," said Redford. "To begin with, the man who just spoke isn't actually a man. He's an extraterrestrial who has given himself the name Tom Vega. He isn't a Tart, but hails from a different species entirely, one calling themselves Vorians—Vors for short. He's their leader here on Earth."

The president's eyes widened as he considered the possibility that he was actually in the virtual presence of a live extraterrestrial, but to his credit, he didn't challenge this assertion or interrupt.

The colonel gestured to Kaitlyn. "This is Kaitlyn O'Connor," he added, "who is also Vorian. She's their chief scientist here. We've come to believe the Vors are an ally of humanity."

McNally studied the two Vorians carefully for several long seconds. "Where are you?" he asked Redford. "You aren't calling from space, I assume."

"No sir, we're right here on Earth."

"Where?"

The colonel winced. "I'm afraid I can't say, sir. This is information the Tarts don't have. There are only a few other pieces of information like this that we'll need to keep from you. Otherwise, we'll tell you everything we know."

"Are you saying you don't trust me with this intel?" asked the president.

"That's not what I'm saying, sir," replied Redford. "Of course we trust you. But we still can't risk it. Just in case the Tarts are ever able to drug you the way they did Secretary Stinnett. Admittedly, this is unlikely, as your personal security is much greater than his was. But too much is on the line to take that chance. And that's why this briefing is for you only, at least at the moment."

McNally thought about this for several seconds. "Understood," he said begrudgingly.

The colonel blew out a long breath. "To continue with the introductions," he said, "the woman seated to my right is named Anna Abbott. She isn't an alien. But she's extraordinary in her own right. It turns out that she's . . . precognitive. *Clairvoyant.*"

"What?" said the president in disbelief. "What does that even mean? That she can see the future?"

"Sometimes, yes," replied Redford.

The president looked alarmed, and it wasn't hard for Anna to guess why. He was willing to be open-minded, but he was now wondering if the colonel was stark raving mad after all.

"I know how this sounds," added Redford hastily, "which is why I'll ask Anna to prove it to you before we proceed. Once she does, you'll be more likely to believe everything else I tell you."

"And how does she intend to do that?" asked McNally skeptically.

"Think of a number between one and a million," said Anna. "And I'll guess it. But once I do, right or wrong, you have to tell us all what it is. Immediately after my guess. I don't read minds, so if you don't remember to tell us—in the future—I won't be able to see what it is."

McNally shook his head. "Surely you can't be serious?" he said.

"I'm very serious, Mr. President," said Anna, and then, with a broad grin, added, "and please, don't call me Shirley."

51

The meeting lasted almost three hours, and the president left a believer. They had told him everything they knew, as promised, except their location and the location of the Vorian portal.

Since Redford now had his command authority restored, he and the president initialized a massive manhunt—although Tart-hunt would be more accurate—to locate and eliminate all Tarts now on Earth. Both knew this would be no easy task. The moment Frey discovered that Nessie would no longer acknowledge him, he and the rest of the Tarts would go further underground.

Redford also agreed to give the president updates at least once a day until the crisis was averted, however long this might take.

Vega assigned two Vors to imprison Stinnett inside a locked room and keep guard outside. The secretary of defense had insisted upon this himself, unsure if there were other, hidden orders he had received that would force him into acts that he would later regret.

Meanwhile, Kaitlyn had been tasked with constructing a wearable signal blocker, so the secretary didn't become a living homing beacon, and was protected from further manipulation by Frey until the antidote did its job.

After they had all eaten, Vega pushed for a meeting to discuss strategies for getting Anna through the portal, as if they were playing a galactic game of soccer, with the Tarts as potential goalkeepers, and Anna the ball. A game in which a single goal would win the day.

Anna agreed to the meeting, but insisted on consulting privately with Steve Redford first, something Vega couldn't refuse. She and the colonel retreated to the Black Ops helicopter, since it was the only location within the compound that they could be certain could not be eavesdropped upon. They sat in the parked aircraft, at the end of the runway, among multiple jets and helicopters owned by the Vors, and used it as if it were a conference room.

Bizarre times called for bizarre measures.

Redford had the nearly irresistible urge to embrace Anna the moment the door to the helicopter was closed, but managed to fight it off. He was a colonel in the US military, with the fate of the world, and maybe more, at stake, not a horny fifteen-year-old behind the bleachers. Yet his body and his emotions didn't seem so sure.

He blinked several times, hoping to erase the puppy-dog look he suspected his eyes conveyed, and studied his clairvoyant companion. "What does your gut say about the Vors?" he asked. "Do you still trust them?"

"I do. For the most part. But not blindly. That would be stupid. They're still alien. They could still have hidden agendas."

"Hidden even from you?"

Anna nodded. "I'm far from infallible," she said. "My intuition has no experience with their species, so my gut isn't reliable when it comes to them. And as everyone keeps pointing out, my visions of the future are sketchy. This is too important, and I don't know nearly enough. And as we discussed, even if I was able to see the *near-term* future perfectly, who knows what the *long-term* future might look like? Especially if I travel to Vor. Maybe their government kept secrets from the people they sent here, knowing that if they did find someone like me, these secrets wouldn't be safe."

"So trusting them is still a leap of faith?" said Redford.

"Trusting *anyone* is a leap of faith. Human *or* alien. But on the whole, as I said, I do trust them. And I'm beginning to have a vague sense of why I agreed to be their admiral. And how other events that have happened recently might fit into the grand scheme of things."

"Is that why you wanted to meet with me in private?" asked the colonel.

She grinned. "That's why I wanted to *speak* with you in private, yes. Later tonight, I'm sure there are other things we can accomplish together in private that have nothing to do with speaking."

"I have no doubt," said Redford with a smile. "To be honest, I'm having trouble keeping my hands to myself even now."

"Good," said Anna impishly.

The colonel sighed and forced himself to stay focused. "So what's on your mind?"

Anna frowned. "As if I only had one. I can tell you what's on my *hidden* mind. My subconscious continues to dictate actions that don't necessarily make sense to me. It wants me to set certain things in motion. But to be fair, it *has* proven itself. My gut told me to surrender to Frey's forces at the Rest Easy Motel, which seemed a horrible move at the time. But if I hadn't done this, we never would have met. And I wouldn't have had the chance to put men who knew I was framed into police custody. Men who can clear my name."

"Do you think your subconscious was able to see these positive outcomes?"

Anna shook her head. "No. They were too far in the future. And the Vors hadn't even improved the functioning of my microtubules at the time. Still, I continue to think I should do what my intuition dictates. Even if I don't understand why. I have to trust that I'll connect the dots at some point. No matter how treacherously complex the pattern made by these dots turns out to be."

Redford thought about this. "I agree," he said.

"Good. So let me tell you what my gut is broadly saying about our current situation."

"You mean the situation on Earth and in the galaxy," said Redford. "Not our *personal* current situation."

Anna smiled. "I can tell you about that, too. My intuition says that you're crazy about me."

"Well, yeah," said the colonel. "But that doesn't require intuition. I told you the same thing just last night."

"Men have been known to lie to a woman to get her into bed," she pointed out.

"Impossible," said Redford, feigning shock. "I've come to believe a lot of crazy things lately," he said, trying to keep a straight face. "But now you've gone too far."

52

The colonel and Anna joined Tom Vega, Kaitlyn O'Connor, and Lisa Moore in the library, as before, except this time with the notable absence of a deck of cards and a timer.

"I'd like to begin by reviewing where things stand," said Vega to kick off the meeting. "We've had some setbacks, but on the whole, things are looking great. Anna has been successfully enhanced. Steve has been restored to his position, and neither the police *nor* the military is hunting for him or Anna. And the president of the most powerful country on Earth is committed to doing whatever is necessary to weed out every Tart on the planet."

He raised his eyebrows. "Most importantly, at least from the Vorian point of view, our portal has reappeared in Albania, and is now active. And Anna has agreed to accompany me to Vor and to become the allied fleet admiral. Finally, since Frey can no longer command the US military, Anna's horrific second vision can't possibly come true."

"Any negatives?" said Anna.

"Not really," said the alien leader. "Everything suddenly seems to be going our way."

"I agree," said Redford, "but the picture isn't quite as rosy as the one you're painting. Yes, the vast might and resources of the US military are being deployed to hunt down the Tarts here on Earth. But the same was true for a fugitive named Osama bin Laden years ago, and it took over a decade to weed him out, even so. So we can't expect miracles. It's true that the Tarts' features and their demon-eyes are quite distinct, and a dead giveaway. But they can keep their light amplification devices off if they have to. And bin Laden was six feet five inches tall, and also very distinctive in appearance, and he evaded the US military for a long time. Worse, the Tarts will be able to deploy technology that we've never seen before, which will make them even more elusive."

"Then why not get every country on Earth involved in this effort?" asked Lisa Moore.

"Good question," said Redford. "You weren't in on the call with President McNally, but we discussed this briefly. The president and I agreed that one of our top priorities going forward will be to decide if, and when, we should share what we know with other world leaders. We could use their help, as you suggest. And that's assuming that the Tarts' portal doesn't reopen, which would make matters even more dicey. Also, it can't be denied that the presence of two alien species here on Earth impacts every human, not just those in the United States."

"So why would you even hesitate?" asked the Vorian genetic engineer.

"There's still a lot to consider before we make such a momentous decision. Possible unintended consequences. If we do spread this to worldwide governments, some will insist on making it public. The president's feeling is that we have enough on our plate at the moment without having to deal with what will surely be the most massive public fallout of any disclosure in history. We both agree we can't put it off for too long, it's just a question of when."

"I think we're going to need to do this very soon," said Anna.

"I agree," said the colonel. "And I'll be making this recommendation to the president when we speak tomorrow. My own belief is that the public has a right to know that we're not alone in the universe. I don't buy the argument that this might incite panic. And I haven't forgotten Frey's threat. He said they have a comprehensive tech library here on Earth, and now have a critical mass of fellow Tarts to implement inventions that will make them invincible. We can't afford to give them time to come to full strength."

"Amen to that," said Anna.

"Thank you for raising these issues, Steve," said Vega. "Does anyone else have any others that we've missed?"

There was silence around the table.

"Then let me return to Anna's second vision," said the alien leader. "The fact that the Tarts were aware of the location of our portal is still highly troubling. They may not be able to make this exact vision come true now, but we can't rule out that they'll find other ways to accomplish the same ends. So I think it's important not to be too hasty. We may only get one chance at this. If we miscalculate, we could, as you humans say, snatch defeat from the jaws of victory. So let's not rush to Albania before we've really thought this through."

Vega paused and nodded at Anna. "I don't suppose you've had any further visions or hunches having to do with your trip to Vor," he said.

Anna shook her head. "You'd be the first to know."

"But we also can't take forever," said Lisa. "The portal could disappear at any time."

"Unfortunately, this is also true," said Vega miserably. "But here's what I'd like to do. I'd like to strategize about how best to get Anna through the portal alive, assuming that neither of her portal-related visions will come true. And also assuming that the Tarts will find out the portal's location and will deploy over six hundred of their people to stop us. This may not be the case, but we'd be foolish to assume anything else."

"Agreed," said Anna.

"Finally," continued Vega, "given these parameters, I'd like to get recommendations from Colonel Redford as to how to proceed. I suspect he's the best military planner here."

Redford nodded. "Give me some time to think," he said.

The room remained silent for several minutes. Finally, the colonel nodded solemnly and began. "I could ask the president to deploy US forces to Albania," he said. "That would be a tough ask, politically and diplomatically, but it could be done. The problem is that the forest location of the portal will render our air and ground power less effective. We could flood the zone with an overwhelming force, but this would raise a lot of questions. It would also require that a large number of people learn the location of your portal. Something I think we'd all like to avoid."

"Agreed," said Vega.

"So I propose we go stealth," said Redford. "The Tarts don't know about your invisibility tech. So let's use it. You and a force of say forty armed Vorians go into the Albanian woods along with Anna. Each of you shielded by your invisibility tech. The Vorian force recons the area, and then creates a kind of corridor, a protected path to the portal. When the portal activates, you and Anna, still invisible, waltz right through."

"Impressive," said Vega. "I like it. And this is good timing. Several weeks ago, I asked Kaitlyn to modify the invisibility generators so that they're portable and can be used to conceal individuals."

"Perfect," said Redford.

Anna nodded. "My intuition is telling me this plan will work," she said. "That an invisible fighting force will more than make up for a disparity in numbers."

The alien leader turned to his chief scientist. "So how are the individual invisibility units coming along?" he asked.

"They've pretty much been perfected," replied Kaitlyn. "I brought two working prototypes with me when I rushed here from Europe to meet Anna. They're in the form of lapel pins, about the size and thickness of a screw-on bottle cap. I put them in the optics lab in building three for further testing, but I'm convinced they're ready to go."

"How do they work?" asked Redford.

"Each scans in the body of the wearer," replied the chief scientist, "and will ensure that this body, and any object being held by it, is rendered invisible, regardless of movement. Ansel Cartwright did most of the work in Switzerland and has the best lab to scale it up for our forces. I'm guessing he and his team can produce forty-two individual systems for the team in a few days."

"Outstanding," said Vega. "I ordered a number of our people to fly here to protect Anna, but I'll have them all diverted to Albania the moment this meeting is over."

"Quick question," said the colonel. "You've used your impressive invisibility tech to hide the facilities we're in now. So why haven't you used it to hide your portal?"

"We tried," replied Vega. "But the portal stubbornly refused to play along. It's the only object we've encountered that seems immune from the technology. Fortunately, when it's inactive, as it is most of the time, it's perfectly reflective."

"I see," said Anna, nodding. "Which makes it nearly invisible on its own. You look at it and you see the reflection of trees and forest undergrowth, which is what you'd expect to see in a forest anyway."

"Exactly," said Vega. "But even if we can't make it fully invisible, I think Steve has come up with a sound plan."

"I hope so," said Redford. "But I should point out the obvious, that this is only a thirty-thousand-foot look at a broad strategy. There are numerous details to be worked out. We need a very precise plan of attack. I can get footage of the portal and vicinity from satellites, but given the forest, this will be of limited value. So we'll need painstaking drone surveillance of every square inch of the forest. I'll also need to know the weapons you Vors can bring to bear and the general skill level of the people you'll be sending to Albania. Then we'll have to organize them into small squadrons and set up the proper command structure for maximum order, cohesion, and versatility. We'll need to choose a staging area. Then we'll have to refine and polish the plan until we're convinced it's as flawless as we can make it."

Vega nodded. "I can't tell you how glad I am that you're on our side," he said. "You clearly have a better grasp of tactics and strategy than we do. So let's get on this. I'll contact Ansel Cartwright in Switzerland immediately to get him started on the personal invisibility tech. I'll have others get the drone survey completed. Colonel, I assume that you're willing to be in charge of further refinements to the plan."

Redford nodded.

"Good," said the alien leader. "Anna," he continued, "are you okay with leaving two mornings from now for Albania? I'd like to be sure that we're in position the moment everything is finally ready to proceed."

"*I'm* okay with it," said Anna. "But I'm not sure about Steve. What do you say?" she asked the colonel.

Redford made a face as though he had eaten moldy cheese. "I'm afraid I can't go with you," he whispered. "I need to coordinate with the president and our anti-Tart forces. Frequently. And I need to make an appearance at Evie headquarters. Settle down some nerves."

He sighed. "Besides, I'm not sure I can take watching you step through that portal. I don't have a problem with a long-distance relationship. God knows no one is worth waiting for more than you are. But twenty-five thousand light-years? The term *long distance* doesn't quite cover it."

Anna's eyes moistened, and a single tear formed in the corner of her eye. "I'll be returning to Earth frequently," she said, although she appeared to be reassuring herself as much as Redford, and everyone in the room knew that the portals were too fickle for her to say this with any confidence. "And look on the bright side," she added, trying to smile through obvious despair, "you won't have to worry about me falling for another guy. At least not a human one."

Redford sighed. "Are you sure you really want to do this, Anna?"

"I don't *want* to do this," she replied. "I *have* to do this. And I know that the timing couldn't be worse as far as our relationship is concerned."

Redford looked shattered, like a little boy who had lost a puppy, but he didn't respond.

Vega opened his mouth to speak, but closed it again.

"Do you have something you want to add, Tom?" asked Anna softly.

Vega still looked uncertain. "I don't want to get too personal," he said.

"Please," said Anna. "Go ahead."

The alien leader thought about this further, and finally decided to proceed. "It's just that, based on my study of human relationships, I'm surprised by how close you and Steve seem to be. You've only known each other a few days, yet you act the way I would expect if you had known each other for much, much longer. What am I missing?"

"Nothing," said Anna despondently, apparently still saddened at the prospect of leaving a man she had come to care for. "You're right.

Most of the time, relationships develop much more slowly. But on very rare occasions, the process can accelerate. Maybe my clairvoyance helped, because we both got a quick sense that our relationship was somehow meant to be. So we let down our guard sooner than we ever would have under normal circumstances. And when we did, we both liked what we saw, and this only reinforced and heightened our emerging feelings. But believe me, it surprises us as much as you."

Redford nodded. "And sorry you have to catch us in this state," he said. "When you're around a couple just beginning to fall hard for each other, it can be nauseating. I know. But when you're the couple, you can't seem to help it."

"I understand," said Vega. "From my reading on human pair bonding, there's a euphoria associated with initial romantic love. And these feelings impact the brain the same way as drugs like cocaine."

"Whoa," said the colonel. "Let's not get *too* carried away. Your use of the term *love* is way premature."

"*Way* premature," seconded Anna.

"But no need to discuss this further," said Redford. "Anna and I will make sure you aren't around when we say our goodbyes, so you won't have to worry about getting sick."

There was a long silence. "Okay then," said Vega. "I guess we're done here."

"Not quite," said Anna. "There is one more thing. Something very important. Earlier, you told me that you had lost five people, and have no idea how. Well I do. At least my gut does. It came to me recently, and Steve and I discussed this at length during our private meeting just now." She paused for effect. "One of the Vors on your team, Tom, is a traitor. I don't know who."

Vega shook his head. "It can't be," he said. "That's the first thing I considered. But I quickly ruled it out."

"Why?" asked Anna.

"Because I refuse to believe that one of our people would actively work against their own species."

The detective nodded. "I considered it, too, when you first brought it up," she said. "And my intuition also ruled it out. But no longer. Now my gut is saying just the opposite. Strongly."

Vega still looked skeptical. "I trust your intuition, Anna," he said. "I do. But I assume you didn't get this from a vision, or you'd know who it was."

Anna frowned. "True enough," she said miserably. "I've strained to find out, but with no luck. All I know is that my intuition tells me there's a traitor in your midst, and that you and I are safe from whoever it is."

"Which makes sense," said Redford thoughtfully. "Now that your clairvoyance has been enhanced, if the traitor tries to kill you in the future, you'll see it beforehand and learn their identity. So they have to lie low."

"I think that's right," said Anna. "But absent any direct move against me in the future, I can't get an identity. Because I still can't direct my abilities. Something comes to me or it doesn't. And I think there are just too many suspects, too many possible futures, and too many other vital things going on for me to sort it all out."

"Keep trying," said Kaitlyn. "I'm sure it will come to you. And your abilities should grow stronger every day." She looked unsettled. "Still, this changes everything. Forty-one out of fifty-nine of us will be in Albania paving the way for you to get through the portal. So the odds are that the traitor will be in this group, working against us."

The chief scientist turned to face Tom Vega. "Shouldn't we delay the mission until we've figured out who it is?"

"No," said Anna before the alien leader could respond. "We just have to count on me being able to see any major surprise before it happens. If they show their hand, I'll sound the alarm right away."

"We should at least warn everyone," said Kaitlyn, "so they can watch their backs. We don't want to sow distrust among ourselves," she added, "but I think all Vorians have a right to know about this."

"I agree," said Vega. "Anna, what do you think?"

"I agree also," said the detective.

"Is there even the slightest chance that you're wrong about this?" the alien leader asked Anna.

"There's always a *chance*," she replied. Then, frowning deeply, she added, "But in this case it's very, very small."

53

Stephen Redford sat at a computer in his bedroom, a room he had once again shared the previous two nights with Anna Abbott, and reviewed the draft of his battle plan yet again. He and Anna seemed to be growing ever closer, and while the term *romantic love* was still premature, it wasn't nearly as absurd as it should have been.

Not that this mattered at the moment. Tom Vega was even now with Anna in a private jet, piloting her on a course to Albania. Redford had said his goodbyes in the wee hours of the morning, had then visited Evie headquarters to reestablish a presence, address his people, and have a new comm implanted in his cochlea, and had now returned. And all of this by late afternoon.

He was exhausted. A state he was long used to, and one that would only get worse until every Tart on Earth had been eliminated.

Kaitlyn O'Connor rushed into the room as if she had seen a ghost. "We have a problem, Steve," she began urgently. "Secretary Stinnett is dying."

"What?" said Redford. "How can that be?"

"I'm convinced it's a delayed effect of the HCS cure."

The chemical compound they were waiting for had arrived the morning before, and Kaitlyn had administered the cure just an hour later.

"But you told us that it was working perfectly," said the colonel. "With no ill effects. And I confirmed this myself when I spoke with him afterwards."

"I know!" replied Kaitlyn. "This shouldn't be happening. I followed the chemical recipe that Tom gave me precisely. And the cure did work. But it must have triggered a delayed reaction. Like the body rejecting a transplant. Stinnett's vital signs started to bottom out thirty minutes ago. Sensors show that his brain is depleted of key neurotransmitters, and he isn't getting proper blood oxygenation. I've managed to stabilize him, but only temporarily. He's currently on full life support. If I don't get him to a hospital with more specialized equipment, we could lose him at any time."

"Where is he now?"

"Two of my colleagues are loading him into one of our helicopters. I can pilot him to the hospital, but I'll need to do this right away."

"What about the portable signal dampener you were working on? Is it ready? We can't have Frey tracking Stinnett's comm."

"It's ready and tested," said Kaitlyn.

"Good. I'll alert the nearest military base to prepare their medical facilities for his arrival."

"The clock is ticking," said Kaitlyn, "and the medical facilities at nearby military installations don't have some of the sophisticated cutting-edge equipment we may need to save his life. So I recommend taking him to Drake Hospital in Salt Lake City. I've cultivated a friendship with a doctor there. A doctor I trust."

"We don't want the state of Stinnett's health to be the lead story in every paper and news channel in the world," said Redford. "Can you get this doctor friend of yours to keep the secretary's identity under wraps?"

"Yes. I'm sure of it."

"Okay, then, take him to Drake. Before you go, do you have any theories as to what happened to him?"

"Only two. First, my predecessors on ancient Earth only used the cure on a few hundred humans during their entire tenure here. Different human beings react to drugs differently. There are any number of drugs developed by your own pharmaceutical companies that have lethal effects on only one in a hundred thousand users. Or one in a million."

"So the secretary could just be the rare person who has an adverse reaction not seen in any of the others."

"Yes," said the chief scientist.

"And the second possibility?"

She hesitated. "Tom was the first to read the log entries made by the original Vorian visitors. I never have. The recipe for the cure was listed there. So maybe he misremembered it when he wrote it down for me. Got it close enough to cure the secretary, but maybe got the concentrations wrong."

Redford frowned. "I thought Vors *didn't* misremember. I thought your superior conscious minds had almost perfect recall."

"They do. But *almost* perfect isn't the same as perfect, and there's a lot going on. I'm also not saying that this is what happened. I'm just saying that it *could* have. If you're thinking for an instant that Tom might be the traitor, I'm telling you this is impossible. There is absolutely no way."

Redford nodded, but didn't respond.

"I have to go now," said the chief scientist. "I just wanted you to know what was happening. I'll contact Tom from the air and fill him in also."

The colonel shook his head. "Don't," he said simply. "I'll take care of it. Tom has a lot on his mind trying to make sure he and Anna make it through the portal. He's still in flight, and reviewing plans. We're scheduled to speak soon anyway, so I'll let him know."

"Understood," said Kaitlyn, rushing from the room.

54

The Vor calling herself Kaitlyn O'Connor landed her helicopter on a smooth sheaf of granite high up on a mountain bluff, one she had scouted out months earlier. Nature's perfect, isolated helipad.

She manipulated a human laptop computer and additional electronics she had brought along so that Stinnett's comm was tied into the helicopter's speaker system, and placed a call through the device implanted in his inner ear.

"Shane Frey, are you out there?" she said.

There was no response.

She repeated this for several minutes before a grating, discordant voice finally blared out through the speaker. "Who is this?" it demanded. "How are you doing this?"

"Hello, Frey," she said. "I've tied into your comm using the connection you built into Wilson Stinnett's comm. But don't bother trying to locate him. I've blocked that part of its functionality."

"Are you going to tell me who this is?"

"You really don't recognize my voice?" she replied. "My Earth name is Kaitlyn O'Connor. Remember now? I was with Colonel Redford and Anna Abbott at Evie headquarters."

"Calling to gloat about your escape, Kaitlyn? Or do you just want to practice your English with a fellow off-worlder?"

"I want to make a deal, Frey."

"A deal?" said the Tart suspiciously. "What kind of deal?"

"The kind that's beneficial to us both. I'm not on the same page as my Vorian brethren. So I want to join forces. You get what you want, and I get what I want."

"So you've gone rogue, is that it?"

"You can call it what you like," said Kaitlyn. "But can I assume you want to hear what I have in mind?'

"Why not?"

"Our portal just reopened a few days ago, allowing two of us through every forty hours. Our leader, Tom Vega, is pulling out all the stops to get Anna Abbott through it as soon as possible. Which has always been his goal, as I'm sure you know.

"So here's my offer. I'll give you the location of our portal, and its precise timing. I'll even give you detailed plans of how Tom plans to get his clairvoyant detective through it. And it's a much better plan than you imagine. Even if I told you the location, and you sent all of your people, she'd still get through. But with the information I can give you, you can stop her."

"And what do you want in return?"

"I want you to leave me and my people alone. You now outnumber us more than ten to one. So I want you to vow not to hunt us down and exterminate us. Do what you want here on Earth. I don't care about the humans. But leave the Vorians alone."

"So you're begging for mercy?"

"I'm *negotiating* for mercy," corrected Kaitlyn. "And you're actually getting the better end of the deal."

"How do you figure that?"

"Do you really want to find out what Anna Abbott can do with a fleet of starships under her command? You get to stop an age-old Vorian initiative, all in exchange for letting a few harmless Vorians live. And you'll need me, even after I give you all the intel I have. Because you can't *kill* Anna. You have to *stop* her. Surround our portal in overwhelming numbers, making it clear to her and Tom that trying to make it through is futile. Suicide. So that neither side engages, and Tom and Anna simply back off. In that way, my people are spared, and your people are spared. And you can leave enough of yours behind to prevent her from ever making it through in the future."

"Remind me again why my overwhelming force and I shouldn't just send a few hundred bullets through her body."

"Because if you kill her in the future, she'll get a vision now, and change that future. She could well see what you intend early enough to figure out a way to kill *you*. It's safer to just go back to the status quo. Which, in your case, is ten to one superiority in numbers."

"Even if you're right, and I decide not to try to kill her, I still don't see why I need you after you give me the portal's location."

"You really don't know what you're up against, Frey. With Anna alive, we're all exposed. You can never be comfortable. The US military, and soon the world military, will be hunting you down. With your tech, you'll be able to survive even this, but not if *she's* around. Trust me, she's your worst nightmare, as I know you've come to appreciate. The ease of her escape from Evie headquarters had to have convinced you of that."

"Once again, this is interesting, but doesn't tell me why I need *you*."

"Because we'll have to work together to devise a plan to eliminate her. I've been working on it, but given her clairvoyance, the plan will have to be complex and wildly inventive. Subtle. Gradual. I'll have to learn a lot more about her capabilities, which is my job anyway. The better I can understand her strengths and weaknesses, the more chance I'll find what the humans call her Achilles' heel. And even after we've killed her, you'll still need me. Since you're leaving us alive, I'll be tipping you off if the Vorians or the Earth's military are about to find you. And since my people will continue their search for additional Annas, I'll make sure they never find one. To be honest, I doubt there's another as perfect as she is anyway."

"Why? Why would you do this? Just to spare the lives of the few Vorians on Earth?"

"I have other reasons also, but why does it matter?" said Kaitlyn. "And just to be clear, you'll be sparing the Vorians here, *and* any who arrive in the future. You can make sure that Anna never makes it to Vor. But those arriving get free passage."

She paused. "So do we have a deal, or don't we?"

"We don't," said Frey. "You've done a good job presenting this fantasy, but there's no way I could ever trust you. It smells like a trap. It smells like a way for you to get me to deploy all of my forces into the teeth of an ambush. I think you're just pretending to be a traitor."

"Is there anything I can say that will get you to believe me?"

"Nothing. So I'm afraid we're done here."

Kaitlyn sighed. She had thought this is where they might end up. Which is why she had gone to the trouble of freeing Stinnett from the Vorian compound. "I can prove that I'm telling the truth," she said.

"How?

"Stinnett. Your previous puppet. Who is now unconscious and serving as our telephone."

"*Previous* puppet?" said Frey. "Does that mean he isn't anymore?"

"No. I gave him the antidote. He's alive and well, and no longer under the influence of HCS. But he was in on all of our planning meetings. He can confirm what I'm telling you. Anna recently announced to all that we have a traitor in our midst. Stinnett can confirm this also."

"And you're that traitor, is that what you're telling me?"

"Yes."

"If Stinnett is no longer under the influence of HCS, why would I trust him any more than I trust you?"

"Because you can put him *back* under the influence," said Kaitlyn. "Do you have more doses?"

"Just one more, recently completed."

"Good. Then that's enough. You can have him confirm the location of our portal, and anything else you want. I'll bring him wherever you want. I'll put myself at your mercy. You can check to be sure I'm not being followed, nullify my comm. Whatever you want to do to convince yourself I'm not part of a trap. Then shoot Stinnett up with HCS, and he'll confirm everything I'm telling you."

There was no response.

"Or let me paint an alternate picture," said Kaitlyn. "You reject my offer. Which means that Anna is guaranteed to get through to Vor. Where her clairvoyance will get stronger, day after day, month after month. And where she'll be dominating battles against the Tartarian Alliance as effortlessly as she's escaped from so many of your foolproof traps."

There was another long pause. "All right," said Frey. "You've made your point. We have a deal. If everything you say checks out, I won't hurt you or any other Vorian. But if it doesn't check out, or if you fail to hold up one nanometer of your end of the bargain, all bets are off."

"Agreed," said Kaitlyn. "And just as a show of good faith, since it will take a while for this to play out, have your people begin preparing for a trip to Albania. That's where our portal is. That way, when you've convinced yourself that I'm on the level, they can travel there without delay."

"Where in Albania?"

"I'll give you the precise GPS coordinates when we're face to face," said Kaitlyn. "So tell me where you want me to go, and let's get this started."

55

Shanifrey Doe ended the connection with Eldamir Kor and returned to his office inside the temporary Tartarian stronghold. His second-in-command would be arriving shortly with the Vorian turncoat and Wilson Stinnett.

Finally.

The stronghold, just outside of Bakersfield, California, was inside a newly renovated factory and was ideal for their needs. It was a perfect, windowless rectangle, one story tall, that housed a hundred thousand square feet of space inside.

Surrounded on all sides by a large concrete parking area and an expansive lawn of grass, forty yards wide, the factory was impossible to sneak up on. Hostiles might hide within a small woods that faced the facility, but given the lawn and parking area, they would have to cover at least sixty yards to reach any door. And Shanifrey had seen to it that they would never make it that far.

A large sign in front indicated that the expansive building was a factory for "Aunt Sophie's Baked Treats, Incorporated," and Shanifrey had even ordered one of his underlings to create a false website for the fictitious company, borrowing content liberally from the web pages of Little Debbie and Hostess Cakes.

The factory had been slated to serve as an impregnable bunker and Foria production facility, both. But Shanifrey had discontinued work on drug production recently after this initiative had been blown. The US government now knew all about Foria and its deadly purpose. Besides, the Tartarians didn't need it anymore. The technologies the large, newly arrived group of Tartarians now planned to unleash on the world would suit their needs far better.

Fully seventeen hours had passed since Kaitlyn O'Connor had contacted him and proposed her deal. And much had happened during this period.

Shanifrey had sent Eldamir Kor and three other Tartarians to meet with Kaitlyn at a site he had selected in Colorado. There, they had confirmed that Stinnett was alive and well, had nullified the Vorian's comm so she couldn't be tracked, and had carefully scanned for anything giving off an EM signal. And these were just the first of the heroic measures they had taken to be certain Kaitlyn couldn't be followed back to the Tartarians' temporary stronghold.

They also allowed the Vorian to make a call to her home base—a heavily supervised call—three hours in, to report that Stinnett was unconscious in a room in Drake Hospital in Salt Lake City. She let it be known that he was expected to make a full recovery, but might remain unconscious for several days, and that she would stay with him until he was fully out of the woods.

Eldamir and his three comrades had then played a lengthy and painstaking shell game, traveling into tunnels and then out again with different vehicles, swapping various helicopters and planes, and taking such a wild, convoluted route to the stronghold that a trip that should have taken three or four hours was stretched into four times this length. But at the end of it all, Shanifrey was satisfied that even if someone had had their eye on the pea to begin with, by the time their shell game was finished, the pea was safely hidden once again.

Not that it would matter if the stronghold *were* discovered. Already, it was all but impregnable, and its armaments had been dramatically upgraded during the past few days. When Shanifrey discovered that Nessie had locked him out of the system, he knew that the US military was now surely activated against his people, so he had accelerated his plans for the site. He had seen to it that lasers and tractor beams were installed to make the factory all but impregnable, even from the US Air Force and any missiles they might choose to deploy.

And just in case the stronghold *was* breached, thick steel barriers could be quickly lowered to enclose Shanifrey's office and a thirty-foot perimeter around it. This would give the Tartarian leader plenty of time to uncover a hidden panel in his office and enter a reinforced tunnel that had recently been completed, allowing him and his top lieutenants to escape to a small warehouse a half mile away that contained three large helicopters.

And this was only the beginning. Soon, they would begin construction of a permanent stronghold in Colorado, built into the side of a mountain. And this stronghold would deploy new and improved technologies, installed as quickly as their hugely expanded team of scientists could jerry-rig human technology to produce what they needed.

Shanifrey prided himself on always erring on the side of caution, and his recent moves were no different. The improvements to his temporary bunker. His plans for an even better permanent one. And the care he had insisted they take while bringing Kaitlyn O'Connor to their stronghold, all were manifestations of this prudence.

But despite his cautious nature, he had chosen to deploy his forces to Albania immediately after speaking with the Vorian turncoat. He had told her that he would ready these forces for such a trip, but wouldn't send them until she and her intel had been fully vetted. But this had been a lie.

In fact, he was sending six hundred eighteen members of his team to this European country, and most had already arrived, or would do so in the next eight hours. Twenty-eight more were now tucked safely away, with him, at the Bakersfield factory, and thirty-three others were spread throughout the world, ensuring that sixty-one Tartarians would remain, even if they lost everyone in Albania.

He felt certain Kaitlyn was exactly who and what she claimed to be. A weak, sniveling Vorian traitor desperate to save the lives of herself and her tiny group on Earth. He had told her otherwise, pretended to disbelieve her and walk away, but this had only been intended to improve his negotiating position and to see how she would react. In truth, he had believed her almost from the start.

She had led off by telling him that the Vorian portal had recently reappeared. This was a vital piece of intelligence she would never have shared if she were simply playing him. And she had no idea that he already knew this was the case. No idea that he had used Nessie to listen in on their conversation while they were traveling to Evie headquarters, and had heard this news for himself.

Besides, there was no reason for her to attempt a charade. He didn't know the location of the Vorian portal, so there was no way he could prevent Vega from taking his clairvoyant prize through to his home planet, uncontested, and completing his mission. Which would be a massive win for the Vorians.

Finally, it would serve no purpose for her to lead him on a wild goose chase to Albania while she was putting her life in his hands. If she had lied, he would soon know it, and she would gain nothing, other than a Tartarian-assisted visit to the afterlife.

He also wasn't surprised she'd become a turncoat, given what he knew about the Vorians. Many were brave and would die for their cause. But others, especially the scientist class like Kaitlyn, were pacifists and cowards.

So he hadn't waited to send his team to Albania. He had sent them immediately, to give them the maximum time to prepare for the decisive battle to come. And while he had agreed to scare the Vorians into beating a hasty retreat, he had no intention of letting Anna and her Vorian allies leave in one piece.

This was his best chance to end this, once and for all. The human detective had proven herself a legitimate threat, probably the only one on the planet, and he wasn't about to pass up a golden opportunity to remove her from the board before she grew any stronger.

56

Kaitlyn O'Connor and the secretary of defense—who was now conscious—were led at gunpoint by four Tartarians into one entrance of a massive factory, so bright inside that it was all but blinding to a human. Both were bound, and both of their mouths were covered with duct tape.

Before they entered, Eldamir Kor removed a pair of ultra-dark sunglasses and slipped them onto Stinnett's face, protecting eyes that were now slammed shut.

They were led across a polished concrete floor bigger than a football field, bereft of most machinery now that the Foria production plans had been halted, and into one corner of the facility and the office that Shanifrey Doe had taken for his own. Kaitlyn wasn't surprised to find that the Tartarians were not using the red, light-amplifying technology implanted in their eyes, as the facility was bright enough to obviate the need.

The alien commander motioned them into his office. "Kaitlyn O'Connor," he said in English, reaching out to rip the duct tape from her mouth. "Thanks for dropping by."

"Hello, Frey," she replied, also in English. "Nice lighting. The first time in years I don't feel slightly anxious."

"At least there's *something* we can agree on," said the alien leader.

"How about untying us?" she said. "I saw a dozen or two of your soldiers milling about this building. And the people you sent to Colorado all but climbed into my orifices with an electron microscope to look for weapons."

Frey nodded at two of the guards accompanying Eldamir, and they made quick work of the prisoners' bonds, but left the duct tape across Stinnett's mouth. A third guard shoved a needle into the secretary's neck and depressed the plunger, which Kaitlyn saw from the corner of her eye.

"HCS?" she said.

Frey nodded.

"How long before it takes hold?"

"Almost immediately," he replied.

They waited in silence for five minutes.

"Wilson Stinnett," said Frey when he was certain the drug had taken effect. "You will follow my every order, and you will only respond to my voice. Nod if you understand."

Stinnett nodded.

"You will not speak unless spoken to," he said, motioning for one of his men to tear the tape from Stinnett's mouth.

"Ask him," said Kaitlyn. "He'll confirm everything I told you."

"Not so fast," said Frey. "I have to be sure he's truly under my control."

"Do your historical records indicate the drug has ever failed?" asked Kaitlyn.

"No. But then again, you might have come up with an antidote that acts like a vaccine, protecting humans from future doses."

"Even though our ancestors never managed this after five hundred years?"

"You can never be too careful," said Frey. He had two of his men separate the prisoners, and they held Kaitlyn tight while he handed Stinnett a gun. Eldamir drew a gun of his own and held it on the secretary of defense from behind, carefully watching his every move now that he was armed.

"Mr. Secretary," said Frey, "shoot yourself in the right thigh."

Stinnett didn't hesitate. He pointed the gun and pulled the trigger, screaming as the bullet drilled a gaping hole in his leg. He might now be a possessed zombie, but that didn't mean he didn't feel pain.

Frey waited for his men to bandage Stinnett's leg, and then handed the secretary a combat knife. "Take off your glasses and very slowly, *deliberately*, bring the tip of this knife to the center of your left eye. When it reaches your eye, shove it slowly through and into your brain. Start when I say the word *now*."

"Really, Frey?" protested Kaitlyn in disgust. "You weren't convinced when he shot himself? No need to prove that you're a sadist on my account."

"Not sadism," said Frey. "Caution. I got to where I am by being careful. And smart."

The Tartarian commander turned to Wilson Stinnett. "Now!" he said, and watched intently as the secretary removed his sunglasses and slowly, carefully inched the knife toward his eyeball, fighting to keep his eyelid open against the blinding brightness.

Kaitlyn looked on in horror, having trouble believing that she was actually working with this barbarian. The tip of the knife was just millimeters away from Stinnett's pupil, and Kaitlyn turned away, unwilling to watch this bulbous orb explode into a mass of fluid and blood.

"Stop!" shouted Frey an instant before the tip entered squishy flesh. "Reverse the knife. Put your glasses back on."

Stinnett did as ordered, seemingly oblivious to how close he had come to losing an eye.

Frey turned to Kaitlyn. "He does seem to be under my control," he said. "Few beings of any kind could get this close to mutilating themselves so stoically if they were just pretending. But I do have one last test."

"You are very, very sick," said the Vorian chief scientist.

"Just thorough. A trait I should think you'd approve of, since you intend to be my partner."

Frey paused. "Mr. Secretary," he said, handing Stinnett the same gun he had used earlier to shoot himself in the thigh. "Shove the barrel of this gun into your mouth and pull the trigger."

Kaitlyn watched in horror as Stinnett calmly opened his mouth wide, ate the barrel of Frey's gun, and depressed the trigger in one smooth motion.

And this time, Frey didn't shout out a last-second reprieve.

57

Kaitlyn braced herself for an explosion that would take out much of the back of Stinnett's head and create a burst of brain matter and blood against the wall.

But neither event came to pass.

"Remove the gun from your mouth and hand it back to me," said Frey to his puppet instead.

Kaitlyn allowed herself to breathe once again as she pieced together what must have happened. "So the gun only had the one round?" she said as Stinnett dutifully did as Frey ordered.

"Correct," said Frey. "Stinnett didn't know that, of course. But he still didn't hesitate to pull the trigger."

"So are we done now?"

"Yes. I have no doubt he's under my control."

"Good, so can we finally get on with it?"

Frey nodded. "Secretary Stinnett," he said, "we're going to have a conversation. I need you to answer truthfully and completely at all times, understood?"

"Understood," said the secretary.

"Kaitlyn says that Anna Abbott has let it be known that the Vorians have a traitor among them. And she says the Vorian portal is in Albania. Are these both true statements as far as you know?"

"They are," said Stinnett immediately.

"Are you familiar with the Vorian plan to get Anna Abbott through their portal?"

"I am," he said woodenly. "Although not in great detail."

"As far as you know," continued Frey, "is Kaitlyn here planning to double-cross me? Is her interaction with me part of a Vorian trick?"

"No," said Stinnett simply.

"Are you aware of any deceit at all that might impact me or other Tartarians?"

"Yes. I believe Colonel Redford hopes to deceive any Tartarian forces in Albania who are trying to prevent Anna from entering the Vorian portal. As part of his military strategy."

Frey smiled. "I don't doubt it. But other than this, are you aware of any other trickery?"

"None."

"Good," said Frey. "Now I'm going to change gears. Kaitlyn is going to fill me in on the precise location of the portal in Albania, the timing of its active state, and Colonel Redford's plans as she knows them. If you hear one word that isn't true, as you understand it, speak up immediately."

"Understood," said the secretary of defense.

Kaitlyn went on to tell Frey and his second-in-command everything she knew. The general plan, which involved the use of invisibility technology, and the possible logistics of the operation. Stinnett didn't call her out on a single lie.

Frey was stunned. Invisibility technology? Apparently, the Vorians had perfected this technology on their home world, and had managed to implement it here. It was a game-changing piece of intelligence. Even if he had known the location of the Vorian portal, without this intel his forces would have been vulnerable. This was yet another indication that Kaitlyn's defection was sincere.

She had also thoroughly described the operation of the individual invisibility units that were being prepared. They were wearable, and when activated would quickly scan the user's body and anything attached, including backpacks, guns, knives, grenades, and so on, making all of it invisible, regardless of subsequent movement—as long as the item remained in contact with the person wearing the generator. If this had not been the case, machine guns and backpacks would seem to float in midair, almost completely nullifying the usefulness of the technology.

"You've told me the basics of the plan and the timing of the portal," he said when she had finished. "But I need more. I need the *detailed* deployment strategy."

"I don't have it to give you," said Kaitlyn. "When Anna announced we had a traitor, Colonel Redford became cagey. Everyone knows the broad plan, but he's keeping the specifics close to the vest. He's developing multiple strategies, and only he knows which he'll deploy. Each subcommander will be given a different set of instructions and won't share them with the others. Everything is being carefully partitioned, and doled out on a need-to-know basis only."

She paused. "But that won't matter. If you encircle the portal with five or six hundred of your people and dig in, there's no way they'll engage. Even though Tom Vega and his army will be invisible, and no matter how clever their planned formations, they'll know there are too few of them to prevail."

"There's only one problem," said Frey. "I've changed my mind. Merely stopping Anna isn't good enough. I intend to kill her after all."

"Were you not paying attention?" snapped Kaitlyn. "Did you not hear what I said when I first contacted you? If you try to kill her, she'll see it coming long before, and it will backfire."

"Normally I would agree with you," said Frey. "But in this case, I think she's *already* seen it coming. And she's already *discounted* it. Which is why it's going to work."

"What are you talking about?"

"I had Nessie listen in to you on your way to Evie headquarters," he said smugly.

Kaitlyn was shocked to hear this, but only for a moment. It should have been obvious once they had learned that Frey could control Nessie. "So what?"

"I heard Anna describing her visions of the portal," said Frey. "And I plan to make her second one come true."

"Impossible," said the Vorian chief scientist. "By now, there's no chance that either one will come true."

"Isn't there?" said Frey. "I think you're wrong. I believe this second vision represents the perfect loophole, one that we can exploit. She's *already* seen her death. She's *already* had her warning. And while she's sure she's taken steps to avoid this fate, I've come to believe she's actually doing the opposite."

"The opposite? What does that mean? You think she's actually bringing this future *about*?"

"Exactly. Without realizing it, of course. And this is the only way to beat her. Her only vulnerability is seeing a perilous future and ignoring it, because she thinks she's made sure it can't possibly come to be."

"But your theory would require that this future plays out precisely the way she saw it."

Frey nodded. "I know."

"You do realize that most of your people were killed in this future, right? Which makes sense, because if you try to *engage* our invisible forces, rather than play defense, the Albanian woods really will turn into the bloodbath Anna envisioned. For my people also."

"Weren't you the one telling me how dangerous this woman is?" said Frey. "Weren't you the one telling me that we'll eventually need to devise a plan devious enough to kill her? She's the ultimate prophet, right? Growing stronger by the day. And you've admitted that you have no idea yet how it's even possible to kill her."

"All of this is true," admitted Kaitlyn.

"So we have to do this," continued Frey. "Even if both of our sides take significant losses. It's the only way to stop her for good. You and I both know that if we wait while she grows stronger, the losses could end up being even greater, with no guarantee we can take her out. So we do this. And when the smoke clears, I'll honor our agreement and leave your survivors in peace. I'll allow future Vorians safe passage here. But this is non-negotiable. This could be the only chance to kill her that we'll ever get."

"But for your theory to be true," said Kaitlyn, "you'd have to recreate *everything* about her vision. If one thing is off, then everything might change, and she might make it through."

"I agree," said Frey.

"But she saw US special forces in the woods, fighting on *your* side," said Kaitlyn. "And there's no way that can happen now. You're no longer able to command the US military."

Frey smiled. "But Stinnett still is," he pointed out. "And I control *him*." He paused. "Or haven't you been paying attention?

There was a long silence as the Tartarian commander shared a smirk with Eldamir Kor, his second-in-command, who continued to stand by his side, gun at the ready.

"What's the matter, Kaitlyn?" said Frey. "No good counterargument? Even you have to admit, it's a bit eerie how events seem to be moving inexorably toward the fulfillment of Anna's second vision. I just have to make sure to do my part."

"Are you sure you can? Right now, your US special forces deployment is just conjecture."

"Let's find out," said Frey confidently. "Secretary Stinnett, can you order the US military to Albania without the blessing of your president?"

"No," said Stinnett. "Not the 'regular' US military. Not to fight. And Congress would need to be notified within forty-eight hours. Deploying our forces without invitation could lead to an international incident and too many questions. I don't think the president would ever agree."

"Not a problem," said Frey, "because the point is for him *not* to know. You said *regular* US forces. What about special forces? Can you deploy these military assets based solely on your authority? And order them to keep this confidential, even from the president?"

"Yes," said Stinnett. "I can deploy up to two hundred of them on my sole authority. A subset of special forces that are technically part of Black Operations. Commandos slated for secret operations in enemy and allied territory both. Forces that we can insist are rogue if everything goes south. In cases like this, it's actually better if I don't brief the president, so he has plausible deniability."

Frey beamed and turned to Kaitlyn. "What do you know?" he said. "Looks like Stinnett *is* able to deploy US special forces to fight on our side. In fact, the use of these forces, the very same forces that Anna foresaw, is the *only* way to deploy the US military in Albania. I knew I could make this happen," he added excitedly. "Because I've *already* made it happen in the future."

Kaitlyn nodded slowly, lost in thought. For the first time, she was beginning to believe that Frey might be right.

"Secretary Stinnett," said the Tartarian commander, "I need you to deploy the maximum number of Black Ops commandos to Albania right now. And make sure they keep this confidential, even from your president, as we just discussed. You can brief them when they're on the way. You'll need to tell them the exact parameters of the coming conflict. That this is a war between two alien species. You'll need to tell them about the Vorians' invisibility, and the fiery eyes of my people. And you'll need to convince them that this battle is vital for the very survival of humanity. That they need to help the Tartarians defeat the Vorians, and kill Anna Abbott, at all cost."

He paused to let this sink in. "Do you think you can do that?"

Stinnett nodded. "I'm sure of it," he said.

PART 6

"You can't connect the dots looking forward; you can only connect them looking backwards. So you have to trust that the dots will somehow connect in your future. You have to trust in something—your gut, destiny, life, karma, whatever. This approach has never let me down, and it has made all the difference in my life."

—Steve Jobs

"Most gods throw dice, but Fate plays chess. And you don't find out 'til too late that he's been playing with two queens all along."

—Terry Pratchett

58

Navy SEAL Commander Horace DeMarco called a halt, and over eight hundred beings swarming though the heart of a ninety-square-mile Albanian forest stopped en masse.

"At ease for the next five minutes," he said through his comm, which reached each and every member of this mixed-species team. "I recommend drinking at least eight ounces of water to avoid future dehydration," he added.

This wasn't something he would need to remind his one hundred ninety-nine fellow Navy SEALs, but when it came to the six hundred eighteen intimidating, red-eyed members of the Tartarian species—who knew? How much water did they need? Had they even brought any with them?

DeMarco was responsible for the preparation of his fellow SEALs, and each was dressed in full-on commando gear, which included body armor, belt-fed machine guns, and vests with dozens of pockets for spare clips, grenades, knives, and so on. But the Tartarian forces, comprised of more females than males, had chosen not to come camouflaged. Even if they had been savvy enough to make this choice, their blazing red eyes would stand out, even in broad daylight.

The never-ending woodland consisted of untold millions of trees, including oak, black pine, chestnut, maple, and linden, although the part of the forest they were in was heavy with chestnut trees, one of the commander's least favorite. He liked the low branches and the small, spiky balls that housed the chestnut fruit inside, but the pollen was now ripe and gave off such a heavy, sweet scent that he felt he was encased in a giant mound of cotton candy. This, combined with the odor he detected when he was too close to a group of Tarts—the smell of rotten eggs—made him wish he had brought a pair of nose plugs.

"Commander DeMarco," said the voice of Wilson Stinnett in his ear, "report."

"As you know, sir," began DeMarco, "we had almost no time for planning and recon, so I'm having to adjust the original plan on the go. We're five miles into the forest from our agreed-upon insertion point, and still four miles from the portal. Given the terrain and the sheer numbers of our combined forces, I've split us up into ten teams. Each consists of twenty SEALs and approximately sixty Tarts. Each team has been assigned numbers, and subdivided by . . . species. So I'm in Team 1, which is divided into Spec Ops 1 and Tart 1. Still un-wieldy, but I don't want to break it down further."

"Understood," said Stinnett. "Continue."

"We'll plan to place all of the teams within five to ten minutes of the portal, spread out. Five to ten minutes at a full run, and taking the dense and uneven terrain into account. We'll make sure we're in position at least an hour before the portal is scheduled to become . . . . active. If we surround the portal with only a fraction of our forces, we'll be sitting ducks for any—"

DeMarco stopped as the weight of what was really happening bore down upon him. He was trying to be professional, trying to pre-tend this was business as usual, but for a moment he couldn't do so. He had never commanded even close to this many SEALs on a single mission, let alone over six hundred others. And he was doing so in the middle of a forest in Albania, where there was apparently a magic portal that led to an alien planet twenty-five thousand light-years away. And he was inserting his unwieldy team into the middle of a looming battle between two extraterrestrial species. Finally, as if this weren't enough, the fighting force of one of the species was expected to come cloaked by perfect, flawless invisibility.

He had been trained to handle the unexpected, but this exceeded his lifetime quota of unexpected by a hundred-fold.

For just a moment, DeMarco thought he might vomit, but he forced his stomach to settle down, despite the pungent, sweet odor of the chestnut trees and the foul smell of sulfur.

"Commander?" said the voice of the secretary of defense in DeMarco's comm. "I lost your signal for a moment. Can you repeat your last sentence."

"Sorry, sir," said DeMarco. "I was saying that if we surround the portal with only a fraction of our forces, we'll be sitting ducks for the ... *invisible* Vor forces, and will take heavy losses. But if we surround the portal with overwhelming numbers, the Vors will likely retreat and call off their mission."

"I'm well aware, Commander. I assumed that's why your plan is to leave the portal seemingly unprotected to lure them in."

"That's right. Hopefully we'll engage and kill Anna Abbott before she gets anywhere near her goal. But if not, just before the portal is due to become active, I'll deploy a handful of my best men to hide in close proximity to it. We'll make sure vibration sensors have been placed before this time to alert us to her presence, invisible or not."

"Good," said Stinnett. "I know I don't have to remind you that killing this woman is *everything*. If she calls off her mission and remains alive, you've *failed*. And even though I can't tell you her exact role in the Vorian plan to destroy humanity, if we don't kill her here and now, the consequences will be *devastating*. Obviously, wiping out all Vors and avoiding losses on our side is a plus. But nobody leaves that forest until Abbott is dead."

"Roger that," said the SEAL commander. "Are you still in contact with the Tart commander stateside?" he asked.

"I am."

"Can you confirm that you're both getting the video feeds from the Tarts' body cameras?"

There was a short pause. "Yes, our computers indicate that the feed from all six hundred eighteen cameras is coming in clearly."

"I recommend that you turn off all but a few of them per team. Over six hundred views of the battle will be too chaotic to make sense of."

"The Tarts have developed advanced algorithms to handle this," said Stinnett. "They've programmed an AI to sort through all feeds and only present those that are most informative. The AI will rotate through various scenes as necessary to give us the most efficient, comprehensive picture of what's happening. We may even get a better sense of the battle than you."

"That may be true," said DeMarco. "Regardless, I request continued full operational control of all forces, human and Tartarian, even after we engage the enemy. I'd ask for you to confirm this with the Tart commander and have him instruct his people to follow my orders without question. Despite your ability to see a video feed, you still aren't on the battlefield, sir, and neither is the Tart commander. And since you're six thousand miles away, there's a communication time lag. It's very brief, but given how quickly events will unfold here, it will likely become a significant hindrance."

The commander paused. "Also," he continued, "our forces have considerable experience fighting in a forest environment. In an *Earth* forest environment. The Tarts, on the other hand, no matter how well trained they might be, are dealing with sub-optimal lighting for their species, and are breathing air that is also sub-optimal."

"Understood," said Stinnett. "I'll discuss this with Shane Frey, the Tartarian commander, now."

Less than a minute later his voice returned. "Your request has been granted, Commander," he said. "Commander Frey has agreed, and is even now instructing his forces to follow your orders throughout the operation."

"Thank you, Mr. Secretary," said DeMarco. "I promise you, sir, that you won't regret it. Nothing will stop me from carrying out my mission, no matter what it takes."

"Thank you, Commander. Of that I have no doubt."

59

Wilson Stinnett sat at a large circular table in Shane Frey's spacious factory office and stared at an eighty-inch monitor attached to the wall, now broken into just eight tiles, each showing a different view of the Albanian forest. Kaitlyn O'Connor was seated next to him, and Shane Frey and Eldamir Kor were directly across, but all could easily see the monitor.

Two Tartarian women stood watch in the corners of the office, their guns ready in case Kaitlyn tried something stupid.

"All teams are in place, Mr. Secretary," said the voice of SEAL Commander Horace DeMarco through a speaker in the ceiling, several hours after his last report. "We've yet to see any sign of Vors or Anna Abbott," he continued. "Not that this is conclusive, given invisibility. But we've laid enough vibration sensors to encircle the portal, about a quarter mile out from it, which will alert us if they pass through. We've had a few false alarms, caused by forest animals, but nothing else."

"Understood, Commander," said Stinnett. "The AI is choosing views from the Tarts' body cams, and I'll be watching carefully. If I see any leaves moving on their own, or twigs being crushed on the ground, I'll alert you immediately."

"Roger that, sir. The portal is due to activate in seventy-eight minutes. So this is crunch time. Abbott has to be in the woods by now, and I need to be in constant contact with individual team commanders. So this will be our last communication until after she's dead. Unless you see something important in the interim and contact me. Tell the Tartarian commander that his . . . *people*, are in good hands."

"Will do, Commander DeMarco," said Stinnett. "Stay frosty."

Kaitlyn tried to remain calm, but without much success. DeMarco had no idea that he was about to walk into a buzz saw and lose nearly the entire force under his command before Anna was killed. Frey, of course, hadn't told his own people that he had sent them on a suicide mission. He hadn't shared that if things worked out the way he hoped, the vast majority of them would be dead, torn to shreds and left as an all-you-can-eat buffet for the insects and creatures of the forest.

But the massacre of at least seven hundred humans and Tartarians didn't trouble Kaitlyn nearly as much as the loss of forty-one Vorians. This left her heartbroken. But Frey was right. If they backed off now to save lives, it would cost them even more later.

Frey was lost in thought, but finally turned his attention to the Vorian chief scientist. "Kaitlyn," he said, "I need you to contact Vega. I'll briefly allow your signal to get through. I assume you've programmed your comms by now for Vorian to English conversion, and vice versa."

Kaitlyn nodded. "We have," she confirmed.

This was one of the first actions protocol dictated, for the benefit of fellow Vorians just arriving on Earth. Their strong conscious minds and memories allowed them to suck in languages very quickly, but there were a number of languages to learn, depending on where they were assigned, so these translation programs helped them ease into the new world.

"Good," said Frey. "Run the translation program through the speakers, so we hear both sides of the conversation in English."

"And why am I talking to Tom Vega?"

"To see if you can glean any valuable information. Try to get him to tell you if he's seen any hostile forces. How far out from the portal he and his team are. Anything that could help our efforts."

Kaitlyn took a deep breath and nodded. "I'll do my best," she said.

* * *

Tom Vega had never walked through a woods with forty fellow Vorians and an irreplaceable human before. And he especially hadn't done so when each member of this group was invisible. But on the whole, he thought it was going well.

Individual invisibility conferred enormous advantages, but it precluded marching in tight formations. They had spaced out enough to prevent endless collisions, and individuals had only run into each other three times over many hours of hiking. They all maintained communication through their comms, and since all but Anna could use these subvocally, communication was largely silent.

"Tom, it's Kaitlyn," said the voice of his chief scientist in his ear, using their native language.

"Kaitlyn?" he responded subvocally. "Why are you calling? Is Stinnett okay?"

"Still unconscious," replied Kaitlyn. "But his vitals are improving. I'm not calling about that. I just wanted to wish you and your team luck. How's it going so far?"

"Good, as far as we know. Colonel Redford is calling the shots from Huntington, and we haven't seen any Tartarians. We've scouted the area many times over the past twenty-four hours, and there's been no sign of them. I expected this to be the case, since they don't know our portal is here. But we had to assume the worst, as you know."

"How long before the portal is receptive?" she asked.

"About seventy minutes," replied Vega. "We're seventy minutes away from achieving a goal we've hoped to attain for thousands of years. It doesn't seem real to finally have this chance."

"Is the portal in sight?" she asked excitedly.

"No. We're still a mile to the northeast. The colonel is about to deploy our forces in strategic positions along this route, to protect us as we approach. So I need to go. Don't contact me again until this is over, even if the secretary takes a turn for the worse."

"Understood," said Kaitlyn. "Sounds like you have everything under control. Good luck, Tom."

Vega walked in silence for almost a minute, while Redford continued to issue orders to various members of the group.

"Tom, this is Anna," whispered a human voice through his comm. "Were you just in contact with someone?"

"How did you know?"

"One of my hunches. Who was it?"

"Kaitlyn O'Connor."

Anna didn't reply to Vega. Instead, she switched to Redford's channel. "It's go time, Steve!" she announced decisively.

The colonel didn't hesitate. "To all Vorians," he announced immediately, "there's been a change of plans. I'm relinquishing complete control of this operation to Anna Abbott, effective immediately. Disregard all previous plans. Follow her every order, no matter what. All status updates and reports should go directly to her. I'm officially out of the loop."

"Thanks, Colonel," said Anna over the general comm channel. "My intuition tells me we aren't in sight of any hostiles at the moment. So I'm now making myself visible. Squadrons A, B, and C, make yourselves visible and find me as quickly as you can. Once you do, hand me your invisibility units. Hurry!" she added when it was clear the stunned Vorians weren't being responsive. "Don't make me repeat myself."

Vega touched the back of a large lapel pin on his shirt and his cocoon of invisibility disappeared. Throughout the nearby forest, the sea of brown bark and green leaves was now punctuated by various Vorians popping into existence as they followed the same procedure.

Vega was closest to Anna and rushed to her side. "What's happening?" he whispered urgently. "Why did the colonel relinquish control? And why are you collecting invisibility units?"

Anna knelt on the ground and removed five drawstring sacks from her backpack as a number of Vorians began reaching her and handing her their lapel pins. "I don't have time to explain, Tom. But you've always trusted my intuition. I'm asking you to trust it *now*. Do as I say and we'll get through this."

Anna quickly collected the invisibility units from the twenty-one members of squadrons A, B, and C and apportioned them out into the five bags, which had each harbored a number of units to begin with.

Vega felt dizzy and slightly ill as he realized just how uninformed he truly was. The fact that Anna and the colonel had felt the need to keep so many things from him was alarming. And it wasn't just them. Ansel Cartwright, a Vorian, had failed to tell him that he had produced many more than the forty-two individual invisibility units they had asked for.

But how many more, exactly? And for what purpose?

Vega resigned himself to the fact that he wouldn't be getting answers anytime soon.

"Squadrons A, B, and C," said Anna, "retreat back to our Albanian base of operations. Since you can no longer make yourself invisible, you're no longer part of this. Get to safety as quickly as possible."

Vega shot a questioning look at the clairvoyant human. "You're dividing our force in half?" he said in disbelief. "Are you *certain* you know what you're doing, Anna?"

"Not *certain*," she whispered back, "but very confident."

Vega nodded unhappily

"Squadrons D, E, and F," said Anna into the general comm channel, "remain invisible and prepare to follow my detailed instructions."

60

Twenty-five minutes after Redford had relinquished his command of the Vorian forces, Orbimel Cain, a Tartarian female, gasped as Anna Abbott and Tom Vega materialized from out of nowhere, fifty yards distant. They were wedged between several large tree trunks in a dense section of the forest, but Orbimel's team, Tart 7, would first have to cross a large clearing to reach them.

The clairvoyant detective stared directly at those Tarts in Team 7 who were visible through the trees, far off in the distance, and smiled broadly. Then, just to be sure she had caught their attention, she waved.

"Tart 7 leader to Commander DeMarco!" shouted Orbimel breathlessly, forgetting to use subvocalizations. "Anna Abbott and the Vorian leader just lost invisibility and appear to be taunting us. We're going after her now."

"Negative!" said DeMarco. "It's a trap. She's showing herself as bait. Stand your ground. We won't play this out on her terms."

"Tart 7 team leader," said Shanifrey in his own language, "go after her now! All sixty of you! Ignore DeMarco. That's a direct order from me."

"Going after her now," said Orbimel in English, letting DeMarco know she was ignoring the SEAL commander's order. She and her fellow Tarts spread out as they headed to the clearing and raced toward the two targets, who began to retreat back through the forest, but far more slowly than Tart Team 7 was approaching.

As the first wave of Tarts hit the clearing, phantom machine-gun fire broke out from all four compass points around them, slicing dozens of them to ribbons. Just over half of them reached the heavily wooded section on the other side of the clearing while their Tart commander viewed the carnage from his factory stronghold.

"Continue tracking her down!" thundered Shanifrey, using a Tart-only channel. "But sweep the area around you with machine-gun fire as you go. They're invisible, not bulletproof."

The survivors of Tart Team 7 swiveled and shot all around themselves as they moved, kicking up bark and leaves and adding to the hellish, deafening cacophony of machine-gun fire coming from everywhere all at once. But they continued to be cut down as if they were sprinting into invisible helicopter blades churning at full speed, drenching the woods with bits and pieces of their bodies and thick black blood.

Every so often, Anna Abbott would duck out from behind a tree trunk up ahead and taunt the survivors onward, making sure the horses were still chasing their clairvoyant carrot through a gauntlet of death.

Despite sustained efforts by the Tarts to spray machine-gun fire all around, the fire heading their way didn't diminish in the slightest, and Shanifrey searched the video feeds frantically for any sign of Vorian body parts or neon green blood that would indicate Vorian casualties.

But there was no evidence of a single hit. It was impossible! The Vorians were invisible, not ethereal.

Only five members of Tart Team 7 remained, now close enough to Anna and the Vorian leader to fire directly at them. But their targets were both concealed behind beefy tree trunks, and their fusillade only managed to whittle the trunks smaller and burst through low-hanging branches.

The Tart closest to Anna took a bullet to her forehead and crashed to the forest floor, and the four Tarts remaining leaped over her body and kept charging ahead.

And inside a stronghold in California, Shanifrey Doe suddenly realized why the Vorian force seemed so invincible. "They're up in the trees!" he screamed, stating what should have been obvious to all. His team had been trying to pick off invisible phantoms by shooting at chest height, while all the while, the Vorians were cutting them down from the safety of the branches above.

"Spray the trees about twelve to fifteen feet up!" he ordered his soldiers, but the order came too late. Before they had a chance to respond, all four remaining Tart combatants were shredded by a barrage of gunfire, causing explosive bursts of inhuman viscera and thick black blood to be splattered onto trees and forest undergrowth.

A deep voice came over the general comm line. "Commander DeMarco, it's Lieutenant Brent Knox, Spec Ops 3 commander. I have eyes on the attempted incursion by Tart Team 7. It appears there were no survivors. We're nearest to Anna Abbott's last known position. Request permission to come at her from behind to avoid the gauntlet she set up to ambush the Tarts. Our Tart 3 teammates are still several minutes to our south, and I don't recommend waiting for them."

"Permission granted," said DeMarco, who then began barking orders at a number of other teams to move closer to the action.

Shanifrey, anxiously watching the video feeds coming from his soldiers, was encouraged. The secretary had done an excellent job of convincing the US forces that the fate of humanity was on the line if they failed to kill the clairvoyant detective. Shanifrey had no doubt they would sacrifice their lives without hesitation to accomplish this goal.

But the US forces had no camera feeds, so the Tart leader could only guess at the progress the human team was making. Which was *maddening*. On the other hand, in Anna's vision, she had been killed by one human and one Tartarian, so he fully expected all twenty humans in Spec Ops 3 to fail. It was all part of a future history that was already woven into the fabric of the cosmos.

"Lieutenant Knox here!" said a breathless, harried voice on the general comm channel, which was also broadcast to the factory in California. "Spec Ops 3 has taken heavy losses! Seventeen down! The last three of us have taken refuge behind a large rock formation. We've been spraying the forest floor *and* up in the trees. And we're wearing advanced body armor. But I don't think we've touched them! It's almost like they know what we're going to do before *we* do. It's uncanny!"

There was a pause. "But we're now very close to Abbott," he added. "And I think I know how to take her out. So stand by. I plan to turn her into paste within the next few minutes."

61

"The humans with the camouflaged uniforms are on their way here!" said Vega urgently to the woman at his side. "And you didn't place any of our people behind us. There's nothing to stop them from reaching us. We need to return to invisibility!"

"We'll be okay, Tom," said Anna calmly. "Trust me."

"But none of our forces are in a position to protect us," he insisted. "We're exposed, and it's just the two of us."

She was about to respond when a deep voice came through her comm. "Move thirty yards due east to be sure you aren't in view of any Tart cameras, and then go invisible—just in case."

"Roger that," she replied aloud to the bafflement of Vega. "Follow me," she said to the Vorian leader as she moved rapidly to their east.

They quickly picked their way among the trees in silence.

"Halt there!" commanded the same voice as before. "Go invisible."

"Going invisible now," said Anna out loud as she manipulated her lapel pin to make this happen, instructing Vega to do the same.

A stream of machine-gun-carrying US commandos broke through heavy foliage twenty yards away and rushed to their general location. Vega raised his machine gun to fire. "Lower your weapon, Tom!" barked Anna, unable to see him, but still sure that his weapon was raised. "They're friends."

"*Friends?*" said the shocked, disembodied voice of her alien companion. "This was all planned? Do you want to tell me about it?"

"I do," said Anna. "And soon. But it's a long story, so not now."

The commandos changed course slightly, zeroing in on her voice. "Anna, I'm Lieutenant Brent Knox," said the man who had directed her earlier. "I need you to lead us to your position."

"Halt where you are," said Anna's disembodied voice. "I'll toss the five bags your way. They'll become visible as soon as I let go."

She made sure the drawstrings on the five bags of invisibility lapels were drawn tightly closed and tossed them toward the ever-growing number of commandos in the forest nearby. "We could only manage eighty-seven units in total," she said. "But that should be more than enough. I assume you've already been briefed on how to use them."

"We have," said Knox, gathering up the five bags and handing them to others under his command. "We have to go now," he said, as the five soldiers holding bags saw to it that he and eleven other members of Spec Ops 3 now had lapel pins.

As he spoke, he and his men began flaring out of existence as they activated the invisibility units. "I'm leaving ten men behind to protect you," he said. "Eight visible and two invisible. But this should be more than enough to do the job. Have your remaining Vorian forces stand down immediately and retreat to safety. Other than that, enjoy the woods, and wait for us to sound the all clear."

"Will do, Lieutenant," said Anna. "*Thank you*. And Godspeed."

Knox rushed off through the woods. "Commander DeMarco," he said through a private Spec Ops channel, "we have the invisibility units. Five of my men are carrying them, and are now invisible. They just activated transponders. Confirm that you're able to track their positions."

"Confirmed," said DeMarco.

"Good. I'm also invisible, as are four others on my team. Since Frey ordered our Team 3 Tart counterparts to follow in our footsteps after I reported that all but three of us were down, they're only a few minutes behind us. We'll engage this team momentarily."

"Roger that," said DeMarco. "But be careful. You're invisible, but they're now shooting at the ground and lower branches indiscriminately."

"Understood. But if my strategy works as planned, they'll be panicking and taking out *each other*. Death by friendly fire. Or a circular firing squad, if you prefer this metaphor."

"Happy hunting, Lieutenant," said DeMarco.

The commander immediately changed channels to one that could be heard by all two hundred Navy SEALs. "Attention, all personnel," he barked into the private channel. "Lieutenant Knox and four of his men will be opening fire on all Tarts in Team 3 momentarily. When you hear this gunfire, take out as many Tarts on your counterpart teams as possible. Move behind them now. Remember, they think you're allies, so maximize the element of surprise. When the survivors have figured out what happened and begin returning fire, disperse through the trees, and I'll make sure many of you hook up with soldiers delivering invisibility units. Those of you who become invisible help protect those who aren't, and systematically finish all Tarts left standing."

Less than a minute later, Knox and his four teammates opened fire as expected, and all hell broke loose in a one-mile stretch of Albanian woods.

Almost two hundred exquisitely trained Navy SEALs fired machine guns in unison, each weapon capable of delivering six hundred rounds per minute, blindsiding their erstwhile Tartarian allies. Given their knowledge of the stakes, none were too proud not to shoot the Tarts in the back, mowing down large swaths of the hostile aliens all at once, littering the woods with their mutilated corpses and filling the air with the pungent sulfur odors of rotting eggs and dead skunk.

A rampage of forest creatures, large and small, fled the area as if a wall of flames were racing toward them. Countless birds were flushed into the sky, along with thick clouds of insects, all mounting a joint exodus from a level of destruction, noise, and vibration that was beyond any life-form's ability to comprehend.

The bark and wood from hundreds of trees splintered into the air as the almost three hundred Tarts who survived the first few minutes of the attack returned fire and the battle was fully joined. But with every passing minute, more SEALs were handed lapel pins, and their training and invisibility, together, gave them an advantage impossible to overcome.

Eventually, thirty-two Tartarians, realizing they had no hope, managed to flee the scene along with the animals of the forest, and would live to fight another day.

But five hundred eighty six others were now dead, in many cases chewed to shreds by dozens of high-caliber rounds. Many dozens of gallons of alien blood had been spilled, adding black to the rich forest palette of greens and browns, along with the yellow-gold of untold thousands of spent shell casings.

After less than ten minutes, the forest fell silent once again, as all hostile forces were either dead or well on the run.

The contrast between the deafening, *terrifying* sounds of thousands of rounds being shot each second during the opening, simultaneous barrage, and the current silence was profound. The entire exchange was even worse for the Vorians, whose hearing was many times more acute than that of humans.

Knox promptly gave Anna and her protectors the all clear, and the detective and her alien companion shimmered back into the visible spectrum.

Vega eyed Anna in wonder. "That was truly remarkable," he said. "Maybe you can fill me in while we work our way to the portal." He smiled broadly. "It looks like nothing can stop us now."

Anna winced. "About that," she began. "I'm afraid I won't be going through right now, after all. I'm really sorry, Tom. One day I will, but not now. I can't tell you how sorry I am to have misled you like this."

"*But why?*" he asked, looking hurt, betrayed, and confused at the same time. "Please, Anna! I'm begging you. We need you. The *galaxy* needs you."

"I'll tell you my reasoning," she said. "And I'll tell you what just happened here. But that will have to wait. Right now, I need absolute quiet. I have to turn my full attention to Steve Redford, who isn't actually in Utah, after all."

62

"Stand your ground!" screamed Shanifrey to the small group of fleeing Tartarian survivors in Albania. "Continue fighting!"

"It's a *massacre*, Commander," replied one of the Tarts in the forest, barely able to speak as she ran, sucking in nothing but the stale, tepid atmosphere of Earth. "If you order us back, we'll return. But we'll die, and nothing will change. The clairvoyant will still get through."

"She's right," said Kaitlyn O'Connor, glad that Frey hadn't yet switched off the Tart-to-English translation program. "We've lost this round. Anna found a way to change something, after all. The US forces are *against* you, Frey. In her vision, they were on your side. And one of them, along with a Tartarian, shot her dead. That's not going to happen now."

"I agree," said Eldamir Kor. "We can't compound our losses. Let them escape. We need as many of our people alive as possible."

Shanifrey's head looked as if it was about to explode, but he still knew he was getting sound advice. "All parties in Albania," he announced to his team, "disregard my previous order. Continue retreating to safety."

He turned to Stinnett and looked ready to rip out the man's jugular with his bare teeth. "What happened out there?" he demanded. "Tell me how this is possible! How could your men have switched sides?"

The secretary shook his head. "I have no idea. You heard every conversation I had with them. I had no reason to believe they weren't carrying out my orders as expected."

"At least now you're starting to fully understand what you're up against," said Kaitlyn. "Why the Vorians have put so much faith in this detective."

Frey screamed and threw a glass paperweight at the wall, where it shattered into dozens of pieces. He drew a gun and pointed it at Kaitlyn. "*You!*" he thundered. "This has to be *your* doing! Stinnett is under my control, but you aren't!"

"I didn't betray you," insisted Kaitlyn hurriedly. "You vetted me, remember? And I was here with you the entire time. You have a right to be furious. You lost most of your people for nothing. But it's Anna who's responsible, not me."

Frey's gun remained pointed at the Vorian chief scientist. and it appeared that he was slowly squeezing down on the trigger.

"If Kaitlyn is responsible," said Eldamir urgently, "then we need to interrogate her, not kill her. We need to find out how she did it."

Frey gritted his teeth and fought himself, just managing to slip his finger from the trigger before the gun went off.

"But we don't have to keep *Stinnett* alive!" snapped the irate Tartarian commander. "The US military is on to him, so he's useless to us."

"*Warning,*" said the voice of the stronghold's AI through the speaker system before Eldamir could reply. "Perimeter alert. Attempted breach of this facility imminent. Defensive armaments being readied and activated."

"Put the relevant exterior footage on the monitor!" yelled Frey to the AI, and the scenes of a forest in Albania, sent by Tartarians fleeing for their lives, vanished, to be replaced by the factory's grounds.

Dozens of US commandos were sweeping forward across the lawn toward the front of the facility, with their assault rifles leading the way.

"Impossible!" screamed Frey as spittle flew from his mouth. He had been so close to ultimate victory, and now everything was coming unglued at once. He had been certain Kaitlyn couldn't have been followed here, but he had missed something yet again. And after he dealt with this attempted incursion, he was going to find out what it was.

He addressed the two Tartarian women in the corners of his office. "Get this Vorian abomination out of my sight!" he barked, gesturing at Kaitlyn. "Take her onto the main factory floor, and shoot her if she even blinks wrong."

Frey shot the Vorian chief scientist a glare capable of melting lead. "When this is over," he hissed at her as she was being dragged away, "you're going to tell me *everything*. You'll be *begging* me for death. But I won't let you die for a very long time."

* * *

Delta Force Captain Damian Hale and twenty-eight Delta Force commandos under his command, in full combat gear, emerged from a small wooded area and charged the massive, rectangular factory. The lawn that surrounded it was dying, and there were only a few cars present in the large concrete lot that abutted the entrance.

The factory appeared to be unprotected, but even so, appearances could be deceiving, and the captain didn't like the smell of this one little bit.

Hale and his men had been rushed to the site near Bakersfield with no notice and no time to recon the site or to make anything other than the most basic preparations. He was placed under the command of Colonel Stephen Redford, who apparently headed up a secret agency having to do with extraterrestrials, and was tasked with attacking what was purported to be an alien stronghold.

Alien stronghold? Really?

All he had been told was that the secretary of defense, Wilson Stinnett, was inside, and couldn't be trusted. That the goal was to wipe out all aliens, who had a distinctive appearance he had been shown, and knock out or incapacitate Stinnett, while keeping him alive. And that he and his men should bring dark sunglasses along. That was about it.

But what was an alien stronghold doing within a baked goods factory near Bakersfield, California, of all places? What were the aliens' capabilities? Their strengths and weaknesses?

And most important of all, why the rush? Why not surround and surveil the stronghold from afar and attack any aliens leaving its confines? Why not take more time to study what they might be up against and prepare contingencies if the operation went sideways?

Why charge the building in broad daylight when they were sure to be seen coming?

Hale didn't have the answers to any of these questions, since there had been no time for a proper briefing. He just hoped that this idiot in command, this Colonel Stephen Redford, now advancing toward the factory next to him, had a reason for rushing headlong into an unknown situation, other than sheer incompetence.

* * *

Steve Redford had maintained constant communication with Anna for several minutes now, ever since she no longer needed to focus on orchestrating and surviving the mother of all battles in the heart of Albania.

"Still no visions or hunches that might help me?" he asked her subvocally as he rushed toward the factory with Captain Damian Hale at his side, and a large contingent of Delta Force soldiers under his command.

"None," said Anna apologetically.

Redford didn't reply. Her abilities were as frustrating as they were extraordinary.

Anna's intuition had indicated that he should let Kaitlyn leave the Vors' Utah compound with Wilson Stinnett, as long as he had her followed to her final destination. Then, despite putting a crack military team on the job of following her, as well as commandeering a satellite to assist in this regard, the Vorian chief scientist had managed to shake all tails and disappear.

And finally, just three hours earlier, Anna had a vision of the secretary of defense killing himself—at Shane Frey's command—in a baked goods factory turned Tartarian nest just outside of Bakersfield, California. The vision had only lasted seconds, as usual, but Anna had known it had taken place in the near future, just minutes after the battle in the Albanian forest had ended.

Redford knew he couldn't complain—this knowledge was priceless—but couldn't her clairvoyance have given him just a little more time? A little more insight as to what to do? The fact that he had managed to get Hale and so many Delta Force commandos onto the playing field in time was a miracle, but he didn't want to push his luck.

But given that Stinnett's death was imminent, he had no other choice but to charge headlong at the factory in broad daylight, having no idea what he was up against, in order to make sure that the future Anna had seen didn't come to pass.

Her vision had been startling in more ways than one. It was the first time she had seen a future that she, herself, wasn't present in. Neither she nor Redford had known that this was even possible, although, given all that was looming, they didn't have the luxury of exploring the implications further.

What did this mean? Was this a rare occurrence? Or would it become commonplace as her powers grew?

If he survived this misguided raid, maybe he would find out.

All of this flashed through his mind in an instant as he and his Delta Force contingent rushed toward the factory's entrance.

Redford was surprised they hadn't encountered any resistance as they crossed the grass field. But as the three forwardmost commandos crossed an imaginary line about fifteen yards from the building, bright red lasers flashed into existence and cut them down instantly.

One moment the soldiers were charging ahead, and the next, quarter-sized holes were neatly drilled through their foreheads, hearts, and testicles—in the blink of an eye—and the men toppled to the ground, dead on arrival. The lasers had shot out from stainless steel soccer-ball-like structures on tripods that had emerged from the roof, piercing the most advanced body armor known to science to reach the soldiers' hearts as if the armor wasn't even there.

"All forces halt!" screamed Redford as loudly as he could, noting that Hale was doing the same. Not that they needed to. The commandos in the lead were already screeching to a stop. The soldier farthest ahead finished braking just beyond the laser threshold, and three holes were drilled into his right foot before he threw himself backwards, screaming, pulling his mutilated foot back to the safe side of the imaginary line.

Redford couldn't help but marvel at a laser technology the likes of which he had never dreamed of, with a combination of power, speed, and accuracy that was breathtaking.

"All forces," he shouted, "concentrate fire at the tripods on the roof and take them out!"

Automatic fire burst forth from more than twenty assault rifles, but not a single round made it to the targets, as the bullets were each slowed by some kind of force field and then nearly vaporized by thousands of precisely guided laser strikes in a dazzling ballet of red light.

It was absolutely astonishing.

"Cease firing!" yelled Redford. No use wasting ammunition when it was clear that the lasers could stop the barrage of bullets indefinitely.

"Recommend launching grenades at the roof!" said Hale. "Maybe they're big enough that one will get through."

"Do it," said Redford. But less than twenty seconds after the captain issued the order, it became clear that this attempt, too, was futile.

The factory's defensive perimeter protected a single building rather than a planet, and operated on different principles than the planetary shields Vega had described, but it seemed just as effective. It was the perfect defensive dome. But the colonel couldn't help but wonder how long it would be until the Tartarians extended the imaginary line of death and went on offense.

"What about an air or missile strike?" he asked Damian Hale.

"I wouldn't advise it, sir," replied the captain. "Based on what I've seen, this could blow up in our faces. Literally. If they can track a fighter jet coming toward the factory and shoot it down, it could crash in population centers. Same for a missile. Bakersfield has a population of almost four hundred thousand. We can't risk it without knowing the capabilities of their system. I recommend breaking off the attack until we know what we're up against."

Redford nodded. He had no doubt that this was the right course of action. But also no doubt that Secretary Stinnett would soon be dead, if he wasn't already. And while the Tarts in Albania had been pawns, Shane Frey, and presumably his top people, were all in this factory. This was their chance to strike a death blow to the Tartarian leadership, a prelude to rooting out the last vestiges of the Tart cancer still on Earth.

The colonel decided there was one tactic left to try, and he refused to back down, even if it killed him. He handed the captain a lapel pin. "Attach this to your uniform," he instructed, "and order your men to surround the two of us so we can't be seen on any surveillance cameras. Then stand by for further orders."

While Hale was doing as he asked, Redford contacted Anna once again. "We're getting nowhere," he told her subvocally. "They have a mix of tractor-beam and laser tech here that we can't penetrate. Three of our team have been killed. But I have an idea. I brought the two prototype invisibility units from the Utah lab with me. I'm betting the laser system uses an optical targeting system. So if I'm invisible, it won't know I'm there."

"You can't be sure of that!" protested Anna. "It could sense vibration, noise, heat, or anything else."

"It's a risk," he acknowledged as dozens of men formed a human wall around him and Captain Hale. "But I'm hereby committing a hundred percent to taking this risk. You do care about me, right, Anna? I mean, if I were to be vaporized, you'd miss me, right?"

"More than you could ever know," she said softly.

"Good. Then are you getting any visions of my death? Any gut reaction that rushing into this laser kill zone is a bad idea?"

"Nothing," said Anna in frustration. "But I'm not infallible."

"I know," replied Redford grimly. "I'm just betting that my death would be devastating enough to you for your subconscious to take notice." He paused. "Gotta go," he finished.

"Good luck, Steve," said Anna, sounding as though she was fighting back tears.

Redford turned his attention back to Hale. "The lapel pin I've given you can make you and your weapons perfectly invisible," he said.

Before Hale could ask questions or express skepticism, the colonel activated his own pin, showing the captain how to do so, and disappeared, knowing that a demonstration was worth a thousand words.

Hale's eyes widened so much they nearly exploded from his face, but he shook his head, as if to clear it, and activated his own unit.

"All personnel," said the colonel, "retreat back into the woods."

As soon as the commandos began carrying out this order, Redford addressed the captain. "Now that we're invisible," he said, "the lasers shouldn't see us. I'll go first. When I'm sure it's safe, I'll let you know to follow."

"Roger that," said Hale. "And I have to say, Colonel, you have bigger balls than I thought."

"I'm not sure if that's a compliment, Captain," said Redford with a grin, "but I'll take it."

The colonel slid a pair of dark sunglasses onto his face. "Hold here," he commanded, setting off toward the laser threshold. When he reached where he thought it began, he inched forward, bracing himself to dive backwards if any holes were blasted through his forward-most foot.

But as he continued shuffling ahead without attracting any fire, he blew out a heavy sigh of relief. "Captain Hale," he said subvocally, "I'm safely within the laser perimeter. Before you join me, put on your sunglasses. My . . . *girlfriend* tells me that it's blindingly bright inside. But also that Stinnett is wearing shades, which are allowing him to see."

"Your girlfriend?" said Hale's voice in his ear, sounding confused. "How does she know what Stinnett is *wearing*?"

"Long story," said Redford. "Just put on the sunglasses, and I'll tell you how I want to play this."

63

Shanifrey Doe continued studying the monitor in his office and noted with satisfaction that every last commando outside was retreating back the way they had come. The newly installed defenses had performed brilliantly, as he had known they would. Even so, he and his people couldn't stay in this stronghold forever. Eventually, the US military would bring such massive forces to bear on the facility that a breach was inevitable.

"All command personnel," he announced through his comm, "meet me in my office immediately to prepare for evacuation through the tunnel. All non-command personnel, spend the next thirty minutes gathering up anything useful—which includes our Vorian prisoner. Then leave through the tunnel in my office as well. Once you're well away from the building underground, activate the self-destruct sequence to blow the factory behind you, and contact me for further instructions."

Shanifrey fought to suppress a rage that kept trying to resurface. They had suffered heavy blows today, but they would regroup. It would take much longer given that he had lost most of his people in Albania, but he could afford to be patient. Now that Anna Abbott had no doubt passed through the portal to Vor she was finally out of his hair. With her gone, he was sure that he would ultimately prevail.

And regardless of what inroads she was able to make while leading the Vorian Allied Fleet, he had no doubt that his people back on the home world would ultimately find a way to stop her. Even though he had failed, a part of him was glad that the clairvoyant detective was now someone *else's* problem.

Shanifrey had one last task to accomplish before he left. It was time to hand Wilson Stinnett a gun and order him to eat the barrel and pull the trigger once again.

Only this time, he'd be sure the gun was fully loaded.

* * *

"Okay, Colonel, I've deployed the sunglasses," reported Hale, as if he couldn't believe this was something he was actually saying. "What's the plan?"

"We'll go in together. Make your way to the left side of the factory entrance. I'll move to the right side. We'll enter on my mark. Upon entering, the first thing we do is take out as many lights as possible. Force them to use the light-amplifying technology implanted in their eyes, which they won't find optimal."

"So we'll only need the sunglasses for about five seconds?" said Hale wryly.

Redford smiled. "Yes, but a very important five seconds. Our goal is to kill as many of the red-eyed aliens as possible, while knocking Stinnett unconscious so he isn't a threat. If you see a woman with softer features, who doesn't have glowing eyes, try to knock her out as well. "

"Understood," said Hale.

"Ideally, we want to be on the move constantly. Make them think they have many more than just two ghosts to contend with. Freak them out. Hope they begin firing at each other in a panic."

"Roger that," said Hale.

"Last thing," added the colonel. "They give off a faint sulfur smell that's pretty unpleasant. And it gets worse once they're dead. Breathe through your mouth if you have to, but let's turn their stronghold into a rotten egg factory."

Less than a minute later, both men were in position on either side of the door. "Three. Two. One. Mark!" said Redford subvocally, and both men rushed through the door, locating the facility's lights and spraying them with bullets. Enough of the overhead lights were shattered to reduce the illumination inside to just below normal levels, but to the Tarts this was a terrifying level of darkness, and they were plunged into an instant panic.

Redford shot three of the hostile aliens before they could even activate their glowing eyes, and Hale downed four others.

The colonel spotted Kaitlyn O'Connor twenty yards away across the polished concrete floor and sprinted in her direction, diving out of the way as a Tart sent random fire in his direction, grazing his arm.

From the corner of his eye, Redford noted that the captain had taken out two more of the armed Tarts, who continued to fire at shadows

* * *

"Just a few more seconds," said Shanifrey to the twelve command personnel who had just entered his office and were huddled near the newly revealed tunnel opening. He extended a gun toward Stinnett, as a precursor to having him end his own life, when several barrages of automatic weapons fire assaulted his ears. Weapons fire coming from *inside* the facility.

How could this be? The commandos had all retreated, leaving no one behind. Even if they hadn't, none of them could possibly have penetrated the laser perimeter.

"Secretary Stinnett," he yelled, "open the door, go outside this office to the factory floor, and stand approximately five feet from the door."

He turned to face his fellow Tartarians. "Wait here!" he commanded.

As the secretary walked to the door, Shanifrey followed. He'd let Stinnett go through first, his canary in a coal mine. If shooters were waiting to carve whoever emerged into tiny pieces, Stinnett would make an excellent volunteer.

The secretary exited the office unscathed, and Shanifrey followed, his eyes now glowing. He took in the scene at a glance. The long, smooth concrete factory floor was in utter chaos, and his people were being massacred. Dead and disfigured bodies were scattered around the facility, lying in pools of their own blood. Kaitlyn O'Connor was also on the floor with neon green blood seeping from a gash in her skull, but Shanifrey judged that her blood loss wasn't enough to be fatal. And while he couldn't make out a single hostile shooter, the Tartarians still alive were mostly shooting blindly in all directions as though they had seen a ghost.

Shanifrey's eyes widened as the truth became obvious. The shooters had made themselves invisible! Which is how they had beaten the laser perimeter.

He wrote off the still-living Tartarians immediately. Even if they managed to survive the invisible attack, as soon as he was far enough through the tunnel to be safe, he planned to blow the self-destruct explosive charges that he'd had placed throughout the factory. This would turn the building to rubble, and kill any Tartarian survivors. Not that there would *be* any survivors, judging from what he was seeing.

And he might not survive either, he realized, if he didn't buy himself a little time. He shoved a gun into Stinnett's hand and gestured to the carnage occurring on the factory floor, thirty yards away. "Run into the center of the firing," he ordered. "Put the gun to your head and shout as loudly as you can that you'll blow your own brains out in twenty seconds if they don't cease fire. Then count to twenty and pull the trigger. If anyone tries to stop you, kill them. Understood?"

"Understood," said Stinnett, rushing into the center of the fray.

Shanifrey ducked back into his office and calmly ordered the AI to lower the steel partitions that would ensure he and his fellow command personnel had plenty of time to escape to safety.

* * *

Steve Redford dived to the floor yet again, feeling like a jumping bean, and took out yet another Tart in the process, but not before a stray round slammed into his body armor, the second such round to hit him since the raid had begun. Once again, it felt as if he had been hit with a pile driver, and he inhaled sharply, sucking in air that was now permeated with the revolting smell of rotten eggs. For all he knew, the bullet had come from Damian Hale, since they couldn't see each other any better than the Tarts could.

From the far corner of the factory, Secretary Stinnett came charging into the center of the room, despite having a bandage around his thigh that was soaked in blood. He put a gun against his head and shouted his intention of killing himself if the attackers didn't cease fire.

Redford had already knocked out Kaitlyn O'Connor with the butt of a handgun, but if he didn't do the same to Stinnett very soon, he had no doubt the man would carry out his threat, making a slightly different version of Anna's vision come true.

Redford charged into Stinnett at full speed, tackling the secretary of defense as if he were about to score the winning touchdown at the Super Bowl. Stinnett was a giant, but they both slammed to the floor, and the secretary's gun went flying, sliding to a stop four feet away.

Stinnett's hands were a blur of motion and the colonel took a number of fierce blows. The secretary was a martial arts master, and even against an invisible opponent he was as formidable as he could be, despite how frozen he had seemed during his encounter with Anna.

Redford rolled away from the secretary, but instead of coming after him, Stinnett dived for the gun. The colonel slammed a fist into the center of the bloody bandages around the secretary's thigh and was rewarded by a bloodcurdling scream, loud enough to be heard over the never-ending gunfire raging around them.

Still, even weak from blood loss and in agonizing pain, Stinnett's elbow lashed out and found Redford's jaw, nearly knocking him unconscious.

Before the colonel could recover, Stinnett found the gun and raised it to his temple. But just as he was about to pull the trigger it was yanked away again, as if it had a mind of its own.

Redford blew out a sigh of relief. Damian Hale must have joined the fight. And not a second too soon.

Only five Tarts remained alive, and two of them were running in Stinnett's direction with guns blazing. Redford rolled to his left and fired, putting both of them down, while Hale wrestled the gun away from the secretary.

Stinnett lashed out and landed a number of blows on the new, invisible combatant, who was caught by surprise by the secretary's skills and ferocity. But just as Stinnett managed to fight off Hale and regain control of the weapon, Redford cracked the butt of his handgun into the hulking secretary's skull and the man went down in a heap on the floor, unconscious at last.

While this struggle to disarm Stinnett was underway, a steel perimeter had slid into place, lowered from the ceiling, enclosing the far end of the factory.

"Shit!" said Redford subvocally to his invisible ally, while picking off a Tart who was now running their way, tipped off to their presence after seeing Stinnett being jerked around by unseen forces. "Frey must have sealed himself off."

Redford was irate that he had allowed Frey to buy himself a reprieve, but knew it could have been worse. He and Hale were still alive, as were Kaitlyn and Stinnett. The same couldn't be said for the enemy. "Take out the last two Tarts while I check out this barrier," he ordered Hale.

Redford ran to the steel perimeter and inspected it carefully, but as expected, there wasn't as much as a millimeter break in the surface, and he knew they'd need to bring in specialized equipment to breach it.

"*Get out of there, Steve!*" screamed Anna into his ear. "*Now!* My gut says that factory will self-destruct and you'll die. Do you read me?"

"Leaving now!" said Redford, racing back in the direction he had come.

"Captain Hale," he said as he ran, "lift Stinnett in a fireman's carry and race out of here like your life depends on it. Hurry!"

Redford screeched to a halt in front of Kaitlyn O'Connor, draped her over his shoulders, and then continued running for the exit. He had made it across twenty yards of concrete and to the start of the lawn of grass when the factory burst into an exploding fireball behind him, creating a furnace of heat that would have baked him had he been ten yards closer. A shock wave blasted him off his feet, and he and the Vorian scientist across his shoulders landed in a heap three yards away, thankfully on the soft grass, which still knocked the wind out of him. He fought for breath as a two-story fireball continued to consume the factory behind him.

"Captain Hale, report!" he said out loud as soon as he regained his breath, deactivating his invisibility generator. Hope surged through him even before he received a reply as he spotted the unconscious form of Wilson Stinnett ten feet ahead of him on the grass.

"I'm battered, but alive," said Hale, who followed Redford's lead and made himself visible once again.

Redford rolled onto his back and drew in several deep breaths. "Outstanding work, Captain," he said in relief.

"Thank you, Colonel. You didn't do too badly yourself. You know, for a deskbound alien hunter."

Redford laughed. "I'm just impressed that we didn't crash into each other a single time in there."

"That's not usually something I'm proud of," said Hale with a grin. "But in this case . . ."

Redford smiled. "You know, Captain, I could use a man like you in my outfit. Any interest?"

"Maybe," said Hale. "As long as all of the missions aren't as boring as this one," he added wryly.

64

Three Vorians and two humans met around the conference table in the Vors' Utah facility only three hours after two protracted battles, on two different continents, had ended. Given the miracle of holographic video conference technology, the same five beings also appeared around a conference table in Albania. In both facilities, it was difficult to tell which were actually present, and which were holograms, and the technology was only getting better.

In Utah, Steve Redford, still in combat gear, sat next to Lisa Moore and a bound and gagged Kaitlyn O'Connor, now conscious, who had a bandage wrapped around her forehead. The colonel had been fully occupied briefing the president while flying back to the Utah compound, and taking care of any number of important tasks he had been neglecting, so he had yet to communicate with anyone in Albania.

The Albania contingent for the meeting consisted solely of Tom Vega and Anna Abbott.

"Why is Kaitlyn bound?" asked the Vorian commander in dismay as soon as the holographic images materialized into place around the table.

Anna sighed beside him. "She's the traitor I spoke about, Tom."

"I don't believe it," said Vega.

"I'm afraid Anna is right," said Redford. "Kaitlyn is here so she can tell us why she betrayed her entire species. But that can come later. At the moment, I want her to remain quiet, which is why she has duct tape over her mouth. I had other Vorians here disable her comm, as well."

Vega opened his mouth to protest, but thought better of it.

Anna turned to the colonel. "As you can tell from Tom's reaction to Kaitlyn," she said, "I've been waiting to fill him in on recent developments. I thought it would be better to discuss this all at once—and together."

She nodded toward the alien leader beside her. "Thank you again for your patience, Tom. After we trade some quick updates, we'll tell you how, and why, events unfolded as they did."

Vega nodded, but looked decidedly unhappy.

"Here's where things stand on our end," continued Anna. A sad expression came over her face, and she shook her head in disgust. "We lost two SEALs and three Vorians. Losing even one member of our team is too many, and unacceptable, and I take full responsibility."

"You can't blame yourself," insisted Vega. "In this same situation, under *anyone* else, all of us would have been killed. And most of the Tarts would have been left alive. With tens of thousands of random bullets being fired, even an Oracle can't prevent a few unlucky hits."

Anna nodded, but it was clear that these words hadn't helped. "On the positive side of the ledger," she said, attempting to move beyond these losses, at least temporarily, "while we can't be sure precisely, we believe we were able to kill all but thirty to forty of the Tart force."

"How many were there to begin with?" asked Redford.

"Six hundred eighteen," replied Anna. "The SEALs knew the precise number. My gut tells me that Frey also held two or three dozen Tarts back from Albania, so as not to put all of his eggs in one basket."

She gestured to Redford. "How many Tarts survived your attack?"

The colonel blew out a long breath. "I don't think more than a dozen or so," he replied. "We were able to take out the majority, but suffered three casualties ourselves."

Redford was as horrified as Anna by these losses, but he knew that in the big picture, things couldn't have gone much better. Losing only eight soldiers while taking out well over six hundred Tartarians, with the odds stacked against them, was a miracle. The kind of miracle that he couldn't blame Vega for wanting Anna to produce in the center of the galaxy.

"I also need to report that we didn't get Shane Frey," he added miserably. "Which was a key objective. And I'm guessing those who escaped with him were key lieutenants. Originally, I thought they had been killed in the explosion. Which in retrospect was a very stupid assumption. After the battle, I scrambled a specialized military team to the site to put out the fire and examine the wreckage. Just before I landed here, I was told that they had found the entrance to a tunnel inside the factory, leading away from it. Remarkably, the tunnel survived the explosion. I'm convinced that Frey and his top people used it to escape."

"Even so," said Vega, "we've managed to knock the Tarts back down to parity with us."

"Almost," said Anna. "My guess is that the Tarts are near eighty in number, and you're at fifty-five. With both sides still having most of their leadership intact."

"But two more of our people can come here from Vor every forty hours," noted Lisa Moore. "So if the portal stays open, we'll exceed their numbers in a month or two."

"Assuming their portal doesn't reopen as well and flood the zone a second time," said Redford.

"Regardless," said Anna. "We're in a hell of a lot better situation than we were yesterday." She paused. "And speaking of that, how is Secretary Stinnett?"

The colonel gestured at Lisa Moore to answer.

"He seems to be fine," said the genetic engineer and medic. "He's still unconscious. But I'm confident he'll make a full recovery. I patched up his bullet wound, and he's receiving human blood in the infirmary right now. I also injected him with a second dose of the HCS antidote. So when he awakens he should be himself again."

"Which is excellent news," said the colonel. "He's had a rough go of it lately. Knocked unconscious, gassed, drugged, and shot."

Anna cringed. "Actually, the first three of those things happened to him *twice*," she pointed out.

"At least this should finally be the end of it," said Redford.

"Anything else particularly noteworthy?" asked the clairvoyant detective. "I'd like to finally let Tom and Lisa know what's been going on."

"Just one last thing," said Redford. "I briefed the president on the way here. He's well pleased by today's success, and sends his congratulations to you and Tom. We've scheduled another meeting for late tomorrow afternoon, and we'd like both of you involved."

"We'll be there," said Vega. "We'll be flying back to Utah right after this meeting ends. So we'll be able to join you in person in the conference room there."

"Perfect," said Redford. "With any luck, Secretary Stinnett will be able to join us also."

"Okay, then," said Anna, locking her gaze on the alien leader. "Let's get right to it. The million-dollar question. How did what happened today come about?"

She blew out a long breath. "It all started when you contacted us on our way to Evie headquarters," she began. "You told us your portal had reappeared, and asked if I would come to Vor to be the admiral of your allied fleet.

"Until that instant, I was going to refuse, for reasons I'll get to. But right when you asked me, my intuition told me to tell you yes, anyway. It _demanded_ that I do so. I hated to lie to you, but my gut gave me no other choice. I had no idea why at the time."

"And now you do?" said Vega.

Anna nodded. "Yes."

"Are you saying that you've been deceiving me from that point on?" asked the alien.

"I'm afraid so," replied Anna with a sigh. "But to continue, just after I agreed, I had two visions of the portal in Albania. Visions of two possible futures. I'm sure you remember that we were baffled as to how this could be. I should see one future at a time. This future should only change if I do something to change it, which couldn't have happened in this case, since the visions were separated by seconds."

"How could I forget?" said Vega.

"Well, I've come to understand how and why this happened," said Anna. "Neither vision was real. At the time I thought they were, because my subconscious didn't let me in on the lie. I'm now convinced that my hidden mind conjured up these false visions to set things up for an outcome like we achieved."

Vega's eyes widened. "Incredible," he said. "As if being able to see _actual_ visions of the future isn't powerful enough. Now you're telling us that your subconscious mind can also slip you *fake* visions of the future. That it's willing to fool even you to manipulate the universe into the shape it wants."

"Apparently, yes," said Anna. "At least in this one instance. I'm not sure if something like this will ever happen again. But I'm convinced that those few minutes in the helicopter set in motion everything that followed. I didn't have any idea at the time, but I was able to gradually connect many of the dots. You might say that I had to use logic and my detective skills to puzzle out my own actions. Steve helped a lot, too. But even if my hidden mind had been able to communicate with me perfectly, I'm not convinced it could have told me what it was doing. I don't think that even it had everything worked out at that point. I think my subconscious mind just saw what it had to do to make a desired future come about, without understanding how or why."

"Which is truly extraordinary," said Vega.

"After I had the visions," continued Anna, "we landed at Evie headquarters and had to deal with a possessed version of Secretary Stinnett, followed by a holographic version of Shane Frey. A Shane Frey who had recently gained full command of an AI named Nessie. I guessed right away that Frey had used Nessie to eavesdrop on us through Steve's comm. And I had a hunch that when we were flying to Arizona, my clairvoyant subconscious *knew* we were being listened to. I had a feeling that my visions in the helicopter were actually for *Frey's* benefit."

"Why would you keep this hunch to yourself?" asked Vega.

"My intuition said that I should," replied Anna. "But to continue, I realized that if Frey *had* listened in, I had given him a lot to think about. If I was able to escape from Evie headquarters, he'd worry that my first vision would come true. And because of this fear, he'd be willing to do *anything* to make the second come true instead, regardless of the cost. Including putting nearly all of his forces in the woods to kill me, since that's how I saw it unfold."

"So your subconscious faked these visions to force him to do what he did," said Vega.

"Exactly. Without the second vision, he'd never have put so many of his people in one place and allowed them to be as vulnerable as they were. He'd have kept them spread out and hidden. He'd continue building more, and ever more impregnable, fortresses. He threatened that the added six hundred of his people would give him the luxury of pushing Tartarian tech to the point that he could wipe us out with ease, and we couldn't touch him. And I'm sure he was right."

"But instead," said Vega, "he sent a huge force to the slaughter, thinking he was fulfilling your vision."

"That's right," said Anna.

"Which allowed us to achieve a rebalancing of the scales," said Redford. "Now the Tarts are relatively shorthanded once again. So we and the US military, or perhaps the world military, have a chance of destroying them before they do the same to us. I believe that if not for Anna's fake visions, the Tarts would have been able to carry out their threat and drive humanity into extinction."

"There's more to it than just the visions, of course," said Anna. "Apparently, we also needed the help of two hundred Navy SEALs to make this happen. Not just two hundred SEALs, but two hundred SEALs that the Tarts would think were working with them. So their guard would be down."

"Right," said Vega. "Which is why your subconscious included hostile US forces in your fake vision."

Anna nodded. "Fake or real, either way, it made no sense that the US military would be on Frey's side. When the president revoked Frey's authority, we all thought this was no longer possible. But then, later, my gut told me two things. One, that Kaitlyn was a traitor. And two, if she thought I'd make it through the portal, she'd betray us and bring Secretary Stinnett to Frey's stronghold."

"Did you see its location?" asked Lisa.

Anna shook her head. "No. And I didn't see anything else, or have any additional hunches. Not why she would betray the Vors, why she would deliver Stinnett, or where they would be. But my intuition insisted that I let her do her thing. And much of what this was leading to became obvious to me. The *conscious* me. The visions had been intended to lead Frey's forces into a massacre. But for him to be comfortable sending so many of his people into the Albanian forest, he had to become convinced he had the upper hand. And being able to add two hundred SEALs to his side—especially since my vision had indicated one of them had killed me—was the tipping point."

"And he needed to have control of Stinnett again to make this happen," said Vega. "Which Kaitlyn kindly made possible."

"Yes. And not to brag about my subconscious, but as a bonus, this would potentially allow us to eliminate even more Tarts and destroy their US stronghold."

"I had Kaitlyn followed," said Redford, "but she managed to lose the tail. Fortunately, Anna had a vision, about three hours before your battle in the woods. She saw Frey making Stinnett kill himself in a factory outside of Bakersfield. And she somehow knew its exact location."

Vega's mouth dropped open and he stared at Anna in disbelief. "But that means you can see a future that you were never part of."

Anna nodded. "Apparently," she said. "At least this once. I don't know if this is an anomaly or not. It may be that my subconscious needs ridiculously high stakes to do tricks like this."

"In any event," said the colonel, "I rushed to Bakersfield, activated a number of US commandos, and attacked, as you know."

"So when you were giving orders to us in Albania," said Vega, "when we thought you were in Utah, you were really in Bakersfield?"

"That's right," said Redford.

Vega frowned deeply and turned to Anna. "So you knew that the colonel wasn't where we thought he was. You knew that Kaitlyn was a traitor. You figured out that your visions were false, and why, and set things up to turn the tables on the Tarts in Albania. You even had Ansel Cartwright make more than forty-two invisibility units. And yet you chose to keep all of this from me," he finished, clearly hurt. "Why?"

"I'm really sorry, Tom," she replied. "But I knew you'd be interacting with Kaitlyn. Quite a lot. And I don't know how good Vors are at acting. I couldn't trust you not to accidentally give it away. I had to be sure your reactions to events, and your interactions with her, came across as genuine. I hope you can understand."

Vega paused in thought. "Actually, I do," he said, surprised she had come up with such a compelling rationale. "And this explains why you waited to take over the operation until the moment after learning I had spoken with Kaitlyn."

"Right. She had to think everything was going exactly the way she and Frey wanted. If you didn't know otherwise, you couldn't inadvertently give it away."

"And because you knew Frey would use the secretary of defense to deploy US commandos," said Vega, "you were able to use them in the perfect double-cross."

"Steve and I discussed how this might unfold," said Anna. "My hunches combined with his knowledge of the military. He knew exactly what steps Stinnett would have to take to get Special Ops forces into Albania. And Steve was in frequent contact with President McNally. The president put out an order to all Spec Ops commanders. He told them that if they were contacted by Secretary Stinnett, they should pretend to follow his orders without question, but then immediately notify the president for further instructions."

Redford smiled. "These guys aren't used to hearing from the president, or speaking with him, so this really got their attention."

"Just remarkable, Anna," said Vega in awe. "The machinations of your subconscious were extraordinary. Far beyond what could be expected given the sporadic knowledge of the future that you actually had. Interlocking deceptions in ten dimensions. It's possible that you and Steve really did just save your entire species."

"Secretary Stinnett played a key role as well," said Redford. "Anna couldn't have done it without his willingness to sacrifice himself for the cause."

"I don't understand," said Vega. "I thought he didn't have any choice in the matter."

"Not so," said Anna. "Steve and I knew that if we let him be taken to Frey, he was facing almost certain torture and death. Especially if we were successful in Albania, and Frey's people were massacred. Frey was sure to take this out on Stinnett. And we couldn't just let this happen without the secretary's permission."

Redford nodded. "So I went to him after he was cured," he added, "and explained the situation. I told him what I thought was at stake, and that I was convinced we could turn the tide. But only if he let himself be possessed for a second time. I told him I expected that he would be tortured and killed, and that while I would do my best to rescue him, I wasn't sure if this would be possible."

"And he volunteered anyway," said Vega, properly impressed.

"Yes," said the colonel. "Which is one of the reasons I risked so much to save him. We owe him a huge debt of gratitude. "

"But it still doesn't make sense to me," said Vega. "HCS is also a perfect truth serum. It's hard for me to believe that Frey wouldn't suspect deception. And the moment he asked Stinnett if this was part of a trick, the secretary would tell him your plan. Would tell him that you *wanted* him to be turned over to the Tarts. There's no way Stinnett could keep that a secret."

Redford smiled. "Turns out there is a way," he said. "That supply of memory-erasing drug you have on hand in your lab. After he volunteered, I erased his memory of everything having to do with our real plans. Everything having to do with any kind of deception. In short, he didn't just volunteer to put himself in great peril, but to have many of his memories stripped away as well. I videoed my meeting with him, so at least I can show him how he came to volunteer."

"Absolutely brilliant," said Vega. "You two really thought of everything."

"We were mostly lucky," said Anna humbly. "But thank you."

She paused. "And I hated keeping you in the dark, Tom. But look what we accomplished by all this craziness. We killed off most of the Tarts on Earth and leveled the playing field once again. By dramatically reducing their numbers, we crippled their ability to produce large supplies of HCS and develop unstoppable technologies. We destroyed their base outside of Bakersfield. A large number of America's most elite soldiers not only know about the Tart threat—the very soldiers who will help us hunt them down—but have firsthand experience with them. We've now had the chance to work closely with the president and the US military on a joint operation that went nearly flawlessly, which will give all sides more confidence going forward. Vors and humans fought together, and, unfortunately, died together."

Anna paused for all of this to fully sink in. "And finally," she added, "we were able to confirm my hunch that Kaitlyn is a traitor."

Vega nodded slowly. "Speaking of which," he said. "I think it's time for us to find out why."

"I couldn't agree more," said Redford, reaching out and tearing the duct tape from the former chief scientist's lips.

65

There was a long silence in both conference rooms, and all eyes were now on the Vorian calling herself Kaitlyn O'Connor.

"So what do you have to say for yourself?" began Vega. "You killed five of your own people. You betrayed everything we believe in. You tried to kill the woman representing the galaxy's best hope to end a senseless war."

"From your perspective, it was a betrayal," replied Kaitlyn in the Vorian language. "But not from mine."

"English, Kaitlyn, please," said Vega. "Or I'll just use the translator program. Our human friends have a right to hear this too."

Kaitlyn sighed and continued in English. "Killing my Vorian brothers and sisters was the most horrible thing I've ever done," she said, her tone anguished. "It haunts me every day. And it will for the rest of my life. But I did it for a higher cause. I did it to save us all."

"Save us all?" said Vega in disbelief. "That's what the rest of us are trying to do. Which is something that you're trying to *stop*."

"I know that your heart is in the right place, Tom," she said. "That's what makes this so hard. But you're doing the *opposite* of saving us. Just because you and most of our governing class believes something doesn't make it true. You're so convinced that a human Oracle like Anna can break the deadlock in this horrible war. And I agree. If only the Gatekeepers would let her."

"The Gatekeepers *will* let her," said Vega. "Her subconscious abilities, because they *are* subconscious, will fly under their radar. I don't understand the math and physics behind it, but this is scientific consensus."

"Well I *do* understand the math and physics," said Kaitlyn, "and it *isn't* consensus. Because I, for one, don't agree. You're all fooling yourselves if you believe for an instant that the Gatekeepers won't notice her. How could they not? You've seen what she can do. And this is only the beginning.

"How can you not be terrified of her potential power?" she continued. "Look what she's just shown us. That her subconscious is clever enough not just to provide her with *actual* visions of the future, but also with *fabrications*, with just the right elements to make something it wants come to pass. Fooling even her. Which is terrifying. And she can see futures of which she's not even a part. You, yourself, marveled at the complexity of what she accomplished, the layers of the onion she constructed. You called it interlocking deceptions in ten dimensions. You can't tell me you aren't a little afraid of what she might become."

"I would be," admitted Vega. "Except that I'm *certain* she's the perfect choice. Anyone else with this power would worry me. Even the humans have a saying about absolute power corrupting. But it won't corrupt Anna. There's something about her that I trust. And I've come to believe in fate. It was fate that we found her."

"You're a fool, Tom. Even if she is the right choice, I come back to the same point. The Gatekeepers can't miss her. Can't! No matter how much you hand-wave about her subconscious being immune from Gatekeeper scrutiny. Even if it is, what do you think will happen if she *is* able to bring our allied fleet to the brink of victory? Don't you think the Gatekeepers will be curious about who's at the helm? How she's able to accomplish what no other intelligent being ever could? So even if she slips under their radar at the start, they *will* find out that she used higher order capabilities to win. And they'll consider this cheating."

Kaitlyn frowned deeply. "So what then?" she asked. "They could destroy our entire fleet, our entire species even, just to make a point."

"So this is how you justify killing five of our people?" said Vega in horror. "You did it because you thought they might be zeroing in on an Oracle, and were worried about Gatekeeper retaliation?"

"That's right. I would never do this if the stakes were any less profound. You're so sure that everyone thinks like you, Tom, but there are dissenters in very powerful positions back home. Dissenters who managed to position me to be among the first to go through to Earth if the portal ever reopened. They and their predecessors have long feared the very thing you hope for, and have long tried to shut down the Earth initiative. And even though they failed, they did manage to send me here as an operative."

"So why didn't you kill me when I was zeroing in on Anna?"

"First, all the other possible candidates you identified turned out to be duds or sociopaths. I thought she would be the same. And then things with her moved much faster than anyone could have anticipated. After your initial meeting, instead of slowly vetting her, slowly bringing her up to speed, as per protocol, you ended up on the run together. Everything was accelerated. Instead of taking days or weeks to vet her, she proved herself in hours. I rushed here as quickly as I could, but she was already having visions, even before being enhanced."

"So you knew that if you tried anything too flashy," said Vega, "she'd likely see it."

"Yes. And that was especially true after she was enhanced."

Vega shook his head in disgust. "I'm truly sad for you, Kaitlyn," he said. "I'm sad that you believe you were protecting our people. You might even be right about the Gatekeepers finding out about Anna. But even if you are, do you really think they'd be vindictive enough to destroy us? Have you ever seen any sign of this? Don't you think that we and every other intelligence has tried to do everything we can to remove the Gatekeepers' shackles?"

The alien leader paused. "We believe they're sabotaging our efforts to achieve transcendence," he continued. "Yet we continue to *try*. We don't kill every scientist with the audacity to go against their will because we fear reprisals. The Gatekeepers have never been known to interfere with any of us directly, at least not overtly, which is why we aren't even certain they exist. So even if they caught us, they'd just stop Anna from being our admiral. They wouldn't take it out on our entire species. Especially since only a handful of the many billions of us were responsible for this choice."

Kaitlyn didn't respond, but her expression indicated that he had scored some points and had shaken her certainty.

"And they've always been in position to wipe us out whenever they like," continued Vega. "So either they find the wholesale slaughter of innocent beings as unthinkable as we do, or they're keeping the many intelligences around for a good reason."

"What reason?"

"Really, Kaitlyn?" he said in disdain. "You know as well as I do that this has been the subject of over twenty thousand years of debate. And you know the predominate view on Vor, which I share. Which is why we're here. I think the Gatekeepers are doing this to force all intelligences to mature. Force us to figure things out. To get creative, and to tame the more aggressive species among us who think the Gatekeepers want war. To demonstrate to all that we won't incur the Gatekeepers' wrath if we have peace. Which is exactly what we hope Anna will bring about."

"You're playing with a fire you can't possibly control," said Kaitlyn. "Two fires. You think the Gatekeepers won't retaliate, but you can't be sure of that. And who's to say that Anna's powers won't evolve to the point where she becomes an even bigger threat than *they* are?"

She turned to the human clairvoyant. "I like and admire you, Anna," she said sincerely. "A lot. You're decent, brave, kind, and for a human being, intelligent. You have very little ego and a relentless determination to do what's right. I can't tell you how many times I wished that I *hated* you. Or that you frightened me. But you don't. You're wonderful."

Kaitlyn sighed. "But that's how you are right now," she added. "Not even you know how you might change. Not even you know if the growing capabilities of your subconscious and your clairvoyance will make you drunk with power." She paused. "Human campers are careful to extinguish their fires," she continued. "But that's not because they don't *like* them. The fires give off light, and warmth, and protection from wildlife. The campers snuff them out because they know and fear the destructive force they might *become*."

Anna stared deeply into Kaitlyn's holographic eyes for several long seconds. Finally, she sighed. "I can't really argue with you," she said. "I have no idea what the Gatekeepers might do if they find out about me. But as to what I might become, you're right to worry. I do too. All I can say is that I'm well aware of the danger, and intend to spend every second fighting against becoming corrupted."

Kaitlyn nodded thoughtfully. "Thank you for that," she said. "I believe that you're sincere. Although I am annoyed at you for making me like you even more," she added with a wistful smile. "And Tom is right. If anyone can avoid corruption, it's you. But I still fear that with the level of power and influence you'll command, this is still inevitable. I guess we'll find out."

"I guess we will," said Anna.

"In any event," added Kaitlyn, "I can't begin to tell you how much I hope you prove me wrong."

66

The meeting participants in Albania and Utah took a short break to attend to biological needs while Kaitlyn was escorted away to a makeshift prison. The Vors didn't believe in capital punishment, but she would become a considerable headache for them to keep imprisoned. Redford suspected she would end up in a human-guarded prison, especially since so many in the US military had become aware of the alien presence on Earth, and so many more would be learning about it soon. Possibly the entire world.

When the meeting reconvened, this time with only four participants, Vega started it off. "So is this the part of the discussion where you tell us why you won't be coming to Vor, after all?" he asked Anna.

"It is," she replied.

"Before you begin," said Lisa Moore, "I wanted to raise one quick issue."

"Go right ahead," said Anna.

"Just out of curiosity," said Lisa, "do you know what I'm about to say?"

Anna shook her head. "I'm still mostly drawing a blank when it comes to reading future conversation," she replied. "Even though it does now seem an easier trick than some of the things I've done. But I'm afraid you're going to have to tell us."

"What you've achieved is remarkable," said Lisa. "But there is one aspect of this I find troubling. Now the Tarts know where our portal is. They didn't before. And now the US military knows, too. Won't this bring about a lot of . . . complications?"

"The Tarts would have found out anyway," said Vega, unconcerned. "If Anna hadn't acted, almost seven hundred of them would have made it their number-one priority to learn its location. I have no doubt they would have succeeded in fairly short order. There is no question in my mind that the gains were more than worth it."

Lisa considered. "You're right," she said. "I suppose the discovery of our portal *was* inevitable."

Vega nodded. "And with the Tart numbers so reduced," he said, "and the US military on our side, we'll be able to protect our people coming through."

Saying this, the alien leader turned to face the woman next to him. "So what is it that's holding you back from going to Vor, Anna?" he said, returning to the pressing topic at hand. "You can't still be concerned about your qualifications for the job, or your ability to lead. You just provided a perfect demonstration of how effective you could be as our admiral. The way you were able to move pieces around the board and orchestrate events was spectacular."

Anna flashed a brief smile. "I have to admit," she said, "I surprised myself. I accomplished more than I ever thought I could, despite having no idea why I was doing what I was doing much of the time. So I'm beginning to believe I really can make a difference in your war. Just not now."

"But the portal could disappear tomorrow," said Vega. "This may be our only chance."

"I hope that isn't the case," said Anna. "But it's a risk I have to take. Before I go with you, Tom, there are a number of things to sort out. First, charity begins at home. Humanity has major problems of our own. It used to be each other, but now it's the Tarts. Their portal could reappear and discharge hundreds, or even thousands of them. Or a portal between Earth and the home planet of one of the other twenty-seven intelligent species could suddenly materialize. Who can say?

"What I do know is that the Vorian portal might disappear after I've gone through. And I know how I'd feel if I learned that while I was off being your admiral, my own species had been killed off— something I might have been able to prevent."

Vega considered this for several long seconds. "I understand," he said finally, letting out a discouraged sigh. "I'm still disappointed, but I can't really blame you."

"Again," said Anna, "I didn't say I would *never* become your admiral. Just not now."

"So when?" asked the alien leader.

"My plan would be to stay on Earth for about ten years," she replied. "Maybe less, depending on circumstances. During that time, our people will get to know your people. We'll work together to eliminate the Tart threat. We'll monitor for other threats. And as soon as I feel comfortable that things are well in hand here, I'll be open to the idea of doing what you ask."

Vega considered. "As long as the portal cooperates, I think this is fair. We've waited twenty thousand years for a game changer like you. We can wait ten more years if we have to."

Anna winced. "I'm afraid there's more to it than that," she said. "A lot more. I have some . . . requests."

The detective paused. "Okay," she continued, "I can't afford to be polite here. They're more like *demands*."

Vega's eyes narrowed. "Go on," he said.

"First, I want to get a much better lay of the land. Understand the details of the galactic situation. The characteristics and histories of the players involved. I refuse to be anyone's pawn until I can figure out for myself who I can trust."

"And how would you propose to do that?" asked Vega.

"With your help. Starting with your allies. Instead of bringing more Vorians here every forty hours, bring two from an allied species. With libraries full of their histories and cultures for us to study. We have a lot of catching up to do."

Anna paused, but Vega chose not to respond.

"And before I agree to become your admiral," continued Anna, "I'll also need to go through your portal and get the lay of the cosmos for myself. Travel to the home planets of other intelligent species. I want differing points of view on the war. Which should have the added benefit of making me a better admiral. I'll also want to talk to prisoners you've taken that represent the forces opposed to you."

Anna sighed. "You say that your goal is just," she added. "And that your side is more deserving of winning than the other sides. My gut tells me you're right. But I'll want to confirm this for myself."

Vega raised his eyebrows. "You've really thought this through, haven't you?"

"You have no idea," replied Anna.

"I guess I shouldn't be surprised," he said "But, please, continue."

"One big problem is that I can't even trust the Vors," said Anna. "My intuition says we're on the same side. But before I become your admiral, you and your allies need to get your houses in order. As Kaitlyn just demonstrated, you aren't monolithic in your thinking. Not everyone will welcome me with open arms. Many will treat me like a savior. But it's also clear that others will try to kill me. Within my own fleet. On board my own flagship."

Vega nodded grimly. "An excellent point," he allowed.

"It's funny," said Redford, "for some reason I thought of the Vors as all reading from the same hymnal. Because you're so much more advanced than us, and all live in peace. But it's obvious to me now that of course this isn't the case. We have peace within our country, but still have huge differences of opinion on key topics. So why should you or your allies be any different?"

"Very few Vorians know about the Earth initiative," said Vega, "or that human clairvoyants are even possible. And while you're right that we don't all agree on everything, I had thought that those who did know about the initiative were all on the same page."

The alien leader sighed. "Apparently not," he added. "So maybe a ten-year wait is for the best, after all. This will give those back home time to ensure that Anna is protected when she arrives. Especially from any Vorians or allies who, like Kaitlyn, fear that she'll bring about the wrath of the Gatekeepers."

"The delay is good for other reasons, also," said Anna. "Did you really want to throw me into the fray right now? I don't know anything about the war, the players, or the workings of your starships. I'm told my powers will only grow stronger. So what's the rush? When I'm not helping our military eradicate the Tarts, you and your people can bring me up to speed. Build a warship simulator to train me. Teach me about historical space battles and common strategies. You can convert additional useful information into audio so my subconscious can absorb it while I'm sleeping."

Vega nodded. "As I mentioned before," he said, "we also have techniques that can implant information directly into your conscious mind. Although this system will take us a few years to recreate here, and modify so it can be used on humans."

"I remember you mentioning it," said Anna. "You said you used it to ensure that you could emulate our expressions and gestures when you arrived here. Did it help you with our language and idioms as well?" she asked. "Because you really do speak like a native."

"Thank you," said Vega. "But we didn't use it for that. English didn't even exist when my people were here last. So no shortcuts, just a lot of hard work and a lot of reading."

The alien leader stared at Anna for several long seconds. "But getting back to your . . . demands," he said, "you win. I'll see to it that they all come to pass."

"Thank you," said Anna. "But I'm afraid I'm not done yet." She forced a smile. "After all, when will I have another opportunity to negotiate on behalf of my species like this?"

"What did you have in mind?" said Vega warily.

"You've agreed to help us eradicate the Tarts," said Anna. "But this is just to prevent something negative from happening." She paused. "My next requests involve going in the *positive* direction."

Vega thought about this. "You want more of our technology, don't you?"

"Good guess," said Anna. "But let me be specific. Invisibility is a nice trick, but I want you to bury that. It's too dangerous. And the optics improvements and algorithms you sold to our companies to raise money are cute, but I'm looking at much bigger fish."

"Just how big are you talking about?" said Vega.

"*Starship* technology big," she said simply. "*Planetary shield* technology big. I'm not asking you to bring us from where we are, technology-wise, to where *you* are overnight. We need to get there on our own. But starships and shields are part of a handful of technologies that I'll insist upon. I want humanity to be able to spread across this sector of space, ensuring our survival, and unleashing our spirit of exploration. And while battleships from your region of space can't come here to attack us, the shield will make sure that no meteors ever hit our planet."

"These technologies are too advanced," said Vega. "You aren't ready for them. You couldn't possibly understand the science."

"I'm not intuitive or clairvoyant," said Redford, "but even I know why that's bullshit. You already told us that *none* of the intelligent species in the galaxy understand these technologies. We'd be no different."

Vega sighed. "Even if we wanted to tell you how to build a starship and planetary shield," he said, "we couldn't. You can't begin to imagine the complexity involved. Our minds are good at retaining information, but there's no way, even collectively, we could recreate the necessary specifications. Any more than you could tell us how to build a supercomputer."

"Come on, Tom," said Anna irritably. "I *am* intuitive and clairvoyant, and you aren't winning points by lying to me. Each one of you carries a technology library tens of millions of pages long, don't you?"

Vega raised his eyebrows. "Now why would you possibly think that?" he said.

"I notice you didn't deny it."

"With you, there's no use. As you've just proven again. But I stand by my question. How did you figure it out?"

"I didn't," said Anna. "Turns out I don't just like Steve for his uniform and good looks." She gestured to the colonel. "Do you want to share how you reached this conclusion?"

"Sure," said Redford. "You weren't there, Tom, but when we were trapped in conference room D and having a chat with our buddy, Shane Frey, he said something intriguing. He wanted us to know just how screwed we were. So he boasted that they had brought a library here to Earth to help them recreate their favorite Tart inventions. He said it was the equivalent of tens of millions of pages. He called it a detailed compendium of all of their technology."

"I have to admit," said Anna, "I didn't really zero in on the importance of this statement the way Steve did."

"When I thought about this later," said Redford, "here's what occurred to me. They obviously didn't carry tens of millions of pages worth of bound books through the portal. I did the math and that would be a stack of books two-thirds of a mile high. And they couldn't have brought it in the form of computer memory. The portal, in its arbitrary randomness, might have decided that a flash drive was too techy to let through. Besides, our computers would likely be so different from theirs that the information could never be read."

"Impressive," said Vega. "This is precisely the analysis we made as we prepared for a possible second visit to Earth. We weren't sure if you had advanced enough to have built computers, but we decided that even if you had, this wouldn't be a viable option. I'm sure the Tarts reached the same conclusion."

"Fortunately," said Anna, "Steve's a bit of a science nerd, and was familiar with information storage alternatives. He realized that the best way for you or the Tarts to transport this much information through the portal was to encode it in your DNA. DNA that you could store in excess cells created for this purpose."

"Even humanity has made backup copies of all human knowledge," said Redford, "so why wouldn't you and the Tarts have done the same? And apparently, all the data on Earth can be embedded in an amount of DNA that can fit inside a *teaspoon*." He smiled. "But I'm sure I'm not telling you anything you don't already know."

Vega sighed. "Very good," he said. "You're right, of course. We all carry a significant amount of extra DNA. Not enough for us to notice," he added, "since, as you said, a little goes a long way. But we already knew from our last visit that our DNA is quite close to yours in construction. Not the same, but close enough that we should be able to modify one of your DNA sequencers in less than a year to decode our library. And ours is at least as extensive as the Tarts'."

He faced the detective and sighed. "So you win, Anna. I'll see to it that your people get the plans for building a starship and a planetary shield."

"So why did you try to lie your way out of it at first?" asked Anna.

"I'm not convinced that humanity is ready to handle this, especially starship technology. But I guess we're going to find out."

"I understand your rationale," said Anna. "But please don't lie to me again."

"Believe me, I won't. And I'm sorry I tried this time."

"Getting back to your library," said Redford, trying to change the subject after this awkward exchange, "I assume it contains non-technical information as well. Like galactic history. Cultural analysis of the twenty-eight intelligent species. Military tactics and strategy. And so on."

"That is correct. We can translate these sections into human languages for you also."

"Thank you," said Anna. "And you'll be happy to know that we're almost done. My intuition tells me that you've developed a way to get unlimited free energy, and to dramatically prolong life. Am I right?"

Vega nodded.

"I want humanity to have both of these," she said.

The alien nodded. "Why not?" he said. "I hoped that you would be open to longevity treatments yourself. I wouldn't mind keeping you young and alive in case the portal disappears and doesn't come back for a century or so."

Vega paused. "Anything else?" he added miserably.

"Last thing," said Anna. "I get to select as many crewmembers for the flagship as I want. If I'm admiral of your fleet, I need people around me I can trust. People I'm comfortable with. And that means fellow human beings. Beginning with Steve Redford. I want him to be my first officer. We're social animals, and I require companionship and intimacy for my psychological well-being." She glanced at Redford and gritted her teeth. "Assuming Steve agrees, of course. Who knows if we'll even be together by that point."

"If anyone would know," said Vega wryly, "I would think it would be *you*, Anna."

Redford laughed. "I don't know if we'll be together when you're ready, Anna," he said, "but if we are, you have yourself a first officer. I mean, you already know how I feel about the chance to sleep with the admiral of a space fleet. It's every boy's childhood dream."

"I thought every boy's childhood dream was to become an astronaut," said Anna.

"That too. But this way I can do both. Travel in space aboard an actual starship, and sleep with a fleet admiral. And you'll have it in your power to help me fulfill my third greatest dream along these lines."

Anna raised her eyebrows. "I'm listening."

"Weightless sex," he said with a straight face.

Anna laughed. "We'll have to see about that, Steve. Sounds challenging."

The detective's smile vanished, and she became serious once again. "So that's everything, Tom. Can I assume we're in full agreement?"

"*Yes*," said the alien leader. "We're in full agreement." He shook his head miserably. "Although it occurs to me that I might have made a rookie negotiating mistake."

"You mean telling me I'm the one being out of trillions who can end a twenty-thousand-year galactic war?"

Vega actually smiled. "Yeah, that's the one," he said. "I could be wrong, but I think this may have strengthened your hand a little bit."

67

Anna and the colonel asked to have a few minutes alone before the video call was ended, and both waited patiently as Vega and Lisa left their respective conference rooms, six thousand miles apart.

Once they were gone, Redford rose from his chair and gazed into the virtual, holographic eyes of the woman who had come to mean so much to him in so little time. "That went well," he said.

"I think so, too," she replied.

"Well done, by the way," added Redford. "On behalf of the human race, let me be the first to say thanks."

"Do you think Tom is right about us not being able to handle having our own starships?"

"I don't," said the colonel. "Maybe if we had them this moment, he would be. But we'll mature fast when we realize that we aren't alone in the galaxy. And nothing will bring the species together faster than a common threat."

He paused. "But I do think he's right about you being chosen by fate. And I do think he's right that you're the one person who will be immune from corruption, no matter how strong you get."

"I'm counting on you to keep me honest, Steve. To be the voice in my ear if I'm getting carried away. As always, assuming we stay together. We barely know each other, after all, so for all we know, it won't last out the month."

"Even the little bit of intuition that I have tells me this won't be the case," said the colonel. "And if it doesn't work out, it won't be by my choice. I've known a lot of women in my life, Anna, but I'll never find your like again in a million years."

The detective smiled. "That's just because you've never dated a woman who could get you a starship before," she said wryly.

Redford laughed.

Anna became serious once again and blew out a heavy sigh. "If all of this *has* been due to some sort of cosmic fate," she said, "maybe you're part of it too. What are the odds that we'd meet the way we did? Get thrown together the way we did? And maybe you really are the key ingredient it will take to keep me grounded. I need you to watch me relentlessly. I need you to make sure I don't get too big of a head, or become too drunk with power."

"I will," said Redford. "I'll be watching your backside every step of the way."

"Don't you mean *back*?"

"No," said the colonel impishly. "When it comes to you, I mean *backside*. But I'll try not to watch it when we're on the bridge," he added in amusement. "Because that would be inappropriate."

"*That* would be inappropriate," said Anna, feigning dismay. "Not the talk of sleeping with an admiral and weightless sex?"

"Hey," said Redford, "you had the vision of us kissing, not me."

Anna laughed. "So what's next?" she asked.

"Good question. I just want to celebrate that we got to this point for a little while. It wasn't too long ago that I was sure I'd never leave my own headquarters alive. And that humanity was totally screwed."

"And now?"

"Now I'm more optimistic than I've ever been," he replied. "Not that we don't have a lot of work cut out for us. A lot to learn, and to figure out. Evie will need to be expanded dramatically, and I think it makes sense for the Vorians to live and work within its confines." He paused. "And you too, Anna."

She raised her eyebrows. "I'm listening."

"I'm sure your good name as an honest detective has been restored by now," he said. "And even if not, it will be soon. But given that you'll be hunting down Tarts, and sucking in all the information the average gal needs in order to, literally, conquer the galaxy, I suspect you don't see yourself going back to your precinct."

Anna grinned. "I guess this would give me an excuse to go out on top," she said. "With my coveted solve rate intact."

"Exactly my thought," said Redford in amusement. "I see you as a civilian consultant at Evie, with sleeping quarters, offices, access to all resources, and the power to come and go as you like. And not just *access* to resources, but authority equal to my own." He smiled. "I really need you to agree," he added, "so I can get *thank you* gift baskets from every criminal in LA."

Anna's smile returned. "You make a compelling offer."

"Good," said Redford, "because I don't intend to take no for an answer. And I forgot to mention the pay. Your compensation will be . . . well, anything you want it to be. I've seen you negotiate, so I'll save us both some time and surrender now."

"You drive a hard bargain, Steve," she said, laughing once again. "Can I have my own parking space?"

He grinned. "You can have your own parking *lot*."

"Okay then," she said. "I'm in."

"Outstanding!" said Redford.

"And you know I was only kidding about the parking space. I don't want to become drunk with power, or a diva. And you're supposed to be keeping me in check. Catering to my every whim is doing the opposite."

"I won't let it happen again," he deadpanned. "Unless you want me to, of course."

Anna was still smiling, but also beaming. "Good to find someone with a sense of humor I can relate to."

"Given what we're likely to face in the future," he said, this time more somberly, "we're going to need a sense of humor."

"There's no one I'd rather face it with," she said. "But I'd better sign off, Steve. Tom wants to fly back to Utah as soon as possible."

"I want you back here as soon as possible, too, believe me. Holograms are nice, but they really don't cut it."

"I couldn't agree more," said Anna.

"Well done, again," said Redford. "The way everything worked out is just mind-blowing. Given everything that happened, everything we were up against, it's impossible for me to even imagine how things could have worked out better."

Anna blew out a long breath. "I hope you're right," she replied. "But to paraphrase a great Zen Master, only time will tell, Steve. Only time will tell."

AUTHOR'S NOTES

Table of Contents

1) From the Author: Thanks for reading *Oracle*. I hope that you enjoyed it. Since a large number of ratings, good or bad, can be instrumental in the success of a novel, I would be grateful if you would rate *Oracle* on its Amazon page, throwing up as many stars as you think it deserves.

Click here to rate ORACLE (and then scroll down to where the reviews begin and click on the link that says, "Write a customer review")

Please feel free to:

- Visit my Website, where you can get on a mailing list to be notified of new releases
- Friend me on Facebook at Douglas E. Richards Author here, or
- Write to me at douglaserichards1@gmail.com (I love to hear from readers, and always respond.)

2) *Oracle*: What's real and what isn't (and why I wrote this novel and chose this title)

As you may know, in addition to trying to tell the most compelling stories I possibly can, I strive to introduce concepts and accurate information that I hope will prove fascinating, thought-provoking, and even controversial. *Oracle* is a work of fiction and contains considerable speculation, so I encourage you to explore the subject matter further to arrive at your own views and conclusions.

With this said, I'll get right into the discussion of what information in the novel is real, and what isn't. I've listed the subject matter I'll be covering below in order of its appearance. So if you aren't interested in an early topic, feel free to skip ahead to one that might interest you more.

- Is *Oracle* the right title?
- Why did I write *Oracle*? (part 1)
- Why did I write *Oracle*? (part 2)
- Are UFOs real?
- Does our subconscious control our lives?
- Intuition
- Microtubules and the hard problem of consciousness.
- Retrocausality
- DNA Information Storage
- The center of the galaxy

Is *Oracle* the right title?

Now that you've read the novel, I hope that you can see why the name *Oracle* seemed so right for the title. But I have to admit to agonizing over this, because it doesn't matter how perfect a title might be for a work if it fails to grab potential readers.

I'm going to admit something shocking: I'm an old guy. (As I always say, you can't teach an old Doug new tricks). I grew up before Oracle, the character from the *Matrix* movies, and Oracle, the software company. So to me the word *Oracle* was always about the Oracle of Delphi in ancient Greece.

But a number of my fans thought otherwise. Many of these have elected to friend me on Facebook, and they are truly amazing. Before I launch every novel, I post a draft synopsis on Facebook to learn what they think, and I've come to treasure their feedback.

This time, a number of my fans weren't thrilled with the title. Some were reminded of the *Matrix*. Some the software company. And even some of those who *were* reminded of the Oracle of Delphi argued that my fiction is about the future, not the past, and felt that this reference was going in the wrong direction.

Yikes! None of them had read the novel, of course. So I couldn't tell them that I had put historical references to the Oracle of Delphi on the very first page, and had taken to calling Anna an Oracle, because of the cryptic nature of her clairvoyance. They had no idea that I had Vega mention that the ancient Vorians had found a few women who confirmed their theory of human precognition, who later went on to become Oracles of Delphi.

Even so, this feedback was troubling, and I thought long and hard about changing the title to something like *Seer, Clairvoyant, Foresight, Delphi, Visionary,* and so on.

After much back and forth I finally, *stubbornly,* stuck with *Oracle.* Hopefully, it isn't too horrible a title, and you aren't the only one in the world who decided to read it. :)

If only I were clairvoyant, I could make sure I made the best decision. I could commit to a title and then look ahead and see how the book did in the future. Then I could commit to another title and see if it did better or worse.

On the other hand, if I really was clairvoyant, I probably wouldn't waste this talent on book titles. If you're thinking I'd use it to buy a lottery ticket, or try to find a single elusive future in which I actually *win* an argument with my wife, shame on you—I'd use it to bring about world peace, of course. :)

Why did I write *Oracle*? (part 1)

Several years ago I wrote a novel called *Game Changer,* which involves neuroscience. While preparing for *Game Changer,* I happened to read several books about the power of the human subconscious. I was blown away. I had no idea just how remarkable the subconscious really is, and how little we're in control of our own actions and decisions.

In any event, the experiments briefly described in this novel with respect to the power of the subconscious are all real, and were actually conducted, including the four-deck experiment, dilated female pupil experiment, and the upside-down funhouse glasses experiment.

The cocktail party effect is also a real phenomenon, and one that I find fascinating.

Chicken sexing is also real, of course, since I couldn't have possibly made this up. I'd like to think I have a good imagination, but I never would have guessed that the early separation of baby chickens by sex was something anyone would ever care to do, let alone just how difficult it might be.

Finally, the power of intuition is also real (more about this in a later section). It may not be as powerful as it was for Anna Abbott in the novel, but it's pretty powerful. I've read biographies of Einstein and Feynman (my two all-time favorite scientists), and both men recognized just how big a role intuitive hunches played in their careers. As I wrote in *Oracle*, I've come to believe that many of humanity's greatest breakthroughs were made by hidden minds, and not the ones we think are in control.

Which brings me to my own experiences. I never know how one of my novels will end until I'm at least halfway through it. I'm stumped on the plot far more frequently than I care to admit, and at least once every novel I become convinced that I can't finish it. I become absolutely *certain* that there is no satisfactory way to complete the work.

And yet I haven't failed to finish a novel yet. So how do I find solutions that I'm so sure don't even exist? The recipe is simple. First, I spend weeks pulling out my hair, and getting nowhere. Then, I spend time pounding my head against the desk. And all along the way, there's plenty of cursing and screaming, and lamenting that finding a solution is *impossible.*

And then the answer comes to me one day. From out of the blue. From out of *nowhere.* It just appears, as if by magic.

My eyes go wide and I think, *Wow! That's it.* I realize that my hidden mind was working tirelessly on the problem behind the scenes, and it just decided to hit me with the answer. And usually this answer is a totally novel way of looking at things, of reaching outside the box I had trapped myself in, of turning the problem on its head. These solutions can take my breath away as it becomes clear to me just how perfect, and how simple, they really are. They were there all along, but my stubborn conscious mind refused to see them.

So over the years, I've grown to have faith that my hidden mind will bail me out. I load up my brain with as much information surrounding the premise as I can. I think about my novel as much as I can, and try to consciously solve the plot. But I almost never do. Thankfully, my subconscious *always* does.

It's humbling to realize that my subconscious mind is a much better problem solver than I'll ever be. For the life of me, I have no idea how it does it.

So I decided it would be fun to introduce a character who really lives this reality. Whose hidden mind makes Oracle-like pronouncements that her conscious mind has to figure out. Whose hidden mind may even have different goals than she does. Almost as if she has multiple personality disorder (now known as dissociative identity disorder).

When this character says she's of two minds about something, she really is of two minds about something.

And then I decided that having a character with extraordinary intuition wasn't quite interesting enough, and that it would be more fun to add clairvoyance into the mix.

This was when I reached the tipping point, and began writing *Oracle*. I only start when my intuition tells me I have enough ideas to fill a novel. Like Anna, I've learned to trust my instincts.

So if you loved this novel, you can thank *me* for listening to my gut. If you hated it, you can blame my hidden mind for fooling me into thinking I really had something here. :)

Why did I write *Oracle*? (part 2)

Ever since I began reading about the technological singularity, post-humanism, and transhumanism, I've come to believe that the human race (or a runaway computer AI) will achieve transcendence within the next hundred years. Given how rapidly our technology is evolving, and given the awesome power of exponential technological growth, it seems inevitable to me (and to many others who are much smarter than me).

I love far-future science fiction and space opera. No power on Earth could keep me away from the latest *Star Trek* movie. But I've come to believe that this future is unlikely. Because if we self-evolve to nearly godlike status in the next hundred years, we'll be unrecognizable as humans, and our motives will be unfathomable. We won't be flying around in starships, like Captain Kirk, and trying to have sex with green aliens. We'll be creating our own universes, or become beings of pure energy.

Ray Kurzweil has a vivid way to compare linear and exponential growth. "If I take thirty steps linearly," he has been known to say, "I get to thirty. If I take thirty steps exponentially, I get to a billion." And while *Star Trek* is the result of the next *linear* step in our development, the reality will be exponential.

I wrote a piece about this for a collection of stories and essays called *Visions of The Future*. My essay was entitled, "Scientific Advances are Ruining Science Fiction," and I've included it at the very end of these notes, after the author bio, for those of you who have interest.

The bottom line is this, as much as I love space opera, I hesitate to write it given what I believe the far future will actually be like. But it occurred to me that perhaps I could have my cake and eat it too. I believe that transcendence is inevitable. But what about a future in which a mysterious entity is actively preventing this last exponential evolutionary leap from taking place? Then I could have my starships, and space battles, and galactic conquest, and also a mystery as to why this transcendence hasn't happened yet.

So the second reason I wrote *Oracle* was to give me an opening to delve into traditional space opera if I wanted, without feeling guilty about it. And I'd like to think that the galaxy I introduced in the novel is pretty darn interesting, also, and can give me plenty to work with if I were to pursue one or more sequels.

So will I write an *Oracle* sequel that leans more toward traditional space opera? One in which Anna Abbott is admiral of the Vorian Allied Fleet? And if I do, will my staunch technothriller fans forgive this space opera dalliance?

If only I were clairvoyant, I could be certain.

In any event, when I make up my mind, you'll be the first to know. :)

Are UFOs real?

Given *Oracle's* subject matter, this is a relevant question, especially now that UFO sightings have become increasingly common and their flight plans increasingly brazen.

So *are* UFOs real? My short answer: I have no idea. My long answer: I have no fricking idea, whatsoever, and I have no idea what to even think about all of this.

None of it makes sense to me. But the evidence has become ever more compelling in the past few years. Every day now military pilots and other trained observers are having close encounters with objects that defy physics. Hard to imagine there's a pedestrian explanation for it all.

On the other hand, if advanced aliens wanted to stay hidden from us, I have no doubt they could pull this off. And on the *third* hand, why isn't there any definitive evidence? I mean ironclad, super-definitive, unquestionable evidence?

Why would aliens toy with us by letting their aircraft get discovered hundreds of times a year? If they wanted their existence to be known, they could make this happen. Hover a few ships over the White House and Times Square, for example, and we'd get the message. Or land in my backyard, show me a futuristic anti-gravity device, and I would find a way to get the national news involved.

And UFOs aren't just an American phenomenon. One would imagine that they are appearing with equal frequency everywhere around the world. So if unmistakable evidence is being hidden from us, does that mean that every government around the world is in on this? And if so, that all of them have managed to successfully keep it from their citizenry? Imagining extraterrestrial visitors is one thing. But imagining this many competent governments is *really* a stretch.

Finally, I'm plagued by the following logic. Members of any species capable of making an interstellar voyage would be so much more sophisticated than we are that they would self-evolve into veritable gods in the blink of the eye. Gods who would have no interest in lowly humanity, or who would be fully capable of sidestepping any of humanity's feeble attempts to discover them.

So none of this makes sense to me. I wish I could give a better answer. It would be cool if aliens really were visiting Earth, but then again, any beings competent enough to make an interstellar voyage could wipe us out in the blink of an eye, and that's a bit disconcerting. Unless, of course, they came through a portal that prevented their tech from passing through with them. :)

I'll leave this section with an excerpt from a May, 2019 article in the *New York Post*, entitled "UFOs have come out of the fringe and into the mainstream," although a simple search will reveal endless others like it.

EXCERPT: You'd have to be living on another planet not to have heard one of the biggest news stories in recent times: After years of denial, it turns out that the US government has a secret program, researching and investigating UFOs.

Details were released of multiple events where UFOs have been tracked on radar and chased by military jets, including a November 2004 incident where the USS Nimitz carrier strike group was buzzed by multiple UFOs. Videos of three of these spectacular midair encounters have been made public, though many more have yet to be released. Also last year, the Defense Intelligence Agency (DIA) briefed Congress on this work. In a January 9, 2018, letter to key members of Congress, the DIA disclosed that they had researched anti-gravity, warp drives, wormholes and other theoretical physics concepts needed for interstellar travel, as part of an effort to understand what they termed "foreign advanced aerospace weapon threats."

Does our subconscious control our lives?

Does our subconscious control our lives? The short answer is yes. The long answer is yes, so much more so than we would ever imagine.

Everything I wrote about in the novel in this regard is true. To learn more about this fascinating subject, I highly recommend starting with a book called *Incognito,* written by David Eagleman, a neuroscientist at Baylor College of Medicine—but only after reading *Game Changer* and the rest of my novels, of course. :) There are also many other books on the subject you can readily find, as well as endless articles with simple internet searches.

We don't realize just how many decisions are being made for us, without our conscious knowledge, because our conscious minds have evolved to believe that they really are in full control. Imagine how embarrassed our conscious minds would be if they had to acknowledge that something hidden from us was pulling our strings with frightening regularity.

There are a large number of experiments demonstrating this truth, and also the lengths the conscious mind will go to fool itself into believing it really is calling the shots. As an example, here is an excerpt from my novel *Game Changer,* which speaks to this point:

EXCERPT: "As we've discussed, if something bubbles up from the unconscious, our minds seize on it and construct a reality, a mythology, to explain it and pretend we're running the show. There are patients whose brains are split, whose left and right hemispheres can't communicate with each other. With these patients there are ways to give instructions to the unconscious without the conscious knowing this was done. Say you instruct a patient who doesn't cook to walk to the kitchen and turn on the oven. His conscious mind doesn't know you gave this instruction. But if you ask him why he did this, he won't confess he has no idea. He'll fabricate a story, a logic, sometimes laughably elaborate, to explain it. 'I turned on the oven to make sure it still worked—in case I decide to sell the house.'"

Below, I've provided excerpts from two articles that I found interesting, among many others.

"Brain makes decisions before you even know it" (Nature, 2008)
EXCERPT: Your brain makes up its mind up to ten seconds before you realize it, according to researchers. By looking at brain activity while making a decision, the researchers could predict what choice people would make before they themselves were even aware of having made a decision.

The work calls into question the consciousness of our decisions and may even challenge ideas about how free we are to make a choice at a particular point in time.

"Consciousness is just the tip of the iceberg," says John-Dylan Haynes, a neuroscientist at the Max Planck Institute for Human Cognitive and Brain Sciences.

"Big Decision Ahead? Let your subconscious choose." (Healthline. com, 2013)

EXCERPT: New research shows that our brains continue solving problems subconsciously when we turn our attention to something else.

The more we learn about our brains, the more we find that they work better without our input. In fact, a great deal of human behavior stems from our subconscious mind. Research into the subconscious has found that it helps to initiate goal-orientated behavior, creativity, insight, memory consolidation, and decision-making.

The funny thing about your brain, as researchers from Carnegie Mellon University (CMU) recently discovered, is that it'll keep solving a problem for you while you do something else. In fact, giving your subconscious time to work makes for better decisions.

Intuition

Much of what is written in the novel about intuition is real. As a handy guide, if a passage seems like it might be real, it probably is. And if it seems like it probably isn't real, it probably isn't. For example, in the novel, Anna can use her intuition/clairvoyance to dodge bullets—but I wouldn't try that at home. :)

I find this subject fascinating. Once again, I'll leave you with excerpts from a few of the many articles I read in preparation for writing *Oracle*.

"Science confirms women's intuition is a real thing" (*New York Post*, 2017)

EXCERPT: Science has finally proven what we have long thought—women are better than men at reading people's emotions. And they can pull off this magic trick just by looking at people's eyes.

Researchers from around the world tested if there were genetic variants associated with cognitive empathy—that is, our ability to be able to understand another person's emotional state just at a glance.

For the study, 90,000 people were shown different photographs of people's eyes. They were then asked to say what they thought that person's mood was. The results: women consistently outperformed men.

"The Science of Intuition: An Eye-Opening Guide to Your Sixth Sense" (Oprah.com, 2011)

EXCERPT: Some people think of intuition as a mystical power. Skeptics write it off as a matter of lucky guesswork. But scientists who study the phenomenon say it's a very real ability that can be identified in lab experiments and visualized on brain scans.

Your powers of deduction, reason, and cognition are all important factors in your perception of the world. But your judgment is working even when you're not conscious of the gears turning—and even when you're not conscious, period.

If you had to guess whether it's easier to take in new information when your attention is focused or when you're distracted, you'd guess the former, right? If so, you'd be wrong. In a study published in *Nature Neuroscience* in 2009 . . . "Our intuitive brains are processing information even when we're not paying attention," says Ken Paller, PhD, a coauthor of the study. "And with the brain's analytical system occupied by another task, the intuitive system—which excels at picking up the gist of a scene or situation—is better able to do its work."

Finally, I'll leave this section with an excerpt from an article suggesting we consolidate memories while we sleep. There is more and more evidence that this is the case. Alas, this still isn't the same as absorbing countless audiobooks in your sleep the way Anna did, but it's fascinating, nonetheless.

"Yes, you can learn a foreign language in your sleep, say Swiss psychologists" (Independent, UK, 2014)
EXCERPT: Subliminal learning in your sleep is usually dismissed as pseudo-science at best and fraud at worst, but a team of Swiss psychologists say you can actually learn a foreign language in your sleep. Well, not from scratch, but research published in the journal *Cerebral Cortex* by the Swiss National Science Foundation claims that listening to newly-learned foreign vocabulary while sleeping can help solidify the memory of the words.

Microtubules and the hard problem of consciousness

I present a lengthy discussion on the nature of consciousness in my novel *Infinity Born*. This is truly an impossible topic that has been debated for thousands of years, and will continue to be debated for many more years to come. To make this impossibly thorny topic even more thorny, a deep dive into this subject matter must inevitably also consider the existence, or non-existence, of the soul. For those of you who are interested, if you Google "the hard problem of consciousness," you will find enough material to last you a lifetime. But be warned, material on the nature of consciousness can be very deep, so don't be surprised if your brain starts to hurt as you read through it.

When it comes to the question of when a computer can be considered sentient, scientists are coming to the conclusion that the Turing test, long considered the gold standard of measuring computer sentience, is no longer a valid metric. This is another topic on which you can readily find endless information and speculation online.

I actually had an epiphany about computer sentience while writing *Infinity Born*. It occurred to me that perhaps "boredom" would be the simplest test. Computers operate at the speed of light, over a hundred thousand times faster than our plodding speed of thought. If we were in this situation, we would literally die of boredom while waiting for a human to provide the next input. I would think that any computer intelligence that could be shown to be losing its mind from boredom, or growing impatient, would have to be fully conscious.

With respect to the role of microtubules and quantum effects in consciousness, everything written in the book is accurate. And Quantum

Biology has become a growing field. The resource that I found most helpful in this regard was a 2018 article in *Discover Magazine* entitled, "Down the Quantum Rabbit Hole: Fellow Scientists labeled him a crackpot. Now Stuart Hameroff's quantum consciousness theories are getting support from unlikely places."

This is a fairly long, fascinating article, and I tried to capture the most relevant points in the novel. I'll excerpt just a bit more of this article below, and then a different article, to underscore the possible importance of recent findings.

EXCERPT: A microtubule is composed of many individual subunits. If they operated in a purely classical fashion, as insulators—like wood, glass, and other common materials that stop electrical current from flowing freely—the amount of resistance across the microtubule should increase. But Bandyopadhyay found something very different when he applied specific charges of alternating current. Resistance levels jumped by a factor of one billion. The microtubule was acting something like a semiconductor, one of the most important development in electronics. He stood there in wonder at his own results.

"Discovery of quantum vibrations in microtubules inside brain neurons supports controversial theory of consciousness" (Science Daily, 2014)
EXCERPT: A review and update of a controversial 20-year-old theory of consciousness claims that consciousness derives from deeper level, finer scale activities inside brain neurons. The recent discovery of quantum vibrations in microtubules inside brain neurons corroborates this theory, according to review authors. They suggest that EEG rhythms (brain waves) also derive from deeper level microtubule vibrations, and that from a practical standpoint, treating brain microtubule vibrations could benefit a host of mental, neurological, and cognitive conditions.

Retrocausality

Retrocausality is real—maybe. :) I'll be honest with you, this subject is like quantum mechanics for me. It gets deep fast, and the more

I read about it, the less I understand it. So I can't really explain to readers what I don't fully grasp myself. (Part of this is laziness on my part—I'd like to think I could get a handle on this if I really put in the effort, but I haven't so far.)

So with this as a feeble introduction to the subject, I'll leave you with one excerpt on the topic that I hope you'll find interesting. This is from a 2010 article in *Discover Magazine* entitled, "Back to the Future: A series of quantum experiments shows that measurements performed in the future can influence the present. Does that mean the universe has a destiny—and the laws of physics pull us inexorably toward our prewritten fate?"

EXCERPT: Jeff Tollaksen may well believe he was destined to be here at this point in time. We're on a boat in the Atlantic, and it's not a pleasant trip. The torrential rain and choppy waters are causing the boat to lurch. The rough sea has little effect on Tollaksen, who grew up around boats. Everyone would agree that events in his past have prepared him for today's excursion. But Tollaksen and his colleagues are investigating a far stranger possibility: It may be not only his past that has led him here today, but his future as well.

Tollaksen's group is looking into the notion that time might flow backward, allowing the future to influence the past. By extension, the universe might have a destiny that reaches back and conspires with the past to bring the present into view. On a cosmic scale, this idea could help explain how life arose in the universe against tremendous odds. On a personal scale, it may make us question whether fate is pulling us forward and whether we have free will.

"Aharonov was one of the first to take seriously the idea that if you want to understand what is happening at any point in time, it's not just the past that is relevant. It's also the future," Tollaksen says. In 1964 Aharonov and his colleagues Peter Bergmann and Joel Lebowitz, all then at Yeshiva University in New York, proposed a new framework called time-symmetric quantum mechanics. It could produce all the same results as the standard form of quantum mechanics that everyone knew and loved, with the added benefit of explaining how information from the future could fill in the indeterministic gaps in the present."

DNA Information Storage

Storing huge amounts of data within the twists and turns of the famous double helix is being worked on now. DNA is stable and compact (thank you Nature), and already carries the entire blueprint for a human being, which is even more complex than a starship or planetary shield. In *Oracle*, Redford claims that all the world's data, encoded in DNA, could fit in a teaspoon.

Did I arrive at this bit of imagery after doing extensive calculations? Actually, no. This information was deeply hidden within a 2015 *Quartz.com* article entitled, "Scientists say all the world's data can fit on a DNA hard drive the size of a teaspoon." (Okay, so maybe it wasn't so deeply hidden, after all. :)) Here is an excerpt:

EXCERPT: Servers, hard drives, flash drives, and disks will degrade (as will our libraries of paper books, of course), but a group of researchers at the Swiss Federal Institute of Technology have found a way to encode data onto DNA—the very same stuff that all living beings' genetic information is stored on—that could survive for millennia.

One gram of DNA can potentially hold up to 455 exabytes of data, according to *New Scientist*. For reference: There are one billion gigabytes in an exabyte, and 1,000 exabytes in a zettabyte. The cloud computing company EMC estimated that there were 1.8 zettabytes of data in the world in 2011, which means we would need only about 4 grams (about a teaspoon) of DNA to hold everything from Plato through the complete works of Shakespeare to Beyonce's latest album (not to mention every brunch photo ever posted on Instagram).

I'll end this section with an excerpt from *MIT Technology Review* entitled, "**Microsoft just booted up the first 'DNA drive' for storing data**

EXCERPT: Microsoft has helped build the first device that automatically encodes digital information into DNA and back to bits again. Microsoft has been working toward a photocopier-sized device that would replace data centers by storing files, movies, and documents in DNA strands, which can pack in information at mind-boggling density.

According to Microsoft, all the information stored in a warehouse-sized data center would fit into a set of Yahtzee dice, were it written in DNA.

The center of the galaxy

I chose to have all known intelligences, other than humanity, arise within the galactic center for several reasons. One, I wanted Earth to be unreachable by starship, so there could be a raging galactic war 25,000 light-years away, but one that couldn't impact Earth—at least not yet. This way I could focus on just two of the twenty-seven intelligence species on Earth, and tell the story I told.

But if I did limit the speed of starships, the combatants would needed to be fairly close to each other, cosmologically speaking, to be able to conduct a respectable war. Having them all reside in the center of the galaxy was the obvious solution.

The fact that this would mean that the residents of Tartar and Vor would be used to nearly continuous light, making them uncomfortable on Earth, and would help pave the way for an homage to angels and demons was a nice fringe benefit.

The little I wrote about the center of the galaxy is accurate. Here is an excerpt taken from NASA's *Web Telescope* website entitled, "What is the center of our galaxy like?"

EXCERPT: If you lived in the center of the Milky Way, you would look up at a sky thick with stars, one thousand to one million times more dense than we're used to seeing, depending on how close you were to the core. For Earth's inhabitants, the next closest star to our sun is about four light-years away. In the center of the galaxy, stars are only 0.4–0.04 light-years apart. This is a region so packed with stars, it's equivalent to having one million suns crammed into the volume of space between us and our closest stellar neighbor a little over four light-years away.

The center of the Milky Way, roughly the inner 10,000 light-years, consists of the region where the galaxy's spiral arm structure has broken down and transformed into a "bulge" of stars. Even if humans could explore the region, it would take us more than 25,000 years to reach it, traveling at close to the speed of light.

So that's it for the notes section of *Oracle*. I hope that you found at least some of this helpful. For those of you interested in reading my essay, "Scientific Advances are Ruining Science Fiction," it appears beyond the "Author bio and list of books," as I mentioned before.

3) Author bio and list of books

Douglas E. Richards is the *New York Times* and *USA Today* best-selling author of *WIRED* and numerous other novels (see list below). A former biotech executive, Richards earned a BS in microbiology from the Ohio State University, a master's degree in genetic engineering from the University of Wisconsin (where he engineered mutant viruses now named after him), and an MBA from the University of Chicago.

In recognition of his work, Richards was selected to be a "special guest" at San Diego Comic-Con International, along with such icons as Stan Lee and Ray Bradbury. His essays have been featured in *National Geographic*, the *BBC*, *the Australian Broadcasting Corporation*, *Earth & Sky*, *Today's Parent*, and many others.

The author has two children and currently lives with his wife and dog in San Diego, California.

You can friend Richards on Facebook at Douglas E. Richards Author, visit his website at douglaserichards.com, and write to him at douglaserichards1@gmail.com

Near Future Science Fiction Thrillers by Douglas E. Richards
WIRED (Wired 1)
AMPED (Wired 2)
MIND'S EYE (Nick Hall 1)

BRAINWEB (Nick Hall 2)
MIND WAR (Nick Hall 3)
QUANTUM LENS
SPLIT SECOND (Split Second 1)
TIME FRAME (Split Second 2)
GAME CHANGER
INFINITY BORN
SEEKER
VERACITY
ORACLE

Kids Science Fiction Thrillers (9 and up, enjoyed by kids and adults alike)
TRAPPED (Prometheus Project 1)
CAPTURED (Prometheus Project 2)
STRANDED (Prometheus Project 3)
OUT OF THIS WORLD
THE DEVIL'S SWORD

4) Essay: Scientific Advances are Ruining Science Fiction

I write science fiction thrillers for a living, set five to ten years in the future, an exercise that allows me to indulge my love of science, futurism, and philosophy, and to examine in fine granularity the impact of approaching revolutions in technology.

But here is the problem: I'd love to write pure science fiction, set *hundreds* of years in the future.

Why don't I?

I guess the short answer is that to do so, I'd have to turn a blind eye to everything I believe will be true hundreds of years from now. Because the truth is that books about the future of humanity, such as Kurzweil's *The Singularity is Near,* have *ruined* me.

As a kid, I read nothing but science fiction. This was a genre that existed to examine individuals and societies through the lens of technological and scientific change. The best of this genre always focused on human beings as much as technology, something

John W. Campbell insisted upon when he ushered in what is widely known as the Golden Age of Science Fiction.

But for the most part, writers in past generations could feel confident that men and women would always be men and women, at least for many thousands of years to come. We might develop technology that would give us incredible abilities. Go back and forth through time, travel to other dimensions, or travel through the galaxy in great starships. But no matter what, in the end, we would still be Grade A, premium cut, humans. Loving, lusting, and laughing. Scheming and coveting. Crying, shouting, and hating. We would remain ambitious, ruthless, and greedy, but also selfless and heroic. Our intellects and motivations in this far future would not be all that different from what they are now, and if we lost a phaser battle with a Klingon, the Grim Reaper would still be waiting for us.

In short, we would continue to be the kind of human beings a writer could work with, could understand. James T. Kirk might have lived hundreds of years in the future, might have beamed down to planets and engaged warp engines, but viewers still had no trouble relating to him. He was adventurous, loyal, and heroic, and he lusted after life (along with green aliens, androids, and just about anything else that could move).

But what if you believe that in a few hundred years, people will *not* be the same as today? What if you believe they will be so different they will be *unrecognizable* as human?

Now how would you write science fiction? You would have to change two variables at the same time: not only addressing dramatic advances in technology, but dramatic changes in the nature of humanity itself (or, more likely, the merger of our technology and ourselves).

In the early days of science fiction, technology changed at a snail's pace. But today, technological change is so furious, so obviously exponential, that it is impossible to ignore. I have no doubt this is why a once fringe, disrespected genre has become so widely popular, has come out of the closet, and is now so all-pervasive in our society. Because we're *living* science fiction every day.

Rapid and transformative technological change isn't hard to imagine anymore. What's hard to imagine is the *lack* of such change.

In 1880, the US asked a group of experts to analyze New York City, one of the fastest-growing cities in North America. They wanted to know what it might be like in a hundred years.

The experts extrapolated the likely growth during this period, and the expected consequences. They then confidently proclaimed that if population growth wasn't halted, by 1980, New York City would require so many horses to stay viable that every inch of it would be knee-deep in manure. Knee-deep! In horse manure!

As someone interested in technology and future trends, I love this story, even if it turns out to be apocryphal, because it does a brilliant job of highlighting the dangers of extrapolating the future, since we aren't capable of foreseeing game-changing technologies that often appear. Even now. Even at our level of sophistication and expectation of change.

But while we can't know what miracles the future will hold, we've now seen too much evidence of exponential progress not to know that Jim Kirk would no longer be relatable to us. Because it seems impossible to me that we will remain as we are. Remain even the least bit recognizable.

This assumes, of course, that we avoid self-destruction, a fate that seems more likely every day as WMDs proliferate and fanaticism grows. But post-apocalyptic science fiction has never been my thing, and if we do reach a *Star Trek* level of technology, we will have avoided self-destruction, by definition. And I prefer to be optimistic, in any case, despite the growing case for pessimism.

So if we do ever advance to the point at which we can travel through hyperspace, beam ourselves down to planets, or wage war in great starships, we can be sure we won't be human anymore.

It is well known that increases in computer power and speed have been exponential. But exponential growth sneaks up on you in a way that isn't intuitive. Start with a penny and double your money every day, and in thirty-nine days you'll have over two billion dollars. But the first day your wealth only increases by a single penny, an amount that's beneath notice. On the *thirty-ninth* day, however, your wealth will increase from one billion to two billion dollars—now *that* is a change impossible to miss. So like a hockey stick, the graph of exponential growth barely rises from the ground for some time, but when it reaches the beginning of the handle, watch out, because you suddenly get an explosive rise that is nearly vertical.

It's becoming crystal clear that we are entering the hockey-stick phase of progress with computers and other technologies. Yes, progress in artificial intelligence has been discouraging. But if we don't self-destruct, does anyone imagine that we won't develop computers within a few hundred years that will make the most advanced supercomputers of today seem like a toddler counting on his or her fingers? Does anyone doubt that at some point a computer could get so powerful it could direct its own future evolution? And given the speed at which such evolution would occur, does anyone doubt that a computer could become self-aware within the next few centuries?

Visionaries like Ray Kurzweil believe this will happen well within this century, but even the most conservative among us must admit the likelihood that by the time the USS *Enterprise* pulls out of space dock, either our computers will have evolved into gods and obsoleted us, or, more likely, we will have merged with our technology to reach almost god-like heights of intelligence ourselves.

And while this bodes well for these far-future beings, it isn't so great for today's science fiction writers. Because what would you rather read about: a swashbuckling starship captain? Or a being as incomprehensible to us as we are to an amoeba?

To be fair, science fiction novels have been written about a future in which this transformation has occurred. And I could write one of these, as well. The problem is that for the most part, people like reading about other people. People who are like them. People who act and think like, you know . . . *people.*

Even if we imagine a future society of omniscient beings, we wouldn't have much of a story without conflict. Without passions and frailties and fear of death. And what kind of a story could an amoeba write about a man, anyway?

I believe that after a few hundred years of riding up this hockey-stick of explosive technological growth, humanity can forge a utopian society whose citizens are nearly-omniscient and nearly-immortal. Governed by pure reason rather than petty human emotions. A society in which unrecognizable beings live in harmony, not driven by current human limitations and motivations.

Wow. A novel about beings we can't possibly relate to, residing on an intellectual plane of existence incomprehensible to us, without conflict or malice. I think I may have just described the most boring novel ever written.

Despite what I believe to be true about the future, however, I have to admit something: I still can't help myself. I *love* space opera. When the next *Star Trek* movie comes out, I'll be the first one in line. Even though I'll still believe that if our technology advances enough for starships, it will have advanced enough for us to have utterly transformed *ourselves*, as well. With apologies to Captain Kirk and his crew, *Star Trek* technology would never coexist with a humanity we can hope to understand, much as dinosaurs and people really didn't roam the earth at the same time. But all of this being said, as a reader and viewer, I find it easy to suspend disbelief. Because I really, really love this stuff.

As a writer, though, it is more difficult for me to turn a blind eye to what I believe will be the truth.

But, hey, I'm only human. A current human. With all kinds of flaws. So maybe I can rationalize ignoring my beliefs long enough to write a rip-roaring science fiction adventure. I mean, it is fiction, right? And maybe dinosaurs and mankind *did* coexist. The *Flintstones* wouldn't lie, would they?

So while the mind-blowing pace of scientific progress has ruined far-future science fiction for me, at least when it comes to the writing of it, I may not be able to help myself. I may love old-school science fiction too much to limit myself to near-future thrillers. One day, I may break down, fall off the wagon, and do what I vowed during my last Futurists Anonymous meeting never to do again: write far-future science fiction.

And if that day ever comes, all I ask is that you not judge me too harshly.

Made in the USA
Middletown, DE
14 June 2021